I0575113

THE WAY YOU SEE ME NOW

A Novel by

MAURY K. DOWNS

The Way You See Me Now

Copyright © 2020, Maury K. Downs
All rights reserved.
ISBN-13: 978-1-7351204-2-3

Published in the United States of America
By Jewel Sky, L.L.C.

Dedicated To

My forever island girl, Lorna who always lives aloha.
Your faith, encouragement, and support
have given me the passion to succeed.

In the words of your gracious kindred, mahal kita.

Bette Jewel, you are so dearly missed.
Possessing an enduring fortitude to live a happy,
rewarding life is the best loving attribute and memory
that I cherish. You live on in our hearts, my beloved mother.

Dad, Ritha, Marcia, Michael, Jasmin, Kristina,
Ryan Kristoffer and Gillian and, their beautiful children,
you are all part of me and profoundly define who I am.

About the Author

Maury Kelly Downs was born and raised in Los Angeles, California. He has had a rewarding previous career working as a health care provider. His responsibilities working as a Registered Respiratory Therapist included the management and treatment of respiratory diseases in patients of various ages. Much of his experience involved working in the Neonatal Intensive Care Unit, Pediatric Intensive Care Unit, and Emergency Department in several acute care medical hospitals in California. Some of his duties also included the management of patients requiring life support on ventilators during hospital to hospital transport, by means of ground emergency medical transport vehicles and air ambulance aircraft. He enjoys all things aviation and he is a certificated pilot. He has experience working as a Certified Flight Instructor greatly enjoying teaching people how to fly. He is an Airline Transport Pilot and thrilled to fly the "Queen of the skies" Boeing 747. He has worked to promote and enhance training and safety standards in the airline industry. When he was a child, he enjoyed telling imaginary stories to his friends and family for their entertainment. He enjoys hearing the humorous cavorts and bold adventures of people's travels. The Way You See Me Now is his debut novel.

Chapter One

Planet earth is a huge and beguiling blue gem shining brightly against the black diamond cloth of deep space. Conceivably guided by destiny, it faithfully circumnavigates a radiating sun every three hundred and sixty-five days. This sculpted and harmonious loop around the bright sole star of our solar system is completed unfailingly in a seemingly timeless orbit. Yet, the very movement produces time in this world, past, present and future, just as it provides day and night to all its inhabitants.

Within the confines of this wondrous planet, there is an abundance of life. Life is present within the vast, climatic atmosphere, on the surface, and all the way to the darkest deep of the great oceans. There is life within the myriad of flowing rivers, the very depths of countless lakes across the lands, and in the tidelands and marshes. Life is present in many forms within the soil, betwixt the compact minerals that comprise the land, and all the rest that encompasses the earth's surface. Practically everywhere, above and below planet earth's vibrant terracotta, life ensues.

Planet earth is colossal in comparison to all the life that makes its home here. Even so, its great mass is measurable. The average man in Northern America weighs 191 pounds. By comparison, the mass of planet earth is approximately 1.36×10^{25} pounds. The earth's relative huge size and mass can be visually appreciated by gazing upon the tallest mountains, beholding the depths of its great valleys, and scouring horizon's end across the seemingly endless seas. Still, the enormity of this world seen with human eyes cannot wholly quantify just how big the earth really is. Standing on the surface, one cannot see the ends of the earth, aside from one horizon to the next. That is because the surface of the earth forms a gigantic globe that stretches outward well beyond sight, roughly 12,416 miles; well past the visible horizon. Considering a few of these uncomplicated facts, our beautiful planet earth is indeed, colossal. It is greatly suitable in size to support all the life that exists here.

In addition to the grand surface of the globe, stretching out over the earth's mean equatorial circumference of approximately 24,880 miles is the vast atmosphere. The seemingly endless blue skies above unquestionably and, befittingly, add to the earth's enormity. The huge atmosphere acts as a gigantic shield, protecting everything within it from the extreme temperatures and the terrific vacuum of outer space. The atmosphere is basically an enormous capsule providing abundant oxygen for all the multitudinous forms of life that need air and a stable environment to survive. Because of the tremendous possibility provided by our vast atmosphere, life can humbly and comfortably exist.

Standing on the ground and looking towards the heavens above, it is very difficult to determine just where the outstretching sky ends approximately 62 miles above. Here is the outer fringe of our enormous planet, the great encompassing border of earthly civilization. Here, at this intangible boundary, outer space begins. This great border yields passage to billions and billions of other planets in infinite bright solar systems located in countless galaxies within the vastness of the universe of incomprehensible cosmic space. Here, where the sky ends, infinity with all its great possibility begins, and earth, in all its colossal grandness, becomes minute.

All of this can be very easily demonstrated without the use of scientific gadgets. All one has to do is go outside on a clear, cloudless night in any open countryside and look straight up. The daytime sky is like a huge curtain over a window, set in place by the gleaming sun during daylight hours. However, at night, after the sun has set, the huge curtain is pulled away and the Earth's atmosphere becomes a transparent window to the beautiful celestial neighborhood above. Revealed to the naked eye is a numerosity of stars. Basically, those are other solar systems not much different from our own, comprising one or more suns and other shining celestial bodies. Infinitely more than can be counted. Question; how many of those other solar systems within the spectacularly visible celestial neighborhood in the night sky above are comprised of a beautiful planet full of life like our own? Simple answer: unknown.

· · · ● ● ● ● · · ·

One summer evening during the first year of the new century, 2001, an unexpected new guest from the celestial neighborhood was about to enter the earth's atmosphere. Already orbiting the earth were hundreds of artificial satellites. Some of these 'earth born' satellites were in operational order, and some were not. Many were remnants of the past. They were launched from the earth's surface during the years of the cold war between the United States of America and the former Union of Soviet Socialists Republic. But this new guest to the atmosphere was in a deliberately decaying orbit around the wondrous blue planet. And while many other foreign objects were in a similar type of decaying orbit around earth that evening in the form of dust particles and tiny rocks commonly witnessed falling to the earth on almost any day or night as falling stars or meteors, this guest was no meteor.

· · · ● ● ● ● · · ·

The date today was Thursday, August 30, 2001. At 8:02 p.m. local time, 0402 Zulu, Senior Airman First Class Herman Gomez was already a few hours into his watch. He sat comfortably in front of his radar screen in the surveillance control room of the Alaskan North American Aerospace Defense Command Region. Herman enjoyed his work on base and his life at the 11th Air Force headquarters located at Elmendorf Air Force Base in

Anchorage, Alaska. He was thinking how the weather would change to more frigid temperatures in a few months. He was used to the warm climate of El Paso, Texas, where he was born and raised. This would be his second winter in Alaska.

Herman was enjoying the routine evening shift when suddenly something appeared on his radar screen. It was a very small target with no other data than it was moving fast! Just a primary radar return originating from the north, probably at very high altitude he thought, as he began trying to identify the radar return signal. His hands moved in steady motion around his radar screen, switching on and turning buttons and knobs on his workspace. He thought about saying something aloud to his commanding officer, who could be heard laughing at someone's joke on the far side of the room.

The Senior Airman opened his mouth to speak, and suddenly, the target was gone. Vanished, just like that, Herman's eyes methodically searched for it. He slowly shook his head in shallow, perplexed thought. *Must be nothing. Maybe I'm just tired and didn't really see it.* His thoughts quickly returned to the upcoming Alaskan winter. The night went on, his shift, quiet as usual. He didn't tell anyone about what he saw, nor did he fill out a report.

· · · • ● ● • · · ·

About 3,000 miles away at 9:26 p.m. local, 0426 Zulu, Clyde Sherman Kauffman sat in a semi-slouched position in his chair at the Los Angeles Air Route Traffic Control Center in Palmdale, California. He was tired from the long day, having painted his garage before starting his evening shift. He was 45 minutes into his eight-hour shift now and was already counting down the clock. The senior controller looked forward to the rest he would reward himself with at the end of his shift; especially knowing the garage was finally painted. Clyde was not too busy that evening. He kept careful watch of the aircraft in his sector. Only six aircraft were passing through the airspace he controlled at the moment. Four of which were large commercial jet airliners. Clyde was listening to the Beach Boys, *Surfer Girl*. The song was quietly playing on a radio located in the far end of the control room. He thought about his upcoming coffee break. Clyde needed another cup. He would have enough time to take a cigarette break, too.

Then, something quite unexpected happened. His eye suddenly caught something moving on his radar screen. It appeared out of nowhere, and its speed abruptly grabbed his attention. Clyde grimaced peculiarly at the seemingly unbelievable occurrence. *What's that? Is this real?* He deliberated in baffled thought. Next thing he noticed was the primary return 'blip' on his radar screen seemed to be immediately decelerating. He was frozen, watching in amazement. *What the…?* He stared at the 'blip' as it remarkably appeared to change course. He wondered again if he was actually seeing this. Years of experience had taught him that anomalies can erroneously show up as actual aircraft. Then, Clyde sprang into action.

"Southwest seven forty-four traffic six miles four o'clock altitude unknown!" Clyde belted out in one breath. His eyes fixed intently on the fast moving, unidentified target on his screen.

· · · • • ● • • · · ·

In the sky above, not far away from the controller's location, Southwest Airlines flight 744 was level in cruise flight in the peaceful summer night sky. The flight crew was talking about the dry weather season and the burning San Joaquin Valley wildfires to the north. The co-pilot, First Officer Janet Lemont had her conversation with Captain John Simon interrupted by the alerting call of the air traffic controller's voice over the radio. She stopped talking mid-sentence and looked over her right shoulder out of the side windows of the Boeing 737's cockpit. She saw nothing at first and, then calmly cued the mike.

"Southwest seven forty-four, looking."

Then she saw it. It was a bright object high in the sky, located above where she was looking for the traffic. The seemingly distant object appeared to her to be falling out of the sky. *A meteor,* she thought to herself. She smiled for a second as the object in the distance swiftly passed behind the aircraft out of her view. Her attention returned to the cockpit, her conversation picking up the words right where she left off.

· · · • • ● • • · · ·

The occupancy on Flight 744 originating from Las Vegas, Nevada was nominal, with passengers filling less than half the seats. Most of these passengers were asleep in the main cabin. There was, however, one little boy sitting near the wing section who also saw the glowing object high above, falling towards earth. The boy's eyes widened suddenly. Six year old Thomas Somers could not believe what he saw.

"Look mommy, a falling star!" he said pulling at his mother's shoulder.

When they both peered back out the little window, there was only the night desert sky to see with its many stars becoming visible now in the darkness. His mother smiled, gave him a kiss on the forehead and closed her eyes to nap again. Thomas pressed his forehead to the window to try and find the pretty, bright shining object again. It was long gone by now.

· · · • ● • • · · ·

Back in the Air Route Traffic Control Center, Clyde lost the radar blip. It vanished just as suddenly as it appeared. He grimaced at the screen and shrugged his shoulders. With a sigh, Clyde's thoughts returned to his upcoming break. He needed it. There would be no more surprises like that for the rest of the evening. He told no one what he saw.

· · · • ● • • · · ·

South of Victorville, California on interstate 15 Barstow Freeway several motorists witnessed a bright object falling out of the night sky. It seemed to be lower in the atmosphere than meteors people usually observed. The flash of the glowing object seemed to disappear quickly, followed by the crack of a sonic boom heard throughout the area. Vehicles traveling in both directions just continued on as they always do. Meteor sightings in the night desert sky were not uncommon. However, those who witnessed the event did not recognize that the presence of a sound shock wave meant that the object had successfully penetrated the earth's atmosphere. Most meteors never make it this far. They simply burn up high above in the earth's sky.

The unidentified flying object was not glowing anymore. It descended out of the sky, decelerating more and more with every second. No one could see the object against the dark night as it speedily approached the surface of the earth. No other radar detected its presence. Although nearly invisible in the dark, the sharp clap of the sonic booms it made could be heard for miles. But anyone hearing them would think the sounds originated from Edwards Air Force Base in the Mojave Desert to the north. There was always some kind of military flight testing going on there. Flight testing occurred at all hours of the day and night. In addition, the Space Shuttle occasionally landed there, too. That meant the 'sonic booms' were really not out of the ordinary.

The alien object gradually descended on its flight path, heading towards a very quiet neighborhood located in the Lake Arrowhead area within the San Bernardino National Forest. As it decelerated, it changed course, making slight adjustments to its flight path. It was headed directly for a sparsely populated region just northwest of Lake Arrowhead. As the dark object approached the area, located within thick forested mountainous terrain, it emitted a strange, very low pitched growl.

Brian Morris was watching the local news and drifting off to sleep when a sudden noise startled him. His eyes widened at the unexpected sound, a deep, undulating humming. It seemed to be vibrating more and more. The strange noise increased to a heavier tone and the windows throughout the house started rattling. The young man tilted his head to one side. He concentrated on the strange, vibrating sounds he heard coming from somewhere outside the house. Brian heard the wind suddenly spring up and begin rustling through the treetops outside. This was very peculiar, because it hadn't been windy a minute ago. From his comfortable, reclined position on the couch, Brian leaned forward and looked around the family room. He saw Mr. Doodles, his mother's cat, bound off the couch and hide under the coffee table. Brian looked around, a bit disoriented. He remembered watching the Los Angeles Dodgers defeat the Colorado Rockies, 5 to 4, on the cable television sports channel network earlier. When the game was over he turned to the local news. He remembered nodding off to sleep. Looking at his Casio watch, he saw the time was now 9:29 p.m.

The humming sound was becoming fainter and the swooshing-wind sounds suddenly stopped. All at once the house was quiet except for the television noise. Brian sat motionless in the dimly lit family room. Most of the other lights were turned off throughout his parent's mountain community home.

Brian stood up and looked around in the eerie calm. He was the only one home. His parents had left for their time share in Hawaii Monday morning on a two week vacation and weren't coming back until next Saturday. He was house-sitting for them. He'd been off today and hadn't done anything but lounge around his parent's home all day, just enjoying a peaceful day in the fresh mountain air. Now, he wondered what the unusual disturbance was all about outside in the stillness of the night.

Where had that noise come from? He walked towards the rear door in the entertainment room and then stopped, hesitating for a moment. The young man was feeling a little uneasy, for no particular reason.

Brian, reached the back door and just barely opened it to look out, thinking that maybe the odd sound had come from the street. He was unsure. He thought for a moment about walking around the rear path to the side gate. Tilting his head to one side, he heard it, again. There was that same hum. It seemed quieter, maybe at a distance farther away. He looked out into the darkness of the back lot toward the direction of the noise. It was so quiet this evening, and very dark at this time of the night, too. Brian remembered the only nearby neighbor to his parent's home was about a quarter of a mile away, and they were gone on vacation, too. *So, who's making the noise? Who could it be? There's no one out in this area but me.* That's why his parents actually bought the house several years ago, to be away from everyone else.

Brian had only opened the rear door a crack when he closed it again. He thought about what to do next and decided, almost reluctantly, to see what the noise was about. He thought he should be prepared, and he remembered there was a flashlight under the sink in the kitchen. Before going there he walked to the couch, grabbed the remote and turned off the television. He did so because his mother always gave him trouble whenever he left the TV on when no one was watching it. Satisfied that his mother would be happy, he turned towards the kitchen. As he walked by the outdoor light switches Brian turned on the patio and rear flood lights. Though they did not light the rear lot far beyond the covered patio well, he felt a little more comfortable with at least some light on. He retrieved the flashlight and grabbed an 8 inch stainless-steel chef's knife out of the deluxe, maple wood knife block. Now he felt prepared for, whatever. *Be a man!*

Brian opened and then quickly closed the door behind him as he stepped out onto the stained concrete patio. He was careful not to let Mr. Doodles out. Clutching the knife in his right hand, he walked forward in the direction of the low pitched humming sound, stepping carefully past several pieces of the Darlee cast aluminum patio furniture set his mom bought this year. At any other time he might have wondered yet again why on earth she bought expensive stuff she couldn't possibly use enough to even remotely justify the cost. But tonight he was focused on creeping toward the humming and didn't give the furniture a second thought other than to avoid tripping on it.

The patio was covered by the upper deck which extended from the master bedroom on the second floor. Flood lights installed on the north corner of the upper deck threw a circle of light out into the back yard but didn't reach past the outdoor fireplace. Beyond that, in the darkness of the summer night, he could hear the soft, low pitched hum. He stepped onto a walkway made from a random, five stone pattern of colonial charcoal brick and lined on either side by well-groomed buffalo grass. Beyond that, the level turf stretched out over most of the rest of the 6,200 square foot lot with intermittent patches of beautiful landscaping that wasn't visible now in the darkness.

Brian figured the sound was coming from beyond the borders of his parent's lot, out where he couldn't see. The flood lights from the upper deck cast his elongated shadow in front of him on the walkway. As he walked, he checked the area around the fireplace, the seating and grill/smoker combination looking strange all covered up against any possible rain, although, California was experiencing a serious drought as of late.

When he passed the stainless steel patio heater at the outer perimeter of the patio area he turned on the flashlight and stepped onto the grass. He walked to the edge of the lot and stood on a custom built retaining wall that was five feet above ground. From there the terrain faded into a forested area to the back of his parent's home. He stood still and fixed his gaze into the woods. The air was cool and refreshing here at 5,000 feet. He took a deep breath and then whispered into the night.

"What am I doing out here?"

He considered walking back inside the house, but something about that humming sound made him curious. It was such an unfamiliar sound. *What type of vehicle makes that noise? Is it possible that it's coming from an all-terrain vehicle? Perhaps someone is stuck out here and needs help. Is it something from the military? Maybe a helicopter crashed landed?* He was not certain what was out there, but whatever it was, the strange humming continued. He looked at the night skyline and could just make out where the mountains and sky met. Looking up, he noticed how clear the evening was. The sky was so beautiful with all the stars aglow.

Brian looked in the direction of the humming sound and sighed deeply. He looked over his jeans, shirt, and the tennis shoes he was wearing and remembered that he'd left his cell phone in the house. He took one look back at his parent's mountain community home. The covered patio seemed far away, now, the flood lights barely lighting the grass and the retaining wall under his feet. He looked ahead into the night forest, listening to the low pitched, unusual humming noise and thought again, *someone might need my help.* Brian was not really scared of proceeding out into the night. He really just wanted to satisfy his curiosity.

He had always been like that ever since he was a child. He was the first kid to jump in the swimming pool during summer days at the park in Pasadena, California and he was the first to dive off the small cliff on Lake Havasu during the Arizona trips he took with his family as a teenager. He got in big trouble for that one. He was also always the first one on point to lead a group during summer camp hiking trips. Some people called him driven. He was not scared of the unknown. He did not believe in monsters. The only thing that worried him was finding someone running from the law, trying to stay out of public eye. *Maybe someone set up camp to hide away for a while?* Possibilities kept running through his mind.

"Hope I don't stumble up on some rave party in the woods," he said in a low voice, trying to drum up a little more nerve to move ahead into the dark of the night.

Brian was careful with the knife and flashlight in his hands. From his crouched position, he pointed the flashlight below to find a landing spot and then jumped down onto a clear patch of dirt. He looked back at the retainer wall and could easily see where to climb back up. He was waist deep in weeds and thickets. He moved forward, training the flashlight on the soil beneath him, careful not to step on anything unsafe, like snakes. He walked slowly for that reason. Truth is, most snakes in the area were small and harmless. Just then his flashlight picked up the shine from a San Bernardino Mountain king snake. *It's small. Barely two feet long, non-poisonous.* He knew, because he watched the Discovery Channel.

"Still," he whispered, "you can never be too sure."

The snake was not the only thing out there in the night forest. Brian could hear a few nocturnal birds and bullfrogs in the distance, and there were other animals making occasional noises, too. He kept walking toward the low pitch humming sound that intrigued him. As he walked, navigating between many different types of mountain vegetation, he was careful not to scrape against anything that might be poisonous. Brian was surrounded by tall, white Snapdragons, Arrowhead Butterweed and Creeping Snowberry. He sensed that the terrain was sloping downward. The night air was still and the stars above and his flashlight were the only sources of illumination. The lack of light meant he couldn't see the details of the landscape ahead of him, but he could see the shadows of the hills rising in the distance and the mountain range in the background. Brian stopped for a moment to look behind him. He could still see the flood lights from his parent's home in the distance. *That will help me get back.*

Brian continued on and on in the cool night, traveling on a westward trek. He wondered how far he had traveled on foot at a steady pace. He guessed, maybe half a mile. As he looked around, he noticed he was well within the tree line of the Western Junipers seen from his parent's patio. Those and, the dark night time shapes of White Fir pines were starting to tower above the earth where he was. The weeds seemed to be getting thicker here, too. His pace slowed a bit. Brian thought about giving up and turning around, but he knew he was very close.

As he walked, Brian's thoughts reflected on the many evening hikes he and his parents had taken in the adjacent area. His mother loved to walk in the early evening. She would usually walk a couple miles every other day after work. If Brian visited overnight, he found himself on some of those short hikes with his mother. Sometimes on the weekends his father joined them. This particular evening reminded him of those times he shared walking with his mother, Linda. Her favorite trail was very close to the house. Although located near the main road where neighborhood cars traveled, the trail offered serenity along its beautiful path. Tonight, however, he was roving quite a ways from any known trail. Brian and his mother never came this way. He even wondered if he could easily find it again. With that in mind this evening hike was, after all, as peaceful as others in the past.

Then Brian stopped and noticed that in front of him, the

terrain changed from what it had been so far. The flashlight showed him a gully that was oriented north and south. He took a deep breath and shone the light around to see a bit better. He was surrounded by trees from all sides. The gully, surrounded by loose dirt and gravel, cut a path between the trees. His eyes, now adjusted to the dark from the walk, revealed the gully was about twenty to thirty feet deep in the center and filled with a variety of vegetation, some of it quite tall. The humming sound stopped, but Brian knew he was very close to the source. He looked around and turned off the flashlight, perplexed. *Now what?* He sat down on the gravel, put the knife down, and took another deep breath. He realized he could see pretty well now. Looking up, the moon was three-quarters full in the night sky, providing some needed light for his adventure. Looking at his watch, the time was 10:21 p.m.

He glanced around, casually looking into the gully. Then he saw something in the center of the gully nestled up under the sagebrush growing beneath a few large Single-leaf pinyons. Something dark, too dark to identify in the light from the moon. He turned on the flashlight but still could not see clearly because of the dense foliage surrounding the object. But something was definitely down there. Brian stared into the dark gully, wondering what he should do next.

· · • • ● ● ● • • · ·

Back at the house, Brian's Ericsson T66 cell phone was ringing for the second time. It was still on top of the cocktail table in the family room right where he left it.

"Hmm… He's not answering," Brian's mother said to her husband.

"Maybe he's asleep already," her husband replied, taking another sip from his Mai Tai. "I'm sure he's okay."

Brian's parents had just finished dinner at The Royal Kona Resort in Kailua-Kona after a day of shopping and walking around the big island of Hawaii. They wanted to relax for a while before returning to their time share not far from there. It was a long leisurely day turning into a quiet evening for the two.

"Well," Linda Louise Morris glanced at her gold, oyster perpetual ladies Rolex.

"It's almost 7:30 p.m. here, so it's about... 10:30 at home?" she questioned and looked at her husband over her reading glasses.

James Morris barely shrugged his shoulders as he signaled the bartender for another round. Linda moved her bar stool a little closer to him and made herself comfortable. She rubbed his legs gently with a little massage and then pulled her Mai Tai a little closer for another sip. The bartender was busy making their second round. James and Linda took in the beautiful tropical evening on the resort's huge, verandah lobby.

· · • • ● • • · ·

Back home within the San Bernardino National Forest Area, at the edge of the gully, Brian sat still. He thought about leaving, quickly and quietly. After the tranquil evening hike to get here, now he was feeling apprehensive in a way he could not ignore. It was fear. Fear of the unknown. He gazed around the immediate area for any signs of wreckage. He could see nothing to indicate an accident had occurred. Satisfied that a helicopter had not crash landed, he began to wonder. His attention returned to the dark object he was barely able to see. He squinted in an effort to focus into the darkness. He wanted a closer look. He had to know what was down there.

As he stood up, he remembered how his father had once slapped a lit firecracker out of his hand. Brian was only eight at the time, and it was the Fourth of July. His older brother, Brandon, had lit the firecracker and tossed it on the ground. Then, without thinking, Brian reached down quickly and snatched the firecracker up with and squeezed the burning end between his thumb and index fingers. Brian could still remember the prickly, burning sensation of the sparkling gun powder covered fuse that was about to ignite the firecracker. He remembered how his father came out of nowhere and slapped the miniature explosive out of his hands. His father, who barely uttered a word, was off balance from drinking several beers that evening during the family barbeque. Brian recalled how his father stumbled and grabbed at him to keep from falling over. The firecracker fell to the ground in front of, and away from Brian. His father stumbled again and fell behind him.

"Brian..!" was all he heard as his intoxicated father fell to the ground spilling his beer on the driveway.

The firecracker landed with the fuse still a dull glow. Brian kept watching as the fuse sparkled to life again, and suddenly the celebratory explosive went off with a loud pop! In his mind, Brian knew he could have stopped the firecracker from exploding. It was at that moment when Brian noticed his brother was staring at him, hand over mouth. Brandon's eyes were wide open in amazement, too. Because, he knew what his little brother was thinking. And, he also knew what his little brother almost accomplished. Brandon just stared, with that same frozen look of astonishment. A tomfoolery stunt that some boys seem to try at least once in the days of their youth. Brandon would have never lit the fuse in the first place, if his little brother mentioned what he was going to do. Nevertheless, Brian was a little hero in Brandon's eyes for the spontaneous feat.

Brian remembered it well. His father, who was trying to pick himself up off the driveway only said.

"Now, Brian, what did you do a fool thing like that for?!"

Clumsily, his father rose to his feet, careful not to spill any more precious beer from the can. He pointed a finger at his son and said drunkenly.

"That should teach you a lesson not to try that again." His dad nodded and brushed himself off.

Brian thought to himself back then, *if you hadn't fallen, I would have put it out!* The father said nothing else to the kids. Brian remembered his dad just stumbled off to see what else there was to eat. So, that was the most lecturing he recalled getting over it. Brian chuckled, recollecting the stunt he pulled that holiday. Just as Brian had to know if he could extinguish the little firecracker, he wanted to know what was down there in the deep gully. Brian was just curious that way.

Brian looked up in awe of the night's spectacular beauty. He heard the distant hoot of an owl somewhere in the night forest. After standing still for a while, his attention returned to the object in the dark deep gully. Brian took a step forward into the steeply descending terrain. Keeping his balance, he picked out a path that would lead him down easily. With flashlight and knife in hand, he continued down into the gully at a slow pace. He wondered how much noise he was making. Brian felt as if each step forward made enough of a disturbance to be heard all the way back to his parents' rear lot. The rainless season had dried the vegetation so weeds and leaves crunched and crackled with each footstep. The flashlight lit the way forward on the dark soil as he moved forward along the narrow pathway. Brian made his way to the bottom of the gully. The stars were bright above, but he was engulfed in darkness, now. The foliage of the deep furrow hindered much of the night skylight above. Brian continued to walk, occasionally raising his head to see where he was headed. He did not want to step on something that would injure him. He kept the flashlight trained in front of his footsteps as he walked at a slow pace.

Then, he saw it.

Chapter Two

Brian looked at the object discreetly situated between trees and shrubs, shrouded overhead by long branches from the large, Single-leaf pinyons within the gully. He tilted his head to one side, trying to figure out just what exactly the object was. Brian had enough room to side step left and right from where he stood. He did so in an effort to get a better view of the object that was about twenty feet in front of him. He shined the flashlight on the unknown object. He noticed it was a dull, dark color. Out of curiosity, Brian stepped closer. He noticed it was bigger than what his first impression was from the top of the gully. What he could see so far was a large ellipsoid object, smooth all around in appearance. It was over forty feet wide and almost twenty feet tall. It also seemed to be about fifty feet long. The overall shape reminded Brian of a stone that would be perfect to skip along the top of the water like the ones he used at Lake Arrowhead on summer picnics. The unfamiliar shape was so beautiful, even in the darkness of the night.

"What in the world is this?" Brian mumbled as he squinted at the object.

He stood motionless with his hands at his side and then knelt down to put the knife on the ground beside him. He shined the flashlight onto different areas of the object in an effort to get clues that would help identify it. He stared at the large ellipsoid thing and then stood back up.

"This definitely isn't a rock," Brian said in a quiet tone, shaking his head slowly. He didn't know whether he was standing at the front or rear of it. He looked around the darkened gully trying to figure it all out, but he still wasn't sure what it was.

"This isn't a downed chopper, that's for sure," he whispered.

It was quiet, now. In the distance, Brian heard the hoot of an owl, again. For a second, he thought he heard something else, too, but his interest quickly returned to the bizarre fixation in front of him. Brian tried to figure out what he had found. *Maybe it's some kind of water tank? But it has no wheels. No tractor treads. No tank tracks. It didn't drive here and nothing drove in here and dropped it off.* He slowly shook his head, perplexed.

Brian slowly reached out to touch the object. At first contact, the surface was smooth, like a glossy enamel finish on a beautiful grand piano. What he touched did not feel like wood, though. The smooth surface did not feel quite like metal, either. It did not quite look like what it felt like. He also realized it was neither cold, nor hot. As he moved his hand over the surface of the object, Brian noticed the texture changed. Visually it was all smooth; however, the tactile surface characteristics differed as his hand moved down across the object. The bottom half of the ellipsoid felt a little rough. Almost, but not quite, like very fine sandpaper. *Maybe, like it is porous, perhaps.* Brian continued moving his hand around in a gentle rubbing motion. He noticed the surface had a 'solid' feel to it, like it was thick, or very dense.

"It almost feels like a rock," Brian whispered.

He knocked on the surface of the dark ellipsoid but no hollow echo resounded from his soft raps. He looked closer. His face was inches away from the surface. With the flashlight shining right on it, he still could not tell what color the object was. He stood up straight and, stared at the unknown thing he had discovered. Given the size of this thing, Brian began to realize it must have been built here if it wasn't towed into the gully. *But... why?* Brian was more perplexed than ever. He touched the surface of the ellipsoid again. Moving his hand around, he noticed the lower area of the object was smoother, now, just like the upper area he had felt. What was once a porous feel to his touch was now smooth. *What? Did that just change?* Brian moved back slowly, frowning in confusion. He touched it again to be sure. And, again, he noticed the lower half was as smooth to the touch as the upper half where his hand was before. He rubbed a larger area, moving forward slowly as he did so. Walking forward, his feet crumpled dried undergrowth in the dark deep gully. He instinctively slowed his pace forward, but, the dried leaves and twigs still crunched with each step. As his hands moved over the upper and lower portion of the ellipsoid, he noticed the same glossy feel. Brian was positive the lower half had a rough texture just before.

He walked along what he thought was the side of the ellipsoid, now to his right. Walking forward, with his right hand moving slowly over the unknown thing, his left shoulder occasionally rubbed against leaves and branches. He stopped at what he thought was the center of the large object and getting down on one knee, reached lower to feel underneath it. It had the same rough feel again. Nodding his head slowly, he stood up to compare what he felt there with the portion above his waist line. Smooth. Brian stood there in the darkened gully and waited for about a minute before kneeling down to touch the same spot he'd touched a minute ago. It was smooth.

"That's weird," he whispered, shining the flashlight on the area he had just touched.

He looked carefully at the surface of the scalene ellipsoid. Visually, everything looked smooth all around, just as before. He stooped down and shined his light underneath the ellipsoid to see if there were pipes or tubes coming from the ground that connected to the object. That's when he noticed something extending from the bottom corner of the object to the ground. He immediately guessed it was some sort of support to hold the object in place. Glancing to his right, on the other end of the ellipsoid object, Brian saw a similar support extended from the other corner. He noticed the support on his right was slightly longer than the one to his left. He studied the object from one end to the other. As he glanced back and forth, he noticed the ellipsoid object appeared to be level. *So, the supports underneath were built to hold the object in a level stance.* He was sure he would find two more supports on the opposite corners underneath the other side. He was convinced that this was some sort of holding tank for water, or fuel, or something important. The strange humming sounds he heard must have been coming from some sort of industrial strength pumps within the large 'tank.' He nodded and sighed deeply. *Why would someone build a strange holding tank in the middle of nowhere?* Brian walked back to where he had placed the knife on the ground.

Probably some kind of secret technological design that turns cow piss into drinkable water. Brian chuckled at the thought.

Retrieving the knife from the ground, he looked up to find the path he'd taken into the gully. Glancing at his watch, he noticed the time was a little past 11 p.m. He figured he could make it back to his parent's house by midnight or just after, if he didn't step on any snakes. The dried leaves and uprooted brush crackled with his footsteps as he walked toward the other side of the deep gully and once again, he wondered how far away his footsteps could be heard. He also thought of the noises he heard when he was aroused from his nap earlier. *What about that windy sound and the trees rustling in the distance that I heard when I woke up? What was that?*

When Brian reached the other end of the gully and started up the path he came in on, something quite unexpected got his attention. The hairs on the back of his neck rose as a light shined from behind him, casting his shadow onto the embankment in front of him. Brian froze. He hadn't seen any lights on the object when he was examining it. He turned around slowly. The light source was bright enough that he could see a small section was sliding open near the rear on the lower half of the ellipsoid. It looked like a door. As it slid soundlessly open, more light flooded the area. Brian stood perfectly still, partly because he was too scared to move. His eyes got even wider when he saw something unfold itself through the door opening. *A ladder?* Brian felt his nerves jangle uncomfortably, but still, he leaned forward to peer at the shiny object, as it extended outward toward the ground with a very soft hum. He took a few steps toward the ellipsoid to get a better look at it and, as he neared the lighted opening, he could clearly see steps on the fully extended ladder that now rested on the ground.

"Not a holding tank, eh?" Brian nervously mumbled to himself, cautiously approaching the steps of the ellipsoid.

They were shiny, clean, and a strange shape. Brian looked up into the opening and saw that the steps led to another door set back about three feet from the outer surface of the ellipsoid. A soft beige lighting illuminated the area around the recessed door.

The unknown fascinated Brian and brought out his curiosity. *Had he found some kind of service entrance to something important enough to be kept secret, hidden away in the woods?* He wanted to know more, and the thought of trespassing into something important and secret is what truly excited him and aroused the same curiosity that almost resulted in being burned by the firecracker before his dad slapped it out of his hands. So he walked closer.

When he was in front of the strange, shiny stepladder, Brian wondered how much trouble he would get into if he continued. *So, is this something that belongs to the military? Is it some kind of hidden experimental chamber? What kind of experiments go on inside? Is this some kind of data gathering equipment?* Questions quickly raced through his mind as he glanced around his surroundings for more information. He looked down at the stepladder and noticed something else. The lowest rung was slightly larger than the rest and had strange markings. The inscription was quite noticeable as it was a neon turquoise color. The foreign markings looked bizarre, yet familiar. The hesitation he had in exploring further was the thought of being where he was not supposed to be. Trepidation about a breach of some type of security worried him, but only a little. The need to explore outweighed any thoughts of misdemeanor consequences. Still, he wanted to be careful. He gave the situation more thought and reasoned he should continue. He looked around to see if any warning signs were posted. There were none. Brian had not come across any fences, security guards, guard dogs or flashing lights to warn him away before entering the gully. No alarms sounded at his arrival. Only the sounds of the nocturnal forest could be heard. The only wall separating him from this area was his parent's rear lot retaining wall. Therefore, nothing had really impeded him from this late night journey and discovery. Why, then, should he be concerned about continuing? Who was there, really, to say no? After all, the door opened when he started to leave. He did not force it open. The door opened on its own.

"What the hell," Brian muttered, and stepped onto the first rung of the shiny stepladder.

With flashlight and knife in hand, he continued up the short ladder. He was able to easily keep balance as the rungs were steadier than they first appeared. Brian looked around once more, grinning as he did not know what he was doing or if he should be doing it. But he pressed on and stepped into the recessed opening and stopped in front of the interior door. It was an off white color and oddly shaped, like an oval, and bore the same type of foreign writing as he saw on the stepladder. He could not see any hinges, or a handle. He looked around within the recessed entry area and saw that a smooth and contiguous concave wall surrounded the strange oval doorway. Brian quickly noticed what a master piece of design this entry space was. There were no seams, or rivets. It all looked fluid, like one piece, beautifully and perfectly engineered. Somehow, the light seemed to be coming from within the wall. But, the concave enclosure wall was not transparent. He could not see any light bulbs behind the swathe concave enclosure. Light softly shined through it all, like a lampshade, filling the recessed entry area with just enough illumination.

As Brian stood motionless, wondering how the entryway was assembled, he suddenly became aware that if the exterior door slid back upward and closed, he could possibly be trapped in that section of the entryway. He looked down to see precisely where the exterior door would slide along the concave grooves to make a seal at the top. Then he was not too concerned as it seemed he would have enough room to stand comfortably, even if the stepladder retracted. He craned his neck, looking all around the inside of the recessed entrance. He thought about ventilation since he did not readily see any way air would ventilate the enclosed area should the exterior door slide up and close. Somehow, though, he thought it probably would be okay. Brian relaxed. He took in a deep breath and turned again to look at the turquoise inscriptions on the inner doorway. The size of each inscription varied, with some larger than others. Brian figured the foreign writing was organized neatly to inform the appropriate persons about safety and such, but he didn't really have a clue what it meant.

"Looks like Chinese, or, Japanese, or, something," Brian said in a full, whispered breath, excited to discover this unknown thing.

Then he noticed his breathing was heavier now, and that his fingers tingled and his throat was dry. In that same moment he wondered if he was all alone with his new discovery. *Did anyone else know of this?* In looking around the entryway again he noticed there were small hand rails alongside the contoured oval walls near the opening. They were the same color as the interior walls and he had simply missed their presence before. He carefully set both the knife and the flashlight on the limited floor area next to him and then, grabbing hold of the small rails for balance, he stooped down towards the entryway to see if anyone was coming. Brian saw no one. He was glad. He wanted to be alone now. Brian remembered how he wished before that someone was sharing the evening hike with him. But now he wanted to take the time to investigate this foreign secret contraption completely, and alone. He began to think that at any minute some Japanese scientist would come running out of the door telling him that this was private property. *He, or she, would probably try to explain that they have a secret experiment in process that converts cow piss into drinking water! Just as I had guessed!* Brian chuckled uncontrollably for a moment.

Brian leaned toward the oval door and looked all over its bizarre surface in an effort to find a button or latch, or anything noteworthy. He wanted in. It was quiet in this space. The only thing on his mind was finding out what was inside. Brian just knew that this secret chamber was the thing making the noise earlier. *Maybe the U.S. Air Force base not far away in the Mohave Desert has something to do with this?* Each question in his mind raised more. *Is this some kind of secret weapon?*

Brian stood in silence as he inspected every inch of the odd shaped door carefully. He started again at the top looking slowly from the left to the right, not wanting to miss any details. When he came across an inscription, he looked at it very meticulously, trying to see if there was a hidden button or something indicating how the door opened. The task made him think of his brother, Brandon. His brother was somewhat of a perfectionist. Sometimes it annoyed Brian, however, his brother's attention to detail helped Brian solve problems which usually saved the day. Brian reflected on one of those particular moments.

When the brothers were younger they had several hobbies as most children do. Brandon and Brian used to build plastic models together for a couple of years during their pubescent youth. They were both quite involved in the hobby. There was a local hobby store in the same neighborhood where they were born and grew up in Pasadena, California. The local hobby store held small, amateur competitions on occasion for the best assembled handiwork. Brian was thirteen years old at the time and very good at assembling model warships. His big brother was very supportive of him. Brian remembered how Brandon encouraged his little brother to compete in the local hobby store contest. Brian loved to put together the exact scale of the World War II era ships. The young boy had many entries that placed in the top three out of dozens of entries from other people.

One of Brian's biggest challenges was an intricate scale replica of the USS Lexington (CV-2) World War II aircraft carrier. It was one of the biggest and most complicated endeavors he ever took on as a young kid. When they purchased the unassembled plastic replica, Brian was a little apprehensive about finishing the model in time for the next competition. He did not want to rush the project and be disappointed with the results. But Brandon had faith in his little brother's talents and encouraged him to build it.

"Come on Brian," Brandon said with a smile, still holding the huge box in both hands after he took it off the hobby store shelf, "The theme is World War II again, and you're the best at it, little bro."

Brandon supervised his brother on the difficult tasks. He gave Brian several helpful hints so his little brother would not become frustrated and overwhelmed, given the size of the project. Brandon often consulted the directions, which he had copied and laminated into a clever master plan board for his brother to follow carefully. Brandon had also visited the local library, and looked at old archive photographs from books they checked out as a resource for some of the warship details. With all the assistance Brandon gave him, Brian was able to concentrate on assembling the model to almost exact specifications. Even in the early stages of the process, Brandon wanted to make sure his little brother got every chance to make it right. Because, when you build plastic models, you really only get one try at each step. Therefore, Brian's big brother would stare at photos from books, and walk over to the model during assembly, checking that most of the details were going to be present and in their proper places. Brandon was quick to point out if something was supposed to be in a particular spot on the model ship while it was still in assembly, too.

"I haven't gotten there, yet," Brian would respond, not wanting to disappoint his big brother.

Brian seriously concentrated on the task at hand every time he sat down to work on it. It was truly remarkable when it was finally painted and finished after all of the sanding and priming and delicate work. In fact, their father still occasionally brags of the marvelous accomplishment in the stories he shares with family and friends. Brian definitely won first place in the competition. All of the other competitors, including the hobby store owner, gazed at the warship wide open eyes and jaws agape. There was a model enthusiast present that day of the competition who was a United States Navy World War II veteran. The gentleman was stationed in Pearl Harbor as an ensign during the war and he saw the real USS Lexington many times. He was so impressed with the history of the aircraft carrier he politely convinced Brian's father to accept $80 for the superbly assembled model. But, it was only after Brian agreed to let it go.

"You want to sell it, or, no? You don't have to son. I know you worked hard on it," his father said quietly.

"It's okay dad." Brian nodded his head resolutely in reassurance.

Brian remembered how the veteran of the historic war, a senior citizen now, shook his hand firmly.

"Well done young man." He had said. "You'd make all the sailors of Lady Lex proud! Great job! I had friends who were on that ship when she sailed to the Battle of the Coral Sea."

The gentleman had the biggest smile. He even took a picture next to the huge model with Brian.

Brandon was so proud of his little brother. His confidence and dedicated assistance is what gave Brian the motivation to succeed. Brian attributed much of his success to his brothers' attention to detail. That is what got the job done. That is what got Brian first place in the competition that day.

I know my brother would have found the button to open this thing up by now. Brian delicately touched the bizarre foreign inscription on the oval door with his fingers. By now, he was actually starting to feel a little tired, and the evening was getting cooler. He was considering leaving. *Maybe I should try this tomorrow. I should bring a camera, too.* He also thought about asking his parents if they knew the strange thing was here. *There was probably mention of this thing in the paper, or... not.* Brian sighed, stretching his arms within the confined space. He turned to leave and reached down to pick up the flashlight and knife next to his feet.

When he stood up he heard a soft click come from the door behind him. The young explorer thought about leaping out of the entryway and running up the other side of the gully, fast. But instead, he stayed right where he was. There hadn't been any 'Do Not Trespass' signs. At least not in English. He had a feeling the door had just unlocked. Brian prepared for an encounter with some foreign scientist. He wanted to ask them what they were doing here on his property. He was curious what type of answer and explanation he would get. It was just his nature to be bold and a bit mischievous at times. He was also a bit of a prankster. Brian stood still and concentrated on having a serious, stern face. He thought it would be the best approach to avert getting in trouble. *Turn things around and make them the trespassers.* He thought about what would happen when he told his mother the story of this evening. She'd get the best laugh of all time out of it. Brian knew his father would also appreciate his sense of adventure, though his dad would have given up and headed home a long time ago.

The door smoothly slid upward on recessed grooves. As the door rose Brian immediately looked down for feet on the other side but, he could not see anyone. The door retracted quickly, barely making a sound. At once, Brian detected a slightly familiar odor. It was very subtle. The young man tilted his head from side to side and sniffed the air. It smelled like a pet.

He was even more curious now, so he stepped into the area that the opened door just exposed. Then he looked back at the ceiling area where the door had disappeared to see if it would automatically come down and close. It did not, so he started to examine the interior of whatever this object was. He was expecting some scientist with a heavy accent to come running out holding a flask of bovine urine in his gloved hands. He smiled briefly at the thought. Brian tried to make light of the situation, but he could not deny the nervous feeling he had deep down inside at the moment. He was quickly sinking into fear of the unknown. The interior area was basically the same off white color but with a slightly darker tinge than the recessed entryway. It was all very clean. The ceiling was slightly higher so it had more headroom than the entryway he'd just come from. He noticed the lighting seemed to be coming from the ceiling in the same manner as he observed in the entryway, that same 'lampshade' effect. Brian noticed two doors to his left that were slightly recessed into the wall. They were as tall as the entry door, but they did not look as heavy. On the opposite side of the narrow room was a duplicate oval shaped door. *That is most likely an entry and exit for the other side, I bet.*

Then Brian heard the gentle sound of air moving, like air

conditioning. He looked around, but saw no vents. He could sense the climate getting just a little warmer and noticeably more comfortable. The surrounding walls joined the ceiling in a slight curve instead of squared corners. The same was true for the floor. Even though it was narrow, the room felt large to Brian, probably due to the lighting. The walls on the left and right had slightly raised darker shaded panels throughout various sections with the same bizarre inscriptions all over. There were soft glowing lights noticeable within the flat panels, but there were no light bulbs to be seen. All over the panels were rows and even more rows of different colored lights in an array of steady and sequentially blinking lights. It all looked unfamiliar. He tried to think of where he had ever seen such an engineering design when he suddenly noticed that the characters on the inscriptions were slightly raised, like Braille. They looked like bronze metal. The raised inscriptions had very narrow pale blue lighting bordering each and every character. The inscriptions and all the blinking lights were astonishing.

Brian walked to the center of the room and looked back at the door where he entered. It was still open. He turned towards the two doors on the side of the wall and reached out. Still holding the knife, he slowly touched the wall next to the door on the right with his index finger. To Brian's amazement, it was kind of soft. It almost felt like firm foam padding. The touch reminded him of a computer mouse pad. He smiled and touched all around the wall in front of him, careful not to press any lights or any of the raised inscriptions. It all felt the same, like one giant mouse pad. He pressed the surface of the door on the right, the closest to him. It felt just like the wall. The young man was amused. Suddenly, without sounding an alarm, the door opened swiftly and quietly, sliding to the right into a cleft in the wall.

Well, I've come this far.

Chapter Three

The door opened, leaving an inch or so visible beyond the cleft into which the door had disappeared. Brian took a fleeting glance at the doorway before entering, not sure if it would close again as fast as it had opened. He looked into the smaller room the open door revealed. It was about half the length of the first room. There was a wall immediately to the left and the room extended on his right. He could see the wall on the other side. The width of the room was about the same as the room he was currently in. He remained still for a moment. At first glance he noticed it was darker than the room he was standing in. For the first time, he felt that this late evening exploration might have been a bad idea. He wasn't sure if it was the darkness, or the incredible silence that disturbed him. Perhaps, it was a combination of the two which only added to his apprehension and the fear of the unknown. He just couldn't seem to suppress his fear. It was such a genuine emotion.

He tried to rationalize. What is fear, really? It is just a normal response humans have when reacting to existent danger. It is a response mechanism to certain stimuli. Fear is what keeps one alert, and often, safe. Because when people are afraid, they often think of a way to escape the situation that conceives the fear. Brian's method of escaping the fear of the unknown was to face it head on. Sometimes, the more you know, the less you fear. But he had to admit that sometimes quite the opposite is true.

He could see a duplicate door on the other side of the room directly across from the doorway where he stood. Several small amber colored lights dotted the right side of that doorway.

Brian stared at the amber lights for a moment and remembered a story he heard when he was a freshman at Bishop Montgomery Catholic High School in Torrance, California. During lunch period one day he overheard a conversation going on at one of the tables near where he was sitting in the cafeteria waiting for some classmates to join him.

"Dude, I'm serious, I couldn't sleep the rest of the night. I kept looking out my sleeping bag every few minutes." Kevin Hearshy, an energetic young freshman, was talking to a few captive listeners at his table.

The kids were huddled around close as he spoke quietly. But, his voice carried far enough for Brian to hear. The skinny young freshman talked about how he and his family went on a camping trip in Joshua Tree National Forest just to the north of Los Angeles County. On the second night after the campfire was put out and everyone was starting to fall asleep, young Kevin witnessed an unidentified flying object.

"Are you serious, Kevin? Sure you didn't get beamed up to the mother ship and have your brain replaced with a gold fish brain?" Tina Reyes, a pretty young girl also in the freshman class, jested as the other kids chuckled.

"I'm telling you what I saw, dude." Kevin's eyes were wide as he recaptured their attention quickly. "There were two lights floating way up in the sky, moving together in a box pattern just like this."

Kevin illustrated their flight with his two fingers moving slowly around in the air. The kids at his table stared at him, listening quietly.

"Then," Kevin said quickly, tilting his head to follow his fingers with a serious gaze, "they shot up into the sky like that!" He suddenly moved his fingers up in the air, stretching his arm over his head straight up, in one rapid motion. The listeners at the table responded with "ooh" and "no way" as Kevin nodded his head silently.

"Freaked me out, man, and I was the only one that saw it, too," Kevin said quietly. "Everybody else had dozed off. I was the only one awake, dude. Serious."

· · • • ● ⬤ ● • · ·

As Brian reflected on the story he heard back in high school, he began to feel all alone in the ellipsoid object. He suddenly felt far away from the comfort of his parents' home. But he took a deep breath and clenched his teeth, regaining his nerve and composure as he stared into the darkened room in front of him. For the first time, Brian spoke aloud.

"Hello?" His voice filled the room. "Anyone here?"

There was no reply. Brian stepped into the smaller room as his eyes started to adjust to the low lighting. Immediately to his right were two objects that took up most of the length of the room. They were located on opposite sides of the room with each positioned horizontally along the wall. They were identical, approximately 4 feet wide and 7 feet long. The height of the objects came up close to Brian's chest, about 4 feet from the floor. The tops were a familiar, basic curvilinear geometric shape. Brian thought they looked like oversized toothbrush containers, the type he always used to travel with. Both were a dark olive color. He stepped in-between the two of them until he was about halfway down their length. From here he could see an array of lights flashing on the sides of the strange cylindrical contraptions, almost waist high. Some of the lights formed the now familiar characters of the inscriptions he had previously noticed. He briefly looked around the surface of both objects for clues as to what these smooth as glass objects were. Brian stuffed the flashlight in his left pant pocket to keep it steady while he investigated. He touched the palm of his hand to the top of the bizarre object on his left and bent over to look at it a little closer.

As he did, something very strange happened. The olive color on the top half of the cylindrical object started to change to an opaque gray precisely where Brian's palm rested on it, and then the entire top half of the object followed suit. Then the gray hue faded away. The effect reminded Brian of how sunglasses automatically change their color and tint when you step inside, away from the bright sunlight outside. As this happened, a dim violet light started to illuminate from within the object and then gradually flood the top half. The hint of violet light changed slowly and then brightened slightly into a diffused ruby red illumination. As this transformation took place Brian could see what was inside the apparatus. A silhouette. The diffused ruby lighting began to gradually change into a very soft white illumination making the top half of the cylindrical object transparent. Brian no longer had to guess what the bizarre, oversized long toothbrush containers were. His jaw dropped open and his eyes widened at the sight of what was in the chamber. He could see what appeared to be a person.

During this process quiet, yet audible sounds like beeps and blips came from the strange apparatus. Brian noticed that the flashing lights on the side panel of this futuristic contrivance were brighter now and they were all flashing in sequence. Next, Brian returned his attention to the inside of the chamber where he could see more detail now since the light inside was brighter than the lighting in the room. He took his hand from the top of the cylindrical chamber quickly, and was very much confused by what his eyes saw next.

This 'being' had very authentic looking amber skin pigmentation, a skin tone he'd never seen before. Brian stared in silence at the delicate, exotic, and entrancing facial features of the person in the chamber. As the soft light transitioned through subtle stages within the chamber, Brian could see this strange, inimitable being was female. She appeared to be sleeping still, her unusual yet appealing face completely expressionless. Her cheeks were slightly prominent. She had an elegantly narrow nose, although it was longer than usual with a defined angle near the eyebrows. The lips were small and delicate, with a slightly deeper shade than her skin color which made them pleasingly extraordinary. The forehead was normal looking and proportionate to the rest of her unusual, yet remarkable facial features. Brian's curious eyes attentively studied how the long, ultrathin eyebrows angled gracefully along the slightly defined supraorbital ridge. Her strikingly humanoid facial features overall were very complementary and not too dissimilar compared to those of any other lovely woman. Her hair was a smooth medium brown with warm gold highlights, short in appearance, falling slightly above her uniform collar. Her closed eyes were rimmed with long dark eyelashes. Brian took in her bizarre, remarkable beauty in awed silence. He was quite enthralled and wanted to see more. The dark, exotic skin pigmentation looked corporeal, natural, and silky-smooth.

Brian leaned forward with his face up close to the sealed chamber. He could see her left hand, the closest one to him, in more detail. The hand was narrow with long fingers. It appeared to be very soft and to some extent, delicate. Despite the unusual narrowness, the hand was not unlike that of any young woman. Brian looked at the fingers and fingertips. The five phalanges looked very authentic, with the thumb a little longer than normal, but in relative proportion to the other four fingers. The cuticles of her fingertips were pushed back and the lunular visible on the thumbnail. He was surprised to see the nails were manicured and looked so healthy.

Then he noticed her long legs, lean looking in a one piece, body-hugging garment a military pilot might wear. He logically assumed this was a similar type of flight suit. It was a dark shade of purple russet with slate gray stripes all along the sides. Then Brian looked at her feet which were together and exposed like the hands, revealing the same deep and silky smooth skin tone. Her feet were very narrow, kind of odd looking, but at the same time, delicately beautiful in appearance. Brian shifted his inquis-itive visual inspection to look at the upper body. The chest area of the snug flight suit was embroidered with the same confusing inscriptions he'd seen throughout, and the collar was high and straight with odd symbols embroidered on them in various spots.

Brian noticed how the fitted jumpsuit revealed the curvature of her breasts. He could see the slight rise and fall of her chest with each breath. He also noticed the accentuated curve of her hips as those flowed down to and blended with those long legs and finally her narrow feet. She appeared to be tall, even lying down in the supine position. Her lean, long physique was very similar to that of a fit athlete. She looked so peaceful, as if time was standing still and she would never change. Brian was in such awe that he did not want to move even the slightest bit, thinking he might disturb her if he did so. He wanted to just stand there the entire night and look upon her beguiling beauty. Never before had he seen such a bizarre sight as the 'woman' within the chamber.

She looks so real. Suddenly Brian wondered if this was all just part of some sort of movie prop. He looked up into the air as he wondered if there were any movies being filmed in the area. Occasionally, various television and movie producers filmed on location, choosing the beautiful scenery of the San Bernardino Mountains for their background. He even tried to recall the last time he saw a film crew up in the area. Brian rubbed his chin for a moment as he pondered. Then, he remembered the pop culture science fiction television series that was filmed on location about a decade ago for a couple seasons. The show was widely popular for a short while. The basic premise was a murder mystery that took place in the immediate area and the detective assigned to solve the case took a little over a year to do so. Each episode divulged the main character's chronological, detailed steps of gathering clues and evidence from other related crimes in the process of solving the main murder mystery. The show made the resort area 'hip' for a while. Tourists visited the mountain community area just to see where the popular television series was filmed. Sometimes, visitors were lucky enough to visit on a day when filming was taking place. But Brian could not recall any film projects in process at the moment.

He looked down at the enchanting and mysterious features once again and was startled to find her eyes were open. Her gaze seemed a bit nomadic at first, as she was noticeably squinting as she looked about. Brian could tell she was trying to focus her vision. The alien woman seemed a little disoriented at first glance. Then, all of a sudden, she made direct eye contact with Brian with a very decipherable, shocked look on her alien face! Without doubt, she was obviously quite alarmed to see him standing there!

Brian was so surprised by her silent, abrupt reaction that

he jumped back and bumped into the chamber behind him. Instantly, beeping noises and flashing lights started up on that apparatus. Brian turned his head to see what was going on and discovered the chamber he bumped was illuminating and becoming transparent similar to the first, but faster. The beeps and blips on the one he bumped into continued while the first one containing the strange female humanoid suddenly opened, the transparent chamber cover smoothly and quickly retracting away into the adjacent side wall. As the cover disappeared into the wall, she scooted to the farthest corner of the chamber and curled into the fetal position in an effort to hide as much of herself behind her long legs as she could. Long arms wrapped around small knees and her narrow, almond shaped eyes locked on Brian without once blinking.

Brian could feel her daunted stare as the other chamber opened and retracted swiftly. He held his breath, not looking at her now, so focused was he on the other chamber behind him. With a subtle hum and hiss it retracted away fully. There was nothing inside. Brian sighed deeply and leaned against the empty chamber, resting his rear end just beyond the center of the apparatus toward the section with the lighted, flashing panel. He adjusted his posture and was almost sitting on the firm padding within the empty chamber. He took his flashlight out of his pocket and held it in his left hand. With the knife still in his right hand, he looked at the mysterious female humanoid. She sat silently across and away from him, her almond shaped eyes were now locked on the sharp object he had in his right hand. Brian immediately felt uncomfortable. Then her eyes shifted back and forth between the flashlight and knife. Brian could see a look of legitimate fear on her face. She was motionless, still hiding most of herself behind those long legs, propped up in the fetal position against the inside corner of her chamber. The exotic female humanoid barely looked at Brian, but from what he could see her eyes were a bright color. They almost sparkled like gems in contrast to her silky-smooth dark skin tone. All her attention was focused on the knife in his hand.

Brian held up the knife with a reassuring smile on his face.

"This is nothing." He shook his head quickly. "Don't worry. I mean you no harm, miss."

He slowly placed the knife down close to his side on the chamber padding. He touched the soft material and quickly assumed it was bedding material.

Brian studied her carefully, almost certain she was in costume for some type of movie production. *But, she looks so real! And, where is the production and film crew? Where are the cameras, and all the other stuff people need to shoot a movie?* He didn't understand this and was a little scared and confused, too. *What could this all be? What does it all mean?* Brian did not believe stories like the one he overheard in the cafeteria of the high school that day. He did not believe in extraterrestrials even though the female humanoid was definitely different. Her physique made a compelling case that suggested she was not from this planet. But however convincing her appearance was, Brian was not yet ready to change his belief.

"What are you dressed up for, anyway?" he asked, trying to break the uncomfortable silence with pleasant conversation. He smiled at her nervously.

"Is this some kind of secret movie set or something?" The humanoid woman did not answer.

"Is all this part of a secret television production?" Brian asked, gesturing with his hands and looking around the dark room for answers. However, the mysterious alien woman only peered over her knees at him in silence.

"Don't be shy, miss, I'm not gonna hurt you," Brian added quietly as he tried to reassure her with a kind, calming voice.

But deep in his mind Brian was starting to realize that he may have discovered something no one else knew about even though he was still not quite sure what this was all about. He stared at her. She stared back at him and shifted her gaze to both of the objects he brought with him, and then looked directly into his eyes again. The room was silent apart from the occasional sounds of beeps from the equipment around them. They studied each other in the silence. Brian shook his head, again and again.

"You look so real!" He finally said softly and then looked her up and down quickly. "You just look _so_ real!" He said, trying to disbelieve what his eyes saw.

She looked back at the flashlight and Brian noticed her fixation so he turned the flashlight on with a click. The exotically beautiful humanoid flinched slightly as the bulb illuminated against the wall. Brian turned the flashlight on and off several times while shining the light against the palm of his right hand.

"It's a light, that's all it is." He smiled at her reassuringly, yet he felt more confused than ever now. _Does she really not know what this is?_ There were no answers coming from the mysterious woman. All she did was stare at him in response.

She studied him carefully, seeing a young, mixed ethnicity African American and Caucasian male, twenty-six years of age. He stood five feet and ten inches tall, weighed 180 pounds and had a slim, athletic build. His clothes were loose fitting and, his face and hands had a healthy mocha skin tone. The young male had no facial hair. His eyes were dark brown. He had short, very curly dark brown hair on his head. His amiable facial expressions displayed candid uneasiness, and there was a hint of fear in his eyes.

Brian could feel her incessant stare probing him from over the tops of her knees. Her gleaming eyes peered through her hair. This was all Brian could see of her behind those long legs and arms. He honestly did not know what to do or say next. He did not want to frighten the strange alien woman one bit.

"I was just out for an evening walk and I found your lab or, movie set, or… uh, whatever this is." Brian looked at her and spoke quietly, careful of the tone of his own voice.

He did not want to distress her any more than he already had. All that he wanted was a few answers for his journey out into the forest this evening. Most people would have given up and returned home long ago. Some would never even have found the strange ellipsoid. Others may have just guessed the ellipsoid was some specialized technological thing and left it at that. Very few would have been intrigued enough to find a way to enter it. Fewer would have explored the inside of the strange ellipsoid and stumbled upon the humanoid woman who was now staring at him. How many, all in all, would stay to get answers? Brian continued to look at her, wondering what he should say next.

"So, um, is this a foreign film?" He searched for a way to get her to talk to him.

"Are you like, living on set so you can get into character or something like that? I know actors do that kinda stuff."

Brian noticed her posture change a little. She brought her head up from her knees and extended her right arm, pointing her thumb at the flashlight in his hand. She spoke. It sounded like complete gibberish, yet there was something slightly familiar about it. Her voice was soft and it carried through the small room like a melody to his ears. Then, she gestured with the wrist and thumb of her right arm at the flashlight in his left hand and the knife next him on the chamber padding. Even though he couldn't understand what she was saying, Brian assumed it was something about those two items. She spoke again, quickly. More gibberish filled his ears. Brian looked at her face and noticed her expression was more relaxed. In fact, she looked self-assured. The fear was completely gone from her body language. The bizarre and beautiful amberous colored humanoid slowly dropped her hands to her sides. For a split-second he thought he saw her eyes shift to his left. *What did she just look at?* He remained silent and perfectly still, almost afraid to move now because all at once he felt uneasy.

Then Brian sensed someone else in the small room. In his peripheral vision he saw a shadowy image slowly approach him. He continued looking at the alien humanoid woman. He noticed her look away, once more to his left, and then she shifted her attention and focused solely on Brian, her gaze confident and content. He saw her composure relax even more. Brian had never in his life experienced what he was going through at this particular moment and just didn't know what to do. Out of fearful curiosity, he slowly turned his head to see what was coming at him from the darkness of the small room. He didn't want to look, but at the same time, something deep inside him had to look. He had to know what was looming in the peripheral of his vision. His breath caught in his throat when he could clearly see. His muscles tensed. His heart skipped a beat and he could feel the hairs on the back of his neck stand up at full attention.

"Oh shit!" The words tumbled instantly and uncontrollably from Brian's lips.

Chapter Four

From the corner of Brian's peripheral vision something emerged from the serene confines of the dark room. Something he'd never seen before. In fact, he couldn't believe what he was seeing. This apparition profoundly challenged his supposition of living beings from another world, just as the humanoid woman had. He had solemnly refused to believe in UFOs and aliens from outer space before tonight. Sure, he had heard and read stories about such things that are unknown to us, and even seen some shows on television about these subjects. Even Kevin Hearshy had an account about this sort of thing that day in high school. However, this was all exceptionally different. He was actually experiencing this himself, and it was so surreal it would be difficult to express the sensation to someone else. How do you explain something that you have no existent knowledge about or, have never actually seen before? How do you begin to convince someone else about a situation like tonight while trying not to make yourself sound crazy? This is what Brian, in a confused state of mind, experienced at this moment. He felt all alone, isolated from all reality even though what stood before him about six feet away was definitely very real.

Brian could not think of, or concentrate on anything else. He only stared in absent minded astonishment as he turned to face it. There it stood for a slight moment within the darkened stillness of the small room staring right back at him, and then the silhouette of the looming being slowly approached him. Brian felt his disbelief fading fast. When he found the alien woman, the experience was a new, exciting realization and, undoubtedly, perhaps a historic discovery. However, looking into the eyes of the being standing just out of arm's reach was immediately and profoundly disturbing. Brian felt an apprehension of unnerving discomfort and fear envelope him like a thick new skin. He was so tense he was unable to move or even hardly breathe. So he stood still in utter shock and awe.

The creature stood about 5 feet and 11 inches tall. Brian was fixated on the most impressive feature at the moment; its teeth. The creature had the distinct semblance of a snarl, much like that of any carnivorous member of the canidae biological family indigenous to earth. There appeared to be a full set of incisors, canines, premolars, and molars; basically, large teeth in full direct view. The gums were a fleshy pink color, wet with shiny clear saliva glimmering on them. Its thin lips appeared black in color, and they stretched around the threatening, sharp, pearl white teeth of the beast. The large head of the creature was wide and long and tapered forward. A low set pair of long, pointed ears was positioned on opposite sides of its wide, muscular skull. The creature also had a very noticeable wide and flat rhinarium with nostrils that flared as it continued to snarl and glower directly at the frightened young man.

Then there were the eyes. Under its muscular, furrowed eyebrows was a pair of large, low set eyes. Visible even in the low lighting, they were ominous and glowering across either side of the creature's long and broad snarling muzzle. The glowing white sclera surrounding the dark iris of each eye left no doubt as to where the creature was looking. As it slowly moved forward into the light cast from the sleeping chambers, Brian could see the color of its eyes. They were a disturbing maroon shade. The prominent color of the irises reminded Brian of the same shade of red identified with arterial blood.

Brian was terrified, and his subconscious fight-or-flight response to this threatening figure was in full effect. But the complete shock and horror of what he was witnessing froze him to the spot. He had never before felt this separated from the comfort of things he was familiar with. He felt like he had no control over the situation now. In an instant, the adventurous excitement was all gone from this night time excursion. With every second that passed Brian came nearer and nearer to a state of pure panic. All he could think about was this could not be happening. It could not be real. *I don't believe in monsters.* The thought echoed again and again in his mind.

The creature stopped about three feet away from the terrified young man. With its menacing teeth still showing, it slowly and precisely focused all its attention on Brian's left hand. Brian looked down and realized the thing was looking at the flashlight he held none too steadily. Without a second thought Brian tossed the flashlight on the bed of the empty chamber. The creature did not even flinch. Brian could sense that it was not happy to find him here tonight, but he also got the distinct impression that it would not be happy to find anybody here at any time. Nothing personal, Brian was just in the wrong place at the wrong time. *Maybe, taking a hike at night all alone in the middle of nowhere just because you hear strange noises isn't the best idea.*

Next, the creature methodically shifted its intent gaze toward Brian's right hand. Brian looked down, unsure of what held the creature's attention this time. He stood perfectly still, staring at his right hand. If he could have physically detached it, disowned his own right hand in that split second, he would have done so. For in that hand, held secure in a tight grasp, was the kitchen knife he must have picked up unawares. His trembling increased until fear threatened to consume him. Brian tried to take a step backwards but bumped his head on the wall behind him, oblivious to the subtle retreat he'd been making since first seeing the creature.

Brian looked up directly into the red eyed, narrow pupils of the beast. The creature furrowed its large brows and snarled even more as it stared the young man down. As it did so, it made a loud gurgling sound very similar to the aggressive growl of a dog. Next, it slowly hunched over, slightly leaning its head and shoulders forward toward Brian. The creature's head tilted to the left as its gaze promptly returned to the knife in Brian's right hand. He nervously tossed the knife on the bed of the chamber as he had the flashlight. The beast did not flinch one inch, but watched every move the young man made with that same disturbing and aggressive snarl. When the knife landed on the bed of the chamber, the beast instantaneously shifted its gaze back toward Brian and locked onto him. It raised its snout as if to make sure all teeth were visible to the young man.

Brian could see the beast very well at this close range. It was muscular all over, tall and solid. The shoulders were a little wider than Brian's. The chest was about the same width in proportion to its hips. It had a small waist which made the upper body look larger than it was. The thighs were long, large, and very firm looking. Both knees and the large calves were brawny extensions of its long muscular legs. The creature had on a similar jumpsuit to the one the mysterious humanoid woman was wearing. The creature's suit was a tight fitting Capri style ending just below the knees. It did not have any sleeves, which allowed Brian to see the solidly toned musculature of the creature's long arms. The forearms were bulky and tense. The wrists were wide and thick. The right wrist had what appeared to be a bracelet with some sort of watch on the top of it. Both hands were large with five long, thick fingers on each. The thumbs were wide and flat looking. The dark fingernails resembled stubby claws. The same was true for the feet on the creature, which were long, with fat, strangely arranged toes with dark and stubby, but sharp toenails. Brian stared at its weird feet as he put it all together in his mind: *The anatomy of the feet, the long snarling snout, the teeth, and those ears. That's it!* The beast had a stark resemblance to what is known in common folklore as a werewolf. In appearance, it defined most of the mythical physical descriptions profoundly and shockingly.

Brian stared into the eyes of the beast. He did not move, and it did not move. To Brian, that was a good sign. He felt lucky he was not dead yet. He noticed more details. The skin of the creature was not as smooth and silky as the alien woman. The creature's skin was a wheat color, with the shade being remarkably close to Brian's own skin. Brian could not see any hair on the creature's legs, arms, or face. His attention again returned to the eerie maroon irises of the creature's eyes. The eyes were not looking anywhere else in the room but at him. Brian took a deep breath and tried to smile. His lips quivered, his hands shook, and his teeth actually chattered from the rush of adrenaline his body had released. But he tried to relax.

The room was silent. The creature's snarl was only slight, now. But it made sure a few sharp teeth were still in full view. Brian stared and the creature stared back. Brian finally spoke with a nervous, crackling in his throat.

"What are you... some kinda hairless werewolf?" Brian tried to smile even though his lips still quivered. His throat was so dry.

The creature only glared at Brian, looking directly into his eyes. Its posture did not change. It was still slightly hunched over with its arms raised at its side, about the height of its hips; like it was ready to pounce at any given moment. Brian, with his nervous posture, tried to relax a little more. He figured if he did not appear afraid, maybe the beast would not kill him. Brian wanted to be strong. But he also had an overwhelming urge to run away as fast as he could. *Is this all really happening? Is this all real?* It sure seemed very real!

Suddenly, the humanoid woman spoke. Again, it was complete gibberish to the young man. But the calmness and melody of her voice was pacifying. All at once, the posture of the creature changed. It stood at attention, face forward with hands at its side. Brian, who had basically ignored the humanoid woman up to this point, now looked to her for reassurance. He still wanted to truly believe that this was some kind of special, exclusive movie set. However, the encounter was numbingly surreal and, confrontationally sublime. Without doubt, deep down inside, he still wanted to run away as fast as he could. But, he also wanted to confirm in his mind if this was all happening for real. He thought he should stay and find out as much as he could. Besides, the tall menacing creature was blocking Brian's only escape route. And where would he run to? He was certain those strong, oversized legs on the beast would run him down for sure.

Brian continued to stare at her. The alien woman had no

expression on her face as she gazed into Brian's eyes. She sat with her long legs crossed beneath her long torso in complete silence. He cleared his throat and spoke.

"Is this some kind of a joke?" There was only silence and the stare of the humanoid woman.

Brian blinked slowly and cleared his throat again. He did not know what to say. After all, how do you start a polite conversation with two completely strange beings you have never seen before?

"So, I'm guessing you two aren't from around here, huh?" He said, nervously chuckled at the sound of his own words.

As soon as he said those words he wanted to take them back. He felt silly for suggesting it. He chuckled again.

"So," he blinked slowly, "this is really some kind of space ship. I mean, it really is, huh?" Brian was trying to make sense of his own words. He wanted to calmly convince himself of the possible conclusion.

Brian had his mouth open, eyes wide for answers, as he asked.

"Or…" he paused as he stared at her, "is this some kind of reality show, some television prank?"

The questioning tone of his words had slowly and clearly proceeded from out of his mouth. Brian wanted to know the truth, although he wanted his own disbelief in extraterrestrials to be that truth. He was honestly still scared for his life. He wanted someone to come out of the shadows with a camera and a crew of people laughing in the background telling him how scared he looked, and this was all actually a joke. But, humans don't look the way these two do. No makeup or costume ever looked <u>so real</u>. Yet, there was no camera crew waiting to reveal themselves to him. He was actually all alone this night, witnessing first hand, something more astounding than he had ever seen before. The incomprehensible was now a fact of life, and a confirmation of existence was standing before him right now. Is it <u>really</u> true that intelligent life exists on other planets? Brian shook his head slowly at the mere thought of it all.

"Come on, man, this can't be really happening." He nervously smiled at the beautiful amberous humanoid, but she remained expressionless.

Brian looked into her eyes, trying to discern what was real and what was cosmetic about her. He was still holding onto glimmers of denial about the fact that this could actually be happening to him.

The alien woman gently brushed some of the hair from her face with both hands to look at him better. Brian could clearly see the luminous bronze colored irises of her eyes in stark contrast to her white sclera, darkened pupils, and her dark facial skin tone. He could see her facial expression had changed to a more relaxed composure. Without looking at the creature in the room, she spoke to it with a clear voice. Her soothing tone broke the silence within the room once again. This time, Brian distinctly heard the creature utter something back. It was slurred, but discernable as language in her native tongue. Brian turned his gaze away from the alien woman to watch in awe as the beast enunciated words that only she understood.

Suddenly, and quietly, the creature turned around and walked on its large, uncanny feet away from Brian. As it turned to leave, Brian could see it had long, straight, platinum blonde hair tied into a ponytail on the back of its head. It exited the room swiftly through the door to Brian's right. The door slid shut without making a sound. Brian returned his attention to the alien woman again. She still had a relaxed posture about her. There was no look of fear in her eyes as before when she first saw him. She watched him in silence, studying him. He knew she sensed his genuine fear a short while ago.

"So, now what?" Brian asked her. There was no expression on her face. She sat motionless. The silence was uncomfortable.

Next, Brian heard the familiar slurred hissing voice of the creature and flinched at the sound. He looked toward the dark side of the room, but, saw nothing. Just the sound of the creature's voice gave him a complete pilomotor reflex, or 'goose bumps'. He reached behind his head and rubbed the back of his neck in an effort to compose himself. The alien humanoid immediately looked up and spoke. Then Brian figured she was communicating with the creature on some type of sophisticated intercom. But the creature's voice was so clear, it sounded like it was right there in the room with them. The two of them continued to converse in their foreign vernacular for a short moment. Then there was silence and the alien woman looked at Brian again.

"You don't understand me, do you?" Brian asked her in a very shy, quiet tone.

He looked at his watch. It was almost midnight. But, it did not feel like it was late. He wanted to know more about the strange occupants of the mysterious dark ellipsoid. When Brian looked up, he noticed the alien woman staring at his watch. He also noticed she was actually smiling a little for the very first time. He was pleasantly surprised. She extended her right arm and pointed with her thumb at the Casio G-shock, model DW 5600 time piece on his left wrist and spoke to Brian softly. What she said made no sense to Brian, but this time when he smiled at her, for the first time she returned a big smile back. That made him very happy and he felt relieved for a moment. He admired her. She possessed a strikingly odd beauty. He looked at her. Again, he studied her face as he had when she was asleep in the chamber. He looked at her prominent cheek bones, her small almond shaped eyes, her delicate narrow nose, and her dainty chin. All of these distinctive features made her seem unusual and exceptionally beautiful at the same time.

"You want to see this?" Brian asked politely in a soft tone of voice.

He leisurely removed the watch and offered it to her, looking up into her bronze eyes. She looked at the watch for a second and then returned her gaze to him. She was still sitting in a cross-legged position, but leaned forward slightly to look down at the watch in the palm of Brian's open hand. She reached out and picked up the watch, bringing it close to her face to study it in detail.

"Hmm." The humanoid woman softly uttered, as she gazed with a fascinated curiosity at the time piece.

She actually gave a short 'hmm', Brian thought, and smiled as he watched her. The alien woman turned the watch around, looking at it from different angles and then offered it back to Brian. He looked at her calm and gently smiling face and could not recall if he had ever seen that same remarkable color and hue anywhere else before tonight. Her skin color had to be authentic. There was nothing obvious that suggested she was wearing some type of cosmetic that made her look the way she did. He stared into her bronze eyes briefly. Her eyes were so strangely beautiful and her facial expression so calm and comforting. Brian felt safe and delighted to be in her company. He sincerely hoped she felt the same way about him. The young man truly meant her no harm. He hoped that she somehow understood that.

She was holding the watch in her open palm, just the way Brian had offered it to her. He noticed how the skin texture of her palm was similar in appearance to any normal hand, although it appeared to be denser, and it was a lighter shade than the dark skin tone on the rest of her hand. What was different was the color, of course. The beautiful flesh colored palm of her hand had a puce hue to it. He stared at her hand. The way her skin tone blended together from her wrist to the palm of her hand looked so real and naturally appealing.

"Unbelievable," he whispered.

Brian reached for his watch and as he did so, he saw her attention shift quickly to his left. Suddenly, Brian saw the creature's large left hand reach in and snatch the watch from the palm of her hand. The humanoid woman spoke quickly in an irritated tone.

You, again? Brian thought to himself as he saw the creature examining the Casio watch intently.

The beast had been so quiet entering the room that Brian never noticed. The creature had the watch up really close to its snout and for a second Brian thought it would eat it. But, it was just trying to see all the details. Brian looked at the floor. The creature examined the watch much faster than the humanoid woman had. It sneered at the small time piece and, with a grunt, it was done with its inspection and quickly handed the time piece back to the exotic humanoid woman, not Brian. She was still in the middle of speaking something in a loud tone of voice when the creature abruptly put it back in her opened hand.

There was silence. Once again, the alien woman offered the watch back to Brian. She did so with the same calm, reassuring smile and he gingerly took the time piece out of her palm. During this quiet exchange, the creature was standing next to Brian who was very much aware of the creature's scrutinizing gaze that watched his every move so carefully. As Brian replaced the watch on his left wrist and fastened the band, the beast moved a step closer to him. He could sense that the creature was standing very close. In fact, it was standing closer to him now than it had been during their first encounter. Brian slowly put his hands down at his side and looked down anxiously at the floor. He stood perfectly still. He could feel the creature breathing on him. Each time the beast exhaled, a warm drift of air gently tickled Brian's left ear and the back of his neck. The resultant timorous sensation made him feel very uncomfortable, all the while realizing there was no way to retreat as he was already backed up against the wall on his right and sandwiched in between two sleeping chambers. The empty one behind him was most likely for the creature. Brian had nowhere to go and there was nowhere to hide from the creature that stood only inches away breathing down on him.

Brian looked at the beast, once again taking notice of the creature's daunting form and well-developed physique. He looked up into the ominous being's creepy reddish eyes and took in every detail. The mouth of the beast was closed, no longer displaying the full set of carnivorous teeth. Brian did not see any seams or wrinkles on the beast's face, like the imperfections found on a costume mask mold. He searched for, but did not see any tell-tale creases or loose threads, either. He did not see any evidence of mascara or any other form of cosmetics being applied. What he could tell at this uncomfortably close distance was that the beast's large menacing snout was in fact, real!

The beast returned Brian's look with a silent, dissecting gaze as it stood composed and silent. Brian studied the musculature and the skin around its head and neck. He could see the prominent outline of several veins underneath various areas of the beast's skin. And there was something else. The creature was perspiring slightly. The glistening, moist, fleshy appearance of the beast's face left no further doubt in Brian's mind that what he was looking at was something definitely <u>not</u> from this world. Brian grimaced with an absolute look of shock and overwhelming awe in his eyes.

"Damn!" was all he could say.

The humanoid woman broke the uncomfortable silence with her unintelligible language and calm voice. She gestured with her right hand as she spoke. Brian had a disturbing feeling that she wanted him to touch the creature. All Brian did was stare at her with a lost look on his face, mouth half open and eyes wide as he considered her suggestion. He was simply astounded. Brian looked at the creature. It appeared to stare back at him with a subtle look in its eyes that dared Brian to try it. For an instant, Brian could swear he saw the creature smirk. Brian felt as if any contemptuous feelings the beast may have for him could all be seen in the daunting stare from those conspicuous, low set eyes.

"Uh," he glanced away from the beast, "I'm not so sure that's a good idea." Brian's voice cracked.

He turned his head and looked at the exotic woman. She answered with something unintelligible to his ears and motioned again with her right hand. She smiled reassuringly at Brian, trying to help him relax. Brian was fond of that smile, and he was already beginning to feel a certain genuine level of trust from her. He considered her suggestion and tried to relax. However, he had an appreciable amount of fear of the creature which distracted his efforts to completely compose himself.

"Right." Brian nervously responded as he continued his perplexed gaze into her mysterious, beautiful, and alluring bronze eyes.

The alien woman sensed Brian's fear of the extraterrestrial being in front of him. She did not speak this time. But she responded with another gesture of her hand and gave a quick nod with her head, similar to a bow. She looked at Brian with a delightful, encouraging smile and he could not help but smile in return. He relaxed.

When Brian looked at the beast and made eye contact, the creature grinned very slowly. It did so in an effort to show off its menacing and full set of sharp teeth. Then he leaned closer so Brian could examine them better. The creature stood still, its snout only a few inches from Brian's face, silently daring him to feel its pointed teeth. Brian could not back up anymore as is back was literally against the wall. He grimaced and started to turn his head away when the alien woman said something aloud in her language in a very sharp tone. At once, the creature stopped grinning. It lowered its head. In his peripheral vision Brian could see the alien woman gesture with her hands again, but he did not take his eyes off the beast in front of him. He most certainly did not want to do anything to make the alien creature angry. But, he did want to touch it. Brian felt like he had to. He started to wonder if this evening hike was all a part of his destiny somehow. Like, he was to be the chosen one that would eventually discover life on other planets, right here in his back yard. Brian was so nervous and curious and fearful, all at the same time.

He reached out a shaky hand and carefully touched the top of the creature's bowed head, timidly rubbing the warm, moist skin and hoping all the while that the beast would not snap and bite his hand off. Brian felt the animate texture of the creature's rough skin and quickly realized it was not a mask. It was not a fancy makeup job, either. Now his mind had to believe what his eyes witnessed. One touch was enough to convince him. The warm, moist, glistening skin of the extraterrestrial beast could not be faked with this much detail by any special effects artist. Maybe it could on camera, but not in the flesh. Not in person. Brian's jaw dropped in amazement as he took his hand off of the creature's head. He stood there in astonishment, momentarily still, as he took in all the detail. Next, he silently and cautiously grasped a hold of the creature's large right hand. It was very warm, dry, and quite firm to the touch. Brian examined the wide bone structure. The creature, which was quite compliant now, raised its arm slightly for Brian to see closer. The young man slowly and curiously took hold of the creature's hand in both of his hands. Next, Brian gently squeezed the hand of the beast and could feel the dense musculature as well as the skeletal form of the beast's warm, solid hand. Then he quickly let go and blinked a couple of times before looking again at the snout of the creature. As if on cue, the creature slowly grinned once again. This time, it was Brian who leaned forward as close as he could to examine the teeth and gums of the alien beast. As he did so, he could smell the warm, slightly pungent breath of the creature. Brian was convinced enough at this point and leaned swiftly back, hands to chest, away from the mouth of the beast.

Oh my God. This is for real, man!

Chapter Five

The local time in Hawaii was 9 p.m. and Brian's mother was plugging her black and silver Nokia 3310 mobile phone into the wall outlet charger. She had just hung up after trying to call her son one last time before going to bed. Brian's parents had returned to their timeshare in Kona from The Royal Kona Resort lobby after enjoying an evening of dinner and cocktails a short while ago.

"He still doesn't answer." Linda sounded a little more concerned than usual now.

"Honey he's a grown man. I'm sure he's okay," James said quickly, a bit distracted.

Brian's father was sitting up in bed with the television controller in hand. He had just changed the channels and discovered an interesting rerun of Hawaii-Five-O he was watching now.

"Besides, isn't it, like, midnight over there right now?" he said, peering to look at the digital clock on the nightstand. "If you call him again, you'll probably wake him up and make him mad." He looked back at his wife and gave her a funny look.

"I know, honey," Brian's mother sat down on the edge of the bed and picked up her paperback book from the nightstand.

"He said he would call me back this evening when I called him earlier today." Linda put on her reading glasses and leaned back on the large pillow against the headboard of the king size bed.

"I just want to make sure he fed Mr. Doodles and took care

of the plants." She stretched her legs out along the bed and gave a big sigh.

"I'm sure he did all of that," her husband responded, eyes on the TV. Linda turned on the nightstand lamp to its lowest setting so she could read next to her husband in bed without disturbing him.

"He probably has a lady friend over." Her husband raised his eyebrows mischievously and leaned his head towards his smiling wife.

Linda chuckled, still holding the paperback novel in her hand.

"Actually, the thought did cross my mind." She raised her eyebrows at her husband in return and leaned on his shoulder.

"At least he is taking advantage of having the house all to himself while we're gone for a while. She opened the book to the spot where she left off. "I know he has his own little place and all, but still, it's nice to get out and have a change of scenery. I hope he is enjoying himself."

"Oh," James interjected quickly with a raised brow, "I know he's enjoying himself at our house. He's young and single, Linda."

His wife chuckled light heartedly in response to his comment. Then, for a brief moment, there was silence between the two.

"Honey?" Linda took a more serious tone as she changed the subject, "Houston's birthday is coming up next month. I still want to have a little get together barbeque on that weekend. I want the kids over."

She put the book down and turned to her husband. "We were gone last year during his fourth birthday because of your silly convention-slash-vacation in Las Vegas. I don't want to miss out on my grandson's birthday this time."

James was looking at the TV, trying to concentrate on the developing plot.

"Linda, you took him and Brandon and Donnette for a two day stay at Disneyland and that California... uh, uh..." he searched for the word while looking up into the air. Then he looked at her.

"California Adventure," Linda said, staring into her husband's eyes.

"Yes, that one. California Adventure-land or something." He pointed at her and gently said, "You guys went there the following week that year." He put both hands up in the air.

"Didn't you get a big hotel suite and all?" His voice raised a couple of notches higher. Linda looked at him for a moment as she thought about it. Then he said, "Sweetheart, he doesn't know what day his birthday is. It's all the same to him. He's still a baby."

"Yes, he does." Linda looked at the television, one eyebrow raised. "It matters to him, and it matters to me, too," she said with her hand on her chest.

"Okay, okay, we'll have everyone over for dinner." He was trying to keep the tone of the conversation passive.

He knew that when his wife got something in her head to talk about, it could last late into the evening, sometimes.

"You can call everyone to confirm it. Talk it over with the kids tomorrow, okay?" James put his arm around his wife's shoulder and gave her a kiss on the cheek.

"Now, read your book and relax for now, okay dear?" He smiled at her and gave her another small peck on the cheek.

James didn't want her to get started talking about how she knew he should have rescheduled his convention meeting for a later date last year, since he could get the continuing education credits he needed for his job at some other meeting. She knew very well that if he had done so in time, they would not have missed their grandson's third birthday party the previous year.

James relaxed against the large fluffy pillow propped up behind him and returned his attention to the television. Linda smiled and picked up the book from her lap.

"I'll do that. I'll call the kids tomorrow. That's a good idea, honey." She adjusted her glasses and returned to the developing love story in her book.

Now there was silence, except for the television volume of the Hawaii-Five-O rerun.

Back inside the ellipsoid shaped object Brian still stood with his back against the wall between the two sleeping chambers. The mere presence of the two mysterious beings was profoundly contradictory to everything Brian had previously known and believed, concerning life on other planets. Without question, this first encounter would change the way he thought, thus making him more consciously aware about existent life outside of his own world. Brian looked back and forth between the two alien beings, his mind completely confounded as he tried to comprehend everything that was happening right now. There could be no more denial. He was the sole witness to a happening that was exceptionally tangible and beyond any doubt, solitarily novel.

"Can you… understand me?" Brian was still a bit nervous, trembling intermittently, his abdominal muscles tensing uncontrollably.

No answer. The two extraterrestrials turned their heads to look at one another. Their facial expressions bore what looked like uncertainty. He took a deep breath. He had to concentrate on making his voice sound less anxious.

"Are you from another planet?" Brian actually felt himself tense up slightly when he asked them the question in a blunt, humorless manner.

He continued to get blank stares in return. Then he had a thought. He wanted to try something simple in an effort to communicate with them. He extended his arm and pointed at the alien woman first. Then, without speaking, he slowly repeated the same motion as he pointed at the creature. Next, the young man looked them each in the eye back and forth as he slowly pointed up to the ceiling of the room. Surprisingly, it was the beast that broke the silence first with a snort, and some indiscernible hissing sound, speaking in the same language as the humanoid woman. The creature looked at the alien woman for a moment. Then, in communal silence, they both looked at Brian and simultaneously lowered their heads in a slow nod.

They did so with the same pause before raising their heads to look at him. Brian recognized this bowing gesture immediately from the moment the alien woman first did it. He assumed the gesture meant yes, or, it's okay.

Brian looked at the floor and tried to clear his dry throat. He was thirsty from his hike in the dry mountain air. He wished he could wet his lips, now. Especially after the rush of adrenaline that surged through his body during the startling encounter with the alien beings. The inside of his mouth was beginning to feel like cotton. He licked his parched lips. The silence in the room was suddenly interrupted when the alien woman spoke softly to the creature. Brian had closed his eyes to try and calm his nerves. He had so much happen to him this evening that would forever change his view of the world. The events of the evening would forever change the way he looked at the sky and wondered if there was life out there. Definitely, this would be a momentous occasion to share with somebody. But who would he tell of this evening's discovery? Who on earth would actually whole heartedly believe him? Everyone that Brian thought of who he could tell about tonight would certainly have serious doubts in the back of their mind about this unique and historic encounter. And it was not just the doubt Brian was concerned about. He also honestly felt that whomever he told would likely try to get psychiatric help for him. He already imagined the look his own parents would give him. Brian was sure his parents would have a discussion about his mental health behind his back.

Who's gonna believe me? Brian rubbed his eyes while immersed in silent thought.

"For real, man. Who's gonna believe me?" He said it out loud this time.

Then he had another thought. *<u>Should</u> I even tell anybody?* Suppose he could get a friend or a stranger to believe him? Suppose someone else had the unique experience and opportunity of a lifetime to encounter these aliens up close and in person like he had? How would that person react? Would they turn and run for the hills, scared for their life? Would they go crazy and try to harm the extraterrestrial beings? Fact is,

Brian knew human nature too well. People as a whole do not really embrace new concepts and ideas or give way to change very well. All you have to do is read a newspaper any day of the week to find proof of this. Many people are frightened by change. They want to hold onto their own narrow perception of the world viewed through their own skeptical eyes. Humans stand firm in their idealistic and pretentious beliefs, no matter what. How then, would people respond to the thought that there is life beyond the boundaries of this world that exists in a different variety of balance than what we are accustomed to seeing every day? Some people are not comfortable with such a drastic change and would prefer that their perception of this world remain the same to them. They are the ones that want to keep life austere and as indifferent as possible. To them, this creed is their version of truth.

There are also many people who will fight over their own versions of the truth, and of faith, and the way they think people should live life. Unscripted adaptation to dissimilarity is often met with conflict. This has historically happened, and it has been recorded so many, many times in the earthly history of mankind. When human intellect is introduced to something unknown, and it challenges what is accepted as socially and politically normal, sometimes there is conflict. Brian knew that this happens among people even if it means conflict to the death and, even if the ones instigating all the fighting themselves are politically wrong. Humans very often react without compromise or compassion for the views and opinions of others. They tend to shoot first and ask questions later. Brian felt that was a good description of the general public and even humankind, for this type of individual made the news headlines every day. They are the people you see and hear about in the news media who are fighting for whatever cause, good or bad.

This all stems from the fact that it is difficult for people to believe in things that do not fit into their personal experience or how they were taught life is supposed to be. Those are generally the individuals who do not believe in anything they cannot see, or maybe have not seen before. To them, in many ways, the world is still proverbially flat. Those individuals cannot see past their horizon of existence without visual proof as fact. Brian, being aware of this poignant actuality, could not deny that in a way, he was one of those types of people. Also, within this group of individuals are those who hold onto doubt, live and judge others by stereotypes, and act out of aggression. They do so merely based on what they believe in contrast to what is known as certain fact. Brian fit somewhere in-between these two groups of individuals. If truth be told, he was a man passionate about what he believed was the truth. He could already imagine based on his own fear and intimidation from the abrupt, surreal extraterrestrial encounter, how the uncivilized humans on earth would react to their own encounter with these very same aliens. He knew these alien beings would be judged against people's own profound and sometimes skewed personal beliefs. Consequently, Brian started to realize that sharing this experience tonight with someone else might lead to serious and terrible repercussions.

Brian, who was holding on steadfast to his own conservative views and opinions, was not too unlike the very same individuals that make newspaper headlines every day. Certainly he did not want to represent the views and opinions and stereotypes of extremists, though. He realized that even though he was privileged, and at the same time frightened by this encounter, he had to be on his best behavior. He had to have an open mind, too. He had a feeling that he was the first human the aliens had made contact with. In essence, with this first opportunistic encounter, Brian instantaneously became the ambassador for all humans on planet earth. At this historic moment, this young man represented all humans on this world. At this juncture of earth history he was the semblance of all mankind. So, how would the alien beings receive Brian with this first contact? If this was their first encounter with mankind, how well then, does Brian represent the best earth has to offer?

Is Brian the best that the world has to offer? He is right now. Indeed, Brian does share the same basic genetic material as those who achieve and contribute wonderful things to society. His mind is composed of the same matter, and he is not dissimilar in deeds as those considered geniuses. Conversely, Brian also shares the same basic genetic material as those who are categorized as degenerates and criminals by everyday society. Brian is a species of Homo sapiens just like the rest of the human beings that dwell on planet earth. He is not really dissimilar to selfless, subservient people or those who religiously dedicate their livelihood in an effort to give all they have to offer of themselves to improve humankind. At the same time, however, Brian is not really dissimilar in physical appearance and overall behavior than those who commit crimes of passion, crimes of aggression, serial crimes, hate crimes, and those that kill for absurd reasons, albeit, even in the name of God.

All things considered, Brian is the best the world has to offer to represent all humankind at this moment.

Brian slowly opened his eyes to find that the creature had left the room. He sighed, partly in relief. He looked at the exotic humanoid woman still sitting comfortably in the chamber in front of him. She had an innocent, untroubled smile on her face. He could not help but stare into her beautiful and mysterious alien eyes. Her radiant bronze eyes captivated his attention.

"All this is so very surreal to me," Brian said. Her beautiful expression remained the same.

"This is unbelievable, man!" Brian continued. "This experience tonight is totally overwhelming me. I mean… I'm not really sure what would happen if someone else had this happen to them instead of me. I don't know for sure how other people would react to this."

She quietly listened to Brian and tilted her head to one side. From Brian's perspective, it was almost as if she could understand his words. She even squinted a little, seemingly very attentive, as if she were sincerely hanging onto every word the young man was saying.

"I…" Brian continued to speak as he looked up momentarily, "I don't believe in Martians, or people from outer space." The humanoid woman was still looking into his eyes as he finished. He looked back into her luminous eyes.

"I'm honestly confused right now. I'm excited, but I feel strange, too. Like I'm a little worried at the same time." Brian was talking directly to her now with the most sincere look deep in his eyes.

All the while, the exotic humanoid woman remained completely silent as he spoke to her.

"I can't believe this is happening to me. I can't believe it's really true that there are other people out there living on other planets. Damn! I mean, I can't believe this!" He finished his words with an intent, solemn, yet, reserved tone in his voice.

Brian's handsome face wore a puzzled smile as he shook his head slowly at her. He desperately wished that she and he could speak the same language. Brian had so many questions in his intrigued and confused mind that he wanted to ask her, but he did not know how or where to begin. He was completely flabbergasted at his inability to think of any simple words to get his point across.

He leaned toward her and asked, "Do you know where you are?" He smiled. "I mean, earth, well, it isn't really a nice place most of the time."

He shook his head and continued to look at her. If this was a prank, he was at his most vulnerable right now to be embarrassed. But he knew, without question by now, that she and the beast were real. It was all so clear and liberating to him in this unique remarkable moment, an evening of historic discovery. Brian, the would-be late night adventurer and discoverer of life on other planets was experiencing this contact, all alone, as Earth's first celestial ambassador.

The exotic extraterrestrial only looked at him as he talked to her with a noticeable expression of curiosity on her dark alien face. Her luminous enchanting eyes kept Brian's rapt attention as he spoke to her. Again he asked.

"You do know where you guys are, don't you? ... Earth?"

Brian was so enthralled with his one sided conversation with her that he hardly noticed the creature again standing in the shadows of the darkened room. The enigmatic alien creature had once again, swiftly and silently, returned through the opposite side door. Without making the slightest sound, the beast was slowly approaching him. Once again, as he had already done several times this evening, Brian slowly turned to look at the now familiar being.

"You again?"

As the alien beast came closer, Brian could see it was holding something in its left hand. Avoiding eye contact, he took an interest in what the beast was holding. The tall creature stood a few feet away from Brian with its reddish eyes trained on him, but Brian avoided making direct eye contact with the alien creature because he was uncomfortable with the way the beast stared at him. The creature stood perfectly still without any expression on its large muzzle of a face. There was no longer a display of teeth from its long glistening hairless snout. Nevertheless, every time the creature was present, the young man was just a little more tense. He knew the beast could sense it, too. Brian adjusted his posture in an attempt to look cool, calm, and collected. *At least it isn't snarling at me anymore.* Putting up with the presence of the menacing beast was worth it, though, for the chance of a lifetime to observe the alien woman.

The humanoid woman said something to the beast. Without a vocal reply, it extended its left hand toward Brian and offered him a dark brown container. Brian stared at it, not sure what to do next. He had a good idea the beast wanted him to take the brown thing from its large hand. Brian could immediately tell the container was for drinking, but he could not tell what was in it. Without a word, the alien woman gestured. Brian was perplexed, because he didn't know who she was gesturing to with her palm facing towards her and her hand sideways with fingers together. She repeatedly fanned her open hand back and forth. Brian tilted his head to the side in amused curiosity as the beast then handed her the container. The humanoid woman took the container and turned it so that what appeared to be a small nipple on the top of the container was now aimed toward her open mouth. Next, she held the dark brown container close to her mouth as she tilted her head back to take a drink. She squeezed the container in her right hand with her mouth wide open without ever touching the container with her lips. A clear liquid squirted out of the nipple into her open mouth. She handed the container to Brian, smiled reassuringly and nodded at him to try it. She looked into his eyes. *It's okay.* Brian thought.

When he reached out to grasp the container, their fingers touched. Brian noticed her fingers were silky smooth with the very brief encounter. He smiled and brought the container up to his face to have a better look at it. On closer inspection, it appeared to be not much different from any other sports water bottle he had seen in local retail athletic stores.

"Nice. Where did you get this from, Sports Chalet?" Brian smiled and said. Of course there was no answer in return, just stares and silence from the two extraterrestrials.

Brian noticed that the sealed bottle felt like the walls of the ellipsoid. It had the same bizarre, cushiony feel to it. Brian examined the small nipple on the flat top of the drinking bottle but couldn't see any holes in it or an apparent stopper to pull open. He looked along the sides to see if he could tell where the top lid began, or find the seam where the lid joined the rest of the container. It was all smooth, one piece.

He looked at the alien woman and, again, she made a smiling gesture to drink just as she had. He did as she requested and, without hesitation, lifted the container and tilted his head back. He opened his mouth wide and squeezed. The cold, wet and refreshing substance instantly satisfied his need for hydration as soon as it splashed on his anticipating tongue. Brian lowered his head to look at the humanoid woman. Her trusting smile was calming and lovely. Brian sloshed the familiar and recognizable liquid around inside his mouth for a quick moment before he swallowed. With raised eyebrow, he concentrated for a moment on the sensation of taste as he gulped it down. It was fresh water. Brian licked his dry lips and proceeded to take another drink. This time he took a much bigger mouthful of the cold refreshing liquid. The water was satisfying and it was just what he needed right now.

"Thank you," Brian said as he handed the container back to the creature.

He couldn't avoid the maroon eyes of the beast as it reached out and took the container from his hand. The creature said nothing, just turned around and walked away, exiting the sleeping quarters on the opposite side of the room. Brian felt himself physically relax a little more. His attention returned to the alien woman.

"Thank you for the water, again." Brian said to her. She responded in her own language in her pleasant, melodious voice. Brian smiled at the humanoid woman, assuming she had said *you are welcome.*

"Well, at least we kind of understand each other." Brian replied, happy they were establishing some form of communication, "That's a good start."

The exotic woman returned a pleasant smile as she brushed a lock of hair from her face. Her stylish brunette hair was quite strikingly beautiful and eloquently similar in style to a fine, straight hair cut coming to just above the shoulders and lightly layered to add volume. The warm golden streaked fringe hairstyle was heavy and homogeneously sweeping. With her head bowed, her beautiful straight hair gently masked her exotic alien features.

Brian scrupulously studied her features in the soft lighting of the sleeping chamber. "Miss, whoever you are from outer space, I gotta say, you're <u>so</u> beautiful." He said, and then he laughed quietly to himself.

"Before tonight, I've never seen anybody with skin color like yours. Damn! It looks so alive and exotic, though." Brian shook his head with a smile and acknowledged, "You have got to be the most beautiful alien woman I have ever seen before. Well, actually, I suppose you're the only one I've seen, so far."

Then he had a thought. *How many more of these aliens are here, right now?* He looked away into the darkness of the room as he thought more about this unique encounter tonight. *Are there other space ships hiding in the woods throughout various parts of the world right now? Are these two the only ones here on earth? Or, are they the first of many more to follow? Is this a secret invasion I stumbled upon? How long have they been out here hiding in the woods? Were they here before tonight?*

He felt dizzy as all the questions filled his head at once and he reached out to grab the empty chamber to his left to balance himself. Suddenly, he felt a sensation of anxiety overwhelm him. Both his hands tingled and his palms were noticeably sweaty. He looked down at the floor of the ellipsoid spacecraft and tried to compose himself.

"Get it together man, take it easy," Brian whispered to himself.

He closed his eyes and tried to concentrate, but noticed his breathing was faster than normal. He was hyperventilating. He concentrated on taking fewer breaths. He mentally slowed his breathing rate a little as he tried to relax. He quickly regained composure, then opened his eyes and yawned. He felt very tired. The hike, including all the exploring late at night, and the overwhelming first contact with the alien beings was all catching up to him now. The young man smiled once again as he looked at the humanoid woman. She looked noticeably concerned. When he looked into her eyes, she said something in her language that sounded like it could have been a question. She repeated the same phrase to Brian and then leaned forward, still with her legs crossed beneath her, to clasp his arm just above the elbow with her long, delicate fingers. Her grip was firm, yet soothing at the same time. She looked at him with concern, watching him carefully. Though feeling tired, he smiled at her.

"I guess this has been a little too overwhelming for me. I actually got myself all worked up for a moment. You see, my world has changed so much by meeting you two here tonight. The entire world will be different, now," he said.

"Things are gonna change. If everyone sees you like I have, things are <u>definitely</u> gonna change!" Brian nodded his head at her.

She kept the gentle hold on his arm and gazed into his eyes a little more serious than before.

Then she spoke, and her melodious sounding words filled the empty space of the darkened room. She looked toward the doors on the other side of the room, articulating something in her native tongue.

Chapter Six

Approximately eighty miles southwest of Lake Arrowhead in a quiet upper middle class neighborhood in Long Beach County, California, Brandon Lyle Morris lay awake in bed. He raised his head off his pillow slightly and glanced at the clock radio on the night stand located next to his wife's side of the bed. It displayed 12:23 a.m. Brandon slowly rolled to his left side and faced away from the clock, trying to be careful not to disturb his wife who was sleeping soundly. He was restless. He inhaled deeply through his nose and exhaled a full breath through his partially closed lips. As he did, his cheeks expanded on exhale as if he was playing a brass wind instrument. The rush of expelled air through his pursed lips made enough of a sound to slightly rouse his wife, Donnette. She moved around a bit on her side of the bed, startled by the sudden sound. Brandon remained completely still for a moment and listened to her breathing settle back into a nice, slow rhythm. He almost sighed aloud with relief that he hadn't woken his wife out of her coveted slumber. *Maybe I'll go get some milk to help me sleep. That should do the trick.*

Brandon started to move, very slowly, starting with his legs. He was already situated close to the edge of the king size bed, so it did not take much to ease both of his legs from under the covers. He waited momentarily, listening for the slightest sound that his wife had awakened. But there was no other sound, save for the slow breathing of her peaceful slumber. Brandon slowly got into a seated position on the edge of the king size mattress as he weighed the chances of getting up without disturbing her.

So far, so good. He thought as he slowly rose to his feet. The box spring made a slight 'squeak' as he got up, but his wife slept on.

The temperature inside the house was very comfortable at this time of night. During the day, outside temperatures were as high as 85°F. But by nightfall, the summer days typically cooled off to a pleasant 66°F. There was really no need for central air in a home like theirs in this part of the city. Besides, almost all the homes built in the neighborhood were constructed without central air during the early 1970s up to the mid-eighties. Brandon and Donnette's house was less than a ten minute drive to the beach on any given weekday. A few open windows and a few smartly placed electric fans were enough to cool the house down from the heat of the summer day by drawing in the evening's pleasant ocean breeze from outside. This was one of the main reasons they had chosen to settle in the Long Beach area.

Standing at the edge of the bed, Brandon could feel the effects of the cool evening air from a gentle flow being circulated from the ceiling fan above the bed. He walked quietly toward the open master bedroom door, looking back one more time when he reached the doorway. Donnette looked so comfortable. He was slightly jealous. He wished he was sleeping so well right now. He stepped into the hallway which was dimly illuminated with a night light a few feet away. Beyond that was the door to his son Houston's room. His son's door was open, and the room was mostly dark. The only illumination came from the soft white lighting of a 'Winnie-the-Pooh' night light near the doorway. Brandon walked to his son's room and leaned against the door frame, watching his son sleeping so peacefully in his twin size bed. Like most parents, Brandon occasionally stood at the bedroom door and watched his son sleeping, so quiet and comfortable. He was often accompanied by his wife on these occasions. Sometimes, soon after their handsome four year old son fell asleep, the couple would spend a coveted portion of their quality 'free' time watching Houston. The proud father smiled as he recalled some of the occasions when he and Donnette had stood there at the doorway together.

This time he stayed only a moment and then resumed walking

toward the kitchen. He passed the door to the guest bedroom on his right, and then another night light. They provided enough illumination to make the journey from the bedrooms to the kitchen without turning on any overhead lights. The hallway on his left held several large framed portraits of his family. He walked straight ahead and entered the family room, an open, spacious and comfortable entertainment area. This is where he and Houston often spent time together watching cartoons early in the morning on weekends. Brandon turned slightly to the right and continued toward the kitchen. He could see the faint microwave light as he entered the dining room area and then followed the wall to his left, which led directly into the kitchen. He turned on the lights and got a glass from the auburn stained oak cabinet next to the black Maytag side-by-side refrigerator. Next, he pulled the refrigerator side of the door open. One thing Donnette did as a stay at home mom was to shop for food a couple times a week to get exactly what she needed for a particular dinner. She enjoyed going to a variety of markets to get fresh vegetables, buying only what she needed at the time. If she needed more for dinner in a day or two, she went shopping, again. The very next day, if need be. She liked to stock up on other food items, too. Donnette always kept a plentiful variety of fresh meat and produce in the refrigerator. Brandon stood with the door open and scanned the contents. He found the milk and poured some in the glass. As he drank it, his thoughts turned to some of the things that had been weighing heavy on his mind lately.

Truth be told, Brandon hardly ever worried much about his work. He was not one to overly stress himself. He was not the type of person that brought home all the troubles of the day. True, he certainly had a lot of responsibility being the senior finance manager at Lexus/Toyota of Orange, California. But, everything was always under control for Brandon. He actually enjoyed his job very much. He was the type of person that any employer would want to have on their payroll. Brandon was an honest, hard-working type of individual. He always sincerely considered how the company could benefit from each of his endeavors and business relations with customers. His efforts were very profitable for the dealership. However, at the same time, he honestly looked out for the rights of the purchaser as well. He always ensured that his customers were happy with their purchase. Each of Brandon's customers was treated with the utmost respect and courtesy when they came in to finance a brand new or previously owned vehicle. He made sure all his customers left with a big smile. Truth be told, when the customers drove off smiling with their new vehicle, the Sales Manager was smiling right along with them. This was because the dealership always secured handsome profits from Brandon's honest and fair-minded transactions. Brandon was the perfect Finance and Insurance Associate. He was meticulous about his work. He poured over every purchase option and package plan in detail. He made sure the junior office associates were just as meticulous as he was in every deal. As a result, his finance team was a spit-shined, well-oiled machine. That was specifically why he never had anything to really worry about concerning his job. Brandon was truly well known and well-liked by everyone at the automotive dealership. Brandon's subordinates and peers considered him one of the best people to work with. The Chief Financial Officer of Lexus/Toyota of Orange sincerely considered Brandon to be one of the best managers in the field, and most certainly one the best in the Long Beach area.

The day to day obligations of his work were not really on his mind, but work was part of the reason Brandon was restless tonight. It was the time spent at work with long hours that concerned him lately. Brandon was spending a lot of late afternoons and a few evenings at his job recently. He knew those long hours spent at work meant less time to spend with his wife and child. Brandon had never heard a complaint from Donnette since he started staying a little late at work over the past few weeks. But he knew she was aware. Whenever he called his lovely wife from work to tell her he would be late, she would tell him not to worry, and she let him know that his dinner would still be ready for him when he got home.

Brandon wanted to spend more time with his wife and child.

He actually had the chance, a recent offer, to take his family on vacation. His close friend Anthony from his college days at the University of Arizona called a few weeks back and offered Brandon a nice opportunity to get away for a week.

"Brandon! What's up, bro?" Anthony said when he got Brandon on the phone.

He was so excited. He'd tried calling Brandon several times during the week prior and was just getting through.

"Nothing much my man, what's up with you?" Brandon said, laughing.

"Bro, don't you listen to your messages? I called you and called, trying to get a hold of you my man." Anthony was happy that at last he had got in contact with his friend.

"Hey Brandon, I wanted to know if you and Donnette would be interested in coming out to meet me and Hillary in Mexico? You know, come stay with us in the condo for a week, bro? Chill out on the beach, relax in the sun, toss a few margaritas back. You know man?"

"Yeah. I know how you do it," Brandon said, listening with sincere interest.

"Definitely, bro!" Anthony said to his buddy. "Hillary and I are gonna head down there in a few weeks. Hey, you can bring Houston, too. I've never seen your son in person yet, you know? I've only seen pictures."

Anthony hardly gave his friend a chance to speak in his happiness at having the chance to talk to Brandon.

"Where is this handsome son of yours, man? I wanna see him. Looks like he has Donnette's eyes. Hey, how has she been, anyway?"

Brandon could not help but smile, and laugh.

"Oh, Donnette is just fine. I'll tell her you said, 'hi', my man." He was wearing a huge smile.

"I know Donnette and Houston would love it. That sounds real good man. I keep telling her I'll take her there, soon. I've just been so damn busy lately." Brandon's tone of voice was a little more serious suddenly and he was not smiling as much.

"Well, you got to get un-busy, Brandon. I'm serious. I'll take care of your plane tickets, too. I'll get you all some first class seats, dude. Okay, my man?" Anthony meant what he said.

Anthony Roy Bornermere was quite the character. He was a tall, handsome Caucasian man at 6 feet and 190 lbs. with an athletic build, brown eyes, curly brown hair, and a goatee. He looked more like he could be the lead singer of any popular 1990's era grunge band rather than an automobile salesperson and businessman. Son of a wealthy mother and father, Anthony was well traveled and very well-liked by everyone who knew him. Always smiling, the man could cheer up just about anyone into a good mood. That personal quality is exactly what made him a fantastic salesperson, too. He was born in Chicago, Illinois, but he had spent a lot of time in the western region of the country when he was younger. He traveled a lot with his parents, especially when he was a teenager. Whenever school was out, if he was not visiting his mother's side of the family in San Luis Obispo, California, he was staying with his parents; often in their second home in Tucson, Arizona. Anthony's parents would escape the Chicago winters and leave their Barrington area home almost every holiday season to soak up the warm sunny Arizona climate. If they wanted to relax in the sun with an ocean view, they would head south of the border to their condominium in San Carlos Bay, Mexico.

Anthony's father, Richard Orland Bornermere, owned several automotive dealerships in the Chicago metro area. Richard, who went by Dick, also owned a dealership in Michigan, as well. After his son Anthony finished college, he immediately made him the Manager of Bornermere Saturn of Saginaw, located in the northern district of Saginaw, Michigan. His mother, Rachael Marie, helped him run the business as an executive administrative assistant for the first year of his 'employment' as Manager of the family owned dealership. Rachael Marie Bornermere was also a descendant of wealthy parents. She came from 'old money'; both of her parents' family's owned several Chicago area textile mills in years past. Anthony did not have any brothers or sisters, and as the only child, he was spoiled. But, he was not 'spoiled-rotten'. His parents took the time to teach him the value of money and the true value of deep, sincere, bonded relationships with family and friends.

"Oh, by the way," Anthony continued, "we got the jib on my dad's boat repaired, so we can do some sailing, too." Anthony hardly gave Brandon any time to think it over.

"So, what day would you like to come to San Carlos? I can pick you up from Guaymas Airport, my man. Hillary's gonna be real happy to see you and Donnette, again."

Brandon remembered his reply to Anthony that day.

"Hillary." He had chuckled to himself, because he knew her well. "How's Miss Hillary? And, how are her doctor mom and dad doing these days, anyway?"

He remembered how snooty they were. However, Dr. Pauline and Dr. Charles Magellan, Hillary's parents, were always very glad whenever Brandon and Donnette came over to stay a few days with them.

"They're all fine, I'll tell them you said hello."

"Uh-huh, sure," Brandon replied in a mundane tone of voice. Brandon cleared his throat and added a little enthusiasm to his next reply, "Well uh, let me see if the wife wants to go. I mean, I'm sure she would like to take a little trip. I'll talk it over with her, and I'll get back to you, Anthony. Okay?"

"Okay bro, but I'm serious. You better get your black ass out there on the beach with me, dude!" Anthony said, as they both burst into sophomoric laughter over their cell phones.

Brandon had known Anthony since freshman year at college. They became best friends, both majoring in finance, and they studied together. Both of them graduated in the class of 1993 with their Bachelor's Degree. Then, the very next semester, they both attended graduate school. After a couple more semesters, Brandon and Anthony graduated again, this time with their Master's Degree in Business Administration. They had a lot in common. Brandon went to a Catholic High School, Bishop Montgomery, in Torrance, California. And Anthony was an alumnus of Brother Rice High School, in Chicago, Illinois. The two of them spent some time socializing with Anthony's friends in Chicago during time off from college. Donnette often accompanied them on trips to Chicago, or she would fly up to meet them later. Anthony, Brandon, and Donnette met Hillary in Chicago at a party of a mutual friend during spring break. That was during Anthony and Brandon's last post-graduate semester of study at the University of Arizona.

The two college buddies talked for a little while longer and ended their conversation with an agreed upon notion that Brandon and family would join Anthony and Hillary, in Mexico. Anthony planned on arriving at his parent's condominium in San Carlos Bay, Mexico on the 8th of September. It was a couple weekends away, so that gave Brandon enough time to sort things out at work, and take his family on a much needed vacation. After the two finished their conversation, Brandon had considered the offer, seriously. Then, he returned to his work.

Brandon recalled the conversation as he drank down the last sip of cold milk. Then he placed the empty glass in the sink, thinking about taking a few days off to meet his friends south of the border next weekend. Truth be told, he sincerely enjoyed both Anthony and Hillary's company. They were a happy, fun couple to be around.

Brandon started back to the bedroom. He flipped off the kitchen light, walked through the corner of the family room and slowed his pace at the photographs on the hallway wall. He stopped to look at the large framed family portrait of Houston and Donnette and himself. It was a beautiful master-piece portraiture taken only a month ago. Brandon and his wife absolutely loved it.

Houston looked so handsome sitting on his father's lap. He was genuinely a happy kid, and he almost always had a smile on his face that would just melt your heart. He had big, beautiful, dark brown eyes and curly brown hair. His face was round and cute with a fair skin complexion. Houston was born on September 24, 1996. His fifth birthday was coming up, next month. He was such a good kid, that the photographer had mentioned several times how he was so well mannered during the photo session.

Brandon looked at his wife in the picture. Donnette had her favorite dress on, and she looked gorgeous. She was a beautiful

African American lady with an exquisite, soft medium brown skin tone. She was a visually lofty 5 feet 7 inches elegant woman, appearing taller than she actually was. She weighed about 129 lbs. and had a shapely figure with wide hips, long legs, and broad shoulders. Donnette had large, appealing, unsullied light brown eyes, and long, straight black hair. She was 32 years of age, and she looked about five to six years younger than her reserved, loving gentleman of a husband. The two met as students at Bishop Montgomery Catholic High School and they had been sweethearts ever since. Friends often described them as the perfect couple; in high school they were practically inseparable. Donnette graduated in the senior class of 1987. Brandon graduated with his senior class in 1989. Brandon followed Donnette to the University of Arizona. She always wanted to be a teacher, and she studied and majored in Education. She graduated from college with a BS, in Education; class of 1992. Currently, she was a substitute kindergarten teacher in the City of Orange Unified School District of California. Brandon and Donnette Dian Price were married on October 3, 1992.

Brandon was very proud, and he smiled as he looked at his family in the portrait. *Wait until both of our parents see this,* Brandon thought to himself in the quiet of the late night. He looked closely at himself in the enlarged portraiture, which was dimly lit from the combined night lights in the hallway and family room. He was wearing his favorite tie in the photograph. Donnette always liked to see her husband dressed up, and when he did, she always told him how handsome he looked. Brandon was 5'11" tall. He was slightly overweight, but, athletic overall. He had muscular arms. His biceps were large. Brandon was proud of his broad, muscular chest. He had firm Pectorals that he could flex, which always made Donnette giggle. He sometimes walked around the house with a tight fitting tank-top tee shirt on, flexing his muscles and grimacing, which made his son laugh aloud. Brandon enjoyed a good meal often, as well as a decent lager. Thus, he also had a slight 'beer' belly. Donnette thought his belly was cute. She told him it reminded her of a Panda bear. That was her cuddly term of endearment for him,

"Panda." Brandon had a smooth, dark mocha skin tone. His eyes were dark brown. He sported a clean, close shaved head, including a demure trimmed moustache, and recently, a goatee. Donnette really liked his goatee and she protested if he even thought about shaving it off.

"You know you love me because I'm sexy," Brandon often said in a soft playful tone.

"You bet I do, Panda!" Donnette would smile back at him with a sultry look in her eyes.

Her husband was a quiet, intelligent, attractive man. Brandon weighed 200 lbs., but it was difficult to guess he was slightly overweight from the way he dressed. Although Brandon and Brian were not twins, their resemblance was rather striking. Brandon was, basically, a slightly heavier version of his younger brother, Brian. He was about four years older than him.

Suddenly Brandon thought about Brian and wondered how he was doing. He had not talked to his younger brother for a few weeks because of his busy schedule at Lexus/Toyota of Orange. The two brothers were very close. He remembered Brian had left a few messages on his cell phone a few days ago. However, Brandon hadn't returned any of them. He had not kept up with his younger brother recently, and that bothered him. Brandon was always concerned about anything that his little brother worried about. The last time the two talked, Brian was having a lot of trouble with his girlfriend, Gina. *I've got to give my little bro a call, soon.* Brandon almost said it out loud. *I bet he's out partying right now at a club somewhere or something like that.* Brandon smiled. He was slightly envious of his brother's carefree bachelor lifestyle.

Brandon yawned as he looked at the beautiful family portrait. He and his wife were very satisfied with it. As he folded his arms in front of him he felt tired all of a sudden. *Time to go to bed.* He turned and walked toward Houston's room to check on him one more time. Houston was comfortably lying asleep in bed, just as before. Brandon smiled and continued walking back to the master bedroom. He felt very sleepy. He gingerly got back into bed, careful not to disturb his wife. He pulled the covers over his shoulders and moved closer to Donnette, resting his forehead against her back. In the tranquil comfort of their bed, he fell asleep. Everything was quiet, now in the Morris residence. The family was sleeping peacefully. Life was perfect here. It was all good.

· · · • • ● • • · ·

Many other families also slept quietly in the immediate vicinity of their neighborhood. That was one of several reasons why Brandon and Donnette chose to settle in this middle-to-upper class beach city area. The neighborhood was peaceful, both day and night. This was a place where families lived happily together. But the same was not true for <u>all</u> people in the surrounding area. Just two blocks to the east there was a domestic disturbance. Police from the City of Long Beach were on the scene at a home responding to a 9-1-1 call. The call came from neighbors who had complained about hearing a lot of shouting and fighting. Before the call was placed, the occupants of the residence in question had been shouting at each other for almost an hour. Next, the neighbors heard the sounds of furniture and other items inside the house being thrown about as a result of an argument. A married couple was fighting over money and finances. Now, the husband, wearing his half torn pajamas, was sitting quietly in the back seat of a patrol car in handcuffs. The rear passenger door of the cruiser was open wide. A police officer shined a flashlight on the husband's face as he asked him several serious questions. Another police officer stood on the porch of the house asking the same type of questions to the angry and sobbing wife of the restrained, pajama clad husband. All the while, the neighbors who called the police department peeked out of their windows in silent curiosity, watching the absorbing drama as it emerged.

· · · • • ● • • · ·

Other neighborhoods were not as peaceful as the Brandon Morris family neighborhood. Only three miles north of Brandon and

Donnette's lovely home was the scene of a crime. Two Caucasian twenty-two-year-old young men sitting in a yellow, modified 1999 Honda Civic were too scared to move. Joshua Hess, the young owner and driver of the barely street legal, 'tricked out' Japanese import vehicle shook nervously. He had never been held at gunpoint before; neither had his passenger, and best friend, Corey Mumfer. The two had just come out of an adult entertainment gentleman's club named 'Topside', the popular local exotic dancing bar. The two young men had spent close to two hours and a lot of cash inside the club and then decided it was time to leave.

The parking lot was still full when the two walked out of the crowded establishment. They walked around the corner to where they parked the car. It was still there, surrounded by several other vehicles parked on the poorly lit section of the street. Joshua got behind the wheel of the sleek yellow Honda while Corey climbed into the passenger seat. They rolled down the custom tinted windows and both lit up a cigarette. Corey turned on some techno music. The pulsing and repetitive staccato sounds of electronic dance music filled the placid summer night air. The two young men talked and laughed out loud as they listened to the music, bobbing their heads to the pulsing beat. Instead of leaving, they decided to stay for a while, to finish their cigarettes, and chat about which of the exotic female dancers was the best looking.

Suddenly, out of the darkness of nowhere, three young men quickly approached the vehicle. The man closest to the driver's side of the car pointed a Taurus PT-92 9mm, blue steel, semiautomatic pistol into the open window of the yellow Honda. The other two young accomplices stood closely behind the man with the gun, looking quickly around the area to make sure no one was watching.

"Don't do nothing stupid! Just give me your money!" That was all the man with the gun said to Joshua and Corey.

"Jack 'em for that ride man, let's take that rice-rocket!" One of the young men standing behind the gunman said, while the other skinny one just snickered at Joshua and Corey.

The two frightened young men inside the car looked down and nervously searched their pockets for cash. They both had their money stuffed in their pockets so they could easily order drinks, and tip the scantily clad servers and dancers.

"Don't do nothing stupid!" warned the skinny young man that had snickered. He leaned forward as he looked around the shoulder of the gunman and added, "Yo, gimmie that watch, too!"

Joshua looked up to see the armed robber motioning for the watch on his wrist. Corey, fearful for his life, handed all his cash, $68.00, to Joshua who added it to his $179.00 and his black and gold Guess watch. He gave it all to the patiently waiting gunman.

"Remember; don't do nothing stupid, boys!" The armed robber said in a humorous, blunt tone of voice as he took the cash and the watch.

Then the gunman and the other two young men walked behind the Honda and quickly disappeared from sight. Joshua and Corey dared not turn around to take a look. They were too scared to move.

A few minutes later Corey finally looked out of the rear window of the Honda. The music was still playing and pulsating into the night air. Corey took his cell phone out of his pants pocket and called the police. Then he looked at his friend and smiled.

"It's gonna be all right, man. Just another day in the city, that's all." Corey tried to calm down his visibly shaken best friend. As he waited for the dial tone on his cellular phone he said. "It's only money."

All Joshua did was nod in response with a tight-lipped smile on his face. Joshua remained speechless, still thinking of the three men that just robbed him and his friend. The clean-shaven-head gunman wearing sunglasses had a small tattoo over his left eyebrow. That was what Joshua remembered the most. The image was stuck in his mind.

·　·　·　•　●　●　●　•　·　·

A few miles to the south of the scene of this crime, Brandon Morris still slept quietly and comfortably at home with his family. The peacefulness of his home only went so far, for clearly, there were other neighborhoods not as peaceful as his. The same was true for many other neighborhoods in the rest of the state of California. The same was true for the rest of the world, for that matter.

Chapter Seven

Brian glanced at his watch as he leaned his back against the soft wall of the darkened room. The time was 12:21 a.m. He shut his eyes and thought about his present situation. *What would have happened if somebody other than me stumbled across these two tonight? How different would things have turned out? What would their situation be like, right now?* He sighed as he thought about those perplexing questions and wondered what to do next.

Less than a minute later Brian slowly opened his eyes to discover that the creature had returned and was standing silently in front of him. The maroon eyes of the beast were staring directly at Brian's face. *You again.* The face of the beast was expressionless as it continued to stare. Then the alien woman spoke to Brian in a quiet tone of voice in her language. She gestured with her hands and arms and then raised her elbows to shoulder height and placed the palm of her right hand on top of the dorsum, or backside, of her left hand, then laid her cheek on top of them and closed her eyes, holding pose for a few seconds. Then, she sat up straight again. The humanoid woman looked into Brian's eyes. It was as if she expected him to reply to what she had just said with her gestures.

"You…" Brian paused in amazement for a moment, "you want to know if I'm tired?" He replied as he repeated the same gesture she had done, with his own hands.

Her response to his question was a slow nod of the head, just as before. Brian smiled in return, satisfied that he got his point across to her. She understood him. Brian knew she could tell he was tired. He realized she could just look at him and almost knew exactly what he needed. Brian considered her intelligence, and he reasoned she was probably no different in cognitive thinking from any other human on earth. Perhaps her intelligence quotient was higher than the average earthly human. Brian wanted to know. He realized these extraterrestrials were truly something special.

"Yes." Brian bowed his head once, as the aliens had done several times to signify an affirmative reply.

"I'm feeling a little tired." Brian smiled at the alien woman.

Just at that moment, the beast began to speak to the alien woman and they conversed back and forth for a short moment. Brian wondered what they were saying to each other. He listened to the way they used inflections in the tone of their voice to each other. The humanoid woman's voice was appealing, not much different from the soft sound of a woman's voice from earth. But the sound the creature made was truly entertaining and fascinating, and even bewildering when it hissed and chattered during conversation with its extraterrestrial companion. Brian could not help but stare at the beast. He watched the way its jaws chopped as it spoke. Brian shook his head, befuddled. *Unbelievable!* he thought to himself.

"Amazing!" Brian couldn't help but interrupt their conversation. With furrowed brow he continued to stare at the strange creature.

"So, that's what it would be like if dogs could talk! Whoa! That's <u>really</u> amazing! The young man was emphatic. "Damn!"

Then there was complete silence as the two extraterrestrials stopped talking and looked at him. The exotic alien woman smiled subtly, in an observably polite fashion. The beast, however, actually looked at Brian with a recognizably perplexed expression on its face as if it were trying to decipher what Brian had just said. The alien creature stared into Brian's eyes, seemingly probing for the meaning of his abruptly blurted comment. Brian quickly broke eye contact with the creature, suddenly feeling very uncomfortable. He looked down at the floor of the darkened room. Those stark reddish eyes were just so intimidating and uncomfortable to look at directly. Then, the beast spoke again.

The conversation went on for a bit. At one point, the humanoid woman listened to the creature without speaking back, as if the beast was trying to explain something to her with its chopping, hissing accent. Brian studied the woman's facial expression and body language as she listened to the creature. From the way things appeared to him, they were making some kind of decision, it seemed to Brian. The creature continued to speak, pointing at Brian with its left thumb. *Okay, I've seen that gesture a couple times. So that must be the way they point at stuff.* Brian was trying to keep track of the gestures the aliens used during communicating. He knew that the two of them were conversing about him, and he began to wonder if he truly surprised them this evening with his late night visit. The young man was wondering if they were supposed to be clandestine. *I bet they didn't expect me to show up tonight. Maybe they are here to watch us.* Brian rubbed his chin and squinted as he pondered what to do next.

Brian interrupted their conversation when there was an opportunistic gap of silence.

"Do you want me to leave?" He said in a raised voice and a faint smile on his tired face. He gestured with the index and middle fingers of his right hand, making them 'walk' on the open palm of his left hand. He pointed to the other end of the dark room where the doors were, and repeated the question.

"Do you want me to leave? I can go back home." Brian smiled and nodded his head slowly.

He stared at them for a moment before adding, "I won't tell anyone I saw you two here tonight." He glanced back and forth at the two extraterrestrials. "Besides, no one would believe me, anyway. For real."

The two alien beings glanced at each other. The beast immediately spoke to the humanoid woman. Once again, she listened quietly to the creature ramble on in its hissing, jaw chopping mannerism. Then she nodded and it stepped backwards and disappeared into the darkness of the room, exiting through the door on the opposite side of the room.

The alien woman began to speak, trying to explain something to Brian. She spoke softly and smiled the whole while. Brian listened, but of course, none of it made any sense. However, he could tell by her reassuring smile that everything would be okay. She pointed at Brian as soon as she finished talking. Next, she gestured with her hands, in the exact manner Brian had done. She held her right hand up, and 'walked' her fingers over the open palm of her left hand. Brian smiled in amazement as he continued to watch her. Then, the alien woman immediately followed that gesticulation with the one she previously did for: 'Are you tired?'

"You want me to go home and sleep?" Brian pointed at himself.

Then, he returned the cheek-to-hand 'tired' gesture, as he replied to her. She bowed her head with a single nod in response.

"Okay." Brian said, "Yes, I will."

We're making some progress communicating. Brian thought. He was amazed how the alien woman was considerate and sensitive to his needs. As exciting as the opportunity had been to meet these extraterrestrials, the thought of leaving the limits of the ellipsoid sleeping chamber was appeasing and reassuring right now. *At least I won't be abducted and subjugated to some type of torturous scientific experiment.* Brian was beginning to feel good about the exotic alien woman's suggestion for him to go home. *But the night is still young.*

Brian watched the extraterrestrial humanoid woman move toward the edge of the bedchamber she was in. She moved silently and smoothly, extending her legs as she pushed herself off the bed and stood on the floor a few feet away from him at approximately the same spot the beast had been for half of the evening. No sooner had she stood up than the alien woman quickly gestured at the young man. She had turned her hand sideways and started to fan her hand toward her. She used the same hand signal when the creature gave her the water container, earlier. 'Follow me', or 'give it to me', the young man inferred.

"I will come with you," Brian said, breaking the silence. He finished the sentence as he pointed to himself first, then her.

She bowed her head with a single nod in response. With the most congenial smile on her lips, she turned and started to walk between the two sleeping chambers in the room. Brian could not help but notice her elegance. Even without shoes, the humanoid woman appeared somewhat tall. The young man guessed she was at least 5 feet 9 inches, or more. Brian looked at the back of her head. The top of her hair made her look almost as tall as him. In the darkened room, he could just barely see the hint of golden highlights in her layered brown hair.

Her flight suit fit appealing snug around her feminine physique. Her broad shoulders and long arms looked a little unusual, but they were uniquely appealing. The sleeves of her dark purple and russet flight suit ended just below the elbow. The pant portion of the elegant uniform stretched chicly around her wide hips and down her long legs, touching the top of her narrow, feet. Like the first moment he saw her sleeping, Brian looked her over from head to toe. He guessed her weight was about 140 lbs. She was slim, and height to weight proportionate in a different, but beautiful way.

Brian followed her closely as they walked in-between the sleeping chambers toward the other side of the darkened crew quarters, concentrating on her legs in the dim light from the bedchambers. He didn't want to bump into her. Just as they passed both chambers, Brian heard the slurred voice of the beast in the darkness. The creature's voice filled the dimly lit room but seemed to originate from right next to Brian. The very sound made Brian cringe for a second until he realized the creature's voice was coming over the intercom.

Next, the door Brian had used to enter the narrow darkened room quickly slid open. As it did, the light filtered in from the narrow room he had been in. It seemed brighter than before. He squinted at the brightness coming at him, now. He was a few close steps behind the alien as he followed her out of the darkened crew quarters into the light of the open doorway. They stepped into the room and the door to the sleeping chamber slid quickly closed behind him.

The humanoid woman turned around to face Brian, reaching

out to take hold of his arm. She spoke to him in her soft, comforting tone of voice. She pointed at him, then pointed at his feet. She seemed to repeat the sentence she was saying, because the words sounded the same to Brian. Again, she pointed at him, then, his feet.

"You want me to stay here for a second?" Brian stood straight as he queried her with his hands stiff at his side. "I stay here."

Then Brian pointed at the floor next to his feet. The alien woman smiled in return. Next, she turned around and stepped quickly toward the door next to the one they had just come out through. The door slid open and closed very quickly behind her. The young man recalled how he briefly thought about entering that first door, instead of the one he ended up going through. Brian wondered if he would have encountered the beast first, rather than the beautiful mysterious alien. Now, as she left, he wondered what was behind that other door.

Brian rubbed his eyes. He stretched as he yawned. Glancing at his watch, the time was now 12:30 a.m. He took a nice deep breath.

"I've got to get my second wind here," he said to himself as he jogged lightly in place for a second. "All that dim lighting in the other room made me sleepy."

He nervously moved about, shaking his arms and legs as he stood in one spot. The truth was; he was beginning to feel uneasy. He did not know what to expect next. *Where are they?*

"I hope they're not talking about eating me up for a midnight snack," Brian mumbled to himself. He was feeling uneasy now.

A few minutes later the door the alien woman went through suddenly opened and she approached Brian, closely followed by the creature. Brian noticed she and the creature seemed to be wearing some very unique apparel. It was sort of a utility vest/backpack combination that looked relatively full. The color matched their jumpsuit uniforms precisely. Glancing down at their feet, Brian saw they both had on some type of fancy, customized utility boots.

The alien woman spoke quickly. As she did, the creature turned toward the large oval shaped doorway Brian entered through and the door silently opened, sliding up as it did for him earlier that night. The creature walked forward through the doorway. Brian could tell the moment the alien beast started to walk down the stepladder that they were definitely leaving the confines of the ellipsoid. Within a few seconds, Brian was standing outside. He took a deep breath in relief. Truth be told, he had not been one hundred percent sure if he would ever see daylight, again. His first encounter and impression of the creature was not an enjoyable one. Then Brian thought to himself, *it's still nighttime, and I am literally not out of the woods, yet.*

Brian looked at the ground. The night was familiarly still and peaceful. The darkness of the gully quickly reminded him how alone he felt when he first arrived. Next, the young man heard something that was also familiar. He barely heard the soft sounds of the retracting stepladder and exterior door. Brian turned slightly and watched as the exterior door slid closed in one swift, smooth process. They all stood there in the darkened gully, as the interior lighting from the ellipsoid entryway disappeared from the fading creases of the exterior sliding door. Now, the only available light came from the stars and moon above, in the late night sky. Brian was silent. He stared at the dark ellipsoid for a moment and then turned around to look at the two extraterrestrials. *Are they really coming with me?*

The young man quickly noticed that the two alien beings were wearing something else. Something that closely resembled sunglasses. They were actually quite fashionable. With only the diffuse, starlit illumination of the night sky as his aid, Brian noticed the lenses had a reflective copper appearance. The humanoid woman was closest to Brian. The young man slowly leaned forward to inspect the strange eyeglasses on her face. He no sooner did so than the alien woman removed the peculiar eyewear from her face and handed them to Brian. She said something to him with an inflection in her voice sounding like that of a question. Brian quietly took the strange looking sunglasses from her hand. He stared at them for just a moment. Even in the darkness of the furrow, Brian could appreciate how stylish the wraparound eyeglasses were. The eyeglasses were somewhat thick, but they were also surprisingly very light. The frame was made of some type of soft material. They were slightly wide at the temple area near each lens. From there, the frame tapered fashionably to a pair of slightly narrow, firm ends. Brian also noticed that there were tiny green pinpoint lights on the inside of the frame, close to each lens. The young man squinted, as he curiously brought the alien technological eyewear close to his face to inspect the bizarre eyeglasses. On the inside portion of the lenses there was a shadowy, blue-grayish glow. However, the outside of the lens was not illuminated.

Without hesitation, he put them on. The view was mind-blowing. It was undoubtedly the most spectacular visual interpretation of the world ever before seen. The young man's visual senses were flooded with enigmatic and stimulating colors as his human eyesight assimilated the visual information from his surroundings. Brian was so overwhelmed he almost lost his balance.

"Whoa!" Brian was astounded.

It was as if he were looking at the world in a strange adaptation of daylight. He could see everything in extraordinary detail. It only took a few seconds before his human eyes immediately adapted to the unusual gray-bluish hue vision of the world as seen through the alien eyewear. The glasses were so light he hardly noticed them on his face. The glasses were form-fitting, snug, and comfortable.

"What are these? I guess some kind of night vision glasses, huh?" Brian said, holding his arms out to look at his own hands and arms.

"Nice!" It was the most impressive technological amazement that he'd ever had the opportunity to experience.

He looked at the alien woman. He could clearly see her smiling face in an animated cerulean shade of cyan. For the first time, Brian heard her chuckle. The sound of her curious amusement made him smile back at her. Next, Brian looked up. The stars were beautiful white dots in a luminescent gray tinged sky. Looking straight ahead the leaves on the trees around and above him shimmered slightly with a dark, aquamarine-greenish hue.

Brian could clearly see in between some of the long branches of those trees. Their dark russet colored branches seemed to stretch out at him in unobstructed sinewy form. Brian looked at the ground. The dry foliage was a dark cinnabar color and the dirt was a dark goldenrod. Everything the young man looked at with the strange eyeglasses on was observed in magnificent, novel optical accord. All the colors and hues mixed harmoniously and in acute depth through the lenses of the eyeglasses. It was all a new, exciting experience and nothing like anything Brian had ever seen before.

"Wow!" he exclaimed in pure amazement.

Then Brian turned his head to one side. Something caught his attention. Something interesting and unexpected, an abrupt sighting revealed by the alien lenses. Brian, still gazing at the ground beneath him, noticed the unique shades of colors within the dirt had revealed several darkened spots, and aligned in a distinct linear pattern that zigzagged from the top of the gully to the ground where he stood. From there, they seemed to continue behind him. Brian was quiet as he inspected this unusual detail revealed by the alien eyewear.

"Are those my footprints… from, when I walked down here earlier?" Brian whispered in absolute awe.

The young man bent forward slightly to examine what he had discovered more closely in the dirt beneath him. He turned and stepped once to his right, as he visually followed where the footprints led. The extraterrestrial night vision eyewear allowed Brian the opportunity to observe how his own imprinted footsteps made their way through the gully and, eventually, toward the ellipsoid. The evidence was absolute to him. He continued in deep thought, observing the tracks he'd made in the dry ground and thinking about how he had stumbled across the mysterious ellipsoid this evening. *What if things hadn't turned out the way they had tonight? What if things had gone badly?*

Then Brian noticed something else. There was another set of tracks. However, these were different from the impression his tennis shoes made in the dirt. The other set of tracks were definitely larger footprints in comparison to his. These other footprints were clearly made by someone else. They paralleled Brian's footpath near the ellipsoid. Observing these other tracks from the ellipsoid, Brian traced how they made their way down the gully. These other footprints originated from a different direction than where Brian's footprints came from. Suddenly, it was all very clear in his mind. There was no doubt in his mind whose footsteps those were. Brian kept looking at the ground as he slowly turned his head toward the spot where the creature was standing now. As he held the alien eyeglasses to his face, Brian gazed at the creature's strange boots. Immediately behind the alien's large sized boots were the exact footprints Brian had just detected.

The young man slowly brought his focused attention up from the creature's boots. His gaze slid along the beast's muscularly fit physique, and when Brian's line of sight reached the creature's head, the young man quickly noticed the extraterrestrial being's wraparound eyewear lenses facing directly at him. Indeed, the creature was looking at Brian the whole while, watching him with its own pair of night vision glasses on. Behind those reflective copper lenses, Brian knew the beast was intently staring at him. Though Brian could not see the maroon eyes of the beast, he could sense the stare. The creature was standing silent and motionless. Brian was certain that the creature knew unerringly just what had transpired, and what the young man saw in the dirt. Brian assumed the creature had also been outside the ellipsoid at some point. However, Brian was not certain when that was.

Brian removed the eyeglasses and handed them back to the extraterrestrial humanoid woman. He squinted as his eyes immediately lost all of the vibrant color and extraordinary detail of the world around him. The humanoid woman gently received the eyeglasses from his grasp and she put them on. She began to speak to the creature, and at the same time, she pointed at Brian. At that moment, Brian noticed that the creature was holding something. The alien beast offered it to the young man. Brian took a few steps closer, and at once realized what the creature was holding. It was the flashlight Brian brought along on the evening hike. The young man took the flashlight from the creature and turned it on. He shined the primitive light toward the ground as he thought about all of the beautiful detail that the alien eyeglasses had provided him just a moment ago. He looked at the ground as he searched for a clear path ahead to walk on. Brian preferred to wear the alien's night vision eyeglasses.

They all stood silently for a moment. The extraterrestrial creature was busy pressing something like buttons on some type of wristband equipment that looked very much like an oversized watch. Next, the creature spoke a few hissing, jaw chopping words in its alien language and then turned and walked toward the incline of the gully. Brian smiled in the dark and gestured for the alien humanoid woman to follow behind the beast. He knew she could see his handsome, welcoming smile with the eyeglasses on. She walked past him to put herself between Brian and the creature in single file. Next, Brian followed the alien woman. With his trusty flashlight in hand, he carefully stepped behind the two extraterrestrials as they started up the gully. Brian glanced back at the ellipsoid one more time as he followed the aliens. He wondered what the aliens would do, now that they had been discovered.

The trio casually made their way up over the loose dirt and gravel that bordered the deep furrow. The creature led the way, advancing in between the contiguous trees. The alien humanoid woman and Brian were close behind. The night air was filled with the airy pine smell of forested evergreens. It was a welcome, accustomed, and refreshing bouquet that filled Brian's nostrils. He was glad to be out in the open, again. He felt more comfortable here. More so than he felt within the boundaries of the sleeping chamber inside the ellipsoid. He took in a deep breath, rejuvenating himself with the mountain air. Brian wondered if the two aliens could appreciate the wonderful scent and the outside world as he did.

The creature was moving at a quick and steady pace, maneuvering around the thickets and waist-high vegetation with ease in the darkness. No doubt the fancy eyeglasses made it a cinch. Brian remembered how using the flashlight still presented a slight challenge in the darkness of the forest when he made his way out here in the early evening. Now, the trio was moving at a faster pace than Brian's initial exploratory hike. Brian and the exotic humanoid woman followed close behind the beast. It was almost as if the creature had traveled the same path many times before. They continued their walk between tall silhouettes of Western Junipers and White Fir pines that surrounded them in the nighttime darkness of the wooded area. It was the same general location Brian passed through on his way to the gully.

Brian looked around as the trio continued to walk. Neither the alien humanoid woman nor the creature was talking. The only sound heard were footsteps traversing over dried leaves and twigs. The group was still together in a tight single file formation. Looking directly up, Brian could see part of the starlit night sky between the canopies of the tall evergreens surrounding him. He wondered which one of those stars the extraterrestrials had come from. Brian told the aliens that he would not tell anyone he saw them tonight. He was telling the truth. Deep inside, he wanted to keep this first contact with the alien beings a secret. Brian was convinced that things would not go well if he shared this encounter with the rest of humankind on earth. Brian felt that in some way, somehow, people on earth would find a way to ruin everything. *I better keep this on the low. I should find a way to keep them hidden and quiet, for now anyway. People are idiots in general. They do stupid stuff. I still can't believe this. It's all exciting, but it's still kind of scary. My life has changed forever.*

·　·　·　•　●　⬤　●　•　·　·　·

In spite of the initial terror Brian experienced with the creature, he wanted to share the overall experience tonight with someone special. He wished he could. He could not help but think of how special it would have been to share this occasion with Gina. Brian felt a little disappointed that the two of them were not together on this adventurous evening hike. Moreover, he felt a little sad that they were not together as a couple anymore. He reflected on the times when the two of them took camping trips together. It was only a few months ago when they last shared a quiet evening like this one. Gina loved the outdoors. She enjoyed discovering new things, and she had an open minded, simple curiosity about life in general. When Brian and Gina were together outside during an evening like this, she would look up at the stars and comment about how beautiful they were. Brian even remembered a few times when she had asked him if he thought there were other people out there on other worlds, looking up to their own sky at night. As the trio meandered on through the night forest Brian thought of different scenarios, and he contemplated how this first contact would have been with Gina at his side tonight. Gina would have really been excited to meet these curious aliens from another world. She would have embraced this moment of discovery, and she would have welcomed the extraterrestrials to her earthly home. That is, if she hadn't run for her life first after meeting the creature.

Brian mulled over his newfound relationship with the aliens. He judiciously considered how things were developing. He was beginning to trust the two beings more. He essentially felt he was in no danger from them, so far. Besides, up to now he really had no reason not to trust them. Brian honestly thought he should have some sort of plan. He did not really know what to do, having this first contact without any prior knowledge, preparation, or warning. This was all so overwhelmingly a shock to his senses. For the time being, he decided that he should just study them to try to find out what they were all about. *What is their mission here on Earth?* He questioned this sincerely. *They most likely have some kind of objective.* The young man turned his head to one side as he thought. *Or, are they lost?*

Brian watched the beast from behind the alien woman as they sauntered on in the darkened forest. Every now and then it looked at the face of the 'watch' it was wearing on its right arm. Brian was curious as to what the illuminated wristband equipment was displaying. He observed the steady pace of the beast and the way it led them through the woods toward his parent's house with a purpose. Brian wholeheartedly believed that the creature was behaving in an honest, responsible manner.

His thoughts kept reflecting on the moment he first saw the beast.

I sure am glad I didn't meet this alien-werewolf from outer space in the middle of the forest tonight. Maybe it was already walking towards the house before I headed out.

As Brian watched the creature hike, he could not help but wonder how the alien beast navigated its way through the dark forest so quickly. *Is that creature really following my tracks so easily with those funky glasses? Or, does it actually know the way back?* Brian thought about all of the strange sounds he heard outside the house earlier that night. He tried to recall if he had possibly seen the shadow of the alien creature looming in the woods. However, he could not recall seeing anything out of the ordinary.

At that moment, the creature slowed its pace and raised its head to look at something in the distance. Brian immediately noticed what the creature saw. It was a light shining not too far away. He knew in an instant that it was the rear lot floodlight of his parents' home. Then, seemingly all at once, Brian noticed the curved pattern, concrete block retaining wall of his parents' elevated rear lot. As they got closer, the wall seemed to come out of the darkness at them in more detail, and the young man started to recognize exactly where they were. Their pace slowed to a shuffle as they stopped in front of the curved concrete block enclosure.

Brian glanced around the immediate area with the beam of the flashlight trained near the base of the retaining wall. *This is about the spot where I…* At that moment Brian suddenly realized he was missing the kitchen knife. *I think this is the spot where I jumped down.* He squarely recognized the moment. He had made the small jump from the retaining wall with both, kitchen knife and flashlight in hand. Only now did the young man remember that he had the knife with him this evening until the creature took it away from him. *What did it do with my knife? Forget about it. I don't need it.* The last thing he wanted to do was confront the alien beast about that knife.

The silence and serene absence of all communication up to this point was finally broken, when the beast began to speak.

It pointed at Brian, and then it pointed toward the rear lot. All that the alien woman did in reply was nod her head once. Next, the creature turned, and looked at Brian. He smiled back at the alien. He knew the beast was staring at him behind those fancy reflective eyeglasses.

"Okay, then," Brian said, "I'll take it from here."

With that, he calmly walked past the extraterrestrials and started his way up the retaining wall. The interlaced arrangement of the concrete blocks made the short climb an easy task. When he made it to the top of the brick bordered edge of the retaining wall the beast spoke, indicating that the humanoid woman should start up the wall. *What are they up to?* Brian wondered. *What are they doing? Are they coming with me to the house… inside?* He tilted his head to one side in amusement.

Brian carefully watched the alien woman's ascent and then instinctively crouched down and helped her up the last segment to the top. The alien beast was silently scanning the entire area with its night vision eyeglasses on, looking in all directions with a speculative gaze. Suddenly it looked down and concentrated on the colorful designs on its 'watch'. Then, all at once, it focused on the task at hand and wasted no time climbing the wall. Brian did not help as he had with the alien woman. Instead, he merely moved back a few steps to give the creature more room. *I'm not helping that hairless werewolf up here.* Brian took another step back when the beast made its way to the top. The creature stood perfectly still for a brief moment as it methodically scanned the area, again. Brian knew it didn't want anyone else to see them.

Brian turned around and started toward his parents' house. Both alien beings followed, with the trio strolling along in single file with the creature taking up the rear. Brian led them quickly past the outdoor grill and fireplace area and then toward the covered patio lit up by the rear flood light on the upper deck. From there he walked across the concrete patio stepping around the beautiful patio furniture and then stopped at the rear door of the house.

Brian took in a deep breath, and sighed.

Chapter Eight

They all stood there in a moment of uncomfortable silence as Brian tried to think of what to do next.

"Well, thanks," Brian said and then joked, "I had a wonderful evening. Thanks for walking me home. We should do it again, sometime."

The alien woman smiled and spoke softly. She gestured with her hands, however, Brian could not figure out what she was implying. As she spoke to Brian, the creature started visually scanning the area again as if something caught its attention. Then the beast grunted and mumbled something in its unintelligible language to the extraterrestrial woman. She stopped talking and both of the extraterrestrials looked away into the dark distance of the surrounding forest. Brian looked too, but he could not see anything in the immediate area. Then he heard the humanoid woman giggle like a little girl and suddenly gasp in a pleasantly surprised manner. Brian looked at her and noticed her expression of astonished amusement. She was smiling and pointing in the direction they had been looking. The creature gurgled, a sound Brian thought might be a faint chuckle.

"What?" Brian glanced over his shoulder, and peered into the night, "You guys see something?"

He squinted in an effort to see into the darkness, and for a moment, he thought he saw someone. The moon lit shapes and shadows of the night forest produced an image in his mind. He saw the image of another alien being. The 'person' was dark in color like the humanoid woman with long legs walking directly towards them out of the bushes and the shadows of the night woods. Brian heard both the creature and humanoid woman chuckle, again. *Is that another one of them?* he thought in disbelief. Brian leaned forward and squinted a little more until he finally realized what he saw was simply the bushes rustling in the distance. He knew he was mistaken.

"There's probably a small coyote peeking at us somewhere in those bushes," Brian mumbled. "Whatever it is, I'm sure you guys can see it with those glasses on." He spoke in a loud, clear, voice as if the aliens could understand him.

Brian remembered his mother telling him she had seen a young coyote around the area at night a couple of times and as soon as she opened the kitchen door or made almost any sound the coyote ran away. Satisfied with the fact that he was wrong, Brian turned around to face the two smiling aliens. Even the creature's thin lips curled up at the edges. *That's a different look on you.* Brian was pleased to see that side of the beast. The sight made Brian smile a little, too.

"Well," Brian said, "I saw your place, so I guess you would probably like to see mine." He opened the rear door slowly, and immediately looked down to the floor.

His eyes searched for Mr. Doodles, who was lying comfortably atop the edge of the family room sofa. Brian pushed the door all the way open.

"Easy, Doodles," Brian said in a soft tone of voice as he stepped into his parents' home.

Brian glanced over his shoulder to find the creature closely following him. The beast had a faint smile underneath the shiny copper lenses of its night vision eyeglasses. It shuffled so close behind that Brian felt its breath on the back of his neck, which resulted in Brian going into the family room much more quickly than he intended. The creature followed, with the extraterrestrial woman close behind. Brian kept a close watch on the cat, still relaxing without a care on top of the couch. Brian stepped aside a little as he continued to lead the way indoors. What happened next was instantaneous. As soon as Mr. Doodles got a full view of the beast, the cat leapt off the couch and scurried under the Queen Anne cocktail table. The precipitate motor reflexes of the little tabby cat startled the beast. Brian noticed an almost imperceptible flinch that he found quite amusing.

He couldn't resist. "Uh-huh," Brian said, barely suppressing a laugh, "you jumped, dog person. I saw it." He barely raised a finger and pointed at the beast.

Then the exotic female alien moved forward and looked around the creature's broad shoulders to see where the cat disappeared to. She immediately started to giggle in her alien voice, and as soon as she did, the beast chuckled in its bizarre tenor of laughter. The two extraterrestrials were staring toward the area underneath the cocktail table where the cat had quickly vanished. After a shared moment of insouciant alien being laughter and amusement, they began to speak to each other quietly. Brian noticed how the beast's vocalizations were actually clearer in a quiet tone of voice. It seemed to hiss and gurgle less. With an intrigued smile, Brian observed how the creature interacted with the exotic alien woman. It was nothing short of stupendous. Indeed, this evening was an occasion that was truly out of this world.

"You guys have cats where you come from?" Brian asked with a smile, as he slowly began to shut the backdoor.

At the first hint of the door's movement, the creature suddenly turned to face Brian. It was expressionless, but quickly pressed the large open face of the 'watch' it was wearing as if it had buttons, which surprised Brian. He gazed at the creature, watching as the large fingers of the beast continued moving in rapid succession as it manipulated the controls of its bizarre, oversized wristband device. *What in the world is that sunglass wearing, hairless werewolf from outer space doing?* Brian wondered, standing perfectly still while holding the rear door ajar. What happened next was instantaneous and made Brian do more than flinch.

From out of the darkness outside, an object shot through the doorway into the room making Brian jumped backwards!

"Whoa!" he exclaimed.

The unexpected movement and extreme close proximity of whatever it was completely startled him. The thing was the shape and size of a billiard ball and right now, it was floating just inches away from his chin. It was dark in color and, just like the large ellipsoid object; it was perfectly smooth all around. It traveled through the air about neck high. The floating orb device entered the family room very quickly, and as soon as it passed by Brian its color started to change to a striped, flat taupe and white camouflage appearance. The two basic color patterns seemed to amalgamate into a dynamic display of striped livery. The disruptive coloration was uniquely disorienting, and allowed the floating object to practically vanish from foreground view. The silent floating drone now melded perfectly with the color dynamics of the surrounding walls and ceiling. The almost instant color transformation was amazing. Within seconds, the object possessed the exact color tinge and light absorbing characteristics of the painted family room surrounding it.

"Whoa! What in the world is that?" Brian said in a high-pitched voice. He stared in pure amazement at the floating object.

"Where did that thing come from? Was that following us the whole time out there?" His tone of voice got louder as he asked more questions with a stark and perplexed look on his face.

"What's it for? Is it some kind of weapon?"

He looked outside into the night to see if there was anything else about to float inside the house and surprise him like that, again. He did not observe anything else strange at the moment. Satisfied with that, he really wanted to close the door. He hastily reached for it, and with his hand on the brass doorknob, glanced at the alien woman. She had just removed her fancy technological eyewear. As Brian began to close the door, she nodded slowly, with a slight, single bow. He swiftly shut the door.

"Hey space-wolf," Brian pointed at the creature and said, "you've got to let me know in advance before you do something like that, again. Give me a heads-up, man."

The beast ignored the foreign, juvenile comment and finger-pointing gesture Brian made. The creature was too busy concentrating on what it was doing. Two of its fingers were practically tap dancing on top of the face of the wristband device. All of a sudden, the beast glanced up at the floating orb and paused for a moment. Next, the extraterrestrial creature looked at Brian and, with one finger it slowly pressed the face of the wristband device once. The strange floating orb drone responded to the command and immediately rose higher and then slowly moved toward the adjacent hallway without making the slightest sound. The alien technological wonder just about disappeared as it progressed into the dimly lit, short hallway, no doubt, because of its perfectly matched coloration and camouflage pattern.

What the hell…

Then Brian was startled by the sudden sound of the humanoid woman speaking in her soothing tone. She stepped closer to Brian and handed him the night vision eyewear. He put them on without uttering a word. What he saw next was astounding. His human eyes were privileged to see what the two extraterrestrials had been observing for some time now. The visual perception he had now was uniquely different than what he observed before in the night forest. He no longer perceived the vibrant colors that had overwhelmed him earlier. The eyewear was no longer functioning like night vision goggles. Instead, the view was familiar, invigoratingly flawless, and remarkably crystal-clear. Through the eyeglasses, Brian could instantly tell that there was an enhanced, wide-angle view. It was as if he was looking at everything through the lenses of some highly advanced video camera. There were small alien symbols flashing about within his field of view. What Brian also quickly noticed was some type of screen presentation affixed to the lower left corner of his view. The effect was a picture-in-picture screen that seemed to 'float' in space within his sight. Brian focused his attention on the small picture frame. He at once noticed something familiar and grinned in disbelief at the sight of it. The small lower left corner picture was a real time view of the hallway that the floating orb drone was actually traveling through. Brian watched in astonishment as the alien lenses showed him what the floating drone saw. He watched as the object floated up the stairway to the second floor of his parent's house. He could see everything in full color and clarity. Brian once again beheld the night-vision presentation that first impressed him. The view from the floating alien camera was amazing. Even with most the house being dark, Brian could see things in remarkable detail. He watched as the alien object floated its way into the darkened master suite upstairs. Brian watched as it proceeded without hesitation toward the master bathroom. The floating drone just continued its travel in the dark, seemingly on a mission. The object methodically turned left and entered the walk-in closet, as well. The night vision display of the small lower left corner picture within the alien eyeglass view revealed how the floating object was scanning the area.

"You're checking everything out, aren't you?" Brian turned to look at the beast. Brian was already convinced. He didn't need a verbal answer, or a single nod. He knew.

The creature looked at him without emotion, as Brian removed the fancy eyewear.

"Here you go. Thanks." Brian smiled as he handed the alien humanoid woman her eyeglasses back. She took them gently from his grasp with an appeasing smile.

"You won't find anything. Nobody's here, just us." Brian shook his head at the creature, and pointed to the three of them in the room.

"There's no one else but us, my man. I mean... my alien-space-dog," Brian said with a raised brow.

There was no response from the beast. The creature remained motionless, standing in one spot. The extraterrestrial being seemed to be staring. Brian was curious to know what the creature was looking at. It was difficult to tell from those fancy, copper lens eyeglasses shining at him. So Brian took a few steps to his right. As soon as he did, the beast turned its head slightly to follow his move.

Whatever. You don't scare me... that much... right now.

The beast continued its conspicuous observation of Brian as it spoke aloud in its celestial native tongue. The exotic alien woman spoke to the creature in return. As she did so, she started to remove the utility vest, backpack combination apparel she was wearing. It must have been somewhat heavy. Brian noticed her grimace a little as she worked her way out of the snug fitting utility garb. A few seconds later, she placed it gently on the polished hardwood floor of the family room. After that, she placed the eyeglasses in an attached receptacle on the rear part of the utility backpack. The beast did not remove its equipment vest-backpack. Brian figured she was tired of wearing it, and the creature was not. Brian knew the beast was physically stronger than she was. He looked the creature up and down. He wondered where the beast was physically vulnerable. As Brian looked the creature over, he noticed for the first time that it had on something else in addition to the utility pack. There was a slender slate gray colored object fastened to the side of the creatures left thigh. The length of it went from the creature's hip to the top of the left knee. Brian did not notice the attached equipment before because it blended in with the flight-suit uniform colors so well.

The two extraterrestrials continued to talk to each other. The creature had turned away from Brian to face her. Brian heard the alien woman slightly raise her voice at the creature as they conversed in their enigmatic language. They seemed to be speaking faster and slightly more impassioned now.

Ah-ha… a heated discussion about something, Brian deduced. *Now what do you suppose it could be about?* Brian was slightly mystified. He came to the obvious conclusion. *Me.*

"You guys aren't leaving anytime too soon, are you?" Brian spoke slowly and clearly as he interrupted their conversation.

Both extraterrestrials stopped talking and looked at him. Brian gestured with his hands in a manner that they understood. He walked his fingers on the open palm of his hand, and pointed at the two beings. Then, he pointed at the door. Brian was also nodding while he communicated with his hands. There was no response from the extraterrestrials.

"I don't think you guys are done with your mission. I bet I interrupted whatever it is you're supposed to do here, huh?" Brian glanced at the two of them, "I sure hope you don't mean us any harm." There was a somber tone to his voice. He started to look worried.

"I hope you come in peace. At least, I thought you did up to now."

The alien creature took a couple quick steps toward Brian, speaking a loud voice to the woman while looking at Brian. Brian just knew the beast's unsettling maroon colored eyes were locked on him. He was happy he could not see them through those reflective copper lens eyeglasses. Brian was feeling more nervous. He did not like the way the extraterrestrial creature faced him down. Something was happening. He did not know what yet, but he could sense it.

"What's going down right about now?" Brian asked as he nervously searched the alien beings' faces for answers. "Is this part of some kind of an invasion? Are we really under attack?"

Brian's mind started to race and his breathing rate increased. He was beginning to really feel on edge.

"What are you guys, a reconnaissance team, or something like that?" Brian tried to remain calm. "I thought everything was cool." Brian wondered if the creature had an ulterior motive.

Why didn't that alien werewolf creature get rid of me when I found them, if this is a secret invasion? Are they at some stage in their plans where they are not ready to be seen? Are they not ready to attack, yet? Did they bring me back so nothing would look suspicious or out of place? So, nobody would come looking for me? So nobody else would discover them out there? Are there more of them? Am I actually in some kind of serious danger right now? Are they really going to kill me here, tonight?

He clenched his teeth. Just then he remembered the Smith and Wesson .357 Magnum revolver his dad kept in the master bedroom dresser. He also remembered his father kept the ammunition right next to it. He started to think about how fast he could make it upstairs and load the firearm with a few bullets. Brian wondered if the floating object he saw would stop him before he could make it to the gun.

The alien beast was standing only a few feet away from him now. Its rigid posture was very intimidating. Brian's mind was in a frenzy, a state of silent panic. He thought of striking first, utilizing the element of surprise, however, maybe that would be a premature feat. After all, he had trusted the aliens up to now, and he was just not totally sure if he was in grave danger at the moment. *What should I do if this really is an invasion?* His mind continued to race. Brian figured he would have to sucker punch the alien in order to get to the weapon upstairs. One clear advantage Brian had, if any, was being closer to the hallway than the aliens. That meant he had a slight head start to get to the handgun.

He considered his options. *Maybe I should go for the fancy eyeglasses and knock them off. That should put the creature at a slight disadvantage. Yes, that's what I'll do. Make your move you hairless werewolf!* Brian tried to silently psych himself up but he did not want to display any of his intentions. He remained quiet and still, trying to hide the genuine feeling of confused anxiety buried deep inside him that was ready to burst like a hot geyser.

The alien creature spoke, again. It looked back at the humanoid woman and made a gesture with its large hands. The beast fanned its left hand back and forth in a gesture Brian had become somewhat familiar with tonight. *Wait a minute.* Brian tried to pay very close attention. *It wants her to do something.* The creature made another fanning gesture with its big left hand. It was waving the exotic female toward where the two were standing. Next, the creature lightly patted its chest several times. Now Brian had no idea what was going on. He had no idea what was about to happen.

Slowly, the beast turned its head to face Brian again. At the same time, the extraterrestrial woman began to walk closer to them. The room was uncomfortably full of unnerving silence as she stared into Brian's eyes. Brian noticed how she stepped slowly and almost reluctantly towards the two as she gently pulled at the long top collar of her jumpsuit. The uniform opened up from the top of her narrow neck down to her cleavage with a couple of crisp 'snaps' from the garment. It was the only sound in the room. Then, Brian noticed her pull something out from underneath the lapels of her uniform. Clasped in her hand was a necklace from which something sparkly dangled.

She was only a few feet away from Brian now, close enough so he could see that what sparkled was an extraordinarily exquisite gem. It was the most breathtaking gemstone Brian had ever seen. The beautiful, pear shaped jewel was almost two inches long and about an inch and a half in the widest part. From where Brian stood, it appeared to be about a half an inch in thickness. The color and resemblance was uncannily similar to that of fine aquamarine.

The perfectly edged facets of the geometrically rounded crystal reflected the ambient light in the most brilliant way. The jewel seemed to emanate more light coming out of it than the room shined upon it. The effect was visually stunning and captivating. Brian could not think of any precious gem, such as a diamond or ruby that possessed as much luster as this stone did. What Brian did not know, was that the alien stone was the rarest celestial gem. Nothing compared to it. Not even the rarest of earthly minerals, such as jadeite, garnet, or grandidierite, which was only remotely similar, at best. By simple comparison, this precious stone was more brilliant and flawless than any jewel on earth.

Brian stared at it in pure and delighted admiration. The alien gem was inimitable. He could appreciate that it must truly have some great value. He was so enthralled with the sight of it that he leaned closer to see the gem better. The dazzling celestial jewel was motionless as it hung beneath the gleaming silvery necklace within the firm clutch of the exotic woman. He assumed the alien ornament must have been quite solid and weighty for its small size. Brian could sense that she used some conscious effort to grab the gleaming necklace at just the right spot in order to lift up the jewel from her chest.

Brian looked deeply into the dazzling aquamarine colored gemstone.

"It's so beautiful," he said sincerely in a hushed tone. "I've never seen anything…" But Brian stopped in mid-sentence for something started to happen.

The gemstone moved on its own! It began rotating just a bit so the entire facet and width of the jewel was completely in view of his gaze. Then, all at once, the jewel started homogeneously losing all its color. The change started from within the very center of the crystal and moved rapidly outward toward the exterior facets of the gem. As this took place, tiny ocher sparks randomly appeared to ignite within the ornament like a dazzling display of minuscule fireworks. It was a fascinating catalytic manifestation to behold. The intensity of the sparking effect increased like an inferno until a slight orange glow emanated from the very center of the spectacularly radiant alien jewel. Brian's eyes grew wide at the sight.

After only a few seconds of watching this internal transformation, a sudden pulse of silvery light flashed from the center of the gem. It was unexpected, and as exactingly intense as a camera flash in stark darkness. Brian instinctively blinked, but his eyes remained focused on the center of the wondrous and beautiful jewel. At the exact moment the flash occurred, Brian heard and felt a single pulsation, a percussion deep inside his skull. It was disorienting and at first, slightly uncomfortable, and in that instant he was not sure if he could move, or if he even wanted to move. He was not certain whether he wanted to look away, or if he was even capable of turning his head away. He could not explain how he felt, however, he knew something was different. Brian involuntarily stood still with his eyes still focused on the center of the jewel. Then a second flash occurred within seconds of the first. The second strobe of bright silvery light also resulted in another single, deep pulsation feeling inside his head. Only this time Brian immediately felt an overwhelming sensation of innate calmness and relaxation, and he also became somewhat drowsy. Brian's breathing slowed a bit and he was becoming less anxious. He was absent of any other thought. Nothing else occupied his mind. He subconsciously concentrated on the center of the alien gem and waited, as if he expected another pulse of light. His body was still in anticipation.

All of a sudden, the exotic alien female lowered the alluring gem to her chest. As she did so, she looked down at the floor of the quiet family room. Brian's eyes were still locked onto the mysterious jewel. The gem was now absent of all color. The crystal reflected the interior lighting of the room with perfection in its purest form. The jewel was so beautiful. It was all that he wanted to look at. He did not care about anything else. He wanted to experience another flash of silvery light. He wanted to feel that pulse surge in his head and overwhelm his senses again. He had become uncontrollably and instantaneously addicted to the soothing hypnotic influence of the radiant, celestial jewel.

Brian felt himself leaning forward. He suddenly felt dizzy. He was off balance. He stumbled a little trying to regain his composure. The beast immediately reached out and stabilized Brian's ungainly attempt to stand straight. Startled, Brian looked at the extraterrestrial creature as he tried to right himself.

"Whoa", he said, "I'm feeling a little dizzy, man." Brian smiled. "I feel good though!" His speech was slightly slurred.

"What is that thing? Some kind of…" He started to fall over.

The extraterrestrial creature stepped forward and put its arm around Brian's waist. Brian leaned against the strong being for some support. Next, the beast actually helped the young man walk. The creature motioned with its left hand in a direction toward the family room couch. The two of them started to walk side by side. Brian stumbled slightly as they walked together on their way. Brian smiled the whole way with a very relaxed look on his handsome face. His eyes were half-closed and his head slightly lowered. They passed the alien woman who was still looking down at the floor. She was silent. When Brian got around to the front of the couch, the beast carefully helped the sedated young man sit down.

"That's very nice of you," he said as he looked up at the alien creature's face with a glazed look in his eyes. "Thank you very much, space-wolf." Brian nodded at the creature.

The beast looked at the humanoid woman. It spoke to her in a calm manner. She immediately responded in a raised tone of voice. Brian looked over his shoulder to see her staring at him. She quickly tucked the beautiful, mesmerizing gem out of sight underneath the bosom of her flight suit and walked over to the couch. She stood behind Brian for a moment, and then leaned toward him. Brian watched calmly as she put her long arms around him and embraced him soothingly. She was soft and smelled like something pleasantly familiar. Brian smiled as she gently hugged him. When she stood up, her hands remained with a comforting soft touch on the young man's shoulders.

Brian pointed one finger in the air as he suddenly recalled her familiar scent.

"You kind of smell like baby powder." Brian's smile was bigger and he chuckled a little with his response. He felt so good right now. He was so relaxed, without a care in the world. He wanted the feeling to last forever.

"Phew…" He turned around to look at the creature as he said, "And you smell like my mom's cat." Brian was pointing at the extraterrestrial beast.

The alien woman leaned towards Brian again and gently massaged his shoulders with her firm, narrow fingers. She spoke to him in a soft reassuring tone of voice. Her words filled his ears, though he had not a clue what she was saying. He just smiled as he listened, and enjoyed the attention he received from her. Brian turned to look at her. She had a reassuring smile on her face. It was an expression Brian enjoyed looking at. She continued to speak as he turned back around. Brian saw that the creature was listening to her as it took off its utility pack.

"Yeah, why don't you guys just chill for a minute? Make yourselves comfortable and help yourself to, whatever," Brian said as his eyes began to shut. He was so tired.

I'll just lie down for a minute to relax. Then I'll be refreshed. He leaned over and stretched out on the couch, kicked off his shoes and turned onto his back.

"Just give me a minute here," he said, "I need to chill for a bit."

As Brian drifted off to sleep, he turned onto his right side to make himself more comfortable. He could hear the two aliens talking softly to each other. He didn't care what they were talking about. He just needed a little nap right now.

"I'm not trying to be rude, I just…" His words quickly faded as he completely relaxed and drifted into a deep slumber.

Chapter Nine

It was the most beautiful evening. The nighttime sky was full of shining, diamond-like stars along with a vivid crescent moon. Gina looked into Brian's eyes. Brian was so happy that the two of them had this opportunity to share such a beautiful night together. She sat across from him on the other side of the small dinner table for two. She was smiling. Brian was trying to remember if she had ever looked so gorgeous.

"You are so beautiful Gina," he said. He could not help himself. He had just told her for the tenth time tonight, all within the last thirteen minutes.

"Brian." She made a funny face at him. "Come on, you're embarrassing me." She started to giggle.

The handsome couple held hands across the small table for two. Between the two lovers a small candle glowed. The light from the candle flickered across their smiling faces and it gave prominence to the look of true love deep within their eyes.

"What a perfect night." Brian looked up into the evening sky.

The outdoor table where the couple sat had a perfect view of the stars above them.

"I'm so glad we're both here right now. I'm so glad you are my lady, Gina." Brian looked into her sultry dark brown eyes.

He took in all her beauty. Her short, straight black hair with dark chocolate highlights was slightly layered in a way that framed her face. The soft candlelight made her silky skin glow as if lit from within. She was youthful and her delicate features were very appealing to Brian. As he silently gazed into her eyes she began to chuckle lightly. She looked away, slightly embarrassed.

Her pretty face blushed in response to his heartfelt gaze. Then, with a slow purposeful motion, she turned her head to give him a deep, alluring look. She lightly bit her lower lip and grinned blissfully. There was a moment of silence, now. Only their eyes communicated how they felt for one another deep inside their souls this very minute.

"So…" They were abruptly startled by their server who was now standing close to their table. He had practically come out of nowhere. The waiter cleared his throat quickly and asked, "Is anyone hungry tonight?" He reached out to hand the handsome couple a pair of dinner menus.

"Or, are we just having cocktails?" the waiter politely inquired with a smile.

"Oh, umm…" Brian was unprepared, unsure of what to say. He smiled at the server and Gina courteously chuckled.

"Would you like some more wine?" the slim, salt and pepper haired waiter asked with a big smile and a pronounced South American accent.

"Well, uh… yes." Brian looked at the two almost empty glasses of white zinfandel on their table.

"Yes, that would be good," Brian responded as he nodded and smiled at his girlfriend.

She playfully smiled in return and gave a quick nod of approval while Brian took the menus from the waiter and gently placed them next to the centerpiece candle on top of their cozy outdoor table.

"I will come back with two more glasses of wine then." The thoughtful server promptly and unobtrusively retrieved the glasses from the table and charmingly articulated, "Perhaps by then you might decide if you want to eat some dinner, too."

With that he very politely smiled, then quietly turned and quickly disappeared into the restaurant. Inside, there were dozens of other tables of various sizes accommodating other smiling and laughing patrons that were enjoying the lovely evening out, just as Brian and Gina were. The inside dining area was nice, but it was a little too noisy and busy to set the mood right. The outdoor dining area had a much more intimate air of romance about it. In addition, there were only a few outdoor tables occupied. It was truly ideal.

When Brian turned back around to look at Gina, she was gazing up into the infinite starlit, nighttime sky. Her mouth was agape, and her eyes wide open.

"Brian." She looked at him, and with curious astonishment asked, "Do you think there are other people out there looking at us right now? I mean, do you think they see our sun with all the other stars around it, like…"

She paused for a slight moment and a look of pure fascination filled her eyes, "…the way we see theirs? Our bright sun is just a tiny shining dot in the sky to somebody else, right? Just think. Our sun is mixed with all those other brilliant stars out there right now." She gestured with all her fingers stretched out, both hands over her head, and eyes wide open.

"Isn't that like, so wonderful when you stop and really think about it?" Gina smiled.

Brian thought for a moment as he looked up high into the heavens.

"Well, I guess so. I think there might be a few alien lovers out there just like us, looking at our sun and admiring how bright and magnificent it is." He looked into her eyes as he finished. "They might be having some kind of a Martian romance right about now. They're probably out on a date looking at our sun this very minute. There's probably at least one little green alien dude trying to get lucky out there tonight." Brian rubbed his chin as he gazed upward.

Gina couldn't help but laugh at his lighthearted pseudo-scientific, romantic estimation.

"You're so cute baby. I like that," she said.

At that moment, Gina gasped. She was looking up, pointing into the air. Brian looked up in time to see a falling star race across the sky for an instant before it extinguished into the darkness above. There were astonished reactions from a few people around them who had also noticed the wondrous though short-lived spectacle.

"Did you see that?" Gina gasped with a smile of pure amazement.

"I sure did. Man, those falling stars are really something. They burn so bright and beautiful."

Then he returned his gaze to his girlfriend's dark brown eyes and said, "You've got to make a wish, Gina." Brian grabbed her hands and gently squeezed. She looked up into the night sky and shut her eyes tight for a moment. Then she opened them and looked at her boyfriend.

The two were having a wonderful time. They were both smiling at each other like they had discovered something wonderful together for the first time. Verily so, what they discovered this night was that they were truly and deeply in love with each other.

"What did you wish for?" Brian said with a curious smile.

Gina opened her mouth wide and shook her head with a teasing look in her eyes.

"Uh-uh no, I can't tell you baby. It won't come true." She could hardly say the words before giving way to mischievous laughter.

Gina giggled as she tried to keep a serious face. She seemed to tense up as if she were expecting something to uncontrollably shock her senses. Next, as if on cue, Brian reached under the romantic table for two and grabbed her left knee. This was a vulnerable, ticklish spot on her that, when squeezed just the right way made her lose control of all practical sincerity in a microsecond. Her reaction was as expected, and she shrieked. The look in her eyes evinced pure ticklish helplessness.

"Brian!" Gina blurted and squirmed to get her knee free from her boyfriend's firm grasp. Both of them erupted into playful, romantic, sophomoric laughter.

"I've never heard of such foolishness. Who told you that?" Brian's face was a full-fledged pearly white smile, although he spoke in a demanding tone as if he were trying to interrogate her.

Gina was still squirming as she finally batted his hand away successfully; her half- muffled attempts to quiet her uncontrol-lable laughter continued as she replied, "My grandmother…"

She couldn't even finish her words as they both looked each other in the eye and erupted into jaunty congenial laughter once more. This was yet another warmhearted and carefree moment that the two lovers enjoyed sharing together, as they usually did. After a respite of only a few seconds, Brian made another fleeting attempt at her left knee to which Gina responded.

"Brian, stop!" in a heavy chuckle as she attempted with all her might to make a serious face.

They were both at the brink of non-stop, uncontainable hilarity by now. Gina fanned herself with her hand, and Brian coughed and cleared his throat. Both of them attempted to gain a little composure. They were so in tune with each other that the slightest mischievous glance from either of them triggered another set of sheer laughter. That is how well they knew each other, and it was also evidence as to how much they truly enjoyed each other's company.

"I'm crazy about you baby, and I can't stop thinking about you. You're always on my mind Gina, for real," Brian said in a confident, sensual tone of voice as the comical mood quickly changed to a more sincere and amorous atmosphere.

"I love you, Brian." Gina responded without hesitation in a sultry voice and an affectionate grin that honestly made him feel the happiest he had been in a long time.

"Gina…" Brian started, but was interrupted by a woman's voice calling his name from behind him. With a confused and slightly frustrated look he turned around to see who had called his attention at the most inopportune moment. Just as he did, the waiter approached their table, stepping between the table where the voice was heard, and the young couple's table.

"Your wine, sir," the server said and promptly placed two glasses of wine on the candlelit table. "So, are we having dinner tonight?" the waiter asked as he slowly clasped his hands together in front of him. He looked at Brian and smiled, waiting for a reply.

Brian looked up at him and replied. "No sir, thank you…ah,

I think we're just having some drinks tonight. Right baby, unless you…?" He turned around in time to hear his girlfriend confirm.

"Yes, wine will be fine, we ate not too long ago." Gina nodded at the server and then smiled at her handsome boyfriend.

"Yes, this is fine for now," Brian agreed, looking up at the server.

"Alright then, keep the menus. I will come back and check on you. If you need anything, don't hesitate to ask." With another big smile the kindly server nodded and turned to walk away. As he did so, Brian looked down in anticipation to see who had called his name prior to the waiter's arrival.

"Bri-an," came the woman's voice again.

She was beautiful. Brian guessed she was of Asian descent. The woman looked to be in her late twenties. She had very shiny hair, as black as a raven, and it was long and straight. Her hair partly covered her face, but Brian could still see her beautiful, alluring eyes. She was slim and lavishly attractive. Even though the mysterious woman was seated, Brian could tell that she had a superb, shapely feminine figure. The woman wore a tight, silky, emerald color dress that stopped just below the knee. Her long legs were crossed and she sat perfectly straight in her chair. Her candlelit table was positioned in a dimly lit corner of the outdoor dining area. The table was set for two people. However, she sat unaccompanied. Her chair was pulled out from the small table somewhat and she was facing slightly towards Brian's direction. The mysterious woman had obviously positioned it to look at Brian, who was situated almost directly in front of her now. She looked at him intently across the outdoor patio dining area.

"Brian, we talk now." Her voice carried over the patio and the background noise of the indoor dining area. The young man leaned forward and squinted as he tried to listen to her.

"Brian, who is she?" Gina all but demanded in a firm tone of voice. "Is she that girl that likes you at the hospital? That nurse from the surgery recovery room I heard about?"

Brian turned around and gave his girlfriend the most bewildered look.

"I don't… uh, I…" he muttered.

"Brian!" Gina glared at her boyfriend, "I know that's her!"

Gina's demeanor was no longer affectionate and romantic. The look in his girlfriend's eyes demanded immediate answers.

"Brian, come talk to me now." The woman on the dark side of the room beckoned fervently in a rather calm tone of voice.

Brian turned once again to look at her. She methodically pointed at the empty chair on the other side of the small table for two.

"Come now, Brian," she calmly insisted.

"Excuse me?" Brian responded with a confused look. When he turned around to face Gina, she already had her mouth open to speak.

"I want to know right now what's going on and don't lie to me. Were you supposed to meet her here tonight? Is that it? Do you have a date with her, too, and you forgot about it? I want to know what's going on, Brian," Gina demanded as she folded her arms in front of her. "NOW!" she blurted with a disapproving frown on her face.

"I have no idea…I" Brian started to answer as Gina quickly rose out of her chair and stood with her hands on her hips at their cozy, romantic table for two.

"Fine!" Gina grumbled and shook her head, "I'm out!"

With that, she began to walk swiftly past her boyfriend on her way toward the indoors dining room, purposefully stomping her high heels as she went by Brian. All Brian could do was watch her with his mouth agape and a confused look on his handsome face. Gina pressed onward and looked straight ahead as she passed the woman seated in the dimly lit corner of the outdoor patio area.

"I'll see you at work, you tramp!" Gina said out of the corner of her mouth without even glancing in the direction of the beautiful woman seated alone.

"Gina?" Brian tried to casually raise his voice across the patio dining area. "Baby what's up?" He helplessly raised his hands in the air.

Brian sensed the stares of others who were curiously watching from nearby tables. A few people behind the large glass window of the indoor dining room were peering at the drama as well. Brian quickly rose to his feet and walked in earnest toward the indoor dining area in pursuit of his perturbed lover.

"Gina wait, come back!" He dispatched his desperate plea like a lasso in hopes to impede his girlfriend's onward high heel stomping exodus. However, it was to no avail, as she simply walked away.

When Brian passed the beautiful woman seated alone, she leisurely looked his way and coolly imposed, "Brian, we talk now. Yes?"

However, Brian did not acknowledge the inviting woman's request. Instead, he ignored her and continued following his lovely girlfriend, Gina.

"Baby what's up?" he implored forlornly. Brian was trying hard not to attract any embarrassing attention. He was behind her now, walking stride for stride, but several feet behind her. Gina did not show any intentions of slowing her pace, and she was quickly disappearing into a small crowd of well-dressed woman and men gathered near the bar. The air was filled with casual laughter and jovial conversation from people socializing throughout the bar. There was also delightful mood music that just began softly playing in the background from a jazz quartet on the far side of the restaurant. The musicians were in view, located across the crowded bar. Brian raised his chin in an effort to see where his girlfriend was heading. It was quite obvious she was making a direct path for the door. As she walked swiftly through the small gathering of people, Brian began to wonder who had driven to the restaurant tonight. He could not remember. All he wanted to do was catch up to her. The anxious young man realized he needed to increase his pace if he wanted to be successful, when suddenly, he heard a voice beckon him.

"Hey!" The voice shot out from behind Brian. "Excuse me, sir!"

Brian turned around quickly to see who was raising their voice at him. He made eye contact with a few people before he realized where the voice was coming from. He looked toward the bar as the sound of a man's voice called out over the jazz music once more.

"Sir, you dropped your phone!" It was the bartender. The gentleman behind the bar fervently pointed toward the floor in an effort to direct Brian's attention there.

When Brian looked down, he discovered that his cell phone had indeed fallen out of his pocket somehow. There it was on the carpeted floor of the restaurant just a few feet behind him. The young man raised his hand and nodded once at the bartender.

"Thank you," Brian said, clearly flustered and self-conscious of his present situation.

He felt as if everyone in the restaurant knew what he was going through right now. He backtracked a few steps and kneeled down to retrieve his cell phone. As soon as he picked it up, the phone started ringing. Brian peered over his shoulder towards the front entrance of the restaurant. At a glance, Gina could not be found. Brian wondered if she was calling him from the parking lot now. He turned the phone over to look at the display face in order to see the caller ID.

Just as he did so, Brian woke up.

· · · • ● ⬤ ● • · · ·

The young man opened his eyes to the sound of his Ericsson T66 cell phone alarm clock ringing over and over again in his ear. Though his eyes were open wide, Brian's focus was off beam. For a moment, he did not know where he was. The cellular phone alarm rang once more as he blindly reached for it right next to him on top of the Queen Anne cocktail table. He quickly found the button to dismiss the annoying alert and in an instant, the family room was silent again. He calmly placed the phone back on the cocktail table without looking at it. Brian's memory was fuzzy. The last thing the confused young man remembered clearly was the sight of Gina walking towards the restaurant's front doorway.

Then, feeling a little less groggy as the seconds passed, Brian gradually recalled the events of his evening with Gina.

He stared at the family room ceiling of his parent's home as he lay perfectly still on their large comfortable sofa. He distinctly remembered the sound of Gina's voice. He could still see her beautiful smiling face in the glow of the romantic candlelight. Brian could recall the moment she got up to walk away from him as if it had just happened. The mental image was so very real to him. *Did we really go out last night? And if we did, how did I get back to my parent's place?* He looked toward his feet stretched out on the sofa. *Yep.* He thought to himself, again. *This is my parents' place for sure. So, did I get drunk and pass out? Did somebody drive me home? Was it Gina? I don't remember!* Brian frowned in the darkness, as he blindly reached for his cell phone again. *What time is it? For that matter, what day is it?* The phone display illuminated the time and date: 5:50 a.m., Friday, August 31.

The cell phone alarm was set to get him up for work. However, he was on vacation. Brian slowly reached over and placed his cell phone back on the cocktail table. This time however, he happened to glance in the direction he was reaching. At that very moment, in the few minutes before civil twilight, he remembered what happened the night before. For, in his vision slightly beyond the end of the cocktail table, was the creature.

The alien beast sat against the wall right next to the entertainment center furniture facing Brian. The celestial creature was putting something into the large utility vest/back pack that it carried around earlier. The beast spoke softly without looking at him. Brian's eyes were affixed on the creature on the far side of the family room. *You again.* Brian rubbed his eyes to get a better look at what the creature was doing.

Just then, the exotic alien woman peered from over the top of the cocktail table at him. She was apparently lying on the family room floor between the cocktail table and the entertainment center furniture. Her head was positioned on the same end of the table as Brian's. He could see her exotic smile. She nodded her head several times quickly as she began to speak to him. Her expression was as reassuringly peaceful as before. The humanoid woman sat up as she spoke, her attention fixed on Brian. As soon as she finished speaking, the creature grunted something and waved its hand once in Brian's direction. *Another conversation about me.* As the twilight of the early morning began to fill the family room, the young man could see that the beast still wore its fancy alien glasses. Out of curiosity, Brian methodically glanced around the ceiling to see if he could find the floating orb drone somewhere in the room. After several seconds of squinting and looking around, he realized he could not see it.

Next, Brian slowly righted himself and sat up. He noticed the beast looking directly at him now. The alien woman continued to smile at him. Brian stretched and yawned aloud.

He looked at the extraterrestrials and bestowed a hearty, "Good morning!"

The young man smiled as the alien woman giggled. There was no reply or expression from the beast.

"Well," Brian said as he slowly stood up, "at least I don't have to work today." Brian walked slowly toward the small hallway. He could feel the two aliens' watchful gaze. He put his hand in the air with his back to the extraterrestrials and jovially stated, "Don't go anywhere, I'll be right back."

Brian headed for the bathroom located immediately to his left just inside the hallway. He opened the door as he took a fleeting glance back at his alien visitors and playfully said in serious tone of voice, "Stay there. I will return, shortly."

He spoke slowly and pointed back at the family room. The exotic woman silently turned and looked at the creature. The beast continued to stare at Brian.

Brian took a few steps into the bathroom and turned on the wall switch light immediately to his left. In that instant he noticed something in his peripheral vision. He turned just in time to see the floating orb drone changing from a dark coffee color to beige. The object was just outside the bathroom and a few inches below the door jam. The floating device silently moved toward him as the color rapidly changed to match the white semi-gloss walls of the guest bathroom. Brian simply watched in awe for a second before realizing what the stealthy chameleon floating drone was doing.

Without thinking twice, and on shear impulse Brian reacted.

"No, I don't think so!" The young man put his hand in the air to block the alien drone as he swiftly closed the door.

The guest bathroom door shut with a 'thud' as Brian simultaneously locked it. Then he turned around and took a few hurried steps toward the other door located to his right. He reached for the brass doorknob and shut the second door hastily. Feeling a little sense of triumph, he quickly locked the door, leaned his head gently against it and, sighed deeply.

The young man stood there for a moment in the quiet of the early morning and thought, *I wonder where dad keeps his tennis racket.*

Chapter Ten

Daniel Ray Kosmor, a registered respiratory therapist on the night shift in the pediatric intensive care unit (PICU) prepared his notes at the only desk in the station. He looked at his watch. The time was 5:55 a.m. Soon, another set of nurses, respiratory therapists, doctors, and other specialists would arrive, signaling the change of shift, and begin taking care of all the ill patients in the intensive care unit and all the other wards in the 400 bed medical center. After twelve hours of non-stop critical care, Danny, as he most preferred to be called, was ready to end the evening shift and go home so he could get some sleep.

"It's about that time." Danny said aloud, and smiled as he continued to study the notes he had prepared for the dayshift respiratory therapist.

"I can hardly wait to go home. I'm so tired," Catherine Smalls, the night shift unit secretary replied. "Are you coming back tonight, Danny?" She turned her desk chair around slightly to face him and anticipated his reply. She already had an idea as to what he would say.

"Yes," Danny said flatly, peering at her over his shoulder. "Unless everybody in this hospital gets up out of bed and walks out today, miraculously healed, I'll be back tomorrow for round number two."

Catherine raised an eyebrow. "I seriously doubt that will happen." She smiled, and he smiled back at her. "I'm coming back, too," Catherine said.

They both had good reason to be tired. Not because they had

worked the night shift. Danny and Catherine were used to that schedule and they, along with many other caregivers on their shift, preferred to work nights. However, last night was exceptionally busy. In the past twelve hours the PICU had admitted six patients; two of which were extremely ill. One of those, the more unstable one, became Danny's patient, along with two others who were not quite as ill.

"Here they come," Catherine announced, looking down the large hallway that led out to the visitor's area. She could see some of the day shift staff approaching the PICU. Danny heard the relief crew walking towards the secretary's front desk area. They sounded happy and ready for another day of work. Some were engaged in light conversation and broke into laughter as the group came up to the secretary's front desk. The small group of people greeted Catherine with a pleasant "Good morning" as they walked passed her. Danny heard the sound of the automatic security door open wide as the day shift respiratory therapists entered the PICU. *Here they come* Danny thought with a bright smile, ready to great them.

"Yo Danny boy, what up?" Jermaine Scott Laws, a hip, young, charismatic gentleman originally from Queens, New York greeted Danny almost immediately as the doors silently closed behind the dayshift respiratory therapists. Lifting his shoulder a bit he added, "I haven't seen you in while my man, where you been?"

Jermaine leaned his head back slightly and looked down through his trendy prescription glasses with Christian Dior stamped on the side of the frame. He leaned forward and stretched out his right hand to shake Danny's.

"I went back to San Diego to visit my mother and father for a week," Danny said, firmly gripping Jermaine's hand with a friendly smile. "I helped them move into their new house. I stayed with them and went to the beach, like every day man." Danny chuckled.

"Oh, okay, okay, nothing wrong with that," Jermaine said calmly with a big, friendly smile. He walked through the station and took a seat next to where his good friend still sat behind the desk. "You got station one and two?" Jermaine asked.

"Uh, yeah let's see." Danny flipped through the few pages of his nightshift list. He looked over his own notes and then replied, "Yes, I had patients Linda Smith, Jimmy Ackerson, Patricia Limond, and Marla Torres." Danny looked at Jermaine as he spoke to confirm that the dayshift list matched the names of the patients he just read off.

"Yup, I got the same ones, my friend." Jermaine nodded as he retrieved a pen from the pocket of his scrub and prepared to write down his own notes for the day's work ahead of him.

"Was that all you had last night?" he asked, knowing that Danny must have been busy by the tired look on his face.

Danny sighed, a look of relief brightening his face at the thought that his busy night had finally come to an end.

"I actually had to give up two other patients from my original list in order to take these new kids. One of the floor therapists took them. Man, it was so freakin' busy last night." He stretched, leaning back in the chair and then yawned. "Hopefully things will calm down a bit for you."

"You can say that again." Catherine overheard the two respiratory therapists and couldn't help but add her own comment.

"Thanks for your two cents, Catherine," Jermaine joked and smiled at the unit secretary.

"Keep the change, honey!" she playfully retorted with a wink. With that, all three of the hospital coworkers chuckled in unison. Their quiet laughter helped ease the tension and seriousness in the intensive care unit.

Everyone at Pleasant Hills Medical Center in San Bernardino, California knew the challenges of working in a critical care environment. Everyone especially knew the particular challenge of working with critically ill children, how psychologically draining it is for anyone, no matter how tough the caregiver may seem. Sometimes, a little light-hearted humor goes a long way for those devoted individuals that become very mentally and emotionally absorbed in this kind of specialized care. A good healthy sense of humor is the type of camaraderie that builds inner strength and is the psychosocial bond that everyone becomes well habituated to in order to help get the job done. It is an intuitive part of a shared, unseen chemistry that each caregiver feels deep down inside, knowing that they truly make a difference in somebody's life; in this case, the life of somebody's child.

Danny leaned towards Jermaine and pointed at one of the names on his newly printed patient workload.

He looked up at Jermaine and said, "That patient you have there, Jimmy Ackerson. He's just like Trevor Lauderson, but not as sick. You remember him?"

"Oh yes, who can forget little Trevor?" Jermaine replied enthusiastically.

"I know," Catherine interposed. "I can still remember how blue he got from those cyanotic spells whenever he got upset. It was kind of scary. But, I guess it was normal for him with his condition. What was the nickname of those cyanotic spells, again?"

"He was born with Tetralogy of Fallot. So, those were called Tet spells. Yeah, it was the weirdest thing to see," Danny commented. "When I first saw little Trevor I was like… okay, should I start resuscitating this kid right now, or what?"

Danny remembered when he saw Trevor for the very first time. He was working his usual night shift and had been assigned to cover the emergency room that particular evening. A Caucasian infant, a little boy, came into the emergency department with a specific type of cardiac disease and was quickly admitted to the hospital. The congenital cyanotic cardio-vascular defect shunted a portion of the child's normal blood flow from one side of his heart to the other side, bypassing the lungs and thereby delivering lowered saturated blood oxygen levels throughout his little body. The infant's name was Trevor Lauderson. He was born at Pleasant Hills Medical Center only a few months before Danny saw him that evening. The hospital environment was nothing new to the baby and his parents. In fact, after a somewhat normal delivery, the newborn had required a brief stay in the medical center because of his rare condition. He was actually doing quite well with his diagnosis and the parents were trained by expert, homecare medical center staff to take special care of him at home. After Trevor's two-week stay in the medical center, he was subsequently discharged from the hospital and allowed to go home with his parents for a short while. The primary care physician wanted the little baby to grow a little more before taking him to surgery to repair the rare heart anomaly. While at home awaiting his turn for surgery, Trevor developed a mild upper respiratory infection. The cause of the infection was the result of a specific seasonal virus. It was a rare virus that normally did not make most children very sick at all.

This was not true in little Trevor's case, however. Consequently, because of the infant's underlying heart disease, he became very ill. The baby was not in the ER long before Danny, who was fairly new on the job at the time, was summoned to assist in taking care of the patient. One thing Danny always remembered was how little Trevor turned an ashen, grayish-blue color every time he screamed and cried when he was agitated. That's what Catherine was referring to. The baby boy had an eerie chronic cyanosis that his body had adapted to live with.

Baby Trevor was immediately admitted to the hospital that particular evening. He received proper treatment and recovered from the respiratory infection. Danny remembered how Trevor finally received the planned corrective heart surgery a short while afterwards.

"Has anyone heard from Trevor's family?" Danny asked. "I haven't seen him in a long time," he said, looking at Catherine and Jermaine.

"Oh yeah, he's just fine," Catherine said quickly. "His mom calls here every now and then to see whose working, and she chats with me every so often. He's been doing great from what I've heard." Jermaine and Danny smiled and nodded, happy to hear the little boy was better.

"Well," Jermaine sighed and said, "I guess I better get the report so I can get you out of here, Danny boy." He smiled at his night shift companion. Jermaine had looked over his assignment list already before talking to Danny, so he had a very good idea how intense today's work would be. "Who's on call today?" Jermaine asked aloud, looking at the night shift unit secretary.

"Doctor Baynor is on call," Catherine stated with a more serious tone of voice as she pointed toward the dry erase board against the wall. Jermaine looked up at the shiny white board and next to a column that read First Call, was the name Dr. Luis Baynor, M.D.

"Okay, that's cool, because me and Doctor Luis will have a good day no matter what. I like him. He's cool." Jermaine nodded several times quickly and asked, "And, who was on call last night?"

"Last night we had doctor Spies," Danny answered with a smile.

"Oh, your boy from San Diego, huh?" Jermaine smiled back as he responded, "Your buddy Brian's favorite doc on the unit."

"Well," Danny kept smiling as he whispered, "I don't know about that. But he was here last night and he did a decent job." Danny pouted his lip and nodded once as he flipped through his nightshift assignment sheet once more. He brushed the curly blonde hair off from his suntanned and freckled face. "He's a nice enough dude, I mean, for a guy that stole somebody's lady, you know."

"Yeah, I know," Jermaine said in agreement and looked directly at Danny through his flashy designer glasses. "I hear you, Danny boy, I hear you. And it wasn't just his girlfriend. I mean, I thought they were engaged."

"What are you guys talking about?" Catherine butted in with a stern, but playful tone of voice. "We're not spreading rumors, are we?" she said.

"No, no," both men replied in unison as they made sure anyone within earshot understood they weren't intentionally spreading something that could be a rumor.

"It's cool, man. It's none of my business, you know. I don't care, man." Danny shrugged his shoulders and shook his head at Catherine.

"Yeah, yeah, man you know how it is... to each his own."

Jermaine shrugged too. "Whatever," he said. Catherine beamed at both of them.

"I don't get into people's personal lives, man," Danny pointed at himself with both his hands and shook his head. "Leave the drama for your mama, dude."

"Yeah, yeah man," Jermaine's urban New York accent was heavy now as he quickly added, "It's none of my business, so it don't matter to me, know what I mean?"

Catherine scrutinized them and then smiled playfully. Then her expression changed. She cleared her throat quickly and said.

"Good morning Doctor Spies, are you ready to go home, soon?"

Dr. Carl Victor Spies, M.D. sighed heavily as he approached the station one desk area. From the two respiratory therapists' perspective, he emerged out of nowhere.

"Yes Ma'am! I'm so tired right now," Carl Spies said as he dramatically drooped over the tall counter portion of the outer desk area. "You just don't know." He raised his head and smiled.

Although he was tired, the end of the night shift gave him a renewed level of energy. He was excited that he made it through the night without losing any PICU patients. At times, it was a challenge keeping everything under control last night. The new admits were a handful, but the young doctor was still smiling with the change of shift now here. He knew it wouldn't be long before he could go home and sleep. "I can't wait to go home and jump in bed. It's funny how the simple things in life can make you so happy. And, right now, all I want is my bed."

"Ain't that the truth!" Catherine quickly responded.

There were a few courtesy laughs from the other three individuals. As the quiet laughter subsided into silence Jermaine asked, "Who's the Attending on call for today?" He turned around, looking at Catherine.

"Doctor Vanderman," The unit secretary answered as the other two gentlemen nodded in agreement.

"Okay. That's good to hear." Jermaine smiled. "He usually likes to hang around for a while after rounds, too. He's very involved with everything. I like it when he's on call. He really likes to teach."

"Yes, he does," Carl replied. "And after morning rounds I should be out of here by, ah…" He looked in the air as if calculating, and then said sarcastically, "Oh, about 3pm." He looked at the small group and added quickly, "Then I get to come back tomorrow morning and do it all over again," he grinned and slapped the papers he was carrying with the back of his hand. "Won't that be fun?" His young, charismatic face lit up as he chuckled. Again, the response was polite but genuine laughter.

"So how've you been, Carl?" Jermaine inquired with a genial grin as the laughter faded. "You plan on running in any more marathons, soon?"

"Well," Carl said as he thought for a second, "I haven't really prepared for anything since I ran the L.A. marathon last March. But some other members of my club are going to run the New York marathon this coming November. They plan on flying out there and staying for several days but I don't have that kind of free time. Many of them going are successful business owners, or retired early."

"What did you say the name of your club was, again?" Danny queried. "Road Runners?"

"Actually," Carl said with a keen smile, "I'm in the Long Beach Distance Club, but our club is a recognized member of the Road Runners Club of America."

"Oh yeah, that's it," Danny said. "I remember you telling me."

"How did you do in the L.A. marathon, Carl?" Jermaine smiled at him. "I don't think you ever told me."

"Oh," Carl looked up at the ceiling, "Uh, I finished in four hours and thirty eight minutes." With a nod of his head he quickly added, "Yeah, that's what is was."

"Wow," Catherine commented, "that's good time, I don't care who you are; professional or not." She added, "There was a gal at my church that ran the L.A. marathon this year, too. She's in really good shape and she did it in just under six hours. She's my age, so that's saying a lot." Catherine laughed lightly with a big smile.

"That's actually very good," Carl quickly responded in a more serious tone of voice. "There were actually a lot of adults older than me running the marathon that day. A remarkable number of them beat my time or came very close to it, believe it or not."

They all nodded in amusement as Catherine remarked, "Hey, age is just a number, right?"

"Yo, it would take me all week to finish running that thing," Jermaine jested. "I would be stopping at fast food joints and window shopping. Last thing I would be doing is running!" They all started laughing as Jermaine added, "I'm so out of shape you couldn't pay me to run in that thing. So age is whatever you make of it. Know what I mean?"

Everyone laughed. "Oh, Jermaine!" Catherine snickered playfully, "Look at you, you're so skinny. Honey, you're not out of shape."

"Trust me." Jermaine rolled his eyes as he laughed. "I'm out of shape."

"Actually, there are thousands of people who come out and walk that marathon for fun and to support various causes," Carl said in a more serious tone. "It isn't as competitive as, say, the Boston or the New York marathons. In those, you have to like, qualify to participate."

"Wow, I didn't know that!" Danny said, looking at Carl.

"Yeah man, the New York marathon is like, a big deal. I don't run, but I know it's a huge sporting event recognized worldwide," Jermaine commented. "All kinds of people from all over the world come out for that one."

"Where are you from again, Jermaine?" Carl asked as he tried to recall where the charismatic African American man with the heavy east coast accent was from. "New York City, right?" he asked.

"I'm from Queens, originally," Jermaine said, nodding. "Born and raised."

"Oh yeah, that's right." Carl said. "You've been out here on the west coast now for a while, right?" He leaned back a little and stretched as he added, "You like it here?"

"Oh yes." Jermaine nodded and answered quickly, "I've always liked it. I have family out here. I've visited California many times while I was growing up. Know what I mean? Yeah, I like it." Jermaine continued to nod slowly. "I've made a lot of friends working here, too. I have a lot of friends on both the east coast and west coast."

Carl smiled politely and nodded in reply.

"Speaking of which…" Jermaine looked directly into Carl's boyish, dark brown eyes and asked, "How's my friend, Gina? I haven't seen her in a long time. I miss working with her. She was one of my favorite nurses to work with. She was my 'compadre'."

There was a moment of uncomfortable silence and then Carl replied with a warm smile.

"Good, she's good. I'll tell her you said, hi." The doctor was quite noticeably fidgeting. He looked down at the papers he had laid out on top of the desk and cleared his throat as Jermaine began to speak again.

"Good to hear. Tell her it's not the same here without her," Jermaine said with a slight smile and the same sincere look.

Carl looked down at his papers, again. Then, with a slight grin, he glanced at Jermaine and said, "I'll tell her you said that." He looked down at his papers again and stated, "That will make her happy. She misses everyone here, actually."

"Tell her," Catherine quickly interjected, "her favorite night-shift secretary says, hi."

"I'll do that." Carl nodded and smiled very politely at Catherine amidst the quiet, speculative stares coming from Danny and Jermaine.

Jermaine looked at Danny. "Hey, where's Brian been hiding, man?" he asked aloud with his thick accent, "I haven't seen him in like, forever." He chuckled, but looked serious.

Danny glanced around quickly, as if he were searching for Brian and expecting him to materialize out of thin air. "Yeah, umm… Brian should be back to work soon. I know he had some time off recently."

"Oh, okay." Jermaine smiled. "I thought maybe he quit or something."

"No, I think he just took some time off to get his head straight." Danny said. "I guess he's been having some personal problems or something." Both men nodded, knowing Carl could hear and read between the lines. Catherine cleared her throat and broke the silence.

"Well," she asked politely, "you ready for morning rounds, doctor Spies?"

"Oh yes." The doctor put on a stoic pose, trying to appear like some kind of juggernaut. "I'm ready for whatever is ahead. I have prepared for my morning rounds, and I'm determined to get out of here by…" he looked up as he thought, "eleven." He playfully stuck his chest out, trying to appear fearless.

"Yeah, right," Catherine laughed quietly. "With Doctor Vanderman coming on?" She chuckled again, "Good luck with that one."

The doctor simply smiled in return and slowly walked away to check on the patient in room one. The young, intelligent, happy-go-lucky resident physician could feel the stares of the group following him.

Chapter Eleven

Brian slowly opened the bathroom door a few inches and peeked into the narrow hallway. He instinctively looked up at the ceiling to look for the elusive floating ball. He just knew the color changing alien camera was out there, somewhere. After a few seconds of visually searching the vacant hallway, he could not find it. Brian knew it was conceivable that he was just simply not able to see it. With that in mind, he shrugged and swung the bathroom door wide open.

Whatever, he thought to himself, and stepped out of the safety of the comfy guest bathroom. *It's around here somewhere.* He just knew the alien thing was watching carefully, moving freely around and about his parent's house. Without a doubt, wherever the alien orb drone floated, the observant eyes of the beast were sure to be watching, as well.

As soon as Brian took a few steps down the hallway, he could hear a conversation between the two alien beings. Brian followed the sound of their alien lingo, treading lightly through the family room first, then towards the kitchen.

"Yo," Brian interposed in a smooth and pleasant tone of voice with a big smile, "what's going on in here? You guys behaving yourselves? What's up?"

The extraterrestrials were facing the sink with their backs towards him as he entered the kitchen area. They turned around to face him, not perceptibly surprised by his return. The beast was still wearing its shiny copper night vision glasses. As expected, the beast was expressionless and quiet.

The exotic alien woman on the other hand, returned his

smile with one of her own, familiar and appealing. She began speaking in an excited tone of voice. Her pretty, almond shaped eyes were opened wide and her teeth were so white in contrast to her exotic skin tone. Brian noticed her vocal inflections, graceful gestures, and feminine posture. Her body language was none the least dissimilar to any typical earthly woman's mannerisms. Without a doubt, she was a mysterious and exotic specimen of femininity and unequivocally and profoundly attractive to behold. She was all 'woman', though extraterrestrial by worldly definition. From the moment he laid eyes on her, he'd been captivated by her strange yet beguiling beauty. The fact was, Brian truly appreciated her. She was beautiful, indeed. Though he could not understand her unfamiliar vocabulary, he understood her demeanor almost perfectly by now.

Brian noticed she was glancing around, pointing at various objects. Her delightful curiosity intrigued him. He stepped closer and focused all his attention on what she was trying to say to him, hanging on every alien word, smiling at the way she expressed herself in the most polite, appeasing manner. He noticed she repeated several words, speaking them slowly as she pointed at the refrigerator and smiled.

"What, that thing there?" Brian asked with a smile. "You want to know what that is?"

He walked to the large kitchen appliance and touched it, then clasped his hand around the handle of the white side-by-side Kenmore refrigerator and looked back at the two extraterrestrials. The creature looked at Brian. The beast seemed a little uneasy and placed its left hand on something attached to its uniform. Brian had not really given too much attention to the long, bizarre piece of equipment before that perfectly matched the dark, purple-russet color of the creature's fitted uniform. The unknown piece of equipment was partially concealed by a component of the garment, but Brian could see it ran snugly along the left thigh of the creature's dark colored flight suit. The reflective, slate gray pinstripes along the side of the uniform were fashioned in such a way that they had, until now, effectively diverted Brian's attention away from the slightly bulky device. Brian tilted his head to one side out of curiosity as he looked at the bizarre alien gadget. Not having a clue as to what it was, he simply figured it was of no concern. Brian returned his attention to the beautiful celestial woman. He smiled as he looked into her enchanting eyes again. That bright smile was ever present on her appealingly narrow face. She nodded slowly at Brian and he opened the refrigerator door.

The beast took an inconspicuous step forward, slightly, but purposefully moving in front of its companion. It was as if the creature was subtly, yet tactically, trying to shield her from something. Brian looked directly at the alien creature and, with puckered brow, calmly asserted.

"It's a refrigerator." He stared at the beast and repeated himself slowly in a louder tone of voice, "Re-fridge-err-a-tor." Brian pointed inside with his free hand.

"Look, see." He stepped aside, holding the door open so both aliens could get a full view, "There's nothing but food inside there. You have nothing to fear except maybe some old grated cheddar cheese."

The alien woman stepped around and in front of the creature. She had a candid expression of keen curiosity. She smiled and stepped closer to examine the contents inside the refrigerator and then intuitively responded in some astonished alien jargon with her eyes affixed on the lighted interior of the open kitchen appliance. There was a slight pause before she spoke again. She lifted her left arm about chest high, elbow and wrist parallel to the floor. Brian noticed something wrapped around her wrist that wound up one quarter of her forearm. It was very similar to a sports band or wrap type brace and was slightly darker in color than her uniform. Brian raised an eyebrow; certain he had not seen that band on her arm until now. She touched the device near the top and the face of the band near the wrist suddenly lit up. Brian hadn't expected that since the wrap looking thing seemed to be just another piece of garment, like her uniform. In an instant, clear, sharp pictures appeared on the face of the device that was now emitting odd sounds similar to beep tones. Brian stepped closer to look at the bizarre equipment. As expected, she was kind, smiling, and willing to show him what she was doing.

Brian looked down at the device on her wrist and quickly recognized various images of the refrigerator flashed on the screen of the armband gadget with the contents inside the refrigerator systematically displayed with alien wording and coding next to them. Brian watched the beeps, flashing symbols and even more images scrolling through the armband display. He was baffled and amused all at once.

"What's it doing?" Brian pointed at the device on her forearm. "Is it taking pictures of the fridge?"

Brian watched as the image of the milk container appeared clearly on the display area of the band. The picture automatically enlarged with more detailed alien symbols around it. To Brian, the device seemed to be analyzing the gallon milk container. He reached inside the refrigerator and retrieved the half-full container of 2% milk then closed the refrigerator door and placed the container on the quartz countertop behind him, leaning against the polished slab of stone.

"Milk." He pointed at the container and simply said.

Both extraterrestrials stepped forward with obviously curious expressions on their faces and spoke between themselves for a moment. The humanoid woman nodded once, and then the creature approached the gallon of milk. The creature looked back at its companion. Again, she nodded once, so the alien beast slowly reached out and touched the container of milk, uttering something to the alien woman before withdrawing its large hand. Brian smiled and reached for the container. The beast was motionless as Brian removed the blue cap, picked up the container with both hands, and brought it close to his face. He sniffed in a slightly exaggerated manner, demonstrating and encouraging the alien visitors to further examine the dairy product. He wanted to let the extraterrestrials freely explore something that was very common to most humans on planet earth.

"Go on, take a sniff." Brian gestured with his hands and nodded once.

The exotic woman stepped swiftly to the counter where Brian was standing. Still smiling in her most delightful manner she looked at the face of her sophisticated armband device, touching the smartly contoured display area as she said a few words. The creature responded by touching the frame of the copper glasses it was wearing. Both of their alien devices beeped and sounded odd, audible cues in unison.

Then, unexpectedly, the creature picked up the milk container and slowly brought the open end towards its peculiar, hairless snout. It sniffed once, quickly. Brian heard the alien woman utter a slight sound like a gasp. He instinctively diverted his attention to look at her armband device. On the display area he noticed symbols similar to bar graphs with other wavy lines. There were bright narrow pink bars, neon green lines and various other brilliant color symbols moving about on the illuminated display. Then the creature took another sniff of the unknown, white liquid in the container. The second effort was a deeper inhalation, more exaggerated. Brian noticed how the creature's narrow, pointed ears stood up more on the second smell and that the graphs on the display of the alien woman's armband device increased in length and changed in color. Her display screen seemed to react to what the creature was smelling inside the cold container.

"Is that thing…?" Brian pointed at her flashing armband gadget and began to ask what he thought he saw when suddenly he was interrupted by the creature.

It began another calm, jaw-chopping conversation with its companion. She listened attentively and nodded a few times. Brian could only assume the beast was trying to explain the smell within the container to its outer space travelling mate. Brian looked at the serious expressions on their extraterrestrial faces and chuckled as he shook his head in amusement.

This is really crazy. I never thought milk could be so mysterious and entertaining.

Brian watched them for a moment. As soon as there was a lull in their conversation he spoke up.

"Milk." Brian said aloud and pointed at the contents of the plastic gallon container.

He kept his finger pointed at the milk for a second amongst the silence and the blank stares of the perplexed and curious visitors from outer space.

"Here," Brian announced as he stepped around the alien woman toward the cabinet where the glasses were kept. "Let me show you what this stuff is for." The watchful eyes of the beast followed his every move. "I usually prefer my milk with some desert, like chocolate chip cookies," he said, sounding like a professor lecturing to brand new students in a science lab just before performing a demonstration. "Some people like chocolate milk. But, we don't have any of that right now." Brian took three glasses from the cabinet.

For no particular reason he glanced to his right when he closed the cabinet door. Located under the corner wall cabinet was his mother's knife block, which brought back the sudden memory of how the previous night began. He had grabbed the chef's knife out of the wooden block for some protection during his evening exploration. He also remembered how he had tossed the knife away as soon as he saw the creature glaring at him for the first time. He thought about that very awkward moment, standing motionless for a few seconds as he remembered how the creature had stared into his frightened eyes during that instant of absolute fear. The maroon eyes of the creature were still a dramatic memory, but then Brian noticed something subtle, yet strikingly odd. The eight-inch chef's knife he took with him on his outing the night before was now, astonishingly, back right where Brian had originally retrieved it before the unforgettable first contact with the alien beings. Not only that, the stainless-steel chef's knife was as clean as the other kitchen utensils in the knife block. It was as if it was never taken outside the house and dropped in the dirt. He wondered for a second which alien put the knife back. He had a good idea.

Brian said nothing. He simply turned around and walked back to the milk container on the breakfast bar. The aliens observed him silently. He picked up one of the glasses and started to pour milk into it, thinking about the knife in the block. He wondered if the aliens had observed that he had noticed.

Brian filled the other glasses, still in deep thought. *I bet the dog person put the knife back.*

"Now, this is what we drink on earth with our breakfast, lunch, and dinner, and with dessert." Brian continued his pseudo lecture, "It has vitamin D and it helps make our bones nice and strong." With a raised eyebrow and a slight grin, he raised the glass to his lips and took a drink.

He felt the stares of his extraterrestrial guests. He had their complete, undivided attention. Brian swallowed the refreshingly cold milk.

"Ahhh…" He smiled and put the glass back on the countertop. "Now you try some." He nodded his head once and made a gesture with his hands, courteously inviting the aliens to partake of the earthly dairy product.

The aliens looked down and stared at the glasses of white fluid in front of them. Brian looked at the extraterrestrials. He could tell the two alien beings were thinking. The humanoid woman was smiling, as usual. She pointed with her right thumb, wrist forward at the glass in front of her on the countertop and said something in her indiscernible alien language. She continued to smile.

"Milk," Brian enunciated clearly as he leaned forward and looked directly into the alien woman's strange, yet enchanting bronze eyes.

Her close proximity revealed the unblemished details of her silky-smooth skin. Living in the moment, Brian smiled warmly as he took in the details of her face.

Yeah, she's real alright. Who knew somewhere out in space there were strange, beautiful women that could walk, talk, and maybe eat like we do here on earth? Then, with a smile he asked her, "You want to try some milk?"

She looked into Brian's eyes, now with a slight grin. To Brian, it appeared she was thinking about something. He sensed she had something to say.

"Beeuk." Her smooth, thin lips pouted as she enunciated the word softly in an attempt to repeat what Brian had described as the mysterious, cold white liquid inside the glass.

Brian leaned back, his eyes wide, and grinned helplessly in pleasant astonishment. She distinctly giggled in response as the delicate muscle definition on her alien face yielded the most beautiful beaming smile. She put her right hand over her smiling, parted lips with palm facing forward as she giggled more. Her bizarre sounding, happy sensation made Brian smile even bigger. Although some of her mannerisms were unfamiliar, she was without doubt, a lady. She was a lovely, alien woman.

She took a moment to compose herself and then said the word again, louder this time. "Beeuk."

"Milk," Brian said aloud, raising his chin so she could observe his lips and tongue articulate as he spoke.

She looked like she was going to say something for a second, but she just giggled again as she stared at Brian's mouth. Her reaction made Brian chuckle, too. His eyes were still wide with intrigued enthusiasm.

"M-i-l-k." This time he repeated himself in a softer tone of voice.

It was almost a whisper, but his baritone voice carried. Brian observed how she squinted and carefully watched his lips. There was a brief second of silence. He grinned and nodded once at her and she chuckled in her alien manner again, leaning forward just a little bit closer toward him.

The alien humanoid woman's lips slowly moved, and her mouth opened as she made her calm, clear reply, "Hmm-e-e-e-y-u-k."

Brian was overcome with delight, and he could not help but giggle like a child. He was charmed by her never-ending smile and soft, sweet tone of voice. He reached for his glass.

"Close enough," he replied with a beaming smile, and with a quick wink, he drank the remaining milk.

The alien visitors were silent and still for a moment. Then, the creature reached for one of the remaining glasses, holding it about chest high.

"Yeah, there you go!" Brian affirmed as he gestured with his hands and encouraged the beast to participate. "Okay, now you try some."

The alien woman raised her left forearm, positioning the strange armband device very close to the top of the glass the beast was holding. She touched the device with her fingers as if she were softly pressing buttons. As soon as she did this, bizarre beeping tones and an array of colors and symbols flashed on the display of her device. She said something and looked at the beast, nodding once. The creature nodded back.

The next thing the creature did was extraordinary to Brian. The beast smoothly and deliberately took a drink from the glass. Brian watched the thin canine animal lips of the creature purse as it touched the rim of the glass, careful not to spill the milk while it carefully tasted the strange earthly dairy product. After taking a small drink, the creature held the glass still in the air and said a few hissing, jaw-chomping words to its smiling partner. She nodded in reply. Then, the beast drank again, finishing all of the remaining milk before returning the glass to the counter. The humanoid woman said something and nodded again, then looked down at the glass of milk in front of her. She stood motionless before slowly grasping the glass in front of her. She looked at Brian.

"Okay, now it's your turn." Brian smiled. "Look." He spoke calmly and pointed at the creature. "The space-wolf liked it. Didn't you?" The young man looked directly at the copper glasses the beast was still wearing.

The creature said nothing and stood still. Brian knew it was staring at him. Somehow, Brian knew it understood what he was saying to the beautiful alien lady. He felt he was making progress communicating with the aliens, now.

Next, the celestial lady took a drink of milk from her glass. It was a very small sip by earthly standards. She smiled as she tasted the milk in her mouth, silent for a moment. Brian knew she was trying to compare the taste to something from her own world. He could sense it by the curious, subjective look in her beaming celestial eyes. She swallowed the milk. Then, her glossy lips parted, revealing her pearly white teeth. Her exotic face had the most curious expression.

"Hmmeeyuk," she asserted with poise.

"Yes." Brian nodded. "And, I hope you liked it," he said slowly, nodding his head once more, "and you're welcome to try whatever you want." He placed the container of milk back in the refrigerator and faced his alien guests. "So, this is the kitchen. It is where we humans prepare our food." The extraterrestrials were watching him attentively. "We usually eat three meals a day. There's breakfast, lunch, and then dinner," he said, lecturing his new students about planet earth. "Maybe we'll try some food later on." Brian cleared his throat and stepped toward the freestanding gas range to his right. He extended his right arm to point at the appliance and said, "This is where we cook our food." He took a few steps closer and pointed at the continuous black grates on top of the stove. "We cook with the heat from small flames." Brian reached for one of the control knobs and turned it on. A small blue flame appeared in the center of the burner and grew taller as he continued to turn the knob. "This is called a stove." He gestured, moving his hand around in a circle over the large kitchen appliance. Then he turned off the burner.

As soon as he did so, the alien guests started talking quietly between themselves. Brian could only guess that their conversation was about how primitive these things he was showing them were. Nevertheless, they also seemed to be captivated, and by the look on their faces, seemed to take extraordinary interest in everything Brian showed them. This was especially true of the beautiful alien lady. Everything Brian said and did was observed by her with a warm smile.

Brian continued his tour of the kitchen, stopping at the full-sized Panasonic microwave beside the gas range. He briefly said a few words about its operation and then continued with his impromptu tour, taking a few steps past the glossy white range towards the corner wall cabinet where his mother's knife block was. He opened the wall cabinets and showed them the various plates, bowls, and glassware inside, then closed the doors and looked down at the knife block. He knew the aliens were staring at him. He could see them in his peripheral vision. He slowly pulled out the same eight-inch chef's knife he had earlier, and set it down on the countertop.

"Okay, I think I should probably show you what this is for."

Brian walked back to the refrigerator. He opened it and took a large, fresh carrot out of the vegetable bin. He brought it back to the countertop and picked up the knife. He was mindful to turn his shoulder so the aliens could see what he was doing as he cut the carrot into several pieces. He looked back at his guests when he was finished.

"This is a tool we use in the kitchen." Brian held the knife up for the aliens to see and then put it on the countertop again. He pointed to the utensil and simply said, "Knife."

The humanoid woman was looking at the beast. The creature was motionless, looking at Brian. He knew that the extraterrestrials figured out what the knife was used for. He also knew the aliens inherently understood it could be used as a weapon. Brian picked up the knife, turned on the faucet at the kitchen sink and cleaned the knife before returning it to its proper place in the wood block.

Brian picked up a piece of the carrot and said, "Now this is a very tasty and healthy vegetable. You can eat it raw, or cook it. In fact, you can even drink it like juice." He bit into the crisp piece and chewed. "Mmmm…" the young pseudo-professor said to his new students, and then exclaimed, "delicious!" He chewed the carrot and then swallowed it before saying, "would you like to try some carrot?" He pointed down at the sliced-up vegetable and promptly added, "It's really good."

The exotic lady, perhaps more trusting by now, was the first to step forward. As soon as she did, however, her forward progress was impeded by the extraterrestrial creature. The beast swiftly grabbed her by the arm. She looked into the copper lenses of the beast and spoke abruptly. The creature said nothing, but released her left arm, all the while looking at Brian. Then she walked straight towards Brian and looked down at the sliced carrot. She picked up a piece and turned to look at the beast, waving the morsel over her armband device. Again, there were beeping tones and displays on the face of the alien gadget. She raised her arm to show the creature the display on her armband device and smiled at the beast. She said something to it and then turned around to face Brian. Still smiling, she placed the piece of sliced carrot in her mouth and ate it. Her smile became bigger, and she nodded her head as she chewed. Brian could tell she was thinking about the taste. She had the same expression on her face when she sampled the milk. Her eyes looked up towards the ceiling and she blinked a few times.

"Mmmm…" was her simple response. She moved her tongue around inside her mouth for a few seconds and turned her inquisitive gaze towards Brian. The alien woman was pleased.

"Okay, looks like we have one satisfied customer," Brian deduced. He picked up another piece of sliced carrot and looked at the alien creature. He raised his hand slightly in a polite gesture, offering the food to the beast. "Come try this space-wolf, you might like it." He waved his hand for the beast to come over.

Just then, strange, melodious beeping sounds emanated from where the creature stood. The beast looked at its large wristband device and pressed on it a few times. The repetitive beeping tones ceased. Then the wolf-like creature covered its right ear with the palm of its right hand and calmly began to speak. The way the creature was acting reminded Brian of what people look like when they are engaged in a phone conversation, especially with wireless phones. Brian watched the strange creature in admiration of the way it spoke.

With a curious grin on his face, Brian peered at the mysterious copper glasses of the beast. *Amazing.*

Chapter Twelve

Brian stared at the creature speaking in its jaw-chopping manner, the palm of its large hand over its ear. He assumed the extraterrestrial beast was communicating with someone. *But who? Are there actually more of these hairless beasts running around here? Are my deepest suspicions correct? Are they hiding in the woods out there?* He contemplated the possibilities and frowned slightly as he began to worry, again.

This was the very first time the extraterrestrial creature exposed convincing proof that there were others out there somewhere and, perhaps someplace in close proximity. Now, the metaphorical wheels of trepidation began to turn and grind inside his head again. The feeling came over him the same way it had inside the ellipsoid object. This notion that there might be other aliens hiding in some secret place brought on an emotion that was straightforward, heavy, and surreal. Up to now, he had done well keeping the thought of an all-out invasion from his mind. There was no need to fear the innocent curiosity of the extraterrestrials. So Brian had been calm up until now. He tried to speak lightheartedly in an effort to make sense of it all and put himself at ease in regards to what was going on in his mind at this very instant.

"Who are you talking to space-wolf? Does your space-wolf-mama want you to come home now?" The openhanded, playful inflection in Brian's rather nervous tone of voice made the alien woman chuckle a bit.

Brian noticed her reaction and raised his eyebrows repeatedly with his head leaned towards the creature. She laughed aloud in her alien manner. It was if she knew what he had commented.

"You do understand me kind of, huh?" Brian asked her with a warm, handsome smile. Just like the moment of first contact within the alien ellipsoid spacecraft, the woman somehow appeased Brian.

He immediately relaxed and even winked at her in return. She tilted her head to one side slightly, and winked back. Brian was at a loss for words at that moment of pure wonder and admiration. *She is peaceful at heart. I know she is.*

Then, the exotic lady suddenly turned to look at her celestial travel companion and said something to the wolf-like creature. It acknowledged her by nodding once as it continued speaking aloud. Then the creature started to walk out of the kitchen still speaking in its bizarre, lip smacking, jaw-chopping, unknown vernacular. The beast calmly walked past the breakfast bar and into the family room. This made Brian very curious. He moved swiftly toward the breakfast bar counter to see where the creature was going. He saw the creature making its way to the backdoor. The wolf-like being turned to look at its companion, who was still in the kitchen. When the creature lowered its hand from its narrow, pointy ear, Brian noticed it was wearing something like an earpiece. The tiny accessory was actually part of the eyeglasses. The hearing device perfectly matched the color of the creature's skin tone around the smooth, hairless region of its pointy ears. The contour of the ingenious equipment anatomically and unobtrusively graced the curves of the creature's ear. Up until now, Brian simply hadn't noticed it. He grinned, staring at the creature. *Very clever, I didn't know you were wired for sound. Every minute I learn something new about you, dog person.* The shiny copper colored lenses of the fancy alien eyewear were trained on Brian. The beast stared back at him in silence.

The extraterrestrial being said nothing more. To Brian's amazement, the beast calmly turned around and opened the door with its large hand, then exited the house. Brian frowned and his jaw dropped in disbelief and even shock as the creature closed the rear door snugly behind it on the way out. The door shut with a solid "clunk" and the beast nonchalantly walked out into the early morning light. The house was quiet. Brian turned his head slowly to look at the alien woman who had silently walked up to stand beside him. His jaw was still open.

"Oh no it didn't!" He said as he shook his head slowly. The young man pointed at the backdoor and said in a much accentuated, ethnic tenor, "That creature did not just walk out of here like it's from earth! If anybody sees it they are going to FREAK OUT!"

The alien lady did not reply in the moment of stillness that followed Brian's outburst. She just quietly stared at the delightfully amusing young gentleman.

As she continued to smile, Brian looked at her face and said, "Maybe we should go get space-wolf and explain that we have to make sure nobody sees either of you. They will freak out and I don't know how to explain you." Brian's eyes widened as he stood motionless, facing the pretty alien woman.

There was a slight pause before she responded in her unknown alien jargon. She spoke calmly, smiling the whole while. Brian stood still for a moment, listening as if he could clearly understand what her words meant. However, he did not know how to respond in her alien vocabulary and he didn't have a clue as to what she just said.

But the look on his face said it all; *I don't think you understand me. That dog person can't just walk out there in broad daylight right now! If somebody sees him, they're gonna FREAK OUT!*

Brian moved quickly. He stepped to one side and swiftly walked around the alien woman, following the smooth contour of the breakfast bar. He hurriedly made his way towards the backdoor and in one fluid motion, swung the heavy, four pane walnut door wide open.

Sunlight poured in, lighting up Brian's desperate gaze that immediately began scanning the area outside the door in hopes of finding the alien creature. He repeatedly looked left and right, trying to find the haughty, sporty eyeglass wearing space alien. But, there was no one to be seen. *Where the hell did that hairless werewolf go?!* Brian had not a clue where the creature could have disappeared to so fast. *It didn't take me that long to get to the door. Surely I'd see something.* He looked left and right again, probing the rear lot as far as he could see.

"Damn!" he finally uttered, "Where did it go?" The perplexed young man started to take a step outdoors. "He can't just…"

The pretty alien lady's gentle, but firm, grasp on his shoulder startled him. Then she took hold of his elbow and pulled him back inside the house, all the while smiling and speaking calmly. She nodded her head several times as she coaxed him back inside. Brian quietly conceded. She was benignly successful in her attempt to re-direct his attention. He pushed the rear entry door closed with one last look outside. There was nothing out of the ordinary that he could see.

The alien woman tried to get Brian to look at something else. She was pointing at the computer monitor on top of the traditional mission-style computer desk. She took a step closer to the large monitor on the brown mahogany desk which was located against the corner wall and to the left of the breakfast bar. Brian stepped closer to stand next to her.

"Do you want to know what that is?" He pointed at the monitor the same way his inquisitive extraterrestrial guest was and remarked, "That is a computer. Well, it's actually the monitor for the computer."

The alien lady began to speak again as she looked closer at the state of the art Dell P1130 21 inch color monitor. During her close inspection, she found where the power cord connected to the backside of the monitor. Then, she noticed the video input connector and cord which led to the PC tower. She leaned to her right and followed the cord with her dissecting gaze. Her eyes followed the monitor cord behind the desk as far as she could see. She leaned forward a little more and then stepped over to the right side of the desk in order to get a closer look. Brian noticed all of this. He was very much amused by her genuine, eager, and innate curiosity. This time she was trying to figure out where all the computer cords were going.

Brian knelt by the desk and opened the large cabinet door to the left. As soon he did, she leaned the other way to look at what he was doing. Brian pushed in the power button and immediately looked up at the dark, inert screen of the black contemporary style computer monitor. After a brief muffled singsong of internal mechanical sounds, the picture tube illuminated with the welcome screen Brian was so used to. This was immediately followed by a very brief, and to Brian, familiar musical preamble heard from the earthly technology. She smiled enthusiastically in anticipation as the computer powered-up. Indeed, she was truly fascinated. The amused smile on her face said it all.

Brian shook his head very slowly and fervently smiled as he thought to himself; *I know she probably wants to laugh at this thing compared to what I've seen so far of their technology.* Brian smirked. *She's probably smarter than anyone I know! But she's very humble. I can tell.* Brian looked her over while she closely studied the computer screen and raised an eyebrow while deep in thought. *She's really cute for an alien space girl, too. I've never seen someone so different and so pretty. It's just unbelievable that there are people out there on another world that look like her. I mean, it's cool, but I just can hardly believe it! Damn!*

Brian looked down at her feet and quaintly noticed she was wearing some type of garment that very closely resembled socks. They were the exact color of her flight suit uniform. He tilted his head to one side. *You guys wear socks, too. You put your pants on one leg at a time, just like us earthlings. Wow, we're so similar, I guess. I wonder what else we have in common.* Brian rubbed his chin as he wondered what other clothes she wore on her planet when she was not busy at work traveling the galaxy.

Brian was startled out of deep thought as she spoke. He looked at her and smiled politely. She reached out and tapped him on the shoulder with her fingers together, as opposed to only one finger as many earthly humans do. Then she pointed several times at the desktop computer with her thumb, wrist forward. The young man was amused by her strange engaging mannerism. He pointed in the air and spoke firmly in his professor tone of voice.

"Now, allow me to show you how this works."

Brian sat in the computer desk chair and pulled out the

keyboard tray. After taking hold of the mouse, he navigated the desktop area of the computer screen with the mouse pointer and opened the Internet application. Brian started to type while the curious alien woman astutely observed how his hands moved busily around, back and forth from the computer mouse to the keyboard. She watched everything he input into the fascinating earthly technology. When the computer made a bizarre noise, she stared even closer at the screen of the large monitor and then quickly glanced all around to see where the sounds emanated from. The peculiar sound she heard was the internal computer modem making its telltale connection with the Internet, through the telephone line. Her head tilted from side to side and she furrowed her narrow eyebrows as the modem established connection with the electronic information superhighway. The connection was made through a confirmation of strings of analogous beeps and amusing, drawn out, high-pitched singular tones. She was delightfully amused by this, and smiled at Brian. Then, the fascinating cyberspace computer program made its final affirmation that the user was ready to surf the net, with the computer speakers emanating a simple phrase; Welcome. She tilted her head to one side. As she did so, another phrase was immediately heard from the computer; *"You've got mail."*

"Okay, we're online," Brian announced, navigating the intriguing web application browser on the large colorful monitor screen in front of him.

He looked to his right and noticed the beautiful, exotic lady leaning forward. She squinted, peering closely at one of the stylish Harmon/Kardon model HK 695 computer speakers to the right of the large monitor. As soon as she did this, the armband device she was wearing started to beep and chirp its own extraterrestrial technological melody. The bizarre sounds immediately caught Brian's attention, and he looked at the strange alien equipment on her wrist. The young man stared as the alien lady promptly stood up straight and gazed at the brilliantly illuminated device on her arm. He was fascinated at how, in comparison, the weird technological audible cues heard from her device were not at all similar to the sounds heard from his father's personal desktop computer. Brian noticed there was a picture of something that flashed on the display screen of the alien gadget, but the extraterrestrial lady raised her arm up closer to her face before Brian could see what the image was. He became more curious at this point. Brian aptly stopped what he was doing and focused all his attention on the mysterious, celestial woman.

Brian logically figured that someone must be calling her based on the melodious beeping tones of the device and her responsive body language. She began to speak aloud, looking down at the illuminated armband device. Then she stopped talking and Brian could hear the sound of the creature's voice emanating from the alien technological gadget. The two alien beings conversed back and forth in short worded sentences for a few seconds.

As soon as Brian got the chance, he opportunely interjected, "Tell space wolf we're not home right now." The young man chuckled to himself aloud and shook his head, smiling. *It figures.*

The young man listened to her casually conversing with the creature and then heard her say a few words that she seemed to be repeating. There was a slight pause between her words and then she said something that definitely sounded similar, as if she was saying something over and over. The young man was staring at the floor when he felt her gently tap him on the shoulder. He looked up into her beguiling bronze eyes. Apparently, she had been talking to him, trying to get his attention.

"Oh, uh, what is it? You need something?" Brian quickly asked with raised eyebrows.

She silently raised her arm and pointed her thumb in a direction towards the front of the house. She looked back at Brian, and at that very instant there was a soft knock heard at the front door. Brian had a blank expression on his face. He was not expecting anyone to visit his parent's home so early in the morning. He wondered who it could be. Even more so, he wondered how the extraterrestrial knew someone was at the door that second. Then, in an instant, Brian got very apprehensive. *Who is knocking at the door? Should I get up? Should I be scared? Is that hairless werewolf being standing out there for everyone to see?* There was another soft rap at the front door. Brian stood up. He quickly glanced into the alien lady's eyes and without saying another word, started to walk towards the front door.

As he passed the breakfast bar he turned and said to her, "Don't move a muscle, I'll be back…" Brian took a few steps backwards, insisting, "…stay right there." He adamantly pointed several times at her long, narrow feet. The exotic lady was silent. She looked at the floor, curious, as Brian turned around and hurried to the front entryway.

"Just a minute, please!" he said and then took the remaining distance with longer, quicker footsteps. Now he was in the beautifully decorated foyer. He stepped close to the main entryway door and peeked through the fisheye lens of the peephole. He relaxed a little when he recognized the person standing on the other side of the mahogany door. He exhaled in relief and slowly opened the door to greet his new, unexpected, human visitor.

"Mr. Webley, what a surprise. How are you today sir?" Brian made his salutation with a warm, welcome smile.

The tall, silver haired gentleman standing on the covered porch immediately smiled in return and acknowledged.

"Well, hello there Brian. I'm just fine young man, and how have you been?" Both men chuckled as Brian reached out to shake the man's accepting hand.

"I'm great sir, just great." Brian noticed Mr. Webley was carrying what appeared to be a package in his left hand. He also noticed that the older gentleman was dressed in his usual attire for work.

"Listen," he said in a warm, gregarious tone of voice, "I got this package in the mail a couple days ago, see. And I've been meaning to bring it by here. I think it belongs to your mother." Mr. Webley handed the small brown package to Brian, who reached out and took the parcel.

"I noticed we got a new mailman a few weeks ago and I think he keeps getting the mail mixed up," Mr. Webley said, shrugging his shoulders. Then he added, "Maybe I should go to the Post Office and say something even though I think your mother already did."

Brian remembered how his mother had complained about the mail service, recently. He nodded his head in acknowledgement as he glanced at the front and back of the small package. His eyebrows rose slightly, with the left one rising a little more than the other. His eyes became more alert and focused on the postal packet. He clearly saw that the parcel was addressed to his mother. It appeared to be some kind of free sample of perfumed lotion from a prominent national television retail shopping network.

After looking the package over once more he said, "Oh yes, I see it's addressed to my mom. I'll give it to her. Thanks for bringing it over here Mr. Webley." Brian smiled.

Mr. Webley thoughtfully smiled in return and asked, "How are your mom and dad doing?" Brian was about to reply, but the tall gentleman coughed aloud a few times and cleared his throat the precise moment Brian was about to speak.

Then, before Brian could say anything, the older man quickly added, "I know your mom kept telling me that she needed to take a vacation."

This was followed by a hearty chortle mixed with another short, nippy set of coughs. Brian laughed lightheartedly but, as a medical professional who had worked with emphysema patients, he quickly discerned that the affable man had quite the smoker's cough.

"My parents are good," Brian answered with a slight nod, "They're actually on vacation in Hawaii right now." Brian looked down and added, "I was supposed to be with them, but I changed my mind. So, I'm kind of housesitting for them right now."

He smiled, almost reluctantly. His very words made him think of the plans he had previously made with Gina. They were both supposed to be in Hawaii along with Brian's parents right now. That is why he had the time off. However, the young couple was no longer together. They parted ways a few weeks before their planned vacation.

He looked up at Mr. Webley and asked, "And, how have you been, sir? How's work?" Brian rubbed his arms a little and folded them across his chest. It was a typical cold summer morning in the Lake Arrowhead resort area.

"Work has been good, life is good!" Mr. Webley affirmed with a nod.

"Good to hear that," Brian responded. He knew his parents' kind neighbor had been through some difficult times as of late with the passing of his wife several months ago.

"Yeah, I can't complain. I keep myself busy, and that's the way I like things." There was a slight pause before he added, "Well, speaking of work, I guess I should be on my way." He put his hands in his jacket pockets and said, "Tell your folks I said hello. And tell them I wish I was out there in paradise right now, and I'm jealous." They both chuckled and smiled at one another.

"I sure will, sir." Brian replied, "You take care of yourself, and thanks again for bringing the mail over."

They both waved once and Mr. Webley turned to walk away. Brian watched him for a moment. The man casually walked the wide concrete pathway over to the connecting driveway to Brian's left. Then, he turned right and proceeded out towards his red, Dodge Ram pickup truck parked on the side of the road across the street. Along the way, Mr. Webley took a pack of cigarettes out of his jacket pocket and lit one, smoking as he made his way back to the truck. Brian watched him get in his truck, start it up, and drive away. He smiled pensively as he took a few steps backward and slowly closed the front door. The warmer confines of his parent's house felt pleasingly more agreeable to him. He thought about Mr. Webley. *Wow, he wasn't even cold.* During their short, neighborly conversation, the older gentleman seemed quite environmentally content to Brian. *Man, I guess I really am a 'flat-lander.'* Brian put himself in the group the rural, resort community population up here called people who lived in the city below the mountains; in the crowded, hectic urban district. He exhaled in relief again and turned around at the precise moment the exotic alien woman stepped into the shadowy hallway. She stood at the other end of the hallway looking down at her illuminated armband device.

"How did you know he was out there?" Brian asked as he

turned slightly and pointed back towards the door. "Is your friend out there watching the house?"

She just smiled in return. Then she pointed at something to her left and began speaking. Whatever it was, the object of her curiosity was out of Brian's view, so he walked quickly through the hallway to see what she was looking at. He walked into the family room and immediately turned to the right. There he saw the celestial lady standing in front of the tall, decorative, picture frame room divider. The glossy, rosewood divider stood close to the wall. Brian's mother had pictures in all twenty-four, 8 x 10 inch frames divided into three panes on both the front and back. No matter what side of the picture frame floor screen was facing out, there were always a dozen pictures that anyone could enjoy looking at. Every couple of months his mother occasionally turned the divider around to reveal the other twelve pictures. She also turned it around for any visiting family members to see during a holiday visit. Each photograph had an engaging story. Most of the pictures in the decorative divider were of Linda and James's only grandson, Houston Morris. He was the most handsome and smart little four year old child anyone could meet. Brian loved him so much, too. The two always played and laughed whenever they found themselves together.

"Oh…" Brian chuckled aloud and smiled as he looked at the picture that the alien woman was pointing at. "Houston. That's my nephew, Houston. Adorable, isn't he?"

The extraterrestrial woman smiled with her long arm stretched out, pointing closely at a colorful picture of Houston when he was just a seven-week-old infant. She lowered her arm and began speaking in her own celestial tongue. Brian smiled as he heard an unmistakable, adoring tone in her voice. He could definitely tell she liked the picture of the baby boy very much. He listened to her calm voice and watched her happy facial expressions. *You must have babies where you come from, too I bet.* Brian stared at her. With a quick brush of her hand, the exotic lady flicked the hair away from her face as she leaned forward to examine all the pictures that were in plain view. It was only a short moment before she returned her attention to the adorable infant picture of Houston. She stared and mumbled something in her alien language. To Brian, it seemed as though she was in deep thought. She stood still for a moment and gazed closely at that particular picture of Houston. Something was definitely on her mind.

She silently pointed at the picture again. Then, she slowly turned her head and looked at Brian. While looking directly into his eyes she pointed at Brian and nodded once. She lowered her arm and stood still. Her colorful, beguiling eyes stayed on him the whole while. From the expression on her narrow face she looked as though she expected a response to her silent, apposite gesture.

"You want to know if that baby is me. Is that it?" Brian inquired while looking directly into her lustrous, bronze eyes. "Is that me?" The young gentleman asked louder with wide eyes as he pointed to himself. She stared, as if she were expecting him to make another gesture. He did. The young man slowly shook his head in an animated expression of few words by clearly acknowledging, "No."

Brian looked at her for a second, and then he pointed to a more recent photograph of the five-year-old boy on the picture frame décor.

"That's him, now." Then he pointed at the same picture of his nephew as an infant.

Then, he pointed at the same photo of the older, handsome young boy. He repeated his gesture. Once again, he pointed at the infant picture, first. Then he pointed at the most recent photograph of his nephew, Houston. The beautiful extraterrestrial lady immediately followed his gesture by pointing at the picture of the infant Houston. Then she quickly pointed at Brian. This time, when she pointed her long, lean thumb forward, as she usually did, she also shook her head; essentially and very simply implying, no. Brian smiled and nodded his head once.

"That is correct, my pretty space-lady friend," he replied.

Brian looked at the photographs in the picture frame divider and noticed there was a recent photo of his older brother Brandon, sister-in-law Donnette, and their son Houston, together. Brian pointed at the three happy family members in the glossy photo. He pointed at the shot of Brandon first, and then Donnette. Brian looked at the extraterrestrial lady as he paused for just a moment. Next, he touched the image of Houston in the same photograph. The handsome smiling little boy was aptly positioned between his two parents in the outdoor shot. When Brian returned his gaze to her, he could see the look of careful intellection in her curious, almond shaped eyes.

Then Brian realized there was another opportunity for his friendly alien visitor to understand a little more about himself. He kneeled down and pointed at a picture of his mother and father together in an indoor setting. Brian looked up at the humanoid woman. She remained silent as she paid close attention to his every move. Next, Brian turned his attention back to the picture frame divider and pointed to a photograph of him and Brandon as young boys. The two young brothers were smiling, giddy, and carefree in that shot taken one hot summer on one of their many family trips to Lake Havasu, Arizona. Both boys had on swim trunks. Their arms were around each other and they were soaking wet. Brian touched the image of young Brandon in the summer photograph. Then, he reached up and touched the older figure of his brother in the family photo he had just previously pointed at with Donnette and Houston. Next, he pointed at the image of himself as a youngster in the summer photograph. Brian looked up at her and then he pointed to himself. He could tell from the look in her alien eyes that she was putting things together in her intelligent, humanoid mind.

She understood. She systematically pointed at Houston in between his parents. She pointed at Donnette, and then Brandon on either side of their handsome son. She switched from her thumb to her long, narrow pinky and softly touched the image of Brandon in the same photo. Then, she pointed at Brandon's parents, Linda first, and then James in the photo that Brian had just shown her. Next, she silently turned to look at Brian. She purposefully reached forward and pointed at Brian, who was still kneeling next to her. She gently pressed her thumb on Brian's chest and smiled. Then, she turned and pointed again at the young man's handsome parents. She identified Linda first, and then she pointed at James in the same photo that Brian had just shown her.

"You got it! Correct again, my space-lady friend," the young man keenly verified.

Chapter Thirteen

Dozens of Lake Arrowhead residents had employed the Aguirre Lawn and Garden business for years and held long-term contracts with them for all their landscape and gardening needs. The time was 7:15 a.m. and Jorge Aguirre was just beginning his morning on the job. He and two work companions had already unloaded their 1998 Ford, XL Super-Cab, F-250 pickup and solid side utility trailer for the first job of the day. It was important to get an early start today because they had several other residences and business locations to work on later. The family- owned business was very successful and very busy of late. The small company was in demand as a direct result of their fervent networking, hard work, and excellent customer service. Some of the wealthy resort area residents had uninterrupted service indentures of more than ten years and counting with the small and hospitable family-owned lawn care business. They treated each new customer as if they were well-known royalty. Gustavo Aguirre, owner of the successful business, knew very well that establishing the best rapport with new customers instilled trust and long-term commitment from his clientele. Almost all these newborn business relationships established another loyal bond, lasting for many years, which, of course, meant many years of abiding revenue.

Jorge whistled aloud as he strolled across the south pathway towards the large rear lot of the beautiful mountain community residence where they were about to work. He walked quickly while carrying one of the two Craftsman gasoline powered string trimmers from the utility trailer. He wanted to get to the backyard and start from there, working his way to the front quickly, as he usually did. Timothy, Jorge's younger brother, had the other powered weed eater. Timothy would start on the north side of the house and eventually work his way towards the front. The two brothers would meet up front and then switch to their gas powered blowers to finish the job. By that time, their father Gustavo would be just about finished mowing the lawn of the large lot with his red Toro, HXL commercial lawn tractor. Each of them had a particular task to accomplish in a timely manner. Each job they went to was a well-orchestrated event. In order to keep to their busy schedule in a timely manner, each of the Aguirre family members had to work diligently.

Jorge was well aware of this and enjoyed keeping a busy schedule. He really enjoyed working outdoors, and he especially admired working in the Lake Arrowhead mountain resort area. Jorge tried to remember if he had enough gasoline in the weed eater, as he whistled and busily strolled along. He was looking down at the grass, steadily making his way to the rear lot of the cozy 1,228 square foot, northwest style home.

As soon as Jorge came around the rear southeast corner of the house, something caught his complete attention. From the corner of his eye, he noticed something against the exterior wall of the rustic mountain home. He immediately stopped in his tracks to look directly at whatever it was. Before him on the beautiful fallow stained, board and batten cedar-sided wall was something Jorge had never ever seen before.

What his eyes subjectively perceived was a very peculiar appearing shadow. In fact, it was actually a mixture of shadow and refracted light. Most of the refracted light appeared at a common focal point at the midpoint of the concentric anomaly of electromagnetic radiation. It was both mysterious and intriguing to behold. From the moment he first detected it, the young Mexican-American could not help but stare at the strange and beguiling occurrence against the wall. The unusual thing before him appeared like a shadowy variance, and was about four feet off the ground. It was uniformly circular all around, and motionless, except for a thin halo of full and then fading grayish light surrounding the midpoint of the anomaly. The subtle, dynamically undulating circumference of the strange anomaly was the very movement he had initially detected in his peripheral vision. The faintly pulsating, indistinguishable oddity that was a mixture of light and shadow had a circumference of about 28 inches, and it was approximately 9 inches in diameter.

Jorge was intrigued rather than just mildly curious. In fact, he was absolutely fascinated. He rationalized that the grayish, waxing and waning image on the wall must indeed be a shadow. Yet, the odd gleaming halo about the image and its auroral center suggested some sort of combined reflection. He stepped closer to the exterior wall of the house and reached toward the unfamiliar shadowy variance. When he did, Jorge quickly noticed the recognizable silhouette of his own hand, as well as the rest of his identifiable solid form against the wall. He slowly touched the odd shadowy image before him, but felt only the smoothness of the cedar siding. When Jorge touched the wall, he intently thought what thing could cast a shadow similar to what he was now looking at. As soon as Jorge realized that the morning sun, that was now rising, was at his back, he knew whatever was casting this bizarre shadow was most likely directly behind him. Jorge stared at the wall for a moment. Then he slowly turned around and looked up slightly higher than the decorative perennial border of Japanese holly toward the rear of the lot. As he did, his eyes initially focused to infinity, but in a split second, they were directly affixed on the <u>source</u> of the bizarre shadow against the wall. He saw it.

"What the hell is that thing up there?" Jorge whispered, nervous and genuinely concerned. He did not move a muscle. He just stood and stared at it. Jorge frowned in absurd bewilderment. "What is that?" he posed.

He stared at it, eyes squinted against the morning sun, and then began to seriously contemplate if he should be amazed, or just plain scared. What his eyes beheld not very far up in the air was simply inexplicable. The thing in plain view in front of him slightly above the horizon had no distinct borders to outline its whole. It was void of color. It was lacking an outside and an inside. In fact, the sky was visible behind it, and the light of day shown easily through it. The only way Jorge was able to really see it was because he happened to look right at it. What he was looking at was more of a visual distortion than an object. What he was looking at was something that occupied space, but was visually devoid of being. Jorge was looking at a focalized yet transparent visual distortion that both appeared and behaved similar to how heat waves emanate from a hot source, like off a road during the height of summer. It was very odd. This optical variance thing had a definite shape, and the shape seemed defined by the very margins of its perceptible visual distortion. Jorge had a little trouble with depth perception, but because of the transparency of the optical variance, he presumed that the soundless hovering anomaly was spherical. This object was, indeed, the distortion casting the bizarre shadowy image against the exterior wall of the house. The distortion observed in the air, and its shadowy image against the wall, were an anonymous product of advantageously refracted light.

"What's up there?" Jorge inquired aloud. He took a step backwards.

In the distance, he could barely hear his father talking to Timothy about something. It seemed they were having a conversation about where his brother should start trimming. Jorge thought about shouting for his father and brother to come see this thing floating in the middle of the air. Perhaps his father has seen something like this before. Surely, his father would know what it was and could explain. Conversely, as he searched for answers deep down inside, Jorge knew this mysterious, transparent, spherical object before him was something beyond anything anyone had ever seen, including his kind, wise father. Jorge wanted to speak up, but for some reason he was too frightened to do so. He felt as though the floating transparent object was watching and waiting for him to do something. He could sense it, as if there was a sign hanging on it that forewarned: Don't move or something bad will happen to you. So now, in this moment of distressed serenity, there was a staring contest between the mysterious hovering object and the frightened young man. Jorge was gathering the nerve to speak when he suddenly heard the sound of his father's voice.

"Santa María! What is that up there?" Gustavo Aguirre exclaimed as he walked around the northeast corner of the house, just past the beautiful, red cedar wood patio deck to see why his older son was not working.

He hadn't heard the sound of the gas trimmer and wanted to know what Jorge was doing instead that would possibly put them behind on their schedule.

"What's going on, Jorge?" Gustavo immediately stopped in his tracks when he noticed Jorge staring up into the air. So, quite naturally, the father looked up in the same direction. When he did, he saw it, too. Jorge turned his head slowly and stared at his father.

"Do you see it?" He cautiously beckoned in a nervous, muffled tone of voice. "What is it, dad?" he calmly pleaded.

Gustavo, eyes wide and eyebrows raised, stood stock still and stared at the strange transparent thing hovering above the ground. He was disturbed, yet amused by its inexplicable, appealing wonder.

"I don't know." he muttered with a faraway look in his eyes.

The kind, wise father assumed that the thing was floating up in the air about twenty feet high off the ground. He also assumed it must be somewhat closer than it appeared to be. From what he could tell by its apparent distorted size, he guessed it was maybe fifteen feet or so away. He looked at his son and tried to think of what to do next. Truth be told, the silent floating aberration was suddenly beginning to worry him. There was something about the distortion of the sky as he looked through it. The refracted, rippling appearance did not at all look natural. The transparent thing was also eerily quiet. It hadn't made a single sound. Gustavo continued to stare at it. It just did not look like it was something of this world. He was correct.

Jorge said nothing, but took a small step sideways towards his father. They both looked up at the strange, floating, hollow sphere and waited. The thing did nothing. It was perfectly still.

The two men perceived only the undulating distortion of the morning sky behind it. They looked at one another again in the stillness of the cool morning air, their tanned faces looking lost, concerned and confused. Jorge looked for answers in his father's eyes, but alas, he found none. Gustavo had not a clue what the strange, transparent, floating thing was. He frowned and looked back at the spherical aberration. Then he squinted and raised a hand to his eyebrows to provide a little shade from the morning sun. Just then, Jorge took two unhurried steps towards his father. Gustavo turned to his son and noticed him point at the floating transparent sphere. Jorge was about to say something when suddenly there was a cracking noise that echoed from the floating, transparent visual aberration. The father looked back at the floating sphere in time to see that the void distortion had instantaneously and momentarily filled with a glistening, metallic bisque color. A fraction of a second later there was a blinding violet-green flash, and before the two Mexican-American males could blink, a sharp, glowing arc of violet-green light very similar in shape to lightning bolted out from the mysterious floating sphere. The magnificent pulse of energy stretched out at the speed of light and made contact with the very top of Jorge's head. There was a distinct whack as the bolt impacted the dark, wavy hair on his scalp. His hair simultaneously and literally stood on end. Jorge instantaneously became rigid and stood up straight when he was hit by the beautifully colored yet mysterious bolt of energy. Then, all at once, he pushed the weed eater away and dropped to his knees. His eyes rolled up to the back of his head as he slowly fell to his left side. Jorge did not utter one word as he made firm contact with the plush, green, fescue grass of the rear lot. Now he lay there peacefully quiescent, out cold.

As soon as it happened, it was over. There was an eerie moment of calm. Only the sound of startled birds taking flight over the tops of nearby evergreen trees could be heard. The transparent sphere was unmoved, hovering perfectly still, just as it had when they first discovered it. In a blink of an eye, it had rendered Jorge unconscious. Gustavo thought of nothing but his beloved son as he looked in disbelief at him lying motionless on the turf. In the next instant, he wondered how this could happen. He wondered what the strange spherical aberration was. He wondered if it was some kind of life form as he looked up at the floating thing with pure terror in his eyes, for he thought the worst had happened to his son. Before he could think of what to do next, there was another brilliant violet-green colored flash and simultaneous cracking sound. His eyes were blinded from the intense streak of light that completely filled his vision. At the same instant the flash occurred, he felt an incredible jolt pound the top of his head. His muscles tensed uncontrollably, and he felt an uncomfortably warm surge of heat shudder through his spine from the top of his head to the soles of his feet. He became dizzy and all at once lost his balance. He stretched out his arms and arched his back in an attempt to stay upright. The world was spinning around and around, but for all practical purposes, he felt like he was still standing upright. The wise father was not even aware he was falling over when the left side of his face firmly impacted mother earth. Gustavo was laid out on his side, unbeknownst to him as the bright spots in his eyes quickly narrowed to darkness. Thoughts of where he was and what he was doing immediately vacated his mind. Within a few split seconds of being struck by the vibrant, colorful arc of energy, Gustavo was out cold. He and his son lay comfortably still on the beautiful green grass they had come to work on. The thick lawn they were supposed to cut down was now their alien inspired, mortal place of rest.

· · · • ● ● ● • · ·

Timothy had just walked to the spot where his father told him to start trimming when he thought he heard something. It was a familiar noise. Like the sound of an electrical short. He ignored it. It was probably nothing. He surveyed the area he was about to start working on. Timothy was standing between a white flowering dogwood tree to his right and a full flowering crabapple tree to his left. The house was to his back. He was looking the gas trimmer over once more before starting it. Just before he powered the weed eater up there was another strange noise, like the first one he heard. The second noise sounded more like something had cracked, like a large branch on a tree splitting apart. Then he thought maybe the first sound was more like the second. Timothy turned around. He did not see his father or brother. He did not hear the power tools they were supposed to be using, either. That was strange. Timothy looked to his left, and then to his right. He said nothing, but laid the weed eater down and started to walk in the direction he last saw his father go. Timothy quietly strolled towards the rear of the beautiful rustic mountain home in hopes of finding where his brother and father were. He listened for their voices, but could hear nothing. For some reason he was beginning to feel all alone and he did not know why; it just seemed too quiet to the teenager.

Timothy passed the steps of the red cedar deck, following the angular lines of its perimeter to the back of the house and then immediately discovered why it was so quiet. Just past the northeast corner of the house, he first saw his father lying on the turf. As soon as he made this discovery, he ran towards him only to discover his brother Jorge laid out as well. The concerned teenager said nothing as he scurried up to his father and knelt at his side. Timothy grabbed his dear father by the shoulder and turned him completely over to face him. His father was just regaining consciousness.

"DAD!" Timothy exclaimed. He looked down onto the wise, aged face of his father, just as Gustavo began to groan.

"What happened?" His father mumbled, putting his hands up to his tanned face.

"Are you okay, dad? What happened?" Timothy queried as he slowly helped his father sit up. The dazed man grabbed hold of his youngest son for a moment as he tried to gather his wits about him. As his father slowly shook his head, Timothy glanced at his brother. Jorge was starting to move around and he also groaned a bit.

"Jorge, you okay? What happened?" Timothy questioned his older brother.

Jorge grimaced as he propped himself up on the plush, green grass. He rubbed the top of his head and looked at his younger brother out of the corner of his eyes.

"I don't know." Jorge frowned. He righted himself a little better and supplemented, "All I remember is coming back here with the trimmer."

Gustavo rubbed his head and gazed at Jorge. "I remember coming back here to see what you were doing." He looked down at the grass for a moment. "I don't know what happened after that." He rubbed his head, again. "I hurt my head doing something is all I know."

"Me, too," Jorge remarked, "I hurt my head, too."

Timothy looked at both of them. He was silent for a moment as he tried to figure everything out. He noticed how close they were lying to each other when they fell. He looked over at the trimmer Jorge was using. It was in close proximity. Timothy quickly looked his brother and father over from head to toe once more and noticed how they were both intermittently rubbing the top of their head. Then he spoke up.

"You two must have run into each other. You guys knocked yourselves out, man." Timothy shook his head. "You have to be more careful." The caring, youngest son gently rubbed his father's back.

Gustavo and Jorge looked very confused, to say the least. They both had no clue as to what had just happened to them. They simply could not recall any of the events just prior to being rendered unconscious. Jorge slowly rose to his feet as Timothy helped his father stand up. The youngest son spoke again in a calm, firm tone of voice.

"Hey man, you guys have to be more careful." Timothy shook his head as he patted his father on the back.

Jorge and Gustavo looked at each other and silently nodded in agreement. Jorge took a few steps and quietly picked up the gas trimmer. He gave it a once over and was satisfied he had not accidentally damaged the fairly new power tool. Gustavo was concerned that maybe he had run into his older son so hard they were both knocked out for a few seconds. Honestly, the kind father was not really sure who ran into whom, but he figured it was his fault since he was the one that came to the back yard to find his son.

He looked at his slightly dazed son and quietly asked, "You okay, Jorge?"

"Yes dad, my head hurts a little, that's all," Jorge answered, rubbing his forehead.

Gustavo pointed at his older son and smiled, "All's okay. Good." He nodded as he looked at his watch. He rubbed his head once more and said, "Okay, let's get back to work. We have plenty of work today."

He gestured with his hand for the two boys to get busy. He waved his elbows around in a circle a few times and stretched his back muscles. He was feeling a little tense. Both his sons turned around and walked their separate ways to complete their assigned tasks. Gustavo rubbed the back of his neck and looked around at what needed to be done. He headed back towards the front of the house so he could start up the lawn tractor. Timothy was several paces ahead of his father. He was making his way back to the same spot between the blossoming trees. As he walked along he remembered the 'cracking' noises and still wasn't sure what had caused them. It was basically a mystery to him. The noises sounded like they had originated somewhere close to the backyard, when he thought a little more about it. As he approached the north end of the lot, he could hear Jorge starting up the gas trimmer. Timothy knew his father would be listening for the sound of his trimmer next. As he got busy with the task at hand, the moment when he heard the 'cracking' sounds and the eerie silence that followed quickly faded from his thoughts. It was no longer of concern. In a few short minutes, all three of them were again focused on doing what they came here to do. They were all very busy now, working hard on Mr. Webley's yard. As they continued to work diligently, the transparent spherical aberration hovered above them, perfectly still and covertly silent. It was much higher now than it was before. Now there was no shadow anomaly to be seen anywhere on the cozy and quaint Webley home below.

Chapter Fourteen

The creature had walked out of the house in broad daylight well over an hour ago. Brian naturally assumed the beast must have returned to the spacecraft out in the woods. He wondered what the extraterrestrial creature was doing right now. He and the alien woman had spent much of their time together looking at pictures after he moved the decorative picture frame floor screen away from the wall so they both could look at all the photographs. It was clear to Brian that she understood the relation between his parents, Brandon, Donnette, Houston, and himself. At one point, she pointed out the chronological order that the photos were taken. She simply used baby Houston as the focal point. She seemed to have a good, reasonable, and basic understanding of human growth and development. The pretty alien had also noticed several other photos on the wide, six-shelf, oak bookcase next to the decorative floor screen. Those pictures were mostly of Linda and James socializing with friends. While she was looking at those, Brian remembered there were more photographs his mother kept of herself and his father when they were much younger. Brian gestured for her to stay where she was and he quickly left the family room. She understood his gesture, and she stayed put, right there.

It only took him a few minutes to retrieve his mother's photo album from the upstairs master bedroom. He returned with a grin on his handsome face. He was eager to see if the perceptive alien lady could figure out who was in the pictures. Brian walked to the breakfast bar and motioned for her to follow him. He pointed at the barstool next to him as he sat in the other one. He patted the dark colored upholstered seat several times, inviting her to sit down and make herself comfortable. She accepted his quiet invitation and walked to the vacant bar stool, smiling as she seated herself close to Brian at the breakfast bar counter. It all transpired without a word uttered between the two. Their new and unspoken inter-celestial communication was becoming second nature, seemingly innate.

Brian opened the pink colored photo album to a specific page that he wanted to show her. He pointed at a picture of his father James when he was in college at the University of Southern California. This was in the fall of 1966. James Brandon Morris was 21 years old at the time, and studying to be a physical therapist. The picture was taken on campus at the university. The reason Brian chose that picture was because of the striking resemblance young James had in the photograph to Brandon. Brian pointed at the picture in the album and then went to the picture frame floor screen they were looking at a few minutes ago and pointed at the familiar photograph of Linda and James together. He leaned forward and touched the image of his father in the photograph. Brian looked back at the alien lady. He could immediately tell from her smiling expression that she under-stood who the person was inside the pink photo album picture. She looked closely at the handsome young image of James in the album. Then, the exotic extraterrestrial looked over at the picture frame floor screen. She was looking for another photo-graph. Brian did not have to say a single word. He knew what she was thinking. He simply pointed at the now familiar photo-graph of Brandon, Donnette, and Houston together. He nodded with a smile on his face and she nodded once in return. She had successfully recognized the resemblance between the handsome son and the young father in the photographs.

Brian was really enjoying every minute he and the alien lady were spending together this morning. He really enjoyed sharing the intimate association of his family with her through all the pictures they viewed together. He wanted to share everything he knew about anything with her. He wanted to show her so much more about his planet. There were so many wonderful things about his home, Earth, that she would really enjoy knowing. He really felt and fully understood the particular role he had to play right now being the sole ambassador of his world. Brian was really considering that this was no chance encounter, and that perhaps this first contact was all part of his destiny.

"Say, are you getting hungry?" the impromptu ambassador asked.

Brian was beginning to feel the effects of staying up almost all night without sustenance. He could feel his stomach grumble with hunger. The only food and drink he had consumed since this whole adventure began was the milk and carrot tasting demonstration.

"You want something to eat?" He jauntily simulated eating and drinking by chomping on air. The humanoid woman delightfully smiled and nodded once. Brian raised his eyebrows and his smile was pearly white as he rubbed his hands together and thought out loud, "Okay then. Let me see now, what should we have?"

Brian walked into the kitchen and opened the refrigerator. He stood there with the door agape and gazed inside the large kitchen appliance with one hand on his chin as he thought about what he would like to share with his fine alien guest. While he was trying to decide what to eat, the humanoid woman flipped through the pages of the pink photo album. She suddenly stopped to look at one specific picture inside the album. Brian quickly noticed her heightened awareness and sudden change in posture. He watched as she leaned in closer to carefully examine the image for a moment. Then, she suddenly looked up at Brian with a noticeable expression of eager curiosity on her face and propped the picture album up for Brian to see. She pointed her slender pinky finger at the photograph she had just examined closely. She uttered something in her strange language and smiled. She seemed to be eager to find out something about the photo. Brian noticed it was a black and white print of a very beautiful baby wearing a cute lace bonnet.

"I'm pretty sure that's a picture of my mom when she was

just a baby," Brian professed as he squinted at the black and white photograph.

The alien lady got up from her barstool and walked towards the decorative, picture frame floor screen. She pointed her thumb and started to move her arm around in a circle several times. She stopped and looked back into Brian's amused eyes. Then she repeated the gesture. Brian stared at her for just a moment.

"Oh," he said, figuring out what she was asking, "you want to know who that is? The baby in this picture?" Brian asked, pointing at the picture in the album on the counter and then walking to where she stood at the floor screen. He pointed directly at his mother's picture. "That's her now. That baby is all grown up, and she's now my mom."

The exotic extraterrestrial looked at the pink photo album for a second. She seemed to be in deep thought. Then she turned her attention to her sleek armband device. She pressed on the display screen several times and the device illuminated like it had been aroused from a short snooze. The hi-tech alien equipment quickly responded to her inputs with strange chirps and beeps. She busily worked the display screen with her long, delicate fingers. Her bronze eyes made contact with Brian's curious gaze as she lifted her arm for him to see what was on the screen. The young man looked down and saw the picture orientation instantly rotate, so that he could see it right side up from his perspective. He looked at the flawless, colorful image on her armband device and quickly recognized what it was, a close-up picture of a beautiful, swaddled human infant. Brian looked at her with a profoundly befuddled expression on his face and bluntly inquired.

"Who's that?" Even though all babies basically looked alike to him, he could at least reason that it was not someone he had ever recently seen.

Just at that moment, her armband device started to beep its strange melodious tones again. Brian looked at the display screen just in time to see the picture change. There were strange animated symbols and colors moving around as the image of the infant quickly shrank and disappeared. Then, another image enlarged and took its place. It was a crystal clear live image of the extraterrestrial creature. Brian raised an eyebrow as the beast noticeably leaned in a little closer to the view screen. With that, Brian also leaned closer to the wrist area display. The fancy sunglass wearing creature stared at him for a brief moment then uttered a strange noise just as Brian spoke.

"Yo dawg, what up?" Brian looked up with a mischievous grin and winked at the surprised and beautiful alien.

She actually stuttered a few of her alien words as she quickly began to speak. As soon as her voice was heard, the image of the beast automatically re-oriented itself back to her perspective of right-side-up on the intricate display screen of her arm garment device. She finished what she had to say, and the creature immediately responded. Its jaw chopping, celestial words were clearly heard from the armband device. Brian could tell from the sound of its voice and the way the beast spoke, that there was an urgent matter being conveyed. Brian gazed up at the alien woman's face just as her expression changed from casual interest to forthright alarm. She was obviously taken aback by whatever the creature had just said. Brian could easily tell from the look in her eyes that she was genuinely shocked by what the beast was saying to her right now. Suddenly, she gasped and put the palm of her right hand over her mouth. Then she put her right hand over her forehead just as earthly humans do when they are flabbergasted. There was no doubt that she was acutely disturbed by the conversation with her celestial travel companion.

The beast continued to talk and the humanoid woman became more agitated. Her bronze eyes widened and she opened her mouth in astonishment. She started to move her lips as if to speak, but she seemed so overwhelmed by the occasion that she just whimpered a few times in a higher octave tone of voice. She looked up into the air as if trying to find some reasonable thing to say while the beast continued speaking. She seemed at a loss for words. Brian could see it in her eyes. With her mouth agape, she looked around the family room. She repeatedly turned her head looking left and right, her anxious gaze seemed to be searching for something. She was subtly breathing faster and becoming more fidgety. She put her hand on her forehead again and looked up in the air. The exotic alien was beginning to panic. Brian did not know what to say because he did not know what was wrong. Definitely, something was wrong. He could sense her emotion. Suddenly, she interrupted what the creature was saying and spoke so fast and so resolutely that it actually made Brian tense up a little. The beast tried to say something else but she interrupted in a much more firm tone of voice. The impromptu ambassador of Earth could not understand what she was saying to her space-traveling friend. Nevertheless, Brian knew it was not a pleasant, casual talk about milk and carrots.

Then there was a pause in their conversation. The celestial lady looked at the floor and silently shook her head several times. Her flowing burnet hair bounced around her face like a silken veil. Even in her distraught state of mind, she was so gracefully beautiful. She had such poise. Brian tried to think of what could possibly be wrong. He wondered if it was something that the extraterrestrial creature had done to make her so upset.

"What did the space-wolf do? Go out and eat somebody for breakfast?" Brian coyly supposed as he pointed towards the back door.

He attempted a bit of lighthearted humor to get information but, alas, she did not know how to speak one word of his earthly language and he certainly did not know how to speak hers. He stared at her as she put her hand on her hip and looked to her left with a faraway gaze in her worried bronze eyes. She slowly brushed some of the hair away from her face and looked into Brian's eyes. As the young man faced her in silence, he could truly sense her distress. For the first time since they met, she actually looked as if she were about to cry. He desperately wished he could talk to her. Then she put her head down and covered her eyes with the palm of her right hand.

"What's wrong?" Brian thoughtfully inquired, but she did not react. She looked to her left again. Brian's gaze followed hers. *She's waiting for something, or someone* Brian intuitively deduced.

She's looking towards the backyard. She's expecting something to happen, I can feel it.

The creature's voice broke the silence. As soon as its jaw chopping words were uttered, the alien woman raised her left arm to look at the view screen on her armband device. The display illuminated on cue, and the image of the beast filled the small screen once more. Brian was standing close enough to the exotic humanoid to see the creature's lips move as it spoke to its distraught companion. She flicked some of the lightly layered hair from her face with a quick turn of her head. Then, she looked down at the screen on her armband device and spoke up. This time her voice was more reserved and melodic, more like Brian was accustomed to hearing her.

As soon as she began to talk to her space-traveling friend, Brian's cell phone began to ring. The surprised young man flinched at the unexpected, earthly technologic salutation. Brian walked slowly towards the sound of the ringing phone located on top of the cherry finish cocktail table next to the sofa. He picked up his phone, taking his eyes off the phone for just a microsecond as he tried to listen to the tone of voice the alien lady was using as she spoke into the armband device to decipher if she was still upset. He looked over at her and just as he did, accidentally knocked the cell phone off the table. It continued to ring as it fell down onto the woven area rug below. He knelt down and picked up the phone off the rug. Brian immediately experienced a profound moment of déjà vu. He paused for a second in reflective thought and then turned the Ericsson T66 cell phone over to look at the display face. At that moment, while staring at his phone with a perplexed frown on his face, he remembered the sequence of his dream. He was looking at the cell phone display now, but he wasn't paying any attention to the incoming call. Brian only thought of that distinct moment in his dream when he tried to follow Gina out of the crowded restaurant. He remembered how he had picked up his ringing phone off the floor of the crowded restaurant to see who was calling. His posture then was very similar to right this second. He flashed back to that instant in his mind and it all seemed so explicit, as if it had all actually happened. He blinked a few times and quickly shook his head. *It was a dream, right?* Brian smiled. *Man, it seemed so real.*

Brian quietly stared at the cell phone as it stopped ringing. Before the caller ID disappeared, he noticed it was his mother trying to call him. It was close to 7 a.m. in Hawaii, now. Brian figured his mother probably got up early to go jogging as she usually did at home. She was most likely trying to see if he was awake yet.

Just then, his peripheral vision picked up movement. The alien woman was walking to where she had laid down earlier next to the large, pine entertainment center. She was doing something with the large utility backpack she brought with her. Brian did not turn his head to look at her. He merely assumed she was packing something into her utility bag. He continued to stare at the mobile phone, realizing he did not want to call his mom back right now because he didn't trust himself. Brian had a feeling he might tell his mother everything. Now was not the time to tell anyone that extraterrestrials really exist. Now was not the time to tell everyone that we are not alone in the universe. People just do not understand, nor do they accept anything out of the ordinary of what they are used to. This is how Brian felt about the issue. He was sure that knowledge of this first contact with his alien guests would not bode well with people on earth. Absolutely no one should know these extraterrestrials were here. He wanted to continue to hide the aliens' presence from view, along with himself.

I can't let anyone know where I am or what I'm doing right now. People on earth are naturally audacious, selfish, and cruel. He gazed at the display of his mobile phone for a moment. It indicated he had one new voice message.

"Where are you going?" Brian turned his head and asked the alien woman.

He had a feeling she was going to leave him. She immediately started to speak in her celestial vernacular, as if, on cue, she was answering the question to his satisfaction and understanding. She paused and stood perfectly still for a moment, looking at him. Her bronze eyes gazed deeply into his eyes as if she was trying to figure out something important and complicated.

"What?" Brian's reaction was innocent and curious compared to her fixated search into his soul.

Just then, her armband device started chirping its weird sounding alerts. She did not look at the display, however. She just stared at Brian. She was obviously preoccupied with something. Now he was beginning to feel a little uneasy. Whatever she was thinking about, it undoubtedly involved him. The open minded, impromptu ambassador of Earth was sure of it. Brian tried to smile, but her solemn gaze into his anxious eyes was too confounding. Next, the beautiful alien put her equipment vest-backpack back down on the polished hardwood floor and walked to where Brian was still kneeling. She stood next to him and spoke softly as she reached out her hand in an obvious gesture to take hold of his hand. Brian slowly rose and quietly put his left hand in hers. The narrow palm of her hand was so soft and warm to the touch. She gently grasped a firm hold of the young man's hand. *What's up?* He thought to himself. The alien woman turned to her right and gently pulled at Brian to follow along. There was no objection from him as he quietly conceded.

Next, she led the bewildered Brian towards the hallway. They silently walked into the guest bathroom with Brian following right behind her. As they passed through the open door he glanced to his left to see the image of the two of them in the large bathroom mirror. Even the mirror asserted her corporal presence, without giving the slightest protest. Brian stared. The sobering reflection beheld staunch proof that there was indeed, life on other planets. The mere sight of her next to him in the reflection was an existential accolade. She looked at Brian through the reflection of the bathroom mirror as she turned around to face him. *Yes, what you are looking at is for real. Yes, I do exist.* Brian could see it in her alien eyes.

Next, she gently grabbed hold of Brian's left wrist and pointed at his watch. She looked down at the black, three-year-old digital watch for a moment and carefully studied it with an intent gaze. Then she started to mumble something.

Brian noticed the staccato cadence of her alien words, and the way she subtly nodded her head once with each utterance. She seemed to be reacting to each second that displayed itself on his watch. *She's counting,* he deduced logically. *She must have a very similar method of keeping time on her planet. She's very observant, and very clever.*

Brian silently smiled at her while she continued to count each earthly second softly in her own celestial, numeric dialect. Then she looked up at Brian and began speaking directly to him. She moved her hands around and seemed to be making gestures about his watch. The alien lady pointed her pinky finger at the 'seconds' display on Brian's sporty digital watch. She looked up at Brian, again. With her right wrist and forearm parallel with the floor and the palm of her hand facing herself she started to count using her long, slender alien digits. She started with the pinky finger as 'one', the ring finger as 'two', the middle finger as 'three', the index finger as 'four' and her thumb represented the number, 'five'. She repeated the gesture and continued uttering her alien words with each tick of a second on Brian's earthly timepiece. Brian naturally assumed she was still counting in sequence, using her same hand to do so. He quickly joined in and counted aloud, starting with the subsequent display of the ring finger she had extended for the second time.

"Seven… eight, nine, ten…" She stopped when Brian announced the number "ten". She raised her thumb up slightly and repeated the same word she had just enunciated, during this second and final interval of the count.

"Ten!" Brian firmly pronounced with a handsome grin.

"Shyurr." Brian distinctly heard her say for the third time. She smiled in return. The exotic woman from another world was making progress communicating with her earthly envoy.

"Shar!" Brian tried to copy her. This resulted in a very pleasant giggle from his admirable alien guest. She nodded once, quickly, and then helplessly smiled at him before starting to speak quickly in her language.

Brian watched her count with her slender amberous fingers once more as she vocalized each number in her own language.

Naturally, Brian counted along with her. This time however, when she got to 'ten,' she kept counting. She smiled to encourage him along. They counted in near perfect unison all the way up to eighty, with Brian doing so in English and the alien lady counting in her own language. She repeated the word for 'eighty' in her language, and Brian did the same in English. Satisfied with that, she emphatically nodded once. Next, she pointed at his watch and then looked into Brian's eyes, pressing her thumb gently into his chest. She spoke quickly, pointing at the bathroom floor in the very same gesture they had used to tell each other to stay put.

"Oh! I got it!" Brian said with a beaming smile. "You want me to stay here in the bathroom for about, eighty seconds!" Brian was excited and he gestured with his hands quickly, as he spoke to her. "Yes, I understand." He nodded once. She smiled and nodded once slowly in return. "Okay, okay," Brian responded fervently.

The extraterrestrial woman kept her gaze on Brian as she quickly moved around him and walked to the bathroom door. Brian remained where he stood, facing the other direction. She spoke aloud and gently yanked at the left sleeve of his T-shirt to get his attention. He turned to his left, just enough to see her reflection in the large mirror on the bathroom wall. They made eye contact through the mirror and she smiled. She raised her left forearm and made a gesture by pointing at her left wrist with her right pinky. *Start timing.* He acknowledged with a single nod of his head. He turned to face forward in the opposite direction again as she silently and quickly shut the bathroom door.

Brian quickly glanced at his watch to note the time; 9:16 a.m. and 22 seconds past the minute. He stood perfectly still inside the quiet bathroom as he did the math in his head. He easily figured he could walk out of there by the time his watch indicated 9:17 a.m. and 42 seconds. As soon as he started observing the time, he heard a faint, familiar noise in the distance. Watching the seconds tick by, which at first seemed like an eternity, he heard the distant sound getting nearer. As the intensity of the sound increased more and more, he was able to recognize what the noise was. Brian looked up at the ceiling as he listened to the sound of a helicopter passing nearby. Because of his location inside the house, he was not able to ascertain exactly where the aircraft was. He wondered if it was a military or law enforcement helicopter. He immediately thought of the aliens. *Surely, they couldn't have been discovered that easy, and so soon. These aliens are much smarter than that.* Brian contemplated as he stood still, listening. He could hear the sound of the helicopter fading away. No cause for alarm. He stared up at the ceiling some more, trying to determine if the aircraft was returning. *Then again, I found them pretty damn easy.* He had second thoughts.

After a few more seconds of silence, Brian was convinced the helicopter was not searching for his celestial guests. He looked down at his watch again and saw that it was now 9:18 a.m. and a few seconds past. He quietly turned around and took a few steps towards the bathroom door, and opened it, very slowly. Brian simultaneously poked his head out of the bathroom and peered to his right. From the way things looked so far, there was nobody present in the family room. Brian cautiously stepped out of the bathroom and quietly proceeded to the family room. As he exited the hallway he called out, "Hello, anyone here?" He walked to the sofa and turned completely around. There was no one to be seen from where he stood. Then he walked to the rear door and slowly opened it. As the door swung open, Brian looked down to make sure his mother's cat didn't make an abrupt escape. The daylight from the beautiful summer morning filled the family room as Brian peered outside. Alas, there was no one out there that he could see. He quickly closed the door.

When he was in the bathroom, Brian had tried to listen for the sound of the back door closing. However, the sound of the helicopter had distracted him. He looked around the family room once more, leaning against the smooth walnut of the back door. The equipment vest-backpacks that belonged to the extraterrestrials were gone. There was no longer a hint of the lip-smacking, outer space, werewolf-creature within view. The beautiful humanoid woman was gone. Brian suddenly remembered how she became upset when she talked to the creature using her fancy, technologic armband device.

I guess the creature must have told her it was time to leave. She probably liked spending time with me, and she didn't want to go. Maybe that's why she got so mad. The young man raised an eyebrow and shrugged his shoulders as he thought. *Maybe they just left.*

· · · • • ● • • · · ·

If the aliens truly did depart this world, then the impromptu Ambassador of Earth felt he had done well. *Time to rejuvenate after all my hard work.* He thought. Brian started towards the kitchen. So much had happened to him in the past twenty-four hours. He needed time to sort out the meaning of all this. Brian was not really one hundred percent sure how he should feel about this first contact. He was elated, yet to some extent, fretful at the same time. He had so many mixed feelings and profound notions stirring deep within him right now. His thoughts were in a complete state of unstrained confusion, clouding his mind like a swarm of agitated yellow jackets. Brian wanted to save all the deep thinking for later, though he remained overly curious about the reason for the aliens' visitation. For the moment, it was just time to eat. He was very hungry and he could not think of much else except food right now.

"Yeah, that must be it," he said aloud as he reflected on the last couple of hours. *Maybe their mission was to observe us for a couple days, or something. Perhaps the two alien beings had already seen enough, and it was time for them to leave. Maybe she and dog-person had a launch time they had to keep, or something. Maybe she had to hurry, and she didn't want to leave, yet. Anyway, I guess she didn't want me to see them secretly blast off, or whatever. That's probably why I had to wait in the bathroom. Or maybe, since I blew their cover last night, they ultimately decided that they <u>had</u> to go home right now. Who knows if they will ever return? I'm sure it costs a lot of money and time to travel in space, even for them.*

Brian rubbed his forehead as he entered the kitchen. He didn't want to do anything else about it right now, at this moment. He definitely was not about to follow the alien woman out the door and search for her and the beast deep in the forest. He was just too tired and hungry for that kind of effort right now. *Maybe I'll look for them later.*

"I don't know. What should I do?" Brian said aloud and then thought, *I have to really think about what just happened last night, before I say or do anything about it. There might be someone or several other people who have had an encounter with these aliens before. Maybe I should find out. Yes, I should probably try and find out if there's any evidence at all of their visit to earth before last night.*

Brian rubbed his head and stared at the refrigerator. What if the aliens were truly gone for good? Who knew for sure? *Well, I guess that's it.* He opened the refrigerator and searched its contents for a good meal. *I bet they somehow know that now is <u>not</u> the time to announce their existence. But who knows? Maybe they will return. Whenever that happens, maybe this world will be ready. I would like to be present and see that take place.*

"Well," Brian said assuredly as he reached inside the refrigerator for a small box of some left over Chinese fried rice next to the container of milk, "before I do anything else, I've got to eat something."

Chapter Fifteen

Jermaine Laws did not really enjoy flying. He did so merely out of necessity. He was especially not enthusiastic about flying in helicopters. Nevertheless, here he was, right back in the very same aircraft that influenced his decision to remove himself from the medical transport team. He was not the slightest bit surprised by that, though. He had seen enough proof of how things always seem to work out that way in his life. He figured, *that's just the way life is.* In fact, that was one of his favorite proverbial expressions.

Jermaine stared at the portable pulse oximeter display, lost in deep thought. He was very concerned about the sick child he and the rest of the medical center transport team had just picked up from Joshua Tree Desert Valley Hospital in Hesperia, California. The medical staff at the small, 80-bed referral hospital had called on the immediate assistance of the Pleasant Hills Medical Center transport team earlier this morning. The call for help from the referral facility came into the PICU not too long after Jermaine received the shift report from his friend, Danny Kosmor. Since Jermaine was working at station one where the unit secretary was located, he was one of the first to know about the request for transport call. The information about the transport was immediately passed along to his department supervisor for the day shift staff. Normally, the respiratory care supervisor provided one respiratory care practitioner to go along with the other two team members consisting of a registered nurse (RN) from the unit and one resident pediatric physician. All three transport team members were usually on call from home, meaning they were standing by and ready to respond within thirty minutes. The Pleasant Hills Medical Center Respiratory Care Department usually had two therapists on call every twenty-four hours who were available to cover all inter-facility transports for the medical center. However, this was not the case for the call that came in this morning. Unfortunately, the respiratory care practitioner in charge for the day did not have anyone available to go on the call. At this particular time, the neonatal intensive care unit (NICU) had two of their own transport teams out on separate calls. Although the NICU had their own registered nurses and physicians on call, the Respiratory Care Department only had the same two therapists available to cover both the PICU and the NICU. Therefore, if there were ever more than two requests for transports, the respiratory care practitioner in charge usually had to get one of the therapists from within the hospital to cover the call. This practice was not uncommon. It was also the reason Jermaine was flying right now. So here he was, sitting very quietly inside the air ambulance helicopter with a slightly perturbed look on his face. Jermaine was just not a big fan of flying.

The flashy green and silver Inland Air Medical Transport helicopter crew consisted of the flight nurse, emergency medical technician (EMT), and pilot. The crew picked up the medical transport team as fast as they could from Pleasant Hills Medical Center for the thirty-five minute flight to Joshua Tree Desert Valley Hospital. There was a very ill patient waiting for them in the referral hospital's emergency department. The patient was a male Caucasian, a nineteen month old named Jeremy Aaron Noble. His worried mother had brought him to the emergency department only a few hours before the Pleasant Hills Medical Center transport team was summoned. The patient presented to the small town hospital emergency department triage nurse with a history of increasing lethargy over the past couple of days. The sick toddler's pediatrician had seen him only four days earlier for a mild fever and upper respiratory tract infection symptoms, including a sore throat. That day little Jeremy was diagnosed with an upper respiratory infection during his examination. The toddler's mother was given a prescription for an oral antibiotic, but unfortunately, the child got worse over the next couple of days. This morning he became more irritable and was much less active than usual. Jeremy was not eating well before his visit to the pediatrician, and over the past twenty-four hours he had been vomiting frequently. His mother noticed in the last couple of days that his urine output was significantly decreased and she wasn't aware of any recent bowel movements. She said Jeremy had a lot of diarrhea about a day ago, but now he had none.

By the time the medical transport team arrived, little Jeremy's vital signs were less stable and, not surprisingly, quite concerning. The emergency room cardiac monitor indicated a steady but fast heart rate of 157 beats per minute. He had a regular respiratory rate of 38 breaths per minute. His latest blood pressure reading taken by the registered nurse in the emergency department was 73 systolic with a diastolic of 47 mm Hg, which was low for his age group. The toddler was also quite febrile, with a core temperature of 104° Fahrenheit. His skin was very pale, and hot and dry to the touch. The mother of the sick child said Jeremy definitely was not himself, and he was complaining of headaches. During the pupillary response examination little Jeremy cried out, and he curtly turned his head away from the small medical penlight the transport team doctor was trying to use. Besides the painful annoyance of the light in his eyes, the transport team physician noticed that not much else seemed to arouse the toddler. The transport team RN, registered respiratory therapist, and physician positively assessed that the toddler had an obtunded level of consciousness, and that this would indeed be consistent with an altered sensorium, as presented by the child's mother. All things considered, it only took a few minutes for the medical transport team to acknowledge that this patient was very ill.

The Pleasant Hills Medical Center transport team collectively agreed that the child quite possibly had a serious central nervous system infection. This meant that the patient needed immediate medical intervention. After the medical transport team finished their initial assessment of the patient, it did not take them long to get Jeremy ready for his quick helicopter flight to the Medical Center. Another intravenous line was immediately started. Next, an infusion of an antibiotic and a corticosteroid followed. In addition, the child was also administered a mild analgesic. The medical transport team physician had spoken with Jeremy's mother, obtained her signature on the consent for transport, and then the transport team members whisked the ailing toddler away on a gurney directly to the helipad. From the moment the transport team arrived, to the second their helicopter lifted off into the air, all transpired quicker than the time it took for the child to initially be seen by the triage nurse at the Joshua Tree Desert Valley Hospital emergency department.

The medical transport team and the air ambulance helicopter crew had just departed the small hospital at 9:15 a.m. for a return trip to Pleasant Hills Medical Center with their patient onboard. Within a few minutes after departure, their MBB/Kawasaki, BK-117-A4 helicopter was already flying southbound over the northwest corner shoreline of beautiful Lake Arrowhead. The lake below was as smooth as glass. The winds were calm, and the morning sky was radiantly blue and unbelievably picturesque. The mountain air was fresh and pure, free of all the hazy pollutants normally found in the overly inhabited Los Angeles basin below and to the southwest.

Jermaine was staring at the portable pulse oximeter display, lost in deep thought as he listened to a conversation between the EMT and the pilot. The two crewmembers sitting in the cockpit of the sporty green helicopter with silver stripes seemed to be doing a little sightseeing on the way back to the Medical Center.

"Look, there's a few more people out on the lake since we came by earlier." The pilot's voice crackled over the crew intercom.

"Yup," the EMT sitting to the pilot's left answered, "and I wish I was one of them."

There were a few chuckles simultaneously heard over the intercom from the rest of the occupants inside the air ambulance helicopter. Jermaine turned down the volume a little on the David Clark headset he was using. He looked down at the cabin floor of the aircraft, trying not to appear too uncomfortable. He took in a deep breath and sighed, which everyone else heard over the intercom. Just then, he felt the hand of the flight nurse lightly touch his left knee. Jermaine looked up at her. She could see more than a hint of nervousness on the young man's face and could tell he was slightly disturbed by something; the flying to be more specific.

"You okay, honey?" Mary Anne Hobalt asked Jermaine in her warmhearted, heavy southern drawl.

She was the nurse manager of the company and one of the nicest flight nurses at Inland Air Medical Transport. She was originally from Houston, Texas, but she loved living in California. Mary had a concerned look about her as she leaned forward and smiled, looking directly into the young man's eyes.

"You feel okay?" she said, lightly rubbing his back.

Jermaine sighed again nervously and replied, "Yeah, I'm cool." He managed to smile back at the kind flight nurse, though he felt like the last place he wanted to be right now was in the helicopter. He delicately adjusted the microphone boom of the headset he was wearing and lackadaisically affirmed, "It's nice to get out of the hospital every now and then, know what I mean?" He had at least made an honest attempt at polite, macho pleasantries.

"Everything okay back there, Mary?" the pilot quickly asked in concern.

The voice activated microphones conveniently allowed anyone to participate in any conversation over the helicopter crew intercom.

"Yes, we're good back here, Chuck," the flight nurse answered Charles Pulaski, a Vietnam War era veteran pilot who was also the most senior employee of the company.

"We'll be landing on the helipad at the medical center soon," Chuck reassured. His voice crackled over the aircraft intercom like a seasoned tour guide.

Mary smiled and nodded at Jermaine, who politely smiled in return. Then she nodded her head towards the pilot seated directly behind her.

"Chuck will take good care of us, honey. He's the best in the business."

Mary's seat faced to the rear of the aircraft, positioned back-to-back behind the pilot in the cockpit. Their two seats were separated by a thin alloy partition. Jermaine's seat was situated beside and to the right of Mary's seat. He was situated back-to-back, behind the EMT. Jermaine's seat also faced to the rear of the cabin. He impassively looked down and stared at the cabin floor of the air ambulance helicopter. As he did, the kind flight nurse gently grasped hold of his hand in a reassuring manner as if to say, *everything is going to be just fine.*

"Oh," Chuck chimed in with a rousing tone in his voice, "it's a great day for flying! Just look at how beautiful it is up here. And, might I add, it's nice and smooth this morning, too."

His amiable proclamation was warmly received by the others. In one word or two, they all kindly and simultaneously agreed over the crisp crew intercom. With that, the EMT and pilot returned to their own quiet, casual conversation about how nice a day it was, and how beautiful Lake Arrowhead is in the morning.

Jermaine looked at the patient who was sleeping on the transport gurney, directly across from the flight nurse. He still wore the oxygen mask. Most toddlers take it off after a few seconds or simply don't allow it to be put on in the first place. The fact that Jeremy did not care either way was actually a sign that the child was not himself and feeling very ill.

"Doesn't Brian Morris live up here somewhere?" Kristen Lagerfeld, the PICU transport team RN casually asked as she wrote down the next set of the patient's vital signs on her aluminum clipboard.

She was sitting comfortably on the medical cabin bench seat directly across from Jermaine. The bench seat faced the transport gurney, allowing quick and easy access to the ill toddler. She continued writing and visually assessing the patient as she prompted the quiet transport team respiratory therapist.

"Jermaine, do you know?"

Jermaine looked at her and answered, "Yes, uh… I think his

parents live up here in the mountains. I know he actually lives in Riverside." He nodded his head at her. "Know what? I think his parents live right by here somewhere, actually."

He looked out of the large sliding door window of the helicopter towards the lush, tall evergreen tree foliage below. He recalled how Brian once told him that his parent's home was not too far from the lake. In fact, Jermaine remembered that Brian's parent's home was located somewhere on the west side of the mountain lake community, which was the region he was looking towards right now.

"Isn't that the guy whose fiancé is now dating one of the PICU residents? Or, something like that?" Doctor Nicholas Kirkpatrick, the transport team resident physician blurted out over the intercom.

The doctor was sitting next to the rear clamshell doors of the rescue aircraft. He leaned forward slightly in order to look past Kristen on his left as he spoke to Jermaine.

"She's a nurse, I think. She's really cute, too." The doctor returned his gaze, looking into a small notebook he was reading from for a second and then glanced up at Jermaine once more, then asked, "What's her name, again?"

"Gina. Her name is Gina." Jermaine's thick, New York accent filled up the intercom. "She happens to be a friend of mine. And Brian is a friend of mine, too." That was Jermaine's polite way of inferring, *careful what you say next.*

"I heard that the guy she's seeing right now… uh, doctor Spies, they used to date before." Kristen looked over at Jermaine, "Doctor Spies and her, weren't they like… high school sweethearts before, or something?" The petite, Caucasian transport team nurse who was originally from Simi Valley, California adjusted the headset she was wearing until it was more comfortable and then added, "I think she just ended up going back with her old boyfriend is what happened." She gestured with her hands and looked to her right where doctor Kirkpatrick was sitting on the other half of the bench seat and articulated, "I mean, I know she was engaged to Brian and all that. I'm not saying it's right. I mean, I really think Brian's a sweet guy and all. But, I know she was in a long-term relationship with her previous boyfriend."

"Whoa, sounds like someone's got some serious issues there," David Ramirez, the flight EMT sitting up front in the cockpit blurted out with a generous hint of lighthearted humor in his voice. His subjective jest was met with several acknowledging chuckles from the others, except for Jermaine. He had no comment. He was quiet.

The conversation was brisk and somewhat pleasant when, seemingly all at once, everyone just returned to their own thoughts. It was quiet for just a moment before the pilot and EMT eventually returned to their discussion, casually sparking up a conversation about the emergency landing this very aircraft they were flying in had to make recently.

Of course, Jermaine could not help but listen in, because the recent event they were talking about happened to be the same flight Jermaine was on. This was the same incident that predisposed Jermaine to quit the transport team.

· · · • ● ● ● ● · ·

The emergency landing occurred almost three months earlier, to the date, and Jermaine remembered it all too well. On the day of the incident the Inland Air Medical Transport helicopter crew flew out from their nearby base to Pleasant Hills Medical Center where they picked up the transport team. They all quickly departed the medical center for a flight to Pomona Community Hospital. The helicopter was enroute to the community hospital to receive a teenager involved in a major rollover traffic collision. The transport team was just a few minutes from making their approach for a landing at the community hospital when their helicopter experienced an engine failure. One of the two turboshaft engines that power the air ambulance rotorcraft suffered an immediate fuel supply loss in spite of the gauges reading an adequate supply onboard. The failure of the aircraft engine occurred due to the fuel vents being completely blocked by some old debris that had accumulated and compacted.

Sometimes, the loss of one engine in a twin-engine aircraft is not always critical. Except, this happened on a warm day, and the air ambulance was heavily loaded. Typically, these are not ideal conditions for many helicopters, especially those that fly low and slow on one good engine rather than the two that normally produce the total power needed for this type of aircraft.

As a result, the pilot had to find a place to land, quickly. Luckily for them, there was a small airport immediately located to the left of their position. Jermaine distinctly remembered hearing the failed engine winding down and losing power as the aircraft descended. Although it was an emergency, the touchdown was almost uneventful, with the exception of there being one less engine running. The unscheduled landing induced a slight delay. The transport team had to wait for a dispatched ground vehicle, commonly referred to as a 'rig' to pick them up. The ground ambulance crew drove them to the community hospital to complete the mission, while the helicopter crew remained behind at the small airport with the failed engine rescue aircraft. When Jermaine finally returned to Pleasant Hills Medical Center safely with their patient, he decided he'd had enough of flying in helicopters.

·　·　•　●　●　⬤　●　●　•　·　·

"Who was flying that day? Who was the pilot?" David asked Chuck, as Jermaine mentally recalled the details of that eventful day.

"Stephan Moure was working as the first call pilot that day. He was flying," Chuck quickly answered, "and Sherry Jones and Paul Keabor were with him." The Vietnam War Veteran added, "Paul was up front with Stephan and Sherry was in the back with the transport team. But I don't know which transport team members were on the flight." Chuck quietly nodded back in response.

"It was Dana Blackwood, Dr. Nguyen, and me," Jermaine quickly spoke up.

"Oh…" everyone reacted in almost perfect unison. Jermaine

had everyone's attention, but he just continued to stare at the cabin floor. He had no further comment.

"That's right, you were on that call," Kristen said, breaking the slight moment of uncomfortable quiet. "I remember, Dana told me." She looked around the cabin at the others as she spoke "You know, she didn't even realize what happened until they landed at that little airport." Kristen gestured with her hands as she smiled and recalled the time she and Dana talked about what had happened that day. "She told me the pilot blurted out something about putting the helicopter down, but she just figured they were landing at the hospital. When they landed at that little airport, Dana was like… 'This isn't the hospital!' She was clueless!" Her animated, candid remark got a few courtesy laughs from the rest of the crewmembers.

"Yeah," Jermaine's heavy accented voice came over the intercom, "she didn't even know what was going on. But I heard him and understood what he was saying. Know what I'm saying? Yo, he said that he <u>had</u> to put it down right <u>now</u>!" The respiratory therapist shook his head as he recalled that moment. "When he said that, I immediately knew something was wrong. Know what I mean?" Jermaine said as he continued to stare at the cabin floor of the same medical transport helicopter he was sitting in that day, remembering the details.

"Well, everything is all fixed now, right Chuck?" Mary quickly spoke up in a confident, reassuring tone of voice. She looked back over her shoulder towards the cockpit.

"Yup, you bet. It was really a minor problem. It's been fixed, and everything is just fine. That landing was really precautionary," the pilot answered on cue. "It's all good."

"See, what did I tell you?" Mary smiled at Jermaine. "It's all good, honey."

"Yeah, it's no big deal." Jermaine looked up at the flight nurse with a content smile and remarked, "That's just the way life is sometimes."

On the outside, he was all smiles. However, deep inside his mind he really wanted nothing else than to be back on solid ground. Jermaine sat in his seat of the helicopter looking forward to a safe landing back at Pleasant Hills Medical Center.

"Wow, it's so quiet on the radio this morning. I think we're the only ones up here right now." The pilot's voice was heard over the intercom as the transport team members continued monitoring their little patient. "I don't think there's any traffic between us and the medical center. I'm gonna check in with So Cal Approach." The subtle, inherent vibration of the helicopter softly reverberated the sound of his professional intonation, as he politely informed the crew, "We'll be landing pretty soon, guys."

The sporty rescue helicopter smoothly sailed across the vast, clear blue sky with little Jeremy onboard and sound asleep. The twin turboshaft engine aircraft was absolutely undisturbed by the slightest hint of turbulence this morning, seemingly hoisted aloft on a perfectly constructed and sturdy pillar of air. Visibility was unlimited above the rolling hills of the evergreen forested terrain from horizon to horizon. The veteran pilot of the air ambulance effortlessly navigated his way over an impressive, breathtaking view of the mountain resort community below. With the considerable exception of Jermaine, each occupant of the rescue aircraft was actually quite comfortable and content. Indeed, this was a very smooth flight. Practically the only sensation of forward movement in the medevac helicopter was evidenced by the flourishing green earth of the mountain community resort passing steadily beneath its path. Chuck, the senior aviator of Inland Air Medical Transport, was definitely correct in his statement about how beautiful the morning was. He was correct to say it was a great day for flying, most definitely. There was no other air traffic between them and the Pleasant Hills Medical Center helipad, less than twenty minutes away now. According to Chuck, the sky was all theirs.

· · • · • • ● ● ● · • · • · · ·

However, the experienced pilot did not have all the facts entirely correct. Technically, they were not really all alone in the sky. As the air ambulance helicopter made its way to the medical center with little Jeremy onboard, a silent, floating spherical aberration systematically followed them. Interestingly, it was the very same mysterious and transparent anomaly Jorge and his father, Gustavo, had unexpectedly encountered. The unseen thing seemed to take an interest in the rescue aircraft flying overhead. It was traveling about 300 feet behind the flashy green and silver helicopter. The silent, anomalous sphere slowly closed the distance on the rescue aircraft and the occupants onboard the medevac helicopter had not a clue.

Chapter Sixteen

uring his morning break, Brandon Morris sat quietly at his desk in a cozy corner office at the Lexus/Toyota of Orange automobile dealership enjoying a fresh, ripe Bartlett pear and reading the local newspaper. He had just taken another bite of the delicious fruit when he noticed someone walking past his office. Brandon glanced up from the newspaper to see his coworker, Gary Purdy, walking casually by on the other side of the full-length glass window. Gary, one of the dealership's salespersons, was a very reserved and friendly gentleman, and Brandon enjoyed working with him. Gary smiled and gave Brandon a quick nod. Through the open vertical blinds, Gary could see Brandon sitting at the desk inside his comfy, finance manager's office. Brandon's response was a quick nod of the head in return, and then he turned his attention back to the newspaper. He had just finished an article about a beautiful young rhythm-and-blues singer and actress who was tragically killed in an airplane crash in the Bahamas several days ago. The sexy and very talented young woman was on the brink of sheer superstardom at the time of her untimely demise. The article in the paper announced that the late singer sensation's funeral was today, August 31, at the Saint Ignatius Loyola Church in New York. Her self-titled third album had just gone platinum barely twenty-four hours before she was being interred.

"Damn," Brandon murmured to himself, "Rest in peace, baby girl. I love you." He shook his head and frowned, "What a terrible shame. We all love you. You'll be missed."

Brandon took a generous bite of the pear and skimmed down

the page to read another article in the local news section of the paper. There he found a brief piece about an armed robbery that occurred not too far from his residence. The article mentioned two young men were held at gunpoint inside their vehicle and robbed of their cash and some personal possessions but were neither car-jacked nor injured. The three suspects were still at large. One of them, the apparent gunman, had a clean-shaven-head, wore sunglasses, and had a peculiar tattoo over his left eyebrow. According to the police, the suspects mentioned in this case fit the description of perpetrators involved in several other similar crimes that had recently occurred in the local area. The Long Beach Police Department requested that anyone who had witnessed this crime or had any additional information to contact the local authorities immediately.

Brandon was about to take another bite of the pear when his red Nokia 8210 cell phone began to ring. The office had been so quiet that the catchy monophonic ringtone he had set for his friend's caller ID startled him. He quickly picked up the mobile phone from the top of his desk.

"Hello." Brandon pressed the cell phone close to his ear with one hand and held the half-eaten pear in the other hand.

"Bro, what's up, man? How have you been, Brandon?" Anthony Bornermere's excited voice filled the wireless device.

His electrified greeting instantly put a smile on his buddy Brandon's face. Brandon leaned back against the camel colored leather of his high back executive chair and answered,

"Hey man, I'm good. What's up with you?" he asked Anthony. "Are you out sailing your yacht around Mexico like you got nothing better to do with yourself?" Brandon chuckled uncontrollably "So tell me, Christopher Columbus, is the world really flat?" They both laughed aloud.

Anthony spoke up, "Actually, that's kind of what I'm calling about." He cleared his throat after the hearty laughter they shared. "Hey man, I just wondered if you still want to bring your family south of the border for a few days. Hillary and I won't be able to get out there in a few weeks as we originally planned. One of Hillary's good friends that she has known since high school was engaged recently. Anyway, a bunch of girls, including the bride to be and Hillary, are all going to Las Vegas for a huge bachelorette party in a few weeks." Anthony cleared his throat again. "So, we're not going to Mexico as planned in a few weeks. We're not totally putting it off, though. We're just gonna go some time after she gets back from Las Vegas, dude."

Brandon leaned forward and put the half-eaten pear on top of the open newspaper as his friend continued to speak.

"So, I just wanted to say, you can still go anytime you want. You don't have to wait for us, bro. We can still meet you down there in San Carlos Bay if you want to go later, too. But don't wait for us. And I'll still pay for your flights, dude." Just then Brandon heard someone else over Anthony's cell phone.

"Hold on, bro…" Brandon heard his friend having a very short conversation with what sounded like an older woman. The soft, elegant voice was familiar. Brandon thought it might be Anthony's mother. It sounded like she was talking about something business related to her son. "Yeah, okay, I'll take care of that one, no problem ma," Anthony replied to his mother and then returned his full attention to Brandon.

"Sorry about that, dude. Anyway, you can still use the condo. I'm just letting you know, bro."

"Okay man, that sounds good," Brandon replied. "I'm going to talk to the wife about it. And don't worry about the tickets. I can get those. I do appreciate it though."

Just then, Brandon heard Anthony's office phone start ringing in the background.

"Oh, hey, I've got to get that." Anthony's tone of voice changed and he suddenly seemed a little preoccupied. He quickly said, "Brandon, give me a call anytime so I can arrange getting your airline tickets before you and the family head down there."

"Okay, but Anthony, you don't have to…"

"Okay bro?" Anthony interrupted in his all too familiar informal and glibly nonchalant tone of voice. "Just give me a call anytime on those tickets. Peace out, bro!" The connection silently terminated. Brandon looked at the suddenly dead phone.

"Okay…well, uh…" he mumbled even though he knew there was no one on the other end. In today's modern world, this way of ending a phone conversation was widespread. Nobody said good-bye any longer. He resolved to just chuckling aloud. Brandon looked up at the ceiling, slowly shaking his head. "Anthony is the most hip millionaire I know," he said out loud. Brandon thought about his best friend. *He's always doing something. Mister-party over here… party over there.* He started to place the mobile phone back on top of the desk when it started ringing again, this time with his mother's caller alert tone.

"Hello mother." Brandon smiled as he answered. How are you this beautiful morning?"

"Aloha Brandon!" He was very happy to hear his mother's cheerful voice. "How's my little bubba?" Linda Morris was of course, referring to her little grandson.

"He's fine, mom. He misses you and grandpa." Brandon smiled.

"Listen, your father and I want to have you all over for dinner. Your father is going to grill outside, and we can give Houston his gift when he comes over." Linda was talking quickly. "So, when do you and Donnette plan to have his party? I will just make the dinner a week later."

"Oh, uh…" Brandon looked up at the ceiling and thought about it.

"Oh listen, I already got his birthday present." Brandon's mother quickly interrupted. In an eager and excited tone of voice, she said, "I got that Dinosaur Land jumbo play set Donnette told me about!" Linda half gasped, "It was on sale at Toys-R-Us!"

"Okay mom, that's real good. That's just what Houston wants." Brandon leaned forward and picked his pear up from the desktop. "He's going to just love that," he said, taking a good bite. Just then, Brandon heard his father talking in the background over Linda's cell phone. He took another quick bite of his pear as he tried to make out what was being said.

"Okay, honey," his mom said softly to her husband.

Brandon was curious, but he could not clearly hear the conversation in the background between his mother and father.

"Brandon?" Linda quickly returned to their conversation and instructed, "I will call Donnette today. Please, make sure you ask her if it is okay to have a little get together the week after his birthday party. I know it's still a few weeks away, but I want to get it planned early for everyone. Okay, dear?" She drew in a quick breath and continued talking before Brandon could make a reply, "Oh, I have an incoming call," she said in a hurried manner. "I think it's your brother. Your father says, hi. Okay, got to go now. Aloha!"

"Oh, okay," Brandon replied with his mouth half full of fruit. "I need to give Brian a call, too." He chewed as he waited for his mother's next response. However, once again the wireless line was silent. Brandon put the cell phone down on his desk and took the last bite of his pear.

· · · • • ● • • · ·

Linda was very knowledgeable about how to use her cell phone. She knew its capabilities much better than her husband knew how to use his. As she quickly answered the call-waiting feature, she thought of how, on occasion, James inadvertently hung up on her when his phone was brand new. She shook her head and smiled in reflective amusement as she answered the incoming call.

"Aloha, Brian! Good morning handsome!" Linda happily greeted the incoming caller ID on her mobile phone. It was indeed, her youngest son.

"Aloha mom," Brian happily greeted in reply, "how's Hawaii?"

"Oh, it's so wonderful, son. I wish you were here. You should have come with us," Linda answered sincerely, although she fully understood when Brian had changed his mind about traveling with his parents after Gina broke up with him unexpectedly. Nonetheless, she still wanted her son to come along. Linda did not want Brian to mope about the break-up and be all alone. She had tried to persuade him the day before they left on vacation, but to no avail.

"I know," Brian said calmly. "It's okay. I'll go next time." The young man cleared his throat and continued. "Anyway, I'm just calling to say everything is okay here. I see you tried to call me a couple times. I listened to your latest message. Everything is cool, mom. Mr. Doodles is fine. Everything is just fine." He kept his voice even to reassure his mom.

"Well, that's nice to hear, dear. I'll tell you what," Linda said. "If you change your mind, you can fly over here anytime. Just let me know and I'll take care of it. Is that okay with you?" There was a slight pause in their conversation before her youngest son replied.

"Mom… uh…" Brian began to speak, but he could not follow through with what he had intended to say.

The words somberly halted at his lips like an oversized window shutting out a cold draft on a blustery winter's day. He had an immense and undeniable compulsion to tell his mother everything that had occurred the previous evening. For a split-second he was actually about to say something about his encounter with the aliens. He really wanted to share this surreal first contact experience with her or anybody else that would listen, for that matter. Brian felt as if he seriously could not contain himself. The secret discovery he had made revealing the existence of intelligent, extraterrestrial life was confounding and overwhelming and he desperately needed to satisfy the urge to tell everything. The compelling urge churned heavily as an aching sentiment deep within him. Brian wanted to scream aloud to the world that the aliens existed. He knew it would disprove and prove many different things, all at the same time. He knew that life on earth would never be the same again. However, he thought of the serious consequences and bare minimum benefits of saying anything. His feelings regarding this matter had not changed since his first encounter with the extraterrestrials. Brian sincerely believed that human society would surely bequeath fear and the wrath of discrimination as cause and effect from this happenstance, extraterrestrial encounter. He could not rationalize or realistically guarantee their safety; either that of the outer space aliens, or the people of earth. He still felt he should mention nothing about the aliens' existence at this point. So he simply could not tell his mother; at least, not right now.

"Yes, dear?" Linda asked calmly. "What is it?"

There was a slight moment of silence before Brian answered, "I was just thinking."

Brian searched for something else to say, but the aliens were all he could think about. He sincerely felt isolated having this new knowledge of the furtive extraterrestrials' unceremonious and unsanctioned visit to planet earth.

"Um…" Brian searched for something relevant to say to replace the thoughts of the newfound celestial existence that he desperately wanted to disclose. He tried to think of anything, or rather something that would not give away what he really wanted to discuss with his mother at this time. Then something came to mind, arriving just in time, like the U.S. Calvary reinforcing a troop against an invading hostile foe. He finally had something to say.

"Would you and dad mind if I purchase a pay per view program tonight? There is a special end of summer concert, and one of the bands will be Matchbox Twenty." The words flowed out of his mouth almost uncontrollably, like a flood waxing down a barren, dry, precipitous hillside.

"Oh, I know who they are." Brian's mother said. "You got me their CD for my birthday last year. What was the other CD I like that I got from you? Um…?"

"Dave Matthew's Band, mom," Brian replied.

"Oh yes, them, too. I like them a lot."

Brian chuckled. "Good mom. One of these days, we'll have to go and see one of those groups in concert in L.A. together. I think you'll like that."

"I want to see Santana!" she replied categorically. "He's been around making noise since before you were born!" Brian began to chuckle aloud as his mother added, "Your dad and I went to one of his concerts a long time ago." Linda could not help but join her son in repartee laughter as she acclaimed, "We were just as hip when we were you and your brother's age, you know. Matter of fact, we still are."

"Yes mom, no doubt. You guys are still cool."

"That's right young man, and don't you forget it."

There was more laughter from the two and then Brandon could hear his father saying something to his mother in the background.

Then his father said loudly, "They wish they were as cool as we are!" There was more laughter. James knew that his youngest son had heard what he just said.

Brian was still smiling and listening to his mother and father laugh aloud when he received an in-coming call. "Oh, hey mom?" he said, "I have an incoming call."

"Sure son." Linda was still chuckling. "I'll talk to you later then. Take care."

· · · • ● ● ● • · · ·

Brian could still hear his father chuckling and commenting in the background as he answered the incoming call.

"Hello? This is Brian."

"Yo Brian, what up?" a very recognizable voice greeted him. "How've you been?"

"Whassup, Jermaine?" Brian emphatically replied.

"Yeah, yeah," Jermaine quickly answered. "I'm good. I'm at work right now. I got shift report from your boy Danny this morning."

"Oh yeah?" Brian was all smiles. "How's he doing?"

"Good, man. He's good." Jermaine then asked, "What are you up to tonight, man?"

Brian casually glanced around the family room and at the computer in front of him before leaning back in the mahogany desk chair. "Nothing much man," he said with a sigh, "Just relaxing here at my parent's house. Why, what's up? What's crackin'?"

"You know Greg Matsudo, the floor secretary for the Mental Wellness Inpatient unit?"

"Yeah, I know who he is. That part-time guy for the psych

ward. The Asian dude that goes to school at Cal State San Bernardino. He's a senior I think."

"Yes, he's a Psychology major," Jermaine added, "That's him. I think he plans on doing an internship at the hospital on the psych ward, too. Anyway, he is like, really into jazz. I think he used to play keyboards in a jazz group a year ago, too."

"Okay, yes I think he told me that once."

"Anyway, he says tonight is the night to go to 'Sparks'. You know, that little club on Hospitality Row."

"That hip-hop spot?"

"Yeah, that's the one. Saturday nights are hip-hop, but Friday nights are live jazz."

Excitement crept into Jermaine's east coast accent. "Well, I'm not working tomorrow and, since this is my weekend off, I'm going to hear me some jazz tonight. And yo, check this out, the owner of the club is Greg's uncle. He's going to hook us up with some drinks and food, and of course there won't be no cover charge. I can't pass that up. Know what I'm sayin'?"

"That sounds like a good time to me. Yes, I'm sure you guys will have a good time tonight." Brian chuckled. "Who's playing, a local band?"

"Yeah, somebody I never heard of. Greg told me, but I forgot the name of the group. Whatever, anyway, I don't care. I'm going out for a good time, know what I mean? And I want you to come, too," Jermaine said sincerely, then added, "Greg knows you, and I asked if it was okay if you could go with us. He said it was cool, man. In fact, he insisted you come along with us, Brian."

"Oh, uh…"

"Come on, Brian. You need to get out. There's no excuse man, you just told me you got nothing to do. And you don't have to pay for nothing. And, if you do, yo, I'll buy it."

Brian thought for a moment before responding. "Okay. Why not? I'll drive down there and meet you guys. Just tell me what time."

"That's what I'm talkin' about!" Jermaine was excited. "Okay, be there at eight tonight man. I'll be there a little early, so

I'll most likely be at the bar. I'll be lookin' for you and, if need be, I got your drinks tonight."

"Okay, see you guys tonight." Brian said.

"Later," Jermaine acknowledged, and hung up the phone in one of the empty PICU rooms he was using to talk to his friend.

· · • • ● • • · ·

Brian felt good. He was happy he had something to do tonight to keep him busy. He needed something to keep his mind off the fact that he and Gina were supposed to be together in Hawaii right now. Brian needed the healthy distraction from the loneliness he felt on occasion. This was especially true during the weekends. He used to spend his free time with Gina so it was natural that's when he felt the worst. Thus, he did not want to be alone tonight. A night out with the boys would be good for a change, but there was, of course, something else to consider. What of the aliens? What evidence did Brian have that convinced him they would never return? Was their mission to earth truly completed? Or, was this the time in earth's history when mankind would become indubitably aware of the existence of intelligent extraterrestrial life? Brian could not help but wonder. He also wondered how many other people had seen them before.

The lower right hand corner of the Windows application desktop toolbar indicated the time was 11:21 a.m. Brian had just spent most of the past two hours searching the Internet, researching everything he could find about extraterrestrial life. Most of what he found was links to books he could purchase about the topic, but there were also various types of scientific literature about the topic, to his surprise. Many of the books and published reference materials had animated caricature drawings of strange looking creatures. However, absolutely nothing even remotely resembled the celestial beings he had encountered. Most everything he read thus far just seemed so fictitious in comparison to his unique, surreal experience. Some of the so-called research articles he'd seen online read more like cheesy tabloid stories found in some low budget periodical that focused on sensationalism. There was nothing really encouraging, and after a while, it all started to look the same; awfully fake.

There's nothing here that's even slightly useful. Brian frowned and silently shook his head. *There has to be something. Or am I truly the only one in the whole world that knows?*

Just then he felt something nudge his leg and then rub against his calf. Completely startled, he almost jumped out of his chair. He looked down with eyes wide and saw his mother's cat snuggling up to him.

"Doodles!" Brian half gasped. "You practically scared me to death." He immediately relaxed, assured there was no creature from outer space grabbing at him from under the desk. Brian reached down and gave the purring cat a little affection.

"How's that little buddy?" Brian smiled, lightly scratching at the back of the cat's neck.

Brian stood up and walked to the large, double-hung window to the right of the rear door. He looked outside through the two-inch eggshell colored vinyl blinds and the slender grill between the double pane glass. Once again, he wondered if the aliens actually went home and whether he would ever see them again. He didn't know what to do next. He stared out into the backyard. *I'll just chill out here watching TV until I go out tonight. Maybe there's something about them on the news or in a special documentary on the public access television channel. Maybe there's even something on the Discovery Channel. Maybe I'll find something related to their visit. If nothing else, I'll just entertain myself for the rest of the day.*

So, in addition to a couple of small naps and a few bathroom breaks, Brian spent much of the afternoon eating snacks and watching cable television. He just did not know what else to do.

Chapter Seventeen

An evening out with the boys turned out to be a very good idea, indeed. It was a lot of fun for Brian and he definitely needed that. He spent the evening relaxing, listening to good music, and enjoying pleasant conversation with his two friends from work. Greg and Jermaine entertained Brian most of the evening by making lighthearted fun of a few people at work, recalling their own innocuous and embarrassing situations, and just talking about anything humorous that came to mind. A good time was to be had tonight for sure, just unwinding in the laid-back ambiance of all the modish people who came to listen to the chic, live jazz music.

Brian didn't have a care in the world when he was with his friends from work. For the first hour of the evening, the young men enjoyed their favorite social beverages. Brian and Greg ordered a couple Guinness black lager beers. For Jermaine, Hennessey Cognac set the mood just right for this jazz-filled evening. By the time the set ended, there was still plenty of laughter to share along with stories about work, leisure, movies, sports, and life in general. The last hour of their evening together found them sipping cups of freshly brewed Columbian coffee. Pleasantly, all of this was had compliments of Greg's happy go lucky and sociable uncle Henry Matsudo who owned the trendy nightspot. By 11:18 p.m., the three gentlemen were outside the nightclub saying their goodbyes. They all promised to make the 'boy's evening out' a regular occasion. Then Greg went one direction, and Jermaine followed Brian in the opposite direction.

"Where did you park?" Jermaine asked as they walked along

the narrow pavement and passed a middle-aged couple holding hands, laughing, and playfully kissing.

"Excuse me," Jermaine said, and quickly stepped around them. The amorously occupied man and woman were oblivious to the minor impromptu intrusion and continued with their smooches and giggles.

"Oh, I think I remember them from inside the club," Jermaine chuckled lightly. "They were sitting at the other end of the bar, practically all over each other the whole night. I swear they were acting like a couple teenagers. Kissing and touching and carrying on. Know what I mean?"

The romantic couple was standing very close to each other, blissfully engrossed in their own little private conversation. They did not notice the two young men at all. Brian paid no attention to the couple as he pointed towards the parking lot.

"I'm over there." He stepped onto the asphalt and looked back at Jermaine. "Where're you at?"

"Uh…" Jermaine hesitated and looked around while he continued to follow his friend, "I think I'm over there, too."

The two friends walked alongside each other in silence through the adequately lit parking lot. Suddenly Brian asked his friend a profound and curious question.

"Jermaine?" Brian paused for a few seconds and then said, "Have you ever experienced something totally out of the ordinary in your life? Something you are sure no one has ever seen or would probably believe?"

Jermaine raised his eyebrows, the right one landed slightly higher than the other one. He looked at Brian.

"What do you mean?"

"I don't know," Brian said, suddenly acting disinterested in what he had just asked. "I was watching something stupid on cable TV. It's nothing." He changed the subject, resolved to be secretive about what he really had on his mind. "Here I am, right here," he said, pointing to his 1999 Toyota Tacoma. The clean and sporty V6 automatic extended cab truck with a surfside green mica paint color was parked just a few cars in front of them.

"Oh, okay." Jermaine craned his neck to the left and then

suddenly spotted his car. "I see my car over there." He pointed at his gold, 1998 Honda Accord LX parked two rows over.

They said goodbye, got into their own vehicles, and drove away. By the time Brian reached his parent's home he felt tired. He parked his truck in the driveway, stepped out of the vehicle, and immediately looked up at the glimmering stars in the beautiful night sky. He smiled as he thought of his alien friends. He also chuckled at a surreal and sobering thought. *I was inside their spaceship only twenty-four hours ago!* Brian gazed into the vastness of the brilliantly starlit night sky. What of the aliens now? Where were they? They were probably well on their way across the vast celestial stretches of the galaxy right now. He chuckled again and leaned against his truck staring into the nighttime heavens, wondering which direction they had taken, whether they were going home, and what part of the galaxy they were from.

He yawned aloud as he recalled all the recent events of his encounter with the extraterrestrials to the best of his memory. He concentrated, carefully trying to recall each detail of everything he had seen. The alien technology he had witnessed the night before was incontrovertibly the most unusual and most fascinating ever seen. There was the black ellipsoid spacecraft, so mysteriously alluring with all its weird symbols and bizarre flashing lights. He remembered the alien night vision glasses and smiled as he recollected how the world had looked so extraordinary with astonishing multi-hued detail through the lenses of the featherweight alien eyewear. Then he laughed aloud as he thought of the small, stealthy, floating chameleon orb drone. Brian's laughter quickly faded into silence as he recalled the first time he saw the creature. His muscles subconsciously tensed.

"Whew," he uttered aloud and shook his head. *That was truly an experience I'll never forget!*

Brian's eyes closed slowly as he precisely recalled each delightful detail of the exotic alien woman. He recollected her unusual and beautiful feminine physique and the way her flight suit hugged every curve of her alluring, mysterious, and shapely alien figure. Her remarkable amberous semblance was, indeed, uniquely captivating. She was so amazingly different and yet so wondrously striking in comparison to any earthly human female he had ever seen.

"Wow!" The young man uttered aloud out of sheer astonishment at the recollection. "She was so extraordinarily beautiful."

He sincerely thought just about any other witness to the fact would agree. Brian looked down at the concrete driveway and thought about how none of his suppositions had changed since the encounter. *I wonder if I will ever find out anything more about them. I wonder if they know everything there is to know about us. I wonder if they trust us. I wonder if they will come back to earth someday and come out of the dark so everyone in the world can see them.* These thoughts completely engrossed him.

A few minutes later Brian stood up straight, stretched his arms out wide over his head and yawned. Then he started towards the front door of his parent's home feeling a little disconcerted. It was actually a little frustrating to him that he did not have anyone else to share his very unique, surreal, and wondrous experience with. The young man felt as if there was no one else in the whole world he could talk to. Nobody would ever believe him, and in fact would consider his claim ludicrous and brand him a crazy person if he said he had seen intelligent extraterrestrial life. He wouldn't be able to share this. He would have to live with this heavy and truly mysterious secret for the rest of his life. If he had another chance to see the aliens, then maybe he could privilege one other very special person to have knowledge of the aliens existence. Then Brian would always have someone with whom he could share the secret of this first contact. However, what were the odds now of that happening? Quite frankly, he was unsure whether he would ever again see his special visitors from outer space.

Brian entered his parent's house and sat down at the computer in the family room. For an hour and a half he searched the Internet, determined to find any information he could about his mysterious celestial visitors. His second search on the information highway was just like the first search earlier that day.

There was nothing even remotely useful. To be quite honest, he was not the least bit surprised. He was becoming somewhat convinced of the distinct possibility that no one had ever seen the aliens before. It was a reasonable assumption by now. Brian did not know what to do next. He paced back and forth in the family room and the kitchen trying to think of where he could find information about someone having an experience similar to the one he had last night.

Maybe I'll go to the San Bernardino Library, or even the Central Public Library in Los Angeles. Brian rubbed his chin slowly in solemn contemplation. *There just might be something related to these aliens' recent visit that no one has any idea about or truly realizes, yet. There might be a strange photograph or a bizarre video, or radar data, or something. Maybe there's something remotely related that someone saw or wrote about in a journal.* He did not want to give up his search for something this significant and historic, not just yet.

Brian finally sat down on the family room sofa after fifteen minutes of pacing. He glanced at his watch. The time was 1:15 a.m. on the first day of the month of September 2001. He looked towards the rear door thinking about what he should do next. He considered going outdoors to see if the alien spacecraft was still where he had last seen it. However, he quickly had second thoughts, and for good reason, too.

"I'm not going out there tonight. That's for sure." What else might he find there in the darkened forest in the middle of the night? What if other creatures loomed in the darkness? "No, I'm not going out there right now. Forget it. Maybe tomorrow during the day, but not now." Brian relaxed, and laid back against the velvet cushion of the sofa and before long drifted off to sleep.

· · · • ● ● ● • · ·

In the late evening hours, a lone truck drove along the windy mountain curves of Highway 189, its headlights the only source of illumination in the still darkness of the wilderness area around Lake Arrowhead. The driver was keenly focused on a dimly lit neighborhood straight ahead of him, about a mile away. The young man behind the wheel was beginning to feel very tired now and he was really looking forward to the end of this long drive home. In a few minutes, he would be there. The only thing between him and a comfortable bed was the winding pavement beneath him, which he steadily negotiated his vehicle along. The tall evergreen trees along the side of the road faded quickly into the night as his headlights passed by.

Something caught his attention. For a split-second, something was visible in the left corner of the rearview mirror. The young man quickly glanced up into the mirror expecting to see something. There was nothing. The only thing visible was the dark winding pavement he had just traversed. The young man quickly looked forward again, making sure he was driving safely within the single lane on his side of the narrow roadway. He prepared to take the curve ahead when something suddenly and unexpectedly appeared in his peripheral vision immediately to the left. He clearly heard the sound of pounding footsteps coming from the blackness of the night. The driver looked out his side window. His heart leapt at the sight of some alien creature running effortlessly alongside his truck at almost 50 miles per hour. The beast growled and leaned forward until its face nearly touched the window, its maroon eyes locked on his. A chill ran down the young man's spine and he jerked away from the window. The creature abruptly slowed its pace. Terrified, the driver watched the beast suddenly dash across the dark and empty opposing traffic lane and come to an abrupt stop, staring directly at him. In that instant the frightened young driver remembered the curve ahead and turned just in time to see he was upon it. *I might not make this.* He hit the brakes, grasping the steering wheel tightly and instinctively turning to the left. The truck started to swerve, tires squealing. He panicked and lost control of the vehicle, sure he would crash into the steep, rocky embankment to the right. All his muscles instinctively tensed and he clenched his teeth. He prepared himself for impact against the large rocks as the truck's tires skidded off the road onto the gravel shoulder of the narrow roadway.

At that precise, frightening moment, Brian awoke. He sat up and leaned forward from the couch all at once, eyes wide open. He looked hastily around the family room and then down at his clenched hands. It was as if he still grasped the steering wheel. The young man opened his hands wide and laid them in his lap. He breathed deeply and exhaled in relief. It was all a dream. *Good Lord!* He rubbed the back of his neck with trembling hands and then leaned back against the cushioned sofa and tried to relax.

"Chill out, man," he said out loud. "It's just a dream." Brian took a few deep breaths and calmed down. There was nothing to worry about. It never happened.

The time on his watch showed 1:49 a.m. now. He walked to the large window beside the rear entryway door and peeked out between the blinds into the dark rear lot, thinking about the dream he just had. Brian could not help but chuckle. *That stupid space-wolf beast is even in my dreams*. He shook his head to clear away the last vestiges of the dream and then walked to the computer to do more research online, but he was just not in the mood. He turned off the desktop PC and monitor and looked around the family room. The house was so quiet. He turned on the television. The background noise of the large twenty-seven inch Panasonic television provided some pseudo companionship.

Brian turned off the lights in the kitchen and the family room and then plopped down on the couch. Only the soft glare of the television filled the room, now. He stared at the television in silence, watching an infomercial about a diet pill made for people interested in losing weight quickly. From what Brian could see, any consumer could take the pill and successfully lose pounds without ever having to exercise. The paid programming advertisement boasted positive results with affirmed testimonials from men and women who looked like they had actually been working out all their life. The overly excited subjects also claimed you did not even have to change your eating habits.

Brian chuckled and shook his head. He was no subject matter pundit, but he reasonably figured that many people would probably buy the infamous diet wonder pills and eventually be dissatisfied. He knew that rather than get a refund, most would just consider it a waste of time. *That's the way this world is. People want something for nothing, and others want to sell you nothing for something.* Brian leaned his head back on the couch and closed his eyes. There was nothing in his world that concerned him.

He thought only of his beautiful extraterrestrial lady friend; her warm infectious smile, her soothing melodious tone of voice, and her mysterious and enchanting alien eyes.

Chapter Eighteen

Brian's forehead rested lazily in the palm of his left hand. His other hand searched through the call log on his cellular phone for the most recent call. He lifted the phone up closer to his face and stared at the backlit display in bewilderment. He was feeling a little confused, because he was positive his mother had called last, but the received calls history was blank.

"You ready for another?" Brian looked up. With a very friendly smile the bartender said, "Would you like another beer?" He leaned forward over the polished wooden bar and pointed at Brian's empty glass.

"Uh…" Brian looked down at the empty glass with a confused look on his face. He looked up at the bartender who was gesturing with one finger in a polite insinuation to deliver another alcoholic beverage.

"Sure," Brian said, happily conceding.

The server nodded once, retrieved the empty glass, and turned towards the beer tap. Brian quickly glanced around at his surroundings. He instantly recognized the place and the bartender. He was back in the restaurant where Gina suddenly became upset and walked out on him the other night. *But, that was a dream, right?* Brian raised an eyebrow in puzzled deliberation and with a very perplexed look on his face, turned completely around on his barstool and surveyed the large restaurant.

"Here you go sir." Brian turned around as the bartender gently pushed a full glass of pale lager in front of him.

"Thanks," Brian responded, and nodded.

"By the way," the bartender leaned forward and discreetly

said, "The lady at the end of the bar would like to speak with you. She asked me to tell you." The bartender squinted and turned his head to one side slightly as he added, "Actually, she said, 'tell him to come sit here, now.'"

He inconspicuously nodded in her direction at the other end of the bar. Brian looked down one side of the polished bar and then the other. Several people were sitting close together, involved in their own conversations. However, it did not take Brian more than a few seconds to see the lady the bartender meant. There she was, staring directly at him and there was no doubt who the woman was.

She was the same beautiful young Asian lady Brian saw that night Gina got so upset. How could he forget the slim and lavishly attractive woman with the shiny black hair that hung like a curtain to her waist? Out of sheer curiosity, Brian picked up his glass of beer and strolled around the bar. He passed other people engrossed in their own conversation as he made his way towards the end of the bar where the mysterious woman sat. She made a polite gesture for him to sit on the empty barstool next to her. As Brian stepped closer, he noticed an attentive expression of sincerity in her eyes. She was very attractive. Brian noticed she was wearing the very same tight, silky, emerald color dress from the first eventful encounter. Her long legs were crossed and she sat up straight and regal, and as glamorous as any consummate lady could be. She continued to stare quietly at him with a demure smile on her face as he settled into the comfortable chair next to her.

"Welcome Brian." Her smooth salutation was heavily accented, yet appealing. "We talk now."

"This is a dream. You aren't real, are you?" Brian interposed quickly. "I mean, I didn't really have an argument with my girlfriend. I mean, uh… my ex-girlfriend."

He stumbled over his words as he looked into her eyes and grimaced in confusion. This moment seemed very real to him, but was it, really? He was not actually sure right now. Perhaps the last time he saw this woman was real. All he could remember to discount this reality was the sound of his cell phone waking him up. However, he could not remember at all what happened right before he fell asleep. When he woke up, he remembered seeing the extraterrestrials in his parent's family room. Brian tried to remember anything related to that bizarre evening, but his mind was foggy with uncertainty. He just couldn't be sure about anything because this moment seemed so real.

Brian held up his hand and said, "Okay, wait a second." She raised an eyebrow. "The last thing I remember is going out with my friends." He looked up at the ceiling as he thought about it some more. "Then, I went back to my parent's place."

"You are with me now, Brian. Your girlfriend is not with you," the woman softly interjected as she continued to stare at him. "Do you understand me, Brian?" Her eyes were locked on his.

"Yes," Brian answered, though he felt confused and unsure if this encounter was real.

He studied his surroundings, taking everything in, and then his gaze settled on the bartender who turned to look at him. Brian suddenly remembered he was the same bartender who told him his phone had fallen to the floor.

"Can I get you something, sir?" the barkeep asked politely.

"No thanks, we're good," Brian answered. But then he turned to the Asian lady and noticed she didn't have a beverage. "Would you like a drink or something?" She paused for a second and then slowly shook her head.

"We talk now," she insisted calmly and politely.

"Sure," Brian said, reaching for his glass of pale lager. He brought it up to his lips. The cold glass felt so surprisingly real that he paused for a moment, uncertain what was real, and what was fantasy. He took a sip. The taste was a veridical delight to him.

"Hmmm…" he said with raised eyebrows, "that's good." He took a bigger sip. *I don't remember drinking the first glass though.* He put down the beer and turned his attention to the beautiful young Asian woman.

"That feels and tastes real!" He smiled and pointed at the glass of beer. He looked down at his arms. He rubbed one and then pinched himself. "Okay, that feels real." He looked up at the quiet young Asian woman who was staring at him with a very curious look on her face. "Here," Brian reached out his arm towards her, "pinch me," he insisted.

The beautiful lady turned her head to one side slightly and stared for a moment. Then she pinched his right forearm. Brian reacted instantly.

"Ouch!" He pulled his arm back. "Okay, I definitely felt that."

"We talk now, Brian," she said, looking into his eyes.

Brian rubbed his arm gently to relieve the pain and said, "Okay, sure. We can start with a formal introduction. Apparently, you know me, but I don't know you." He held out his hand. "My name is Brian, as you already know, and you are…?"

"My name is Baouzhe." She looked down and stared at his open hand for a slight moment before slowly reaching forward to take his hand in a mutual shake.

"Bah-oozhh." Brian attempted to say her name.

"Baouzhe," she replied without expression. Her pronunciation was exacting and crisp in her foreign tongue.

"Forgive me, but I don't think we've met before. I'm sure I would remember meeting someone so pretty." Brian tried to make pleasant conversation. He had no idea who she was. "Do you work at the medical center?" he inquired politely.

"You know who I am." The young man stared closely at her face, trying to place where he could have possibly seen her before.

"I'm sorry," he said and shook his head, "I can't remember meeting you, Miss Baouzhe."

She sat perfectly still, just staring into his brown eyes. There was not much expression with her reply.

"I am here to represent what you have seen. You know who I am."

"Okay." Brian chuckled. "From where? From here? This bar?"

The woman paused for a moment. Then she slowly raised her left arm and pointed up over her head towards the ceiling.

"Okay, so…" Brian looked up at her finger and then returned his gaze to her mysterious and beautiful eyes. "What does that mean, exactly?"

At the precise moment he said it, a feeling of acute presentiment overwhelmed him and he realized what she was trying to say. He stared into her beautiful dark brown eyes as she squarely responded to his courteous reservation.

"I am here to represent who you know. I am here, so we can talk now."

He wanted to believe her. He really wanted to see the aliens again, especially the mysterious but kindly humanoid woman. He felt he was just getting to know and understand them when they simply left. Just as unceremoniously as he had found them, they departed.

"Are you kidding me?" he said with equitable skepticism. "You don't look like them at all. Are you really one of them? Is this beautiful woman-look a clever disguise so you can hide among us humans?" He gestured in animation and then said, "Are you some kind of android spying on us?" He frowned in confusion. "What exactly do you mean by, I know who you are? I beg your pardon, but I am positive that I have never seen you before, miss. I would definitely remember if I had met a pretty lady like you." He winked at the unsmiling, mysterious woman.

"This first conversation will be to establish our intentions and make sure we can trust each other. We must make it known what we are thinking by our communications here." She gave Brian an attractive, agreeable smile. The young man automatically smiled in return. Baouzhe was kindly trying to convey much sincerity. "You believe me, yes?"

"I…" Brian did not know how to respond. He looked at her smiling face with his mouth agape, searching for words.

"You must trust me, Brian."

"Well…"

"Yes? Do you have a question for me? What would you like to know first? I will share some information to help you understand. It will help us build a relationship. We need to, because we talk now. We must establish trust, Brian." She calmly encouraged him. The young man finally had something to say.

"The last time I saw you my girlfriend Gina got upset with me." Brian looked down towards the floor. "Funny thing about that. See, I'm not with my girlfriend, uh, fiancée anymore. I mean, it all seemed so real at the time, just like now. But we split up several weeks ago. So, some of this doesn't make sense. Also, I can't remember how I got here last time, or how and when I left. I don't know how I got here right now, for that matter. So, this must be a dream, right?"

He returned his gaze to the mysterious Asian woman's eyes for some answers to his very logical query.

"Brian, you must trust me." The beautiful lady leaned forward and said, "We mean you no harm. We must continue our mission. It is a mission of peace. I think you can help us." Brian opened his mouth to speak, but did not know how to respond. "I know you have many questions." Baouzhe continued, "I will respond to all your questions." She leaned back very slowly and smiled.

Brian was beginning to feel a little more anxious right now. His mind was in a complete state of disorder, like an old dilapidated belfry filled with crazed bats.

"I don't know what to think," he replied, reaching for his beer. He took a good-sized swallow and followed that with another smaller gulp of the brisk golden lager. "I don't know if this place is real or not, but I can say that I do like this beer!"

Baouzhe had no reply to that. She simply looked at the glass with a curious expression on her face. She slowly returned her gaze to him.

"You trust me, yes?"

Something about the way she said that, and the way she was staring at him now made him feel even more anxious.

"Sure," Brian replied, although deep down inside he knew that Baouzhe knew how he really felt.

Brian did not trust, nor believe what he heard. He felt this was simply all just a very intense dream. The young man figured he would make the most of it while he was here, though. He quietly reached for his glass of beer and took another generous drink of the cold beverage.

"Mmmm, I'm really liking this brew, man." He placed the glass back on the bar. He felt the woman watching his every move. "Miss Baouzhe," Brian said, "you don't really say much, and you stare a lot. You are a very mysterious and beautiful woman. I get the feeling you are studying me."

"I am sorry. "I do not mean to make you feel uncomfortable," she insisted pleasantly, "I am here with you in peace. You can trust me, Brian."

"It's all good," the young man smiled and replied, "I just want you to know I also mean you no harm. You don't have to get your guard up." He leaned forward a little and added, "You seem a little uptight. You know what I think? I think you need to have some of this beer and relax." Brian pointed at his beverage.

The young Asian woman leaned toward Brian, again. She raised her voice a little as she spoke.

"Brian, you must trust me so we can work together. If you help us, we can do something for you that can benefit your people. We are happy to do that for you. We are here on a mission of peace."

Brian smirked. "The best thing you can do is stay out of sight." His face changed to a much more serious expression. "Many people don't really like change. They don't accept things that they can't understand or things that are very different. People are generally selfish, and if you try to do something kind, it would just backfire. This society is dangerous to itself."

He reached for the glass of beer and took another drink. It did not matter to Brian if he said what he really felt. He figured this must be happening in a dream; a dream about everything he had been thinking of recently. He figured this intense delusion was a direct reflection of the feelings of frustration he held bottled up tight inside his mind. Maybe playing out this dream was a way of releasing his feelings of frustration, along with his anxiety. Brian's response surprised Baouzhe.

"What are you saying, Brian?" She widened her eyes slightly.

"You will not help us?" she inquired in a perplexed tone. "You will not trust me?"

"Of course I'll help." Brian smiled reassuringly. "I'm just saying don't do anything special for these people here on Earth. We don't need anything right now from you. Besides, people would just find a way to take advantage of your generosity and mess things up. Seriously, I really mean it." He shook his head slowly. "Whatever you do, please don't involve anyone else."

Baouzhe just stared at him.

"But, I'm happy to help." He patted himself on the chest. "So," Brian raised his hands in a sincere gesture of goodwill, "what can I do for you?"

"You will help us, yes?" There was a hint of a smile on her face.

"I'll do whatever I can until I wake up, and then all of this won't really matter." His hand gestured to the two of them. "But hey, maybe I'll feel better about it somehow."

The woman raised an eyebrow and replied quaintly, "I believe, in order to get your full cooperation, you must do something simple for me, Brian." She put her hands on her lap and raised her chin a little. "You will look at me."

"Girl, I've been looking at you all night!" Brian quipped charmingly. He chuckled at his own jejune pun, but he stopped appropriately when he realized he was the only one humored by his response. Baouzhe stared at him in complete silence. He cleared his throat. "Okay, seriously, what do you want?" he calmly inquired, still smiling.

"First, you will look into my eyes closely Brian." Baouzhe moved her long and silky raven-black hair back away from her face and lifted her chin up so the young man could see clearly. Brian obligingly leaned forward to do so. The irises surrounding her pupils were a gorgeous dark brown, and they seemed to gleam like polished ornaments in the dimly lit bar setting.

"Come closer, tell me what you see, Brian," she encouraged.

"Uh…"

"Look closer," she said, and firmly grasped his arm.

The woman gently pulled him closer and suddenly Brian's

face was intimately close to hers. Dream or not, the experience was making the young man feel a little bit self-conscious right now. Regardless, he could not help but closely appraise her perfectly fair skin tone, her long thick eyelashes, her cute little narrow nose, her appealing small mouth, her glossy red lips, and how her beautiful and yet mysterious dark brown eyes shimmered. He blinked several times quickly as he casually took a couple precious seconds to draw in her delicate and delightfully arousing perfume through his nostrils. Dream or not, the experience seemed real enough for him to fully admire this treat to his senses.

"Brian," she said again, holding his arm firmly with one hand and holding her hair behind her neck with the other hand. "My eyes. Look into my eyes." The Asian lady was insistent on having Brian's complete attention to the matter. Baouzhe could immediately sense his mind was in a whirlwind wander, as he was not making direct eye contact with her. He was gazing about her face. "Can you see?" she asked, holding him close to her.

"Wow. This is some dream." Brian was very much enjoying this very atypical enchanting circumstance. His eyes were full of her, and he greatly approved of this delight.

He was in the midst of enjoying what seemed to be a rare and enchanting moment when Baouzhe very unexpectedly grabbed hold of his jaw and chin with the palm of her left hand. Clearly, she was a spontaneous and aggressive woman when need be. Brian was just a little taken aback by that at first, but then he found it subtly enticing. Having hold of his face in her hand, she suddenly and firmly replied, enunciating every word clearly.

"Look into my eyes, Brian!" The young man responded to that. He instantaneously made direct, wide-eyed contact with her. "Please, pay close attention to me." She relaxed her grip on his jaw a little. "Now, tell me what you can see."

"Okay." Brian replied in a slightly more serious tone of voice.

Baouzhe was still holding his face close to hers, so close that their noses touched. He could actually feel her gentle breathing on his lips. Although it was a delightful distraction, he tried to concentrate more on the task at hand as she had requested.

He peered deeply into her stunning dark eyes and immediately discovered some very interesting and distinguishing details. There were miniscule, hairline streaks of maroon color dispersed within the shimmery dark brown irises of the Asian woman's beautiful eyes.

"Oh, okay I see. Hmmm… that's kind of unusual." She released her hold on his face as soon as he acknowledged the fact. Brian stayed close for just a moment to get a thorough look at the unusual detail of her irises, sensing a poignant hint of familiarity. "You have very interesting eyes, Baouzhe," Brian said as he leaned away from the inviting closeness of her dark, shimmery eyes and her subtly arousing posture. "I mean that as a compliment. They're remarkable."

"Now, you look at me." She boldly and confidently smiled at him.

"Uh… I just did, didn't I?"

There was a slight pause before she spoke again. "I want you to look outside." A slight smile graced her luscious red lips. Her posture was sophisticatedly erect and she exuded nothing but complete confidence about her alluring, womanly semblance. "You will look at me now."

"From outside?" Brian raised his eyebrows and pointed towards the outdoor dining area.

"Yes, Brian." Baouzhe nodded her head once slowly. "You will look at me."

"I will look at you now." Brian repeated her request. "I will look at you now. I will talk to you now, and look into your eyes." He flamboyantly gestured with his hands as he smiled and took another sip of what was left of his delicious beverage. Then, he analytically supplemented with poetic charm, "I am helping you now."

"Yes," she agreeably affirmed with a smile in return. "You will help me now."

The perplexed young man shrugged his shoulders. "Okay, if it makes you happy."

He stood up from his chair and casually walked away from the bar area. Brian just knew that the mysterious woman was watching his every move as he walked out onto the rear patio dining area. It was the same place he and Gina had sat when they first saw Baouzhe. Brian walked around a small table where a couple was sitting close together, engaged in an intimate conversation. He stepped in-between their table and an empty table to his left, being careful not to disturb the couple or anyone else in the outdoor dining area. Brian then looked indoors through the grand rear windows of the restaurant towards the bar where he had been with Baouzhe. To his surprise, she was not there.

He quickly looked around the restaurant in an attempt to find her. *Okay, now what?* He shrugged his shoulders and sighed heavily, then turned to walk away. A sudden sharp tapping sound came from the other side of the large glass window next to him. He instinctively turned back to discover Baouzhe standing very close and directly in front of him on the other side of the large window. Brian grimaced slightly. He was completely perplexed as to how she had come so close to the window and so quickly, without him noticing. He just stared in amazement as she continued to rap on the large window. She smiled at him as she tapped a little louder on the glass. Brian squinted at her. The tapping noise seemed unusually loud now. It echoed slightly and almost seemed as if the reverberation was coming from inside his brain. The sensation was a little disorienting. Brian looked down at the floor and gently rubbed his eyes.

As he did so, he woke up.

Chapter Nineteen

Brian awoke suddenly, half startled. His head still rested against the couch cushions, but now his eyes were wide open, gazing at the dark ceiling above him. The soft illumination of the television filled the family room. The sound of an infomercial about hair restoration quietly prevailed over the eerie calmness of the dark, early morning hour. Then Brian heard something else, a purposeful tapping noise against one of the family room windows. When he lifted his head off the couch, the noise stopped. He stared at the rear windows for a moment. The noise came again.

Brian quickly realized the sound was coming from the window to the left of the rear entryway door. He thought for a moment, glancing at his watch. The time was 2:42 a.m. early Saturday. *Who could be out there at this hour of the night?* Brian had second thoughts about getting up, mostly because he was so tired. He sighed aloud as he leaned forward and rubbed the top of his head. When he stood up from the couch, the tapping noise started again. Someone was obviously trying to get his attention.

"Who is it?" Brian said, a bit of nervousness evident in his voice.

There was no reply. It was silent for only a moment. Then there was another purposeful rap on the window. The young man took a few cautious short strides towards the rear window, which was elegantly sheltered behind the closed mini-blinds. Brian queried once more, his voice a little louder this time.

"Who is it? What do you want?"

There was no reply to his apprehensive request so Brian

slowly took hold of the twist-control rod for the mini-blinds. He truly wanted to believe his amberous alien lady friend was out there waiting for an invitation to come inside. Without a doubt, the unique and momentous first contact experience still consumed him. Perhaps the dream he just had that seemed so real was, indeed, the legitimate result of his incessant thoughts of the extraterrestrial lady. There was so much more he wanted to know and felt obliged to know about her. This need to know was a yearning interest that kindled something within his soul like an inexorable and inflammable catalyst. Brian had a sincere desire to know everything about her people, her culture, her planet, and her life on another world. He felt sure that she wanted to know exactly the same things about him, too. Brian was convinced there had been an immediate, definite and insightful connection when they first met that dark and quiet evening inside the mysterious ellipsoid. He had honestly enjoyed her amiable company, not to mention her engaging, curious manner. Brian felt he had really begun to understand the humanoid woman quite easily. He sensed she could easily understand him, as well. He felt as if they were making great progress getting to know each other and becoming more acquainted as they spent time together. Now, it seemed that the more time that passed since he'd seen her, the more Brian missed her. Now he was beginning to feel her exodus was somewhat unmerited, for her to have disappeared the way she did, and so soon. As quietly as he discovered her existence, she was gone. There was no formal farewell. There was only an abrupt silence to signify that the aliens had departed. Brian was content with that at first. He had tried to logically reason why she vanished so quickly. Yet, how could the kindly and inquisitive extraterrestrial woman just disappear without a trace? How could she just leave him naively standing in the bathroom staring at his watch and counting the seconds going by? Should he have peeked out the bathroom door to see what was going on? It did not matter now. He had consented quietly and deferentially to the way she had departed; unprompted and surreptitious.

All the same, he hoped she would return to earth and visit him again soon. For surely that's not the way they would say farewell, is it? Or would that be the last time he ever saw her? Surely not. Indeed, would such a historic moment in this modern century simply go unnoticed? Without commemoration? Without any spectacular crowd pleasing pyrotechnics or any marching band to celebrate the event? Indeed. The unceremonious circumstances of the departure of the extraterrestrials had left Brian feeling a bit forlorn and confused. He felt a bit disappointed, and there was a definable emptiness inside him. There was no doubt that he wanted to see the mysterious alien humanoid woman again.

He slowly twisted the rod to open the mini-blinds and could see there was, indeed, a person standing outside in the dark. The starlit summer night cast just enough illumination to allow Brian to see the silhouette of someone standing very close to the window. Suddenly the person started to move. Then, quite unexpectedly, a light shone below the face of the individual who leaned in close to the windowpane, outlining their prominent facial features. The wide angle light starkly revealed a distinctly broad and smooth muscular jaw. Immediately noticeable in the wake of the fluorescent glow was the familiar prolongation of the nose, strikingly analogous to a canidae snout, and one that was all too familiar to Brian. It was the alien beast!

The mere sight of the beast standing close to the window in the dark was indeed more than subtly shocking to Brian's tired nerves. He had to consciously resist the knee-jerk reaction of leaning away from the window. Instead, he watched the extraterrestrial creature raise its left arm slightly to bring the light from its wristband device up to shine across its long and narrow, yet prominent eyebrows. Now Brian could clearly see the large, low set eyes of the alien and immediately noticed there was something distinctly different about the beast; specifically its eyes. This time the irises were not the disturbing arrant maroon shade, such as when he first encountered the beast when it was angry. This time Brian saw miniscule maroon colored streaks dispersed in the large and surprisingly dark brown irises of the portentous creature. Brian silently examined the eyes of the alien beast who stared back at him from the darkness of night on the other side of the glass. He stood close to the window and gawped out of curiosity at the unusual detail in the eyes of the celestial wolf-like being. In fact, he was so close to the glass, he could see the pupils of the beast constrict from the light shining across its face. An immediate and peculiar sense of déjà vu swept through Brian, for the eyes of the beast were the same as the beautiful mysterious Asian woman in his dream. Brian's eyes widened at the acute realization and without thinking, took a few small steps back away from the large family room window.

"What the…" Brian uttered, as he grimaced at the disconcerting face of the creature a mere few inches away on the other side of the windowpane.

The young man simply could not believe what his own eyes beheld. No, as Brian had ingenuously and incorrectly assumed, the extraterrestrial was not a million miles away by now, gone into outer space forevermore. *So, you're still here!*

Suddenly, the pristine white light illuminating the face of the creature extinguished and the creature's silhouette became noticeably less distinct. In fact, everything beyond the borders of the large window seemed to be getting perceptibly darker and more obscure. Brian squinted, trying to discern any detail of the extraterrestrial creature, but the beast just seemed to vanish into the night right before his eyes. Brian instinctively stepped to the rear door, wanting to know what was going on. Besides, where was the beautiful alien? If the wolf-like creature was still here on earth, then she must be here, as well. With only a faint hint of apprehension, Brian opened the door.

What happened next completely surprised him. A cold mist immediately permeated the family room from outside, seeping through the full height of the large doorway opening from top to bottom. Startled, Brian instinctively leaned away from the cold vapor wafting around his body. He grimaced and batted his eyes several times, trying to peer through the dense mist. The air had suddenly become thick with the strange wet vapor to the point that Brian could not see an honest inch past his nose. He stood in the doorway for a moment trying to remember the last time mountain fog had rolled into the area so quickly. *It's so weird.*

The strange cold mist almost completely engulfed him and then clouded over the family room with a serendipitous fog. Such an abrupt weather event might ensue during the winter months in this mountain wilderness region, but he could not recall this type of climate occurring during summer. Actually, Brian could not recall ever seeing any type of extreme foggy weather like this. For that matter, he had never experienced any thick fog that could actually penetrate someone's home the way smoke can.

Then he noticed something else was happening. All the shrouding mist suddenly began to dissipate rapidly. Brian looked around the room and then out the rear doorway again, at a loss for words. His jaw dropped out of sheer disbelief, for in an instant, the dense cloud of mist was completely gone.

What the…? How could such a phenomenon occur? Brian raised an eyebrow and shook his head. The fog had vanished just as quickly as the creature had.

In that instant he realized what must have occurred. *How clever!* Brian grinned. He was rather impressed by what he had just seen. Mountain fog had not rolled in unexpectedly; not at all. Brian intuitively realized that the dissipating mist was a diversion tactic. Indeed, the outer space beast used a proverbial smoke screen as a veil that allowed it to vanish before Brian's eyes.

Brian chuckled aloud. "So, you got a few tricks. Very clever, space-wolf," he muttered humorously and closed the door.

He thought about the alien creature's eyes. The mental image of the beast staring back from the other side of the glass pane was still so vividly clear. Then he remembered his dream. He took a deep breath and slowly exhaled, trying to relax and sort things out. He felt confused. Was his subconscious mind somehow enlightening him that the aliens had never left the planet and were, in fact, still nearby? As bewildering a notion as that seemed, Brian was even more perplexed about how a dream could alert him that the alien creature was actually lurking about just outside the family room window. *Okay, now that's really, really weird and, actually it's kinda scary.* Brian stood perfectly still as he thought about it some more. He quickly recalled how

Baouzhe wanted him to take a close look at her eyes. Her irises were a striking resemblance in color and detail compared to the wolf-like creature's eyes. Brian looked down at the floor as he reflected on the details of his dreamscape conversation with Baouzhe and in particular something she had said to him;

"You know who I am, Brian."

Her sultry voice was still so very clear and distinct in his mind. He also remembered other parts of their conversation.

"I believe in order to get your full cooperation you must do something simple for me, Brian…", "You will look at me…", "Look into my eyes, Brian!", "… tell me what you can see."

The young man continued to stare at the floor in silence. *It's no coincidence, is it?* Brian knew now, without a doubt, precisely what Baouzhe wanted him to notice. The celestial beast showed him the same thing. Brian came to the sobering conclusion that the mysterious, attractive Asian lady in his dream was actually trying to get him to wake up and literally look outside the window.

But, how could that be? Brian scowled and shook his head in confused thought, "That was just a dream!" he professed to himself and stepped away from the rear door. He almost stumbled backwards over the couch. "I was dreaming." He shook his head fervently again. "Wasn't I?"

It did not take Brian long to figure it out and put two and two together. After what he just experienced outside the family room window tonight, he needed no further convincing. He realized his dream was not some subconscious manifestation of the things going on in his life right now. No, his dream was definitely no ordinary dream. This realization was poignantly clear to him now. If that was true, it meant that the mysterious woman in his dream was obviously telling the truth.

"Son of a bitch!" Brian uttered as he returned his bewildered gaze to the darkness beyond the rear window.

He stood still for a moment, not knowing exactly what to do next. Indeed, acknowledgement of the fact that the beast had a method of communicating with him was intriguing, yet at the same time, a little disquieting. In addition to that, recognition of the fact that the creature was capable of appropriating the image of a human being in order to communicate in someone's dream was honestly a bit discomforting to Brian. This intimate mode of communication seemed slightly disingenuous to him. It also seemed to Brian to be a slight invasion of his privacy, not to mention his mind.

Brian was honestly not sure how he really felt about this, but he found himself articulating, "Oh my, space-wolf, you definitely got tricks!"

Brian felt a bit more anxious right now. He scratched his head and tried to think, not knowing what to do about what he had just seen. *Why would the aliens leave in such a hurry, only to come back covertly in a dream?* He suddenly was not sure if the alien creature was really trying to openly communicate, or subversively trying to take over his mind, and eventually the world. *Should I consider the dream a warning sign? Does the alien space-wolf have an ulterior motive?* Brian couldn't help but wonder.

He took a few steps closer to the window and hastily shut the blinds, and then practically ran upstairs to his parent's room. He flicked on the lights, shut the door, and then nervously locked it. His hands were shaking. He went to his father's dresser and with no thought for anything else, hastily retrieved the blue steel Smith and Wesson .357 Magnum revolver from the top drawer, then grabbed the small box of ammunition next to it. With both items in his possession now, Brian quickly trotted through his parent's luxuriously airy master bath and proceeded directly into the large walk-in closet. Once inside, he turned around and pushed the door of paneled mirrors shut. He used his elbow to turn on the light switch inside the walk-in closet and then, apprehensive and confused, he knelt down on the carpeted closet floor.

So, what's my plan now, seriously? What should I do next? Should I talk to someone now? Or, should I still keep this a secret? He clenched his teeth, shut his eyes tight, and slowly shook his head. He shrugged his shoulders in agitation. *If I don't talk to someone now, then when should I?* Brian's uncertainty made his thoughts go round and round.

"I don't know. Damn, I can't think straight. What should I do now, seriously?"

He looked at the 4-inch barrel of the weapon in his hand and winced. He gently placed the heavy revolver and ammunition on the carpet, sat down, and then buried his face in his open palms. A wave of confusion and apprehension such as he had never felt before washed over him, followed immediately by a tangible sense of isolation and anxiety. He felt so distant from the life he'd always known that he may as well have been standing on the moon all alone, looking back through empty space to earth below. He felt as if he was standing alone beyond the abyss of blackness without a soul to share the moment with, and with no hope of companionship. Indeed, there was not a single person in the world who knew what he was going through at this precise moment. He very much wanted to tell someone what he was going through. However, he still did not know whom. This feeling was becoming familiar, poignant almost, for he'd had this intense feeling ever since the very first moment he saw the extraterrestrials with his own skeptical, earthly eyes.

Brian rubbed his forehead and stared at the revolver. *I'm no different than everyone else. This is precisely what I'm afraid of, too. This is how people are going to react when they become aware of the extraterrestrial's existence. This is the welcome those aliens will get from us. I just know it. I can picture it. This is exactly what will happen.* He shook his head as he contemplated. *People will undoubtedly find a reason to distrust them and, eventually will speak out in one voice to try and get rid of them.* Brian clenched his teeth and gently knocked on the top of his head with both fists, trying to think of what he should do next. Nothing came to mind. He only knew that he would honestly not mind having another chance to see the alien woman again.

At that moment, Brian suddenly became aware of what he was doing, and was ashamed of his reaction.

"What am I doing hiding in the closet like a frightened little child?" He shook his head. "Damn, and with a gun!" Brian picked up the sturdy firearm and the ammunition, and then he stood motionless for a second as he wondered about his experience with the extraterrestrials up to now.

For some reason, these aliens are trying to make contact with me about what they are doing here. It's something important. I need to find out what it is they need me to help them with. I can't do that by running and hiding in fear. Besides, if I won't help them, they just might go find somebody else. I have to keep in mind that the next person will probably not be as open minded and rational as I am. I don't want them to come across someone that's unintelligent, insecure, and dangerously immature… pretty much like the way I just reacted. That could end up being a huge ignorant mistake; one that could get the aliens into trouble. That's a mistake that could get us all in big trouble. So I need to be smart about this. I need to be their contact person here on earth. Nobody else will understand them like me. Besides, they've already taken the next step in trying to work with me. They're actually trying to communicate.

"This is ridiculous!" he blurted out and reached for the closet door.

He pulled the door open and quickly made his way back to his father's dresser. Without saying another word, he placed the revolver and the ammunition where he had originally found it in the top drawer. Brian closed the dresser drawer and just stood there for a moment. He still wanted to talk to somebody about this unique and momentous first contact experience. Then he had an idea.

"I'll keep a journal about it!"

If he could at least write about the experience, he'd have a way to express what was going on. Documenting the events that occurred to date would help him stay calm and reveal the facts of this very historic occasion, and it would help keep him sane by sharing his thoughts and innermost feelings, even if it was in words written in a journal. This was the solution to what he should do next.

By 4:56 a.m. Brian was writing down all he could remember of the events that took place on the eve of his first contact experience with the alien woman and the creature. He was sitting at the computer desk in the family room with a pencil in one hand

and a cold glass of milk in the other. He had a small notepad directly in front of him with recent dates, a nearly exact estimate of times, and a thorough summation of most of the events that occurred on that historic Thursday night. He had several pages of information documented already, which included a general description of both extraterrestrials. Brian was very proud of his new journal, and the more he wrote, the more he remembered. He had most of the details written down, but there was no mention of the celestial jewel encounter. Brian simply did not recall the transfixing and intoxicating event at all.

To the right of the notebook he was currently writing in, was another larger notepad. Brian decided he would use that second notepad for the documentation of his dreams. He drank some more and tried to recall the events of his first dream, the one when he first saw the beautiful Asian lady. That was the same dream Gina was in, and the first time he had encountered the dreamscape manifestation of the creature. The young man felt he had a very good recollection of the extraterrestrial induced nocturnal delusion, because the experience seemed so very real to him. Brian moved the large notepad directly in front of him and started to write down the events that took place in that very first dream. His right hand wrote the first couple of sentences slowly before the pace picked up rather dramatically, and with reason.

The seemingly real events that took place in his first dream were indeed very clear in his memory; as if they had just happened.

Chapter Twenty

It was another hazy Saturday morning in the Inland Empire, a morning that was really no different than the other days of the week that came before, and in all probability a precursor for the weekdays to follow. The time was 6:44 a.m. now, and with the early sunny California sunrise came an assured promise of another bright and hot summer day for the inland valley. For most healthcare professionals at the hospital, like Danny, this beautiful summer morning picturesquely and precisely marked the end of another rewarding evening of hard and productive work. This collective work process of the hospital's skillful, intelligent medical staff was a sincere corollary of selfless fortitude and heartfelt dedication to help the less fortunate who were greatly afflicted with illness or injury.

Danny was just heading out of the hospital after completing his change of shift report and saying his farewells to the day shift and the few remaining night shift staff. Due to staffing needs, the lean, blonde haired respiratory therapist was not able to keep his familiar patient workload in the PICU, and was instead assigned to the emergency department last night. The long, twelve-hour shift was made all the busier by the constant calls coming in on the emergency pager he wore. Danny walked briskly out of the automated sliding glass doorway of the Pleasant Hills Medical Center Emergency Department, or ER as it is more familiarly known, into the waking, early morning sunshine.

Danny walked past a red, brightly polished San Bernardino County Fire Department paramedic rig parked to his left. There was also a sporty silver and green colored, Inland Medical

Transport ambulance just a few paces ahead to his right. The rear doors of the ambulance were wide open. Danny noticed there were two EMTs present, one still inside the vehicle, and the other one was standing at the rear. They were busy unloading the lightweight collapsible transport gurney with a patient on it. The elderly patient was sitting up comfortably on the gurney wearing an oxygen mask. He did not appear to be in any pain or distress at the moment, at least from Danny's perspective. Danny recognized the crew and he nodded at them with a smile as soon as they noticed him walking by. They politely acknowledged his presence and quickly returned to the task at hand. As they prepared to wheel the patient inside, Danny remembered that this new patient must have been the last incoming call he overheard on the ER radio. He recalled that there would be at least one patient arriving right on time for the morning shift, an elderly Caucasian male experiencing chest pains.

As Danny faced forward and continued walking, he indistinctly noticed something just out of the top corner of his vision. He looked up and promptly noticed a couple of pigeons flying towards him almost directly overhead. The birds were not very high up, so the sound of their wings flapping in the early morning sky captured his attention. Peculiarly, there was something else that caught his eye this morning besides the pigeons. As the birds flew past, Danny noticed something unfamiliar up in the air almost directly over his head. At first glance, there seemed to be a very small, blurry, transparent spot high up in the sky. Danny blinked a few times and squinted as he tried to focus on what he thought he saw. However, as he peered upward, the bizarre finding seemed to vanish. Just like that, the blurry spot was gone. Danny stopped walking, stood perfectly still, and stared more intently. He was certain that for a second he had seen something strange, but alas, he simply lost track of it. His eyes searched high in the summer morning sky for the strange blurry aberration, but he could see nothing at all out of the ordinary. There was only the beautiful golden colors of the bright summer morning filling his acutely inquisitive vision. Danny shut his eyes briefly and softly rubbed his forehead and eyebrows for a second. *I'm so tired, my vision is getting blurry.* He blinked a few times and then continued quietly on his way to the parking garage. Danny got in his car and drove home. That was that.

·　·　·　•　●　⬤　●　•　·　·

By 7:46 a.m. Brian had written down an impressively detailed recollection of all the encounters he'd had with the aliens thus far, including the most recent interaction with the creature at the family room window several hours ago. He also had completely documented the events that occurred in his very first dream of Gina and Baouzhe. As soon as he completed that, Brian began thinking about documenting the second dream of Baouzhe. There was no plan or thought in his mind to write about the very short dream that he had in-between the other two.

Brian did not write anything about the dream he had of the creature chasing him on the winding mountainous road at night. He simply did not recall having it. All things known to him and considered, he was very satisfied with his journal so far; but alas, he felt he could do more to enhance the revealing experience of his unique and enlightening adventure. He wanted to provide some physical corroboration in order to substantiate his work he was meticulously documenting, and any future experiences he would encounter, as well. He propped an elbow on the table and rested his chin in the palm of his hand, absentmindedly rubbing a finger over his lips while considering what else he could do. Brian's gaze searched the family room for any clue that could help him achieve his elemental objective. Then he had an idea.

Brian walked to the pine entertainment center and pulled open the large pocket doors in search of his father's camera. He already knew that the Nikon N60 35mm camera would not be there. His father and mother had taken it on their trip to Hawaii. What he was looking for was the other camera, the Polaroid SLR 690 instant camera. An instant camera meant instant proof. With the Polaroid, there was no need to have the film developed in a lab, which meant nobody else would have the opportunity to see the pictures. The Polaroid photographs would be exclusively for his eyes only, for now. Brian smiled. That camera would be an excellent tool to help document this historic first contact experience.

"Now why didn't I think of that sooner?" He shook his head and chuckled.

It did not take him long at all to find the fancy Polaroid camera. Brian remembered his mother had given it to his father as a birthday present several years ago on May 24, 1996. The camera was actually a well-calculated and timely gift. In essence, Linda and James had smartly prepared themselves for the much-anticipated arrival of their first new grandson, Houston. He was born several months later that same year on September 24th.

Brian retrieved the brown leather book bag from inside his truck and loaded it up with a few snacks, a pullover sweatshirt, and the instant camera, of course. By 8:25 a.m. Brian was outdoors once again in the evergreen forest area of his parent's home, surrounded by tall white Snapdragons, Arrowhead Butterweed and Creeping Snowberry. He walked briskly along as the sunrise diffused into the brighter, more intense light of mid-morning. His progress was much quicker this time since he could see the entire landscape instead of relying on the narrow beam of a flashlight to guide him through the dark.

Before he knew it, he had arrived at the gully that was oriented north and south. In the light of the morning sun, Brian could more readily appreciate the actual size of the gully. It was much wider and deeper than he remembered from his perception in the dark. He fully recognized where he was at that point, and with careful haste, began to make his way down the steep furrow. As he descended into the deep gully, Brian glanced around to see if he could spot the ellipsoid spacecraft. He clearly remembered where he had first seen the strange dark thing and how it was discreetly nestled under the gathering of sagebrush and large single-leaf Pinyon foliage. He remembered the bizarre spacecraft was located in the center of the gully. Brian slowed his pace a bit as he gazed beneath the trees in the heart of the steep, gravelly furrow. To his distinct recollection, that is where it should be, except the ellipsoid was no longer there.

Brian steadily made his way to the bottom of the shadowy gully. The foliage of the deep furrow hindered much of the sunlight overhead. However, there was enough light to notice that the ellipsoid spacecraft was indeed, missing. Brian walked directly to the spot where he knew the spacecraft had been and looked around at his surroundings. He figured he was standing approximately in the middle of where the space vehicle was supposed to be. *It's obvious,* he hypothesized, *they must have moved their spaceship.* Brian was reasonably somewhat disappointed, but he was not the least bit surprised. He simply shrugged his shoulders and methodically began taking a few pictures of what he would eventually denote the extraterrestrial landing zone. Next, he quickly hiked back up the narrow ravine to the soft graveled edge. Brian snapped a few more pictures and secured the camera and photos in his book bag. He took one last quick look around his immediate surroundings, and then made his way back home.

By 11:55 a.m. Brian had taken a hot shower and eaten a filling breakfast consisting of two eggs over easy with hickory smoked bacon, wheat raisin bagels with cream cheese, and a refreshing cold glass of orange juice. Now, after cleaning up the kitchen, he sat down with his notebook to write about the second dream of Baouzhe. He thought he was more than ready by now, and he was very much looking forward to it. He placed his journal notebook and Polaroid photographs in front of him on the computer desk to prepare for the task. Suddenly he started to feel very tired. He was exhausted from being awake so early in the day, not to mention the hike through the woods. The hot shower and full meal had completely relaxed him. Brian got up from the desk and walked to the couch in the family room. Without thinking much about what he was doing, he simply plopped down on the comfortable velvet sofa and fell fast asleep.

· · • ● ⬤ ● • · ·

"It's good that you can meet me now, Brian. We can get much accomplished."

Brian looked up from his lap to see Baouzhe sitting comfortably on the other side of the small table. It was the very same table he had sat at with Gina in that first dream. Now, he and Baouzhe were the only ones outside in the cozy patio dining area. Brian gazed into the Asian woman's beautiful eyes for a second as he gathered his thoughts for a reply. He looked around the all too familiar surroundings of the establishment. Then, he spoke.

"I'm back here, again, with you, again."

"Yes, we…"

"Yes, I know, I know. We talk now." Brian waved his hand in the air.

Baouzhe attentively observed the young man as he leaned forward and rubbed his forehead. "Are you too tired to talk to me now, Brian?"

"No, no." Brian emphatically answered as he put his hand up. "I'm just a little disoriented." He shook his head a few times and promptly responded, "I'm cool." He smiled and pointed at the beautiful, enchanting woman. She smiled at him in return.

"So," Brian nodded as he spoke up, "what's up space-wolf?" He raised both hands and shrugged his shoulders as he supposed aloud, "I mean, that's who you really are. Am I right?"

There was a brief moment of uncomfortable silence and darting stares from the beautiful woman before she spoke again.

"You think I am a…" Her alluring eyes gazed upward into the romantic starry night air as she calmly inquired, "a… wolf-like creature?"

Brian noticed that when Baouzhe looked up for a second, the light coming from the indoor dining area hit her eyes at just the right angle and intensity, making the faint hairline streaks of maroon just barely visible in the brown of her appealing and mysterious Asian eyes.

"Well," Brian cleared his throat and said, "in my dreams you're a very attractive, exotic foreign lady." He chuckled aloud.

"But in the real world, well…" Brian looked directly into her probing gaze and coolly implied, "You're not."

"What are you saying, I'm not attractive?" Baouzhe asked with a presumptuous grin.

"Well," Brian raised a brow and pouted his lips as he chose his words carefully, "let's just say you look very different in person. Here, you're a sexy woman, but in reality you're a hairless werewolf alien being from outer space," he calmly asserted, rubbing his chin.

The attractive young lady across the table just grinned a little more and, entirely composed, said, "Is that really what you think of me? Is that what I am to you, Brian?"

Brian's brazen comment was an open and honest conjecture from the heart. At the moment, he felt he could speak candidly because this was his dream and, being so, he felt he was in complete control of things. In the real world, the alien beast was quite intimidating. The mere presence of the creature usurped his manly authority. Not here, however. Here, Brian felt he could say anything he wanted to say because, in this dream-scape world, the beast was just another dainty, pretty, young lady. In this surreal dreamscape world the creature was human, very feminine, and seemingly vulnerable.

"Well…" Brian started to speak, but just as he did, the pretty lady interrupted him.

"The way you see me now is the way I am perceived on my home planet," she said with the same presumptuous grin.

"Oh-kay." Brian widened his eyes slightly in response and smiled as he looked down at the small table they were sitting at. Then, intrigued, he inquired, "So, you come from a planet where everyone looks like you?"

"Yes." Baouzhe answered with a smile and then articulated, "Well, to be honest, not everyone looks like me. There are several other species of people on my planet. For example, the other female you saw with me on this expedition is from my planet. So, I suppose she is verification of that fact."

"Okay." The young man slowly nodded his head in agreement

and surmised, "So, let me get this straight, you're a female, and on your planet, you're like, well… gorgeous, basically."

"As I just told you, the way you see me now is the way I am perceived on my home planet." Brian just stared as she inquired, "What's wrong?" With a demure smile she contended, "Is it so difficult to believe, Brian?"

"No, no." Brian raised both hands in a pacifying, diplomatic reply, "I mean, uh, I believe you. It's just… well, I don't know."

The young man scratched his head a few times as he thought intently for a moment about what she really looked like outside the romantic dreamscape world they were experiencing right now. He clearly remembered how the mere first sight of the beast had utterly shocked and intimidated him into a real feeling of terror. Truth be told, to Brian, it was the most fretful, yet exciting moment he had ever experienced, for sure. Nonetheless, with that sobering colossal episode behind him now he tried to be a little more objective. He recalled her tall, sturdy physique. Yet, after briefly considering, he realized that she was actually taller than she was stocky.

"I guess you really don't look that masculine." He also recalled how her waist was, indeed, noticeably small for her size, and that maybe in an uncanny way she was somewhat shapely, too, though Brian would not dare acknowledge that fact aloud. He thought about other details of her anatomy. The arms of the beast were long, but not overly muscular. He remembered how her hands, though large, had comparatively long fingers with narrow nails. Then Brian reflected on the looks of the alien beast, the glaring facial expressions, or more accurately, lack of expression. Brian chuckled amusingly, "I didn't really think of you as a female because you didn't really act like it to me, I guess."

Baouzhe smiled and then chuckled. "Your perception of me as a fierce animal creature is intriguing and in some regards complimentary. Now that I am thinking about it, I can see how it is easy for you to judge my demeanor as such. But I can assure you, Brian, I am actually quite the opposite of the way you perceive me."

"Well, forgive me, but I didn't realize you're such a hottie, Baouzhe!" The young man's expression became much more animated and colorful as he smiled and asserted, "With those looks," he pointed at her and supposed, "I bet on your world you can get just about anything you want. Damn, girl! I guess I got it all wrong." Brian winked and smiled. "How was I to know? Sorry Baouzhe. My bad!"

She leaned forward in her little chair and made direct eye contact with him.

"You can say and think what you wish. Like I said, the way you see me here is the way I am perceived on my world by other people. But know this, Brian, I'm one of the smartest and most talented females in my career discipline on my world, and I am fully qualified for this mission. That is why I'm here. I was not assigned this important, historic mission just because I'm beautiful, as you see me now in a familiar Homo sapien appearance." She stated frankly.

"I meant no disrespect by what I just said Baouzhe, really." Brian raised his hand to his chest in earnestness. "I'm sure you've got to really know your shit and be the best because our own astronauts from this world are really, really smart and the training is pretty tough from what I understand. In fact, I've heard it's like really hard to get selected to be an astronaut. Even after you're lucky enough to be selected, I've heard there's no real guarantee you will even get to go to space. So, if your space program is anything like ours, I know you two are most likely very special." He nodded with raised brow sincerity.

"Yes, the same is very true on my world," Baouzhe smiled in reply. "It's nice to know you appreciate that, Brian."

"Look, I apologize. I'm truly sorry if I've insulted you, Miss Baouzhe. I mean, we earth humans are used to only seeing and communicating with other earth humans. We aren't used to a world full of walking, talking, dog-people. We don't have a variety of other intelligent species walking around with us who don't look at all like us. Now, don't get me wrong, there are a variety of intelligent animals here on earth. But, it's just not the same. It's not the same at all, at least from what I know and have seen so far."

"I see." Baouzhe understood what Brian was trying to say.

"People on earth would actually totally freak out if they saw you, or your other female space alien friend, for that matter. And, to be honest," Brian raised his finger as he articulated, "you kind of scare me a little, Baouzhe. I mean, you always look like you're about to bite my head off or something." He shook his head. "Frankly, you're kind of intimidating when you want to be. Maybe if you try smiling for a change, I might see a better, more agreeable side of you."

"Very well Brian." Baouzhe calmly replied with a single nod. "I will try. I mean you no harm. I admit, sometimes I might be a little overly cautious and critical about certain things. I have to, for our own protection. We are far from home on a very hostile planet. But, do not take that personal, or as a sign that I don't like you in particular." There was a generous and considerate look of compassion in her eyes and a beautiful smile across her glossy red lips.

"You come in peace, right?" Brian pointed and smiled at the young lady.

Baouzhe humbly smiled and quietly nodded her head again once, slowly, in an earnest reply. Brian looked up into the air for a moment.

"Well, now that I think about it, you do have long hair, your shoulders aren't really overly muscular, and your fingernails are kind of feminine looking," Brian said, "so, I guess that's normal for a wolf-girl from your side of the galaxy." Her face was an expressionless reply to his brief attempted pun. He thought for a slight moment as Baouzhe silently stared at him.

"So, what do we humans look like to you?" he inquired.

Baouzhe grinned as she continued to stare, and then very tranquilly replied, "You all look like an oversized, hairless chimpanzee."

"Touché." Brian nodded with raised brow in deferential reply. "I guess I should have seen that one coming." The young man leaned forward just a bit. "So, you know what a wolf is, and what a chimpanzee is. What else do you know about this world, my world, Earth?"

"We know a lot."

"Oh-kay." Brian broke the ensuing silence. "Well, I know very, very little about you and your world. Actually, I don't know anything except what I've seen so far. And, I'm guessing nobody else on this planet knows about your existence. Otherwise, I'm sure this visitation of yours would have gone very public in a hurry, already." There was a slight moment of empty silence as Brian patiently waited for a thoughtful reply to his assumption.

Baouzhe simply smiled in reply.

"Okay, so," Brian gestured freely with his hands, "are we, meaning the citizens of planet Earth, going to become aware of your existence formally, anytime soon?"

"Perhaps."

"Oh-kay." Brian was still waiting for a more indulged reply and explanation to his polite inquiry. But, there was no verbal reaction. The beautiful lady just stared in a very familiar way, just as the creature did in the waking world, the world outside of the dreamscape that the two were now sharing. Brian could fully sense and recognize that probing gaze right now. Surely, this figment across the table was clearly the manifestation of the beast.

Then Baouzhe spoke. "I know you have many questions, Brian. But the one thing you don't ever have to question is your safety. Please, do not fear us. This beautiful blue planet you live on and every living entity here, large, or minutely small, is not in any danger from us at any time. There is nothing to fear from the people of my world, not presently, and certainly not in the future. I will tell you right now Brian, we are not here to invade or start a war. My people are intelligent, ethical, and a very peaceful society. We are an integrated society of different wonderful species living as a whole, united in beliefs and principle. This current expedition is a mission of fact and data gathering. It is, or was, a secret mission. That is, well, until you discovered our presence."

Brian stared at Baouzhe, observantly hanging on every word she uttered, intently listening to all she had just said.

"Okay," he replied, his mouth half agape, and his eyes trained on her pretty face. Brian wanted to hear absolutely everything she said. "This is really, really interesting. I need to know this. Yes, I do have many questions my strange, beautiful friend. You're definitely right about that. Yes, indeed."

"I will answer your questions, Brian. I know you must be very confused about many things. Since the night you discovered our existence, your view of life on other planets may have changed, or perhaps confirmed your suspicions. Regardless, you now have proof. My guess is you most likely want to know the reason for our visitation. I can understand that you have many questions and concerns about that. Yes, I know your mind must be very confused about many things. And I can sense you are very frightened at times, too." Baouzhe leaned forward to assure the young man. "Brian, you must believe me when I say you have nothing to fear. You and the people of this planet are in no danger from us." She leaned against the back of her seat again and supplemented in a monotone tempered voice, "You are only in danger from yourselves."

"Ain't that the truth." Brian chuckled as he mentally digested her solemn words. "Very interesting." He looked directly into her eyes.

"So, Miss Baouzhe, if you don't mind telling me, just who are you, and where do you and your companion come from, exactly?" Brian asked the most imperative question he had wanted answered since he discovered them in the dark forest that historic night. He assumed the pair of explorers was from another solar system and, of course, from another habitable planet, but he was curious from where, exactly. "I know you're from outer space, but where exactly is your home world?"

Baouzhe was quiet. She only smiled at him. To Brian, she appeared to be suddenly distracted, as if she was thinking of something else entirely dissimilar to their present conversation. Then, all at once, she closed her eyes and touched her forehead with the extended fingers of both hands. She was obviously concentrating on something, but Brian had no idea what she was contemplating. Brian waited for an answer from her, which came almost as quickly as she closed her eyes.

"We are not too far away by our own technological means." Baouzhe looked into his eyes and continued, "However, we are a very great distance away, by comparison to your own peoples' antiquated and limited capability."

"I see." Brian continued to rub his chin and almost whispered in reply, "Indeed."

"We are a very peaceful, intelligent civilization, and we're practically your nearest neighbor. That is all you honestly need to know and, it is really the most significant concern for now, Brian." She smiled in a very courteous manner at him and then looked down at the small table and closed her eyes again. She was obviously distracted about something else on her mind.

"What's wrong?" Brian asked, grimacing slightly out of sincere concern after observing her brief, distracted behavior a moment ago.

"I must go now." She stared directly into his eyes. "We will continue our conversation later, Brian." Her face was now expressionless as she suddenly rose to her feet and turned to leave. Brian stared and was practically at a loss for words as she began to walk away. Her well-fitting emerald dress hugged the curves of her slender body and she moved gracefully on attractive, athletic legs. With her back straight, shoulders firm, and chin held high with alluring confidence, she glided swiftly away in her glossy black high heels. "Goodbye for now," she uttered aloud without looking back. Her pace picked up as she hurried through the patio doorway of the romantic restaurant.

"Everything okay?" Brian quickly got up from his chair and out of naive curiosity started to follow her. However, by the time he stepped through the patio doorway, Baouzhe had already disappeared into the crowd of happy and jocular socialites and the smartly dressed patrons at the bar.

"Baouzhe?" Brian looked around, but she was gone.

Chapter Twenty One

At approximately 12:30 p.m. that Saturday afternoon, a young couple was enjoying their weekend jog along one of Linda Morris' favorite trails. This one was close to the main road where neighborhood vehicles often traveled, and also ran very close to her house. Although it was close to the road, the trail offered a great deal of serenity as it wound through a lush and endless montage of brightly colored floral and vividly aromatic plants such as Musk Flower, California poppy, Bigelow's Coreopsis, and Mustang Mint. This was one of several reasons Brian's mother enjoyed running along that beautiful path, and that was basically why the young, upper-middle class couple was jogging along it now. The handsome young couple was about thirty-five minutes into their jog this afternoon, heading north, when they spotted something quite out of the ordinary.

The man was the first to see the strange thing. Aaron Spechlard, an attorney who worked for a very successful private, public interest law firm, slowed his pace and grimaced as he peered into the thick shrubs to his left. He just caught a glimpse of something he perceived to be very peculiar. He came to a sudden stop.

"You okay?" the woman with him asked when he suddenly stopped running. Janet Hillrem, Aaron's fiancée who was also an attorney at the same law firm then said, "What is it honey?" She could not help but notice his bewildered expression. She instinctively turned her head towards the thickened shrubbery in the direction Aaron was looking.

"You see that?" Aaron pointed into the woods.

Janet squinted, covering her forehead with her right hand to take some of the summer glare out of her eyes, then peered intently in the direction he was pointing.

"See what?" she queried with more of a concerned expression on her face than she had just a second before. "It's not a mountain lion is it?" Janet's hand moved to the trendy and posh neon pink fanny pack she used for running. She started to work the zipper pocket open where she kept a small can of mace ready, if needed.

"What in the world..." Aaron curiously said.

Amid the thickets and trees, the sun's rays had pierced the canopy and highlighted some type of visual distortion. It was more of a rippling, wavy aberration than a thing. Aaron had a little trouble with depth perception because of the obscuring shadows cast by the tall foliage as well as the bleary visual effects of the odd optical variance. Nevertheless, the shape seemed to be defined by the margins of the perceptible distortion. Judging only by what was visible in-between the shrubbery, the blurred and wavy optical aberration seemed to have a very peculiar shape similar to that of an egg. From where Aaron stood, the bizarre peculiarity seemed to be about the same size of an all-terrain vehicle or perhaps a very small automobile. He made this simple assumption by comparing the optical variance to the relevant size of the immediate surrounding vegetation. However, since he was standing in bright daylight looking into thick, deeply shaded foliage, he was just not one hundred percent sure if the oddity was a shadow or an actual object. He even wondered if this unexplained and wavy aberration was a figment of his own imagination. He wanted to get a closer look.

"What are you looking at? What...?" Janet took a few steps closer to Aaron as he very cautiously advanced towards the edge of the scenic trail. "What is it honey?"

She positioned herself close behind him and followed quietly in-step. She took another glance around his shoulder and saw a shadowy, wavy visual distortion straight ahead, about 40 to 50 feet off the winding trail. It was very difficult to see. From any other angle than exactly where they now stood, it would simply not be visible. She was surprised that Aaron had caught a glimpse of it. Janet figured he must have looked right at it by sheer happenstance.

"Do you see it?" Aaron raised his arm again and pointed straight ahead into the deep shadowy vegetation, directly towards the darkened, blurred visual oddity. "Right there, under those trees, right in-between the large bushes." His face wore a look of juvenile curiosity.

"I think so." Janet grimaced as she peered around his shoulder. "I can see something is there. It's dark. What is it? Is it a bear?" Her grip tightened on the small can of mace in her hand. "Honey, we have to scream and make a lot of noise. We have to make ourselves look big." She practically whispered this all the while firmly pulling at his right arm with her free hand.

"I'm not sure it's a…"

Just then they heard and felt a strong vibration. Janet gasped aloud and clenched Aaron's arm tightly. Aaron stood straight up and, without a word, was ready to grab hold of his beautiful lady. The noise grew louder. At that moment, from behind them, a large moving and storage rental vehicle rumbled by on the roadway adjacent to the jogging trail. Janet and Aaron immediately turned almost completely around as soon as they heard the rental truck pass by. Their eyes locked on the bright yellow truck and they sighed together in relief, knowing there was no wild animal ready to pounce on them from out of the forest. The truck sped by, gone as quickly as it had shown up and surprised them.

"Good Lord!" Janet exclaimed in relief. She sputtered and then chuckled with glee, looking into Aaron's reassuring eyes. "That truck almost scared me to death!" The distraction caused them both to chuckle lightheartedly.

Next, something else quite unexpected happened. At that precise moment, simultaneously and almost on cue, Janet and Aaron looked down. They did so because they both felt something cold and tickly on their bare legs. Aaron raised his elbows up high and took a few steps back. Janet basically did the same as she kept hold of his arm.

"What the…?" The tall, handsome gentleman with the

narrow jaw took a few more steps backwards. "Where is that coming from?" Aaron curiously mumbled, looking down at the cold mist shrouding the ground where they stood. The startlingly cold vapor was about knee high and a second later, almost chest high.

"Aaron, honey what's happening? Where is this fog coming from?" Janet wrapped her arms around her man and hugged him tight. The mace was still clenched in her nervous hand, ready for use on whatever they needed defense against.

"I have no idea," Aaron said, looking up at the huge wall of cold, odorless mist coming at him, obscuring the foliage they could see only a second ago.

In another second or two the couple was fully engulfed in the dense mist. The strange, wet vapor was so thick light couldn't penetrate, so suddenly, the area where they stood became black as pitch. Janet and Aaron could not see even an inch past the end of their nose. Then the couple noticed something else. Just as soon as the shrouding mist completely engulfed them, it began to dissipate quickly and before they knew it, the mist was completely gone.

"Okay, what just happened?" Janet looked solemnly into Aaron's bewildered eyes.

"I really, really don't have any idea," Aaron replied, eyes wide and looking uncertainly around him.

The two were now standing quietly, embracing each other on the bright sunny trail. They both simultaneously looked into the woods in the general direction of where the bizarre oddity was. There was no wavy aberration, nothing out of the ordinary.

Without further ado, Aaron grabbed Janet's hand firmly and led the way in reverse direction on the beautiful scenic trail.

"Okay, I don't know what that was, I don't know where all the steam came from, and I'm not even sure I actually saw something moving around in the bushes in the first place." He said.

They walked briskly as he talked. The couple started to pick up their southbound pace heading back to Aaron's new Range Rover SUV parked approximately two miles away.

Then he said, "All I know is, if it was a bear moving around in the shadows, then we need to get out of here! Like, right now!"

"Okay, here honey," Janet replied, handing him the can of mace.

He took it quickly, without uttering a word, and then clenched it tightly. The two continued hastily on their southward trek without a single look behind them. The only things following them were their own shadows cast by the sun and a peculiar looking shadow several paces behind them.

This other peculiar shadow was uniformly circular all around with a faint, grayish halo radiating from its center. This other mysterious shadow gave chase for a few minutes. It purposefully followed the retreating couple and then suddenly stopped and zoomed away in a northwesterly direction. It was gone. The handsome young yuppie couple never saw it, and they never realized it was virtually right next to them the entire time they were peering into the woods at the other strange, dark and blurry thing.

More importantly, they never saw the source of that shadow, the mysterious, floating, transparent spherical aberration Gustavo Aguirre and his sons had encountered. That same thing had silently positioned itself almost directly overhead the handsome couple the whole while. They never knew.

· · · • • ● • • · ·

Miles away another handsome young couple was enjoying some time together on this beautiful Saturday afternoon. They, however, unlike the startled and retreating yuppie couple, were not jogging in the woods. The summer sun was shining bright and the temperature was near the forecasted high of 85°F in the city of Long Beach. Many local people were at the beach or the harbor, shopping, dining, and just enjoying the outdoors amongst the crowd of visitors and tourists who were doing exactly the same thing. It was a beautiful day to be outdoors in the beach area. Nevertheless, Donnette and Brandon decided to spend time enjoying each other indoors. They were fully relishing a rare moment of intimacy as the lovers they once were, and still are.

Brandon lay on his side gazing at Donnette, taking in all of the sensuous beauty of his lovely wife through his very relaxed and satisfied eyes. The couple had shared a quiet and cozy late breakfast together. Now, they were in bed enjoying the comforting, loving embrace of each other's arms after a dutifully appropriated opportunity of spontaneous, intense lovemaking. It was easy now for the two to release all of the pent-up energy and conjugal passion they enduringly had for each other. It was easy now for both of them to verbalize aloud the way they made each other feel without the curious ears of their wandering four-year-old child to hear, and then lead Houston to inquire what was going on.

Brandon took this moment of tranquil matrimonial sanctity to remember and appreciate everything Donnette was to him in his happy life with her. He took this stolen moment of togetherness to just look upon her and take in every bit of her incontestable naked loveliness. Now, lying next to her, he gazed at her beautiful, unembellished and shapely figure. She was as desirable to him now as she always had been since the very first time they ever made sweet, passionate love together. His adoring, visual immersion of her corporeal womanly virtues was extremely obvious, yet comfortably flattering to Donnette. She was without doubt quite aware and fully content with his silent, loving appreciation of her. She turned her head to look at him with those unsullied, light brown eyes of hers, and smiled.

"What are you thinking about Panda?" She giggled aloud as she leisurely pushed back a long lock of her straight black hair.

"I'm thinking about how beautiful you are to me right now, just like the first time I saw you baby," Brandon replied as he grabbed her hand and gently kissed it.

"Brandon, that's so sweet. Honey, I love you." Donnette kissed him on his lips.

"I love you, too baby." Brandon rubbed her hand gently and then held it close to his naked and slightly perspired chest.

He enjoyed this blissful moment of togetherness they were

sharing. He knew they needed more time together as a loving couple. He also knew he needed more time to be with his family. Brandon thought about the offer his best friend Anthony had made recently. A family trip out of town would be perfect and lots of fun for his son and his wife, not to mention himself. Donnette and Brandon both always enjoyed Anthony and his girlfriend, Hillary's company. They were definitely a happy, genuinely fun, and gracious couple to be around. Indeed, Donnette would really appreciate and enjoy a little getaway.

Brandon even considered finding out if it would be okay to bring his brother Brian along, too. Perhaps that would make his younger brother feel better. Brandon heard his brother had canceled his plans and hence, did not travel with his parents to Hawaii. For that reason, Brandon thought his younger brother could really enjoy a little time away, as well. Brandon rolled slightly towards his left to lay on his back as he shared his idea with his lovely wife.

"Baby," he kissed her hand again and said, "Let's take that trip to Mexico before Houston starts school. You know, before he goes to kindergarten."

"Really? That trip coming up that you mentioned about?" Donnette inquired with a big curious smile.

"Yeah, let's take the kid," he chuckled, "and the other kid for that matter, my brother."

"Sure, that would be great. Is Brian still house-sitting for your mom and dad?"

"Yeah he decided to stay, since, well, you know." Donnette nodded in realization and agreement with a slightly pouted lip as her husband talked. "He was supposed to be gone with them to Hawaii. Hell, he could probably use some time away. He's probably bored to death up there in the woods, all alone."

"Okay, why don't you give him a call? I think it would be nice to have him come with us. I know he was supposed to go to Hawaii with Gina and your parents. For whatever reason, it didn't work out. So, this would be a nice consolation." She rubbed his firm chest and then pulled herself closer to him. "You should call Brian. He might like that."

"Yeah, I will. Thanks honey." Brandon looked into her eyes and gave her a kiss.

"Panda, baby?" Donnette continued to caress his chest gently. "Do you mind if we do a little shopping before we pick up Houston later today?"

Their little handsome four-year-old son was at the babysitter's house since this morning. Donnette dropped Houston off earlier so he could enjoy the day with some other kids they knew from preschool. The babysitter, Karla Smith, was a former employee at Sunshine Coast Preschool where Houston was previously enrolled for day care. He would go to the preschool on days when Donnette worked as a substitute kindergarten teacher for the Orange Unified School District. On those days, Houston had fun at preschool with Karla and the other kids in her class. Karla quit her job last May and returned to summer school to finish pursuing a degree in psychology. She was well liked and quite popular at the day care center. As a result, she was able to keep in touch with some of the parents and babysit their children part-time. Karla occasionally liked to babysit for parents on weekends because she knew it gave the parents some quality time to be with their significant others, and the parents always paid her very well to have such an opportunity. The kids loved to visit her, too. The children really looked forward to visiting Karla's large, spacious home, because she had lots of toys and fun things for them to do. Karla simply loved children, and Houston was definitely one of her favorite little pupils from the preschool. Houston was about to start kindergarten at Worldcrest Elementary School this coming fall. Although he had left the preschool, his mother remained friends with Karla. She was the best babysitter Donnette ever had, besides Houston's grandparents, of course.

Now that Houston was visiting his favorite former preschool teacher and playmates, Donnette was thinking of taking advantage of having some free time to shop for herself without having to bore her little son to tears while browsing through department stores for discounts and other exciting special sales. The youngster really disliked going to department stores, especially shopping for women's clothes, or any clothes for that matter. Unless he and his mother were at the mall and happened, by chance, to pass the Disney Store; well now, that was different.

"You don't mind, do you baby?" she coaxed with a smile. "It won't take too long."

"Sure baby, whatever you want. It's the weekend." Brandon smiled in reply.

"Yay!" She clapped her hands and giggled. "Because, there's this really cute and simple dinner dress I saw the other day, and I would like to maybe buy it for Mexico." She gave her husband an insinuative, sultry smile. "Maybe we could go out for dinner one evening while Brian watches his little nephew? Wouldn't that be nice?"

"Yeah, that would be really nice." Brandon raised his eyebrows at her and smiled.

"You're so good to me baby," Donnette acclaimed with another carefree giggle as she pulled herself up on top of her loving husband. They both chuckled aloud, tickling and playfully wrestling each other for a brief moment before the same passionate kissing that had brought them to the bedroom started again.

·   ·   ·   •   ●   ●   ●   •   ·   ·   ·

Miles away at the Lake Arrowhead Branch Library of San Bernardino County, at approximately 3:35 p.m. in the afternoon, Brian had just finished writing the details about the second and the third dream of Baouzhe. He had been very busy writing about the dreamscape encounter with the alien beast in human form and researching any books he could find about extraterrestrial life for almost three hours now. Although the books and literature he found were several decades old, Brian still considered at least some of the theory sound. He was actually able to find a few books about the possibility of extraterrestrial life, the feasibility of earth visitation, and what alien beings probably looked like. He had many books at his fingertips available to read in the cozy library, however, there was absolutely nothing that mentioned the same type of encounter he had experienced. There was nothing even remotely similar, for that matter. Many of the old science and astronomy books and several dated technological magazines he skimmed through had material that was more focused on the topic of alien abduction. Almost all the material he found was copy written in the early 1970s. It came as no surprise that every book he selected and took enough time to quickly look through seemed to be based more on fiction and fable than scientific fact.

Brian leaned forward and rested his forehead in the palm of his right hand. He stared at the table and rubbed his eyebrows as he thought deeply about the historic alien encounter. The same concerns filled his mind. *What does it all mean, and how will humans on earth really react as soon as everyone finds out that we, indeed, are not alone in the universe?* He still felt burdened to be the only person that knew of the aliens' secret visit to his planet. He wished there was another witness he could share the experience with. Brian wondered again if it was time to tell someone else, but alas, if others found out, he felt it would only cause panic. He felt he needed to find out more about the extraterrestrial visitors' mission before even considering informing someone else about what was going on. Therefore, he thought maybe now was still not the proper time. *But, when is it a good time? And, who should I tell first? I want to talk to someone about this, but who? Who is going to believe me? And who can I trust to keep it a secret, like me?* He shook his head. For now, his pen and paper would be the only witness.

Brian was tired from searching, reading, and then searching again for more books and other literature at the library. He sighed heavily as he folded his arms and rested his heavy head for a moment. He wanted to relax for just a minute or two. Brian slowly closed his gently fluttering eyelids as he brought to mind the pleasant recollection of the mysterious alien humanoid woman. Once more, he precisely recalled each delightful detail of the exotic celestial female. Brian recollected her unusual, though strikingly beautiful, feminine physique, and the way her flight suit hugged every curve of her shapely alien figure.

I wonder why she's not with Baouzhe in my dreams. "Hmmm…" He curiously pondered. *I wonder if she thinks of me. And, I wonder what a handsome male looks like on her planet. Hey, maybe she thinks I'm handsome… for an earthling, that is. Maybe she thinks so; the same way I think she's so beautiful.* Brian smiled as he thought about the celestial alien woman. *Baouzhe never told me her name. I've got to remember to ask about her, now that I know we're actually communicating.* His tranquil thoughts pleasantly reflected on her extraterrestrial smile and he soon fell asleep at the library table.

· · · • ● ● ● • · · ·

The next thing Brian was fully aware of was opening the door to the guest bathroom on the first floor of his parent's house. As the door swung open, the young man heard the sound of the shower being turned off. The bathroom was generously misted and comfortably humid from the steam generated by the hot water. The colorful shower curtain was suddenly flung open from the faucet side of the tub. Brian stood perfectly still. What he saw was quite surprising and very tantalizing to his senses.

There she was, completely wet and perfectly naked. She was facing the ceramic tiled faucet side of the combined shower and tub. From that perspective, Brian could see her entire alien backside. Though her unusual, yet proportionately lean celestial body was somewhat different compared to humans, she was, nonetheless, enthrallingly appealing. Her sopping wet burnet hair with subtle golden highlights fell straight and narrow along her long, slender neck just above her befittingly wide alien shoulders. Her silky-smooth and incredibly exceptional amberous skin tone glistened from the abundant tiny water drops, just like glitter all over her alluring naked humanoid body. She was, without doubt, a desirable female by even the most modest earthly standards. Brian's jaw dropped in slightly less than innocent marvel of this welcome and appeasing amazement, as his probing gaze made way from north to south of her bewildering extraterrestrial, feminine physique. The elegant small of her back, exaggerated by her extraordinarily small waist, gave way to erogenous wide hips. Brian's mischievously curious, roving gaze continued from there. He was keen to notice how her long and shapely thighs very pleasingly delimited her exposed, glistening, wet alien buttocks. She stood very straight and purposefully still, with her long, athletically slender legs close together. It was as if she knew he was there watching, and she wanted him to get a good look at her.

Then she slowly turned her shoulder to look at him. Brian could distinctly see a slight, agreeable, and contented smile from the left side of her face as she precisely turned her head to glance behind her bare left shoulder. He felt speechless until she purposefully turned to make full eye contact with him. Then Brian almost gasped. For an honest moment, he felt like running out of the bathroom and slamming the door shut, but he did not do so. His mind suggested it was time to leave, but his feet stayed put. Now Brian found himself looking directly into her beautiful almond shaped, luminous bronze eyes. He was simply captivated by her incredible celestial womanly splendor in its complete and wonderful naked form. She was fully exposed to him now, allowing Brian's curious eyes to wander wherever. The subtle smile on her face openly invited his unmitigated visual examination of her unique, primal womanhood. Her alien body was a remarkable sight to behold, as it was gracefully and athletically toned. Her naked breasts were firm and very modest in size and proportion in comparison to many healthy women on earth. This modest sized appearance was in most part due to her very wide shoulders. The generously rounded areolae and prominent nipples of both of her round and delightfully formed breasts were an appreciably darker pigmentation.

Next, Brian's unrestrained probing gaze quickly progressed downward along her midriff area, slowly passing between the distinctively accentuated curves that elegantly defined her narrow waist. Her abdomen was flat and firm and, Brian could even distinguish some of the sculpted musculature definition underneath her gleaming wet skin. He also noticed another interesting and significant anatomical symbol of her mammalian species, which was exactly similar to earthly humans. She had a cute little 'innie' bellybutton. The full, uninhibited view of her was beguiling. Brian was unaware that he was involuntarily smiling as he continued his rousing exploratory gaze.

He was awfully delighted to advantageously observe how the exceptionally curvy thighs of her unusually wide glistening pelvis was just as enticing from the anterior view as it was from the posterior, rear view. Then Brian's more than curious gaze eventually, though not subtly, found its way to her soaked mons pubis. Much to his surprise the dark pubic hair of the alien humanoid woman's genitalia was actually well trimmed, and there was something else even more peculiar. The burnet color was appealingly divided by a prominent, straight, golden-blonde streak situated almost directly down the center. Brian very coolly raised an eyebrow at the arousing discovery of this. *Now that's something you don't see every day, for sure.*

He continued his visual survey of her exquisite alien femininity, searching down her long, dripping wet legs to the top of the tub where they vanished behind the white porcelain. She remained perfectly still during this entire process, with her arms at her side, and with nothing to hide from his gratified inspection. Next, his eyes made their way back to hers. She was still agreeably smiling.

"Damn!" Brian uttered aloud out of sheer, enthralled astonishment. "Uh…" he stumbled on his words, grinning from ear to ear. "I mean," he cleared his throat, "excuse me, I didn't mean to intrude."

He shook his head and slapped his cheek, trying to extinguish the juvenile grin from his face. As he courteously bowed his head towards her, Brian firmly grabbed the bathroom doorknob and turned his shoulder to avert his eyes from the very privileged exclusivity he had already visually partaken of. He continued to turn around and pull the door shut with haste to make a charming and swift exit, when all at once he was confronted with an unexpected and dreadful obstruction. Directly in front of him was the wolf-like being. Brian found himself face to face with the menacing snarl of the beast, just inches from his own nose. The creature's eyes were blazing red, and the aggravated growl of the alien suddenly filled the young man's ears like the sound of a roaring, breaking wave on a low tide beach. Brian opened his mouth to scream.

· · · • • ● • • · ·

"Dude!" Brian opened his startled eyes and quickly raised his head off the library table. "Hey, bro." There was a hearty whisper from across the table. Brian, still in a daze, looked over to see a young man with long, bright red color treated hair and a tattered baseball cap staring directly at him. Tattoos covered his arms and his oversized black 'Megadeth' T-shirt practically swallowed his long, skinny torso. Brian grimaced at the sight of him, and the young man across the table gawked back. Brian did not know if he should answer or ask him a question. "You're snoring dude." The young man raised his finger to his lips and looked directly into Brian's dazed and dreary eyes.

"Shhh… Keep it down sir. I'm trying to read here."

Brian noticed several skate boarding magazines spread out in front of the young man on the large library table. He rubbed his eyes and face for a minute to wake up, and then decided he was alert enough to stand. He rose to his feet, checked for any belongings on the table he may have left, and then quietly exited the building.

Chapter Twenty Two

Brian wanted to clear his head. He felt he needed to do something to keep busy in an effort to distract himself from the continuous thoughts of the recent alien visitation. So, after he left the library he drove towards the lake. He tried to rationally re-think the benefits and consequences of telling someone about the aliens, verses keeping everything a secret. He even considered asking the creature if it was okay to let one more person know about their visit to earth. Brian weighed the pros and cons of disclosing everything he knew, but alas, who would really believe him? Probably no one.

Brian decided to park near the lake and go for a walk to help him unwind a bit. So, that is precisely what he did. He walked for an hour along the lake, but still could not help thinking about the unique encounter. Brian stopped by the shore of the lake to observe a large party of people laughing and playing in the shallow water. He stared at them for a while in silence and entertained the thought that those people did not have even the slightest clue about the alien visitation to earth. He shook his head slowly at the thought of it all. *People are going about their lives without the slightest clue that we have visitors from outer space here today! Damn!* He laughed aloud. *If they only knew! I bet there would be widespread panic. Everyone would go absolutely out of their minds.* He continued to stare at the large gathering of people laughing and playing on the shore. *There would probably be utter chaos amongst us right now.*

After the long walk and the idle time he spent people-watching by the lake, Brian was very hungry. He picked up some Mexican take-out for dinner from a well-known restaurant in the resort area and brought the delicious food to his parent's house. He dined alone in complete silence. His mind was full of thoughts about the kind, though furtive aliens; especially the humanoid woman. After he finished his meal, he paced around the house for half an hour. He thought again of the consequences of telling someone he could trust, or maybe the local authorities and the media about his terrific first contact encounter. But eventually he came to the same conclusion; that he would only be made a fool of unless he had indiscriminate proof of the unbelievable alien visitation. No one would believe his firsthand accounts of what happened. Not to mention the dreams. Especially, no one would believe the dreams.

He was feeling restless again so he walked out the front door and went for another stroll. Ironically, his travels took him south, into the vicinity where the young engaged couple had enjoyed their weekend jog earlier that day. He was near his mother's favorite hiking trail, practically at the very spot Janet and Aaron had sighted something very bizarre in the woods. However, Brian saw nothing, because, there was nothing to be seen. There was no bizarre, dark shadowy peculiarity hiding in the shrubs, and there was no strange, blurrily transparent thing hovering over his head, for now.

After forty-five minutes of walking outdoors in another effort to clear his thoughts and relax his mind, he went back to the house. The sun had just set and it was getting dark. There were no street lights in the immediate area of the neighborhood. Thus, it was safer to be indoors than outdoors alongside the unlit road this time of day. Brian decided to watch every television news channel he could find to see if someone else had accidentally discovered the extraterrestrials and reported their clandestine presence on earth to the broadcast media. However, the only repeated story on several news channels was about the withdrawal of Israeli troops from the besieged, occupied Palestinian town of Beit Jala after two days of intense fighting. There was nothing about aliens from outer space being discovered in the San Bernardino National Forest, or anywhere else in the world, for that matter. No one had reported a unique, surreal encounter with the extraterrestrials. That was gratifying to a certain extent since, truth be told, Brian did not want his alien friends to be discovered by just any random person. He was actually quite relieved that no one else had done that yet.

After watching over an hour of repetitive cable news television, Brian started pacing around the house. He really wanted to talk to the aliens again. There were many questions on his mind that he wanted to have answered, and the more he paced, the more he thought about those questions. He glanced at his watch and noticed the time was 9:05 p.m. Just then his cell phone rang. He recognized the ringtone and picked up the cell phone off the breakfast bar in the kitchen.

"Hey Brandon, what's up?" Brian merrily greeted.

"What's up little bro, how're you doing these days man? Sorry I haven't called you, I've been so busy. You know how it is," Brandon responded.

The two talked about the usual things; Brandon's wife Donnette and their son, work, saving up a little money, and the latest technology they planned to buy with their extra cash. Brandon wanted the latest cellular phone upgrade, and Brian wanted to buy a new notebook computer. The two talked about their parents and their vacation in Hawaii. Brian danced around the fact that he and Gina were supposed to be there on vacation with his parents right now. Brandon knew his brother was supposed to be enjoying some tropical sunshine with Gina. He knew they were having some trouble in their relationship, but what was more, Brandon could sense that his younger brother felt dejected. Brandon knew his brother had a healthy ego, however, he definitely knew the young man also had feelings. He knew his younger brother was deferentially competitive in a lot of things he did. Brian took on success in everything in life as a very personal challenge. Brandon's little brother was one you could count on to always rise to any occasion and get something done, whether the task was big or small. Brandon knew that Brian could be trusted to help him with anything he needed. Now, it was Brian who needed a shoulder to lean on, though the younger brother would never admit it. So, Brandon made a wholehearted effort and suggested his brother accompany his family to Mexico. Brian was happy to hear that, and he said he would sincerely consider it. To Brandon, that sufficed as a mental 'man hug' for his dear brother. It served as a good, emotional 'pick me up'. Even if he decided not to go, at least the offer was there, and it still stood.

Towards the end of their conversation, Brian actually considered telling his brother about the visiting aliens from another world. He felt if he could not trust his own brother, then whom could he trust? They'd had a close relationship since they were children, and they understood each other very well. Surely, Brandon would believe him. *My brother always has my back.* The young man mentally deliberated, but alas, he revealed nothing to Brandon by conversation's end. *It's probably better I remain quiet about it for now, just a little while longer. Besides, I can probably help the aliens better if I keep their visit a secret. That was kind of my latest plan of action, anyway, I guess. I should probably stick to that plan. I think I'll know when it's time to speak up about it.* Brian laid the cell phone on the computer desk after he and his brother said their goodbyes. Maybe some other time he would say something, but for now, that was that.

After enjoying a couple of light snacks and watching a few hours of situation comedies like *The Cosby Show* and *Home Improvement* on *Nick at Nite*, Brian felt very drowsy. By 11:15 p.m. he was prepared for bed, and by the time he lay down on the comfortable queen size bed in the guest bedroom downstairs, he quickly fell asleep. *Time to go visit my alien friend.* Brian thought; *maybe I'll even get a beer, too.* He closed his eyes and it did not take long for him to drift away. His muscles began to completely relax, his heart rate slowed a bit, and his body temperature dropped slightly as his body prepared to enter the deep sleep associated with rapid eye movements.

·　　·　　•　　●　　●　　●　　●　　•　　·　　·　　·

The next thing Brian was aware of was sitting outside in the cozy patio dining area at the same table of the dreamscape restaurant. Baouzhe sat contentedly across from him. Brian gazed into her beautiful eyes just as before, gathering his thoughts for the anticipated conversation.

"Nice to see you again, Baouzhe," Brian said. "I was expecting we would be here tonight, as usual."

"I've been ready to meet with you, Brian. It is very good to see you, too." The beautiful woman of his dreams politely answered him.

"Well," Brian was encouraged and spoke up with much enthusiasm, "Let's get to it, shall we?" He clasped his hands together and rubbed them vigorously. "I've got a lot on my mind, girl."

"I'm sure you do," Baouzhe calmly responded. "Let me first apologize for leaving so hastily last time we spoke." She adjusted her posture slightly. "You third-planet-homo sapiens are so very curious."

"Third-planet-homo sapiens?" Brian inquisitively raised an eyebrow.

"Yes, well, that is a term some of my people use to describe your kind. You humans live on the third orbiting planet of your solar system's single, bright-white star."

"You mean third planet from the sun?" Brian politely responded.

Baouzhe replied with a smile. "Yes, third planet from the sun, or bright-white, as we like to call celestial thermonuclear masses similar to yours, that is."

"I see." Brian rubbed his chin. "Anyway, what do you mean by saying humans are so very curious?"

"The last time we met here at this place Brian, some other humans almost discovered my actual, physical location." Baouzhe spoke in a very sincere tone. "I can't afford to have another being from this planet know about our whereabouts and our mission, Brian."

"What happened, exactly?" Brian asked. He hoped no one stumbled upon the aliens as he had done. Brian could only imagine the terror of seeing the alien creature at first sight, especially the way he had experienced meeting her. "Did somebody accidentally find your spaceship, again?"

"To be honest, I was not inside the interstellar vehicle that you discovered. I use another vehicle for travel within this atmosphere that is much smaller and more clandestine." The beautiful semblance of the creature smiled slightly. "Anyway, my presence was not successfully discovered."

"The spaceship," Brian asserted, "you moved the ship. I know, because I went back to find it again. I'm certain of where I last saw it and hiked back to the same spot. But the ship was gone." There was a discernible moment of silence in their conversation as they stared at each other. Then Brian politely inquired, "So, where is it now?"

"I'm sorry, but I cannot disclose that information to you, Brian," Baouzhe calmly replied. "Surely, you can understand why."

"Listen up lady friend, as long as we are communicating, albeit in a dream," Brian quickly spoke up, "and, as long as there is at least one person, me in particular, that knows you guys are here, then, your mission is not a secret, baby. It is not clandestine, anymore."

"I should tell you, the board of high command rank officers and chief executive personnel for this mission in unison with and supported by all the leaders of my world are fully aware of all occurrences that have transpired upon our arrival, Brian. They are all unanimously agreed upon and they have duly determined your knowledge of our existence to be an assessable, tolerable risk." The beautiful lady of Brian's dreams spoke without the slightest hint of apprehension, "We have been authorized to continue the mission as planned."

"Because nobody's gonna believe me, is that it?" Brian quickly countered. "Who's going to believe one person saying he saw some alien creatures from another world out in the woods late at night? I certainly can't prove your existence to anybody based on a story alone. People will just think I'm making things up." The young man shook his head. "We have a word for people who openly talk about stuff like this happening to them here on my world. Crazy." He pointed at the young lady and said, "Somehow you realize that fact. That's why you're not too worried, huh? No wonder you didn't try to knock me out or something when I discovered you guys were out there. I bet that's probably why you two just walked me back home. So you could just disappear into secrecy again. You don't need to do anything about it simply because nobody's going to believe me anyway. It's a tiny problem that kind of conveniently solves itself, doesn't it?"

There was no verbal reply from the bewildering exotic dreamscape woman sitting across the small table. Nevertheless, Brian could not help but notice the compelling affirmation in her mysterious eyes. It was a look of silent, insightful accord in regards to what he had just professed. He felt sure he was, indeed, correct in his assumption.

Truth was, Brian wanted someone else special to know, partly so that he could convince himself this was not simply a contrived fantasy that he had colorfully created in his own mind. He really wanted to have some type of factual validation and consolation by having another person on this planet know what he had discovered. However, the circumstance was quite the contrary. There was no one else who had this exclusive knowledge right now except him. The circumstances were such that he was the only person on earth who knew of the aliens' existence. True, it was difficult to remain quiet, but it would probably be more complicated and maybe even more consequential to acquaint someone else with what was surreptitiously happening right now. Brian knew he would have a very difficult time convincing someone else that there were alien visitors from outer space here on earth unless he actually introduced the celestial visitors to somebody in person. *Not a good idea right now.* For now, his pen and paper would remain the only witness.

Brian was just about to say something else when he noticed someone approaching their table from the left. The person walked swiftly, coming directly from the indoor dining area. "Good evening. My name is Alfred and I will be your server tonight. Would you like to start with some wine or cocktails before dinner?" the waiter asked with a big smile and a distinct South American accent.

Brian recognized the gentleman from the first dream he had, the one that included Gina.

"Oh, uh," Brian replied promptly, "yes sir, two beers, please."

"We have several varieties on-tap and in bottles. What do you prefer, sir?" The kindly server politely asked in his familiar smooth, baritone voice.

Brian looked at Baouzhe as he replied with a smile, "You know what?" he sniffed, "Make it a Red Wolf for me and the beautiful lady, please. That's all we want, Alfred. No dinner tonight, just Red Wolf."

"Very well sir, I will be back with your beer. Here are some menus in case you change your mind." The server smiled and handed them each a menu before whisking away into the indoor dining area.

"Red Wolf?" Baouzhe chuckled. "I suppose you ordered that in my honor? Sounds interesting, Brian." She could not hold back her amusement and chuckled aloud.

Brian grinned like a dastardly comedian onstage in front of a rapt, giddy audience.

"Baouzhe!" The young man playfully retorted, "You're smiling. You're actually laughing and smiling right now, amazing!"

They both shared that charming moment of laughter together, allowing them to simply relax and enjoy the jovial similarities they both shared as intelligent beings from different worlds. This is exactly what they both needed right now.

"I told you I'm not as uptight as you make me out to be." Baouzhe leaned forward. "Brian, if you ever get the chance to come and visit my world, I will show you how we have a good time."

The young lady gave him the warmest smile he had ever witnessed grace her beautiful face. It was a display of benevolent emotion, an expression he had never seen before this surreal moment they were sharing.

"No doubt." Brian was impressed by what she said. It was a sincere offer, and he really appreciated the fact that she wanted to socialize with him on her home planet. He quickly extended the same courtesy in a manner of speaking. "If things were different here on earth, we could have a really good time on this world as well, Baouzhe."

She gave him a bright smile and a single nod in kind response.

"Baouzhe, I have to be honest with you." Brian's tone changed back to a slightly more serious vibe as he said, "I've been going back and forth in my mind about telling someone else about you guys being here. You don't know the dilemma it has caused in my head. I just keep thinking, should I, or shouldn't I. But deep down inside, I know it would probably be a bad idea. So, all things considered, I will honor the significance of your mission and keep what I know a secret. Besides, you have assured me your intentions are good, right?"

"Yes, that is correct, Brian. I thank you on behalf of all the people of my world for your consideration and cooperation." Baouzhe nodded her head respectfully.

"Baouzhe, I want to be your only contact here on earth, for now. Public knowledge of your existence will most likely cause widespread panic. So, let's keep it that way. It's best nobody knows you guys are here."

"Except for you, Brian." The beautiful semblance of the creature smiled at the young man. "It is okay for you to know, so we can help learn about each other better, yes?" She raised an eyebrow.

"Okay, that's cool with me." Brian cleared his throat. "So, tell me Baouzhe, who are you? I mean, what do you call yourselves?"

"The best translation of the words from our language to give you relevant meaning would be to call the people of my world, dwellers of the lifeful planet." Baouzhe smiled as she explained. "We literally associate ourselves with the world we live on. It is a blue-green planet full of abundant life and energy. It is very much as big and beautiful as the world you live on, Brian. There are many similarities. In fact, our planet is also the third orbiting satellite of our solar system's bright star." She smiled. "Our planets look very much alike, Brian. Our oceans also cover most of our planet, just like yours, deep and blue. And our mountains are just as tall and grand. The atmosphere on our world is also capable of sustaining organic life, just like yours, except, ours is not polluted. You see, the way we live in our world is quite different from the way you people live in yours. We do not saturate the waters, soil, and skies with filth." She frowned. "If your people only knew the way this world you and your people live on is truly reacting to the combined exploitation of its natural resources." The lovely lady looked up into the dreamscape night air as she thought for a moment, and very calmly yet sternly conveyed, "The best way I can put it is, this planet is tolerating your presence."

"Interesting." Brian crossed his arms.

It was all he could say and do in response. How does one react and honestly reply to such an argument when you know it is probably not very far from the truth? The young man wanted to point out the faults of most of the careless people of the world, but how could he do so when he was part of the very same equation? In the grand scheme of things, Brian considered himself just as responsible as everyone else.

"The humans of this world seem to generate so much useless waste in comparison to essential material that is produced, Brian. There appears to be so much energy inharmoniously employed and then negligently expended just to generate a comparatively and quantitatively smaller outcome as benefit."

"Okay." Brian was attentively listening to what she was saying.

"It is something we have observed over much time."

"You mean like, when we make stuff?" Brian assumed, "Making what for example?"

"Everything," The beautiful dreamscape semblance of the creature asserted forebodingly. "Everything you make, use, and waste is in vast excess."

Brian concurred. "Well, I can't really argue with you on that one. I agree that it's probably very true, Baouzhe. What can I say?" He shrugged his shoulders.

"But, I see you are also a very intelligent society, capable of doing many wonderful things." Baouzhe turned her slight frown into a warm, genuine smile. "We have observed how people work together on a common goal for the good of others. You remind me of our own people in many ways. It is a known fact. I have studied much about this world."

"Is that what you and your people think of us?"

"Yes Brian." Baouzhe replied. "The people of my planet respect the people of this world. You are all so very honored by my people. Yes, we realize many groups of people on this planet do not believe the same things or have the same practices. We observe the violence that spawns from differences in political and religious beliefs. However, despite the wars and generations of anger, you all seem to coexist in peace more often than not."

Baouzhe leaned towards Brian. "The people of my world consider this planet you live on a holy place. And we consider the people of your world the chosen ones who will someday soon bring love and serenity back to this part of the universe." She supplemented with the most beautiful smile. "My people believe that in the beginning, this was the perfect planet where unconditional love was masterfully crafted into guiltless, flawless living. Our written history reveals that your planet was a very beautiful place a long time ago. It once had The Garden." She leaned back in her chair with a contented reflection of humility upon her face.

Brian was at a loss for words, completely dumbfounded. His contorted face exhibited that fact. At first Baouzhe talked about how wasteful humans are, and the next moment claimed humans are more or less hallowed.

Brian winced and frowned a bit as he said, "Baouzhe, I'm sorry, but I don't know what the hell you're talking about. Just what are you trying to tell me?"

"When the words of the sacred scrolls are fulfilled, True Love will return. Then The Garden will essentially be as once before, perfect! You'll see, someday." Brian raised a finger and pursed his lips to respond but suddenly their polite server arrived.

"Your drinks," the smiling man calmly announced and placed two tall glasses and two bottles of darkened red lager beer on their cozy dinner table for two. "I will check on you in a little while to see if you are hungry, okay?" His thick Latin accent broke the conciliatory silence.

Brian simply nodded in acknowledgement. The kindly server poured the frothy dark lager into both glasses. No sooner had he done that the server walked away with the same gracious smile.

"Okay now," Brian said, insistent but polite, "just what in the world are you talking about?" He stared at her. "What are you trying to tell me? This planet is a perfect, sacred place, like a beautiful enchanted garden?" Brian chortled. "I got some breaking news for you. This planet is called Earth, and it is very far from holy my friend! It's just a huge ball of hostility and deprivation. And, let me say, it is also the official home of the have and the have nots!"

He shook his head at the state humanity was in. Baouzhe seemed a little taken aback by his reply.

"This may not look like the same world now that was perfect in the beginning. Nevertheless, this is the same place, Brian. And someday it will be the same beautiful world it once was."

"Say what?!" Brian grimaced and reached for his beer. "What are you trying to say? You're not making any sense. Girl, what've you been smoking? Are you high?" Brian giggled for a moment and then he said, "What do you mean by a perfect world, and garden, and all that? It was perfect in the beginning... the beginning of what? You talk about this planet like it's some kind of special secret place, like it's supposed to be, I don't know, like it's supposed to be the..." his eyes searched overhead as he tried to find the appropriate paradigm, "...the Garden of..."

No sooner had he said that than his jaw dropped and his eyes widened as the wheels of spiritual realization turned in his oblivious mind. He clumsily placed the tall glass back on the small table without that much anticipated first sip. He let go of it so abruptly that some of the cold and frothy red lager breached the rim of the glass and spilled over his tightly clasped fingers. In that moment Brian suddenly and profoundly realized what Baouzhe was implying.

"Good God!"

Chapter Twenty Three

There was a moment of awkward speechlessness on the romantic restaurant patio as the two individuals stared at each other. Baouzhe still had that same contented reflection of humility upon her face. Brian remained completely dumbfounded and definitely looked every bit as much. Then he broke the discomfited moment of silence.

"You're talking about the…" Brian grimaced and lowered his voice, "…the Garden of Eden." He shook his head in a moment of agitation and then rubbed the sides of his face. "Okay, hold on…"

Then, Baouzhe spoke up, suddenly interrupting him.

"Brian, do not be discouraged. Someday, this world will find sanctity and peace, when True Love returns. It is written. It is the will of the Sacred Creator."

Brian opened his mouth, paused, and then pointed his finger at the prophesying, alien dreamscape lady. He leaned forward and made direct eye contact with her.

"Now wait just a doggone minute…" He was promptly interrupted by Baouzhe as she continued to speak.

"Do you not believe, Brian? Don't you know by now in this stage of your young mortal years? We are basically taught everyone on this planet has at least some knowledge of the Sacred Creator and His infinite existence and divine authority. Can't you see His grand labor of love around you? The Sacred Creator paints like a brush on a perfect canvas with his beloved spoken words. The atoms and the elements respond to that indefinable preeminence, taking shape, fluid in motion from the mere sound of His great majestic voice. With the immeasurable inspiring might of His sounded words, they are commanded to take form into organic and inorganic material. From spoken words they become the essence of life." The reflective words of tranquility poured out from her glossy red lips like a gentle flowing mountain stream in the pure quiet of early dawn.

"This is how it was in the very beginning, Brian. Are you not familiar?"

Brian just stared mutely at Baouzhe from the other side of their small cozy table for two.

"Brian?" Baouzhe prompted as the young man finally blinked, his eyes wide and staring. "Are you not familiar?"

Brian rubbed his entire face with one hand and then sighed heavily.

"Sacred Creator? Do you really know what you're talking about? Do you know what you are saying? I mean, do you really believe what you're telling me right now? I thought you might be joking at first, but you're not, are you? This isn't just a theory you have? You're really serious. You're not mocking religion. Instead, you seem to have religion. You actually believe what you're telling me, huh?" Brian blinked several times with his mouth slightly agape.

"The Sacred Creator..." he muttered with a hint of a discomfited grin.

Baouzhe smiled politely as he cleared his throat and appealed for some affirmation.

"He's God, one and the same, yes? That's what you're telling me, and that's what you really believe?"

"Of course, why not?" she responded with a profoundly curious look.

"Wow!" Brian rubbed the back of his neck and then looked intently into her inquisitive dark brown eyes. "Look, I was raised in a Catholic home and I went to Catholic Church and Catholic school, and all that. And, most of my friends are also Christians for that matter." Brian sniffed. "I mean, I think it's beautiful, I really do." The young man could not help but chuckle a bit as he quickly composed himself and then said, "It's just that..."

"Christian," Baouzhe politely interrupted once again as she looked up into the night air for a second. Then her gaze returned to Brian's skeptical eyes. "Yes, that is the name for those on this planet who believe in the works and teachings of the one you call, Savior. I'm very familiar with that terminology and reference." Baouzhe smiled.

"You know of the Savior?" The inflection of surprise carried in the young man's voice as he leaned forward again and bluntly asked, "You know who He is?"

Brian was very eager to know her response, to say the least. Baouzhe nodded her head once slowly with a blissful smile upon her face.

"His wondrous works on this planet is the greatest story ever told."

"You're not kidding, are you?" Brian gawped at her, his words testing her resolute state of content.

"Brian, who doesn't know about the Son of the Sacred Creator and the eventual, altruistic sacrifice He made for everyone?" Baouzhe's humble words continued, "We call Him the Righteous Son in our own language. On this planet your people call Him Jesus and the Savior. Yes, Brian. Everyone, including me, knows who He is on my world. He is True Love."

"Whoa, okay, okay," Brian responded, as he started waving his hands fervently about, "I think I really am dreaming now!" He cleared his throat while gathering his thoughts. "Wait a second here. So, what you're telling me is you're a Christian." He coughed to clear his throat again. "You're basically, like, a Christian, alien, dog-person from outer space." He gestured a bit wildly and then began to chuckle and shake his head. He was confused, delighted, and flabbergasted all at the same time at this alien lady's revelation. What she was saying settled in his mind like an avalanche of enormous boulders. "You, you're really serious about all this, aren't you?" Brian smirked with a hint of misgiving and amusement.

"Yes. Why? Do you have doubt, Brian? Do you question my own beliefs and faith?" She turned her head to one side in a quaint, reflexive query.

"Well, Baouzhe," he replied with a clap of his hands, "I tell you what. I think it's the most beautiful thing to hear, but at the same time, this is all quite a shock! But, I guess it's shocking in a good way. However, my beautiful dream lady friend, I have to say this may not be so pleasantly shocking to other people here on Earth. In fact, some might even say its sacrilege. You see, you're going to confuse a lot of people by saying what you just told me. There are a lot of people in this world who will attest that evolution is truly a fact when they get their first look at you and your friend. People will point and say, 'Ah-ha, there it is! There's your proof that we all evolved from pond scum!' But, man, I'd like to see the look on their faces, everybody's face, when you start talking to them about The Garden and the Sacred Creator like you just told me." Brian started to laugh.

"I mean, it's really wonderful, Baouzhe, but it's kind of weird." He shook his head. "It's almost downright hilarious, actually." He shook his head. "I guess I always felt there was intelligent life out there somewhere. But, well…" Brian grimaced, "I never gave any thought as to what other intelligent life would believe in as far as religion is concerned. I just figured we would be the only Christians, I guess. Maybe that's an arrogant concept now that I think about it, huh? I mean, the people of this world use to think this planet was the center of the universe many generations ago. But we learned we're not. So, I suppose soon, we may all learn there are other people out there who believe in God just like many of us here on Earth do."

"Surely everyone knows of the Sacred Creator and the Divine Trinity," the pretty lady contended with a warm smile and a delightful nod. "There is the Sacred Creator, the Righteous Son, and the Comforter."

"OH BOY!" Brian scooted his chair very close to the small table for two. "Okay, look…" He leaned as far forward as he could when he spoke. "Divine Trinity, eh?" He almost whispered that last bit, then a little louder said, "Look, Baouzhe," Brian fidgeted and his eyes darted around the quaint patio as he searched for the proper words to say to her, "I have no doubt you believe what you believe. Heck, sounds like it's really what lots of us here on Earth believe, including me! And, Baouzhe, it's really wonderful. I really mean it, too. I mean, I'm shocked, but like I said, in a pleasant way."

Brian quickly reached for her dainty left hand and took hold of it in his fervent masculine clutch.

"Baouzhe, listen very carefully to me, okay? I mean no disrespect by what I have to say. But listen, you have to stay out of sight, and don't say a single word to anyone about what you're telling me right now! Don't go to any churches, synagogues, mosques, tabernacles, revival tents, prayer meetings, ice cream socials, or, whatever! You hear!? Don't go to our President! Don't go to any law enforcement agencies. Don't go see any other government leaders, or political figures. Don't visit any social gatherings, no matter how big or small. I mean nothing, not even a freakin' Girl Scout meeting! Stay completely out of sight! Do not make contact with anybody on this planet except me! Stay out of sight, do you hear me? Stay - out - of - sight!"

"Brian, it is not our mission to…"

"I mean it!" Brian interrupted, "If you make yourself known with all this evangelical when-the-saints-come-marching-in hullabaloo, you're gonna turn this confused as it is world UPSIDE DOWN!"

"Brian, we…"

"Baouzhe, please, promise me you won't let anyone else know you guys are here and who you are. Don't go knocking on people's doors with your sharp teeth and long pointed ears asking if they've heard the Good News!" he pleaded. "Please, PROMISE ME!" He squeezed her hand tight.

The very beautiful dream-world semblance of the female alien, wolf-like creature just stared with wide eyed amazement. "They told us you people would probably react this way," she replied in a hushed voice. "But, I don't understand why. This is the holy place."

"No!" Brian shook his head enthusiastically, "It is certainly not! Look, if you tell everyone you're here and start preaching, some people will probably be cool with that. But let me tell you right now, most people probably will not. Listen up. First of all, you guys are aliens from another world. That alone will cause much confusion and probably much panic. Then, when you start talking to people about the Sacred Creator like you're a bunch of space-traveling-later-day-saints, people are going to go into mass hysteria. Here's why. Some will shout hallelujah, some will second guess and want to interrogate you, some will denounce you and want to burn you like witches, and the rest won't know what to think. Next thing you know, people are arguing and taking sides. Next, there's fighting and escalating to world war. Then, next thing you know, we're all hurling nuclear bombs at each other in the name of whatever we separately believe to be true. And just think about it, you guys haven't said one threatening word to actually start it all." They both stared into each other's eyes. "You follow?"

"I personally do not understand why, Brian. But, I…"

"Exactly!" he exclaimed, pointing directly at the appealing semblance of the space alien creature.

She stared at him for a moment and then said, "We are here on a scientific mission of peace, Brian. We are here in secret to learn more about your world. We will not disclose our presence to anyone else here, as we have agreed. Brian, we mean you no harm. I have told you that, already. You can trust me. I promise."

He nodded and reached for his beer. "So, tell me, have you been to Earth before? And, if so, how many times? When? And how often?"

Brian took a generous drink of the mildly bitter beverage. It tasted and felt soothingly good to him. He felt he really needed it now.

"I can tell you we have been monitoring your planet and the people of this world for some time. We dispatched the very first satellite probe to start scientific data gathering for research over fifty solar earth years ago," Baouzhe said. "There have been several more probes dispatched to this solar system to monitor and gather more data from this world since that first one. We have learned much about this world and the life forms that inhabit it, including your humankind. There is much that we know now without ever having made ourselves formally known to the people of this beautiful planet." She raised an eyebrow and smiled. "Brian, we know now is not the time to come forth and make public contact and formal introductions with the people of this world. You probably will not be surprised to know that we judged that action would result in complete chaos. We are intuitive and wise enough to know that making ourselves known here would be a bad idea right now. We actually figured that out a very long time ago."

"Good!" Brian said and took another generous drink of his beer. Baouzhe curiously watched as he gulped the lager down. Brian noticed her watching him, and responded with a prompt gesture for her to join him. He pointed to her glass and raised his eyebrows several times while still drinking. Then, he returned the half empty glass to the table and belched. "Excuse me." He looked at her glass. "You got some catching up to do girl."

Baouzhe looked at her beverage for a moment. Then she reached for the glass of frosty cold beer and took a drink.

"That's what I'm talking about," Brian said with a grand, handsome smile.

"Not bad." She grinned. "It has an invigorating bitterness that I find quite enjoyable, actually." She took another ladylike swallow. Brian chuckled and drank with her.

"So, in answer to your question," Baouzhe set her glass down, "yes, we've been observing your kind from the shadows, so to speak, for quite some time now. And, someday, we do hope to make ourselves officially known to your people. Someday soon, I hope, but not now, Brian. I've been told many times your society is not mature enough yet. I really can't understand why people would panic, though. I mean, honestly Brian, doesn't everybody see all those countless brilliant stars at night?" Baouzhe pointed up to the romantic starry heavens. "Don't the people of this majestic world realize there are other people looking back at them from out there?" She returned her gaze to Brian's brown eyes and smiled.

"I guess. I mean, well, I don't know." Brian scratched his chin.

"You amaze me, Brian," Baouzhe replied sincerely. "The

people of this world are so naive, so irresponsible, yet so intelligent and so caring at the same time. You all seem to have a unique quality of self-preservation and survival, even when you turn your anger towards each other." The pretty young lady grinned. "Regardless of your inherently violent nature, there are many admirable traits that my people acknowledge and respect about you and this consecrated civilization."

"So, you don't think we're just a bunch of hairless chimpanzees walking around?" he joked with a warm smile. "You really do suggest we are a holy people, to some degree, anyway?"

"Please forgive my insulting analogy." She humbly bowed her head. "And, yes, this society of humans is revered by my people, Brian. You have a special prominence and purpose regarding the future of this universe. It is what we believe, and we would never do anything to disturb what we solemnly believe to be true." She smiled graciously.

"Interesting," Brian observed, "you think we are primitive and a danger to ourselves to some extent, yet we are holy, or at least, very special?"

"This is the holy place. And, to be completely honest, I believe you are a divine people."

She humbly bowed her head, again.

"Forgive me, please. Sometimes, I am too critical of you and your kind, Brian. You see, I am quite familiar with the innate nature of human beings. Therefore, I was not sure I could trust you at first. I didn't know how you would react seeing us right in front of your face, without already having knowledge there is intelligent life on other planets. I understand your anxiety. You are not used to living with different species of peoples. It was much more shocking to you when you first discovered us, than when we first saw you face to face. We already knew humans lived here. But, you didn't know about us. That is why I was not sure if you would try to hurt my companion and me in the forest that night. I had to be cautious, as you probably already assumed."

"Hmm," Brian smiled at her, "I understand what you're saying, Baouzhe." He chuckled. "Yeah, I was a little scared of you at first, girl. No offense, but at first sight, you kind of look like a monster to the people of this world. Trust me on that one. You do."

"I am not." She looked intently into his eyes with a heartfelt gaze of innocent susceptibility, one that only a sincere woman could truly evoke. The moment turned intimate, with deep appreciation and a mutual understanding. Brian was effectually captivated by her exotic dreamscape semblance. She was surreally fantastical, and by every definition of the word to him, she was dreamy. Indeed, she was a very beautiful woman, albeit a contrived fantasy within his sleeping mind. Brian could not help but concede to the realization that he was infatuated with this exotic fantasy woman even though he knew she was pseudo-physical.

He put his head down and rubbed his eyes as he forced himself to remember what she looked like in the waking world. He was preoccupied by the sight before him now. Although she was strikingly attractive, Brian had to try and remember to really keep in mind what she actually looked like when he was awake. She was, after all, a creature from another world. She was something he had never ever seen before. He was telling the truth when he told her she had the appearance of a frightening monster at first sight. Nevertheless, she was not, by honest definition, really ugly to look upon in the real world. She was just uniquely different. Brian was okay with that. All things considered now, she was not, after all, the ferocious beast he had made her out to be in his mind.

He tried to replay the words she had just uttered to him so that it all clearly made sense within his REM sleeping mind. There was so much to reflect on. This meeting between the two of them had, overwhelmingly, been the most pertinent of them all. He was learning so much about the alien visitors, their mission, and their intentions. For that reason it was important for him that their relationship continued to mature, both in trust, and in clear understanding of each other as distinct individuals. They were representatives of their respective societies. This was a deeply intriguing moment for both of them to be in each other's company right now. Brian certainly wanted to make the best of it. He looked again into her alluring eyes.

"I'm sorry for the derogatory things I have said. You're not a monster, Baouzhe. You're just very different from what I am used to seeing in this world. Please forgive my careless insults."

She smiled at him. Brian reached for his tall glass and took another generous sip of his beer. Baouzhe did the same. He smiled at the fact that she was really enjoying herself, albeit, in a dream.

"So," he said, "you were as surprised to see me as I was to find you guys out there that night, I bet."

"It was, well, quite an awkward surprise, to put it mildly." Baouzhe smiled. "You see, I was extremely preoccupied with a system integration procedure regarding our spacecraft's semblance articulation equipment and a molecular-anatomical, all-inclusive biochemical analysis of the earth's ambient atmosphere."

"Huh?"

"We were experiencing a slight problem trying to match the artificial intellectual, polynomial taxonomy verifier data received with another verifier in contiguous orbit."

"Say what?" Brian's face contorted as he tried to comprehend what she was saying.

The beautiful lady gazed at him from across the small table for a moment.

"We had a minor software glitch that I was busy working on," Baouzhe said, courteously translating to laymen's terms so he could understand what she had been doing that night.

"Oh, okay, I see." He took another sip of his delightfully tart, amber brew. "Go on," he said, "Tell me more."

"Well, I was so busy working on that issue, that for a moment I lost my situational awareness about our landing site's immediate topographical environment. You see, I accidentally set all the close-proximity perimeter alarm limits to a much lower sensitivity. It is not easy for me to concentrate on something so technical when there are several other audible indications all going off in unison in my ears. Most of the other alerts flashing and sounding off were just rudimentary utilities. So, by mistake, I adjusted them all to a quieter volume, including the perimeter alarms." The beautiful young lady shrugged her shoulders and glanced down at the table and said meekly, "It was basically my fault we were discovered that night."

"Hmmm, is that a fact?" Brian replied astutely.

"Yes, Brian." She made direct eye contact with him, again. "It was a mistake and it was quite the embarrassing surprise to find you standing there in our interstellar vehicle's berth, right next to our sleeping compartments. I was only alerted to your presence by an urgent orbital communications transmission. I got up at once, as soon as I realized what had happened."

Baouzhe shook her head and glanced down at the table, again. "I was so upset with myself for allowing that to happen. I will most likely be reprimanded for that incident when I return home. That, I can say, is most certain."

Brian was silent for a moment. He felt she was being completely sincere and he actually felt responsible for taking a long walk in the woods that uniquely serendipitous and historic evening. He hadn't meant to disturb them. On the other hand, when he discovered the mysterious ellipsoid object hiding in the deep ravine, he really wanted to know what that unfamiliar mechanism was.

Brian finally replied, "I thought you knew where I came from that night. I thought maybe you knew where I lived."

"I knew approximately where your physical domicile was located. Your house, that is." Baouzhe said. "I did a quick, close walk-around inspection of our interstellar vehicle to see what was immediately around us after we made successful surface contact. Then I returned to the vessel. Our atmospheric observation modules showed me everything else I needed to be aware of within several miles proximity of our surface landing position. There was nothing to be really concerned about based on the remote locality and tenable concealment. I could clearly see we were mainly surrounded by small, naturally occurring animal life residing in the very dense vegetation there. We were never in danger from anything from where we were situated. We were not in danger from being discovered by any mass gathering of curious and potentially hostile human earth dwellers, nor were there any dangerous large wilderness creatures close by. The weather climate was also quite agreeable for our terra surface locality. I am actually very impressed that the interstellar mission planning experts and subordinates considered the present environmental conditions so precisely. I will have to commend them for that in our mission debrief when we return home."

"Okay, I guess. Well, good for you guys on that one." Brian nodded.

"You see, Brian," Baouzhe continued "there are many, many things that can go dreadfully wrong on a long, complicated mission such as this one. A mission that is specifically so historically important, too." She smiled. "All things considered, it is still going very well. There have only been a few unexpected incongruences to mission planning."

"What do you mean by 'incongruences'?" Brian asked.

"Oh, well, um…" she started to answer, but then gasped as she looked up into the night sky. "Oh, look at that." She pointed up into the air and said, "What a brilliant falling rock!" She smiled at the delightfully timed incinerating distraction. "They look so different from this view when they enter the atmosphere. They really do shine like the brightest stars. It is so beautiful!"

Brian glanced up just in time to see the brilliant meteor zip across the atmosphere before it was quenched by the blackness of the vast, romantic nighttime sky. Brian sensed a solemn hint of déjà vu at the spectacular occurrence. He could not help but think of the moment he and Gina witnessed the same wondrous event in the first dream. He sat there, staring into the dark, star spotted heavens, as he reflected on that intimate moment. He had no comment.

Baouzhe broke the silence. "You miss her, your lady friend, yes?" Brian looked into her eyes. She smiled and said, "She is a very beautiful lady."

"Yes." Brian nodded and answered, with a hint of a smile.

"So, Brian," Baouzhe asked in a soothing, informal tone of voice as she quickly changed the subject, "what were you doing out there that night? How did you know we were there? Tell me."

"I should be asking you the same thing. What were you doing out there in the forest that night?" Brian chuckled.

"I told you." The beautiful semblance of the alien calmly replied with a genuine smile. "We are here on a scientific mission of peace." She leaned towards him and in a soft, slightly sultry voice asked, "Now, what were you doing out there?"

"I went out that night, because…" Brian looked up in the air and tried to recall exactly the reason. "Well, I just felt there was something different." It was all he could say.

"Did you hear us make our surface landing?" She softly inquired, almost cautiously so, with her heavy accent.

"Well," Brian looked at her, "I heard something strange in the night. It was as if… well, it just sounded, strange."

"Maybe then, we should have changed our landing site." Baouzhe looked down at the table. "There was some debate about it."

"Who debated about it?" Brian leaned forward towards Baouzhe. "You? Your companion?" Brian smiled, "Tell me about her. Why was she sleeping when I found her?"

"Why was she sleeping?" Baouzhe responded with an amusing gaze. "Because she was tired. Interstellar hyper-travel is very, very exhausting, Brian."

"Yes, of course it is. Oh, I definitely agree on that one." Brian took a swallow of beer.

"How would you know?" she asked with a smile.

Brian laughed, almost spitting out his beer. He managed to return the glass to the table without spilling it.

"I'm just playing. I have no idea." He wiped his lips.

Baouzhe sat erect in her small chair and then began to speak in a more serious tone.

"Brian, you want to know more about what we were doing in the forest that night." She stared into his eyes as she disclosed the information. "Well, I will tell you now. Brian, we have been sent here to try and find out more information concerning one of our… subjects. The subject is part of a study, from one of our earlier observation missions."

Brian was curious. He raised an eyebrow and, with a faint smile said, "One of your subjects? From an earlier mission?" He definitely wanted to know more about this.

"Do tell."

Chapter Twenty Four

Baouzhe leaned forward a little and, with the hint of a smile, answered him.

"Yes, Brian. She was the last subject we were collecting data from. We lost contact with her on May 21, 2001. Her domicile is in the same region where you dwell now. In fact, her residence is very close to yours. Or, it was. Just before we lost contact, her residence had changed for a very short while. Her last dwelling was located at an establishment not very far from her permanent domicile. If my calculations are correct, I believe she was residing at one of your infirmaries for a while."

"Infirmary… you mean a hospital," Brian supposed, intrigued.

"Our data suggests that she was ill at the time of her change of residence. We think, very ill." Baouzhe said, "Her mortal life force may have terminated. I must confirm if that is true."

"No shit." Brian looked at her, wide-eyed.

"We started monitoring her in the recorded earth calendar year of 1948. She was a very healthy female infant at that time. She was an excellent subject."

"Really? No shit." Brian pinched the meaty part of his chin absently as he listened.

"Shit?" Baouzhe paused for a moment. That is an earthly allegory for defecation, yes? It is… a vernacular. But, I do not understand your query, Brian." Baouzhe tilted her head to one side, perplexed at his use of the word.

"Oh, uh, yeah, it's just a stupid slang response, sorry. I'm just really impressed and surprised by what you are telling me right now. It is very interesting, Baouzhe."

Baouzhe nodded in reply and then continued, "Her cumulative recorded data has proven to be an edifying, historically scientific event to us, to say the least. There was much to learn from it all, specifically in regards to how your divine human body matures and carefully ages with the passing of time. Our scientists are very, very intrigued by your species' existence, and how you have adapted to the wonderful world you live in. You are truly a divine people," she said, bowing her head a little in respect. "Brian, now as I am telling you this, I reflect on the way I have reacted to your hospitality and can only say I am no less than thoroughly embarrassed by my speculative, judgmental, and at times, arrogant attitude towards you. Again, please forgive me." She bowed her head.

"It's cool, space-wolf… I mean, Ms. Baouzhe." She smiled at his reply.

"Brian, I suppose you have many questions and want to know more about that particular historic mission as well as this current, significant mission.

"I really don't know where to begin, to be honest with you. And, yes, you are absolutely correct, Baouzhe. Like I said before, I have many, many questions."

"Let me explain a bit then, Brian. Perhaps I can answer some of those questions."

Baouzhe sat erect and continued in her thick, accented voice. "We made our first surface contact on this planet several decades ago with a specific purpose and a carefully determined plan. There was much to do. Much like your nation's intra-solar space travelers did when they visited your nearest satellite many years ago."

"You mean, when we sent astronauts to the moon back in the 1960s?" Brian asked.

"Yes, Brian. Your nation of people sent several crews to that ancient satellite several times between your earth calendar years, 1969 to 1972, I believe. I know for a fact you sent several teams to collect mineral rocks and study the lunar surface. I remember during my indoctrination and conditioning training, I was required to watch declassified data chronicles taken from our covert observations during that time." Baouzhe looked at Brian. "I watched every recorded mission and considered your space travel capabilities quite rudimentary and the trip extremely risky for your people to attempt at that particular period in time. Nevertheless, the scholastic experts and scientists on my planet insisted it was probably the greatest milestone for your kind. Indeed, I do suppose you could say that mission officially marked the beginning of human space travel. You successfully ventured out past the boundaries of your own planet and actually landed somewhere else. I know how impressive it must have been for the people of your world to watch such a thing during those days. I respectfully acknowledge that fact, Brian." Baouzhe nodded once.

"Uh, thanks, I think." Brian responded to her frank complimentary reply.

"We have been observing all of your travels into space, both manned and unmanned, including all rocket launches from every nation for quite some time now. We continually monitor those missions, as well as your overall combined technological progress. Your people have noticeable potential, enough to someday successfully and consistently reach beyond the borders of your solar system."

"We people of earth are natural born explorers. There are a lot of people here with the same audacious spirit as I have, Baouzhe." Brian beamed proudly.

"Your space travel program is quite rudimentary, but effectual, nonetheless. You have had many successful launches and many failures. Regardless, your humankind continues to make small progress. In fact, we are still monitoring and categorizing data from your nation's slow traveling vehicles, including the Pioneer and Voyager probes dispatched several earth decades ago. The Voyager 1 continuing mission, in particular, is still the topic of a many great scientific discussions on my world." A small smile pulled at the edges of Baouzhe's lips. "I suppose I should commend your people's successful effort to explore far beyond your horizons."

"Uh, okay, yeah, thanks."

"You should be proud of your people's accomplishments, Brian," the beautiful young lady said sincerely. "At least you did not use all that technology to try and completely annihilate each other."

"True. Well, not yet, anyway." Brian rubbed his nose. "I guess that's something to be proud of, indeed." He was actually very impressed that she knew so much about earthly space travel. "You have an impressive knowledge of our space program."

"It would be inspiring to see humans continually develop and use this technology for the good of everyone and not just invent more powerful and deadly missile weapons of mass destruction. Space travel technology should be used to better a society, not destroy it. Your industrial and technological developments should bring you closer together and unify civilization. It is possible. There is always hope that you will eventually live in total harmony with one another." Baouzhe smiled. "I always hope for that. I pray for it."

"You do?" Brian responded with enthused intrigue. "Really?"

"Yes, Brian. Of course I do." She smiled.

"Well, thanks, again."

"You are welcome," Baouzhe replied politely, and then resumed disclosing a little more information, "Our second surface contact mission…"

"Whoa!" Brian said, holding up a hand. "How many times have you guys been here?"

Baouzhe paused for a discreet moment before answering. She gazed at Brian, seemingly undistracted by his query.

"…our second surface contact mission was the most recent one, until this current one in progress, Brian." Baouzhe coolly continued. She tilted her head to one side and asked, "Is that a satisfactory answer?"

"I guess." He was puzzled by her answer and sensed she was guarding something. However, her answer sufficed for now.

"We made successful surface contact to start the scientific

monitoring process of our second planned subject near the end of your calendar year, 1971. We began collecting data when that subject was an infant, as well. Just like the first subject, we gathered much useful data over many solar earth years from that human, until the subject's unfortunate demise earlier this year."

"Say what?" Brian's eyes widened. "What do you mean? What happened to that person?" He sat close to the small table so he didn't miss a word she was saying.

"That male subject's mortal life force was accidentally extinguished on January 26 of this current calendar year. He was dwelling in the city named Bhuj, in the land of Gujarat, India at the time of his unfortunate death. There was a terrific seismic episode of your measured magnitude 7.7 which devastated the entire area where he lived. Many of your human kind perished there, I believe over 19,000 initially. Many others soon fatally succumbed to their inflicted wounds, or they soon perished from additional consequences of their condition as a direct result of that terrible tragedy."

"Yeah, you know what, I think I remember reading something in the news and seeing something about it on TV earlier this year," Brian vaguely recollected. "That many people died, huh?" Brian tried to remember the television news report he had seen about the incident.

"You see Brian, almost all of our work learning more about your human kind has come from the indispensable data received over many years from both of those excellent subjects. We realize humans can live a very long and healthy lifespan. Yes, we can theoretically see that. But, we have not yet recorded and officially documented enough substantiated data to support that as fact. You see, it is one thing to look at something and make a determination based on observed, visual substantiation. On the other hand, if you can formulate and prove, or even argue a hypothesis based on known or even unexpected, quantum variables, in precise simultaneous concurrence with well-established, congruent and duplicable polynomial solutions, well, that is something completely different." She slowly leaned back in her chair.

"I see." Brian nodded. He tried to follow along as best he could.

"Brian, I need to determine the condition of the older female subject's health and her present whereabouts. She is all we have left regarding this great, historic, ongoing study of ours. Some of us think the subject is still alive, and some of us think she is not. We are just not certain. Regardless, we definitely are not receiving any more data. I must at least address that issue. It is possible, and has been considered by my superiors, that our synthesized, organic micro-biotelemetry implant device has malfunctioned. If it has temporarily ceased to operate there may be a way for me to rectify the situation. However, if there is no malfunction, then, it is reasonable to assume the subject has terminated. And, if that is true, then, we have lost our only two human subjects… both within the span of a year!" Brian nodded his head in acknowledgement as Baouzhe asked, "Do you understand what I am trying to say?"

"I think so," he said. "You want me to help you find her?"

"Yes, Brian!" She exclaimed with appealing glee. "We talk now, and you will help us now. I am happy to report this to my superiors soon. We are making a lot of progress, Brian, yes?"

"Yes we are." Brian smiled. "I'm happy to help in any way I can, seriously. I mean, it's all for the good of science I guess, as long as no one gets hurt or anything."

"Oh yes, Brian, it is for the good of both our worlds. It certainly is. Our observations have been extremely informative, and the method is so completely harmless. Both subjects have no clue they are being studied by us. I know we have no formal permission to do this, and I do apologize on behalf of my people for the lack of formal consent. But, I can promise you as a show of good faith, we already have an official plan to reciprocate. We will leave a couple subjects from my world here for as long as your humankind wants to study them, when the time is right. We are happy to do that, Brian. We want your people to greet us, accept us, and learn everything about us. We look forward to that when the time comes that we can share our world and our culture with you. I hope, someday soon."

"That sounds really good, Baouzhe, someday soon. But, not just yet." Brian looked down at the table and shook his head. "I mean, I hope the time will be right in my lifetime, but don't do it now. We definitely aren't ready, yet."

"Agreed." Baouzhe said, her face expressionless.

"Well," Brian smiled, "I'm happy you guys are at least visiting us here in peace, and there's no alien invasion about to happen." He cleared his throat and then asked, "There aren't a million other space-wolves out there waiting to invade at your command, are there?"

Brian leaned forward in his chair and peered at Baouzhe in a jesting manner.

"Brian," she retorted, "we are not a violent society. We are not a brood of nomadic warmongers! We are an intellectual, spiritual people. We do not seek to invade a holy place and ruin a divine society. What would that gain? We are not that kind of people!" Baouzhe attested. "Besides, an attempted land invasion and hostile occupation would be imminently futile... for us. We would not be a superior advisory to you."

"Are you serious?" Brian chuckled, "With all that technology you have? I mean, from what little I have seen so far, I can only assume your weapons are even more impressive."

"It is not the weapon that makes one superior. It is the will and spirit to fight."

"Hmm..."

"Brian, I need you to learn an effective and very practical new method of communication. We will use it so we can understand each other, and help with our coordination efforts during this investigation. We will be able to understand each other outside of your subconscious, extrasensory sleep cycles." She smiled. "I think we are now at the proper juncture where I can rapidly and successfully teach you."

"You mean, so we can talk to each other without dreaming?" Brian stared at her for a slight moment.

"In essence, yes." She nodded her head once.

"Wow!" A puzzled frown settled on his handsome face for just a short moment before he said, "Hey, wait a second, how are you able to do all this anyway?" He pointed around them, waving his finger back and forth several times. "How are you able to meet me here in my sleep? How are you able to communicate with me right now while I'm dreaming?"

Baouzhe smiled humbly and looked down at the cozy table for a slight moment, seemingly searching for the most basic terminology to explain the method.

"Well, Brian, the best way I can explain it is, well, I have what you call, a certain talent. A gift, you might even say." She gestured with her dainty hands. "I am well practiced. I have been trained to enhance my extraordinary capability, which just happens to be a very, very rare and fortuitous trait of my species."

"No shit." Brian's eyes were fully locked onto the beautiful, exotic woman of his fantastical dream world.

"I have specially designed devices customized for only me to use because of my special abilities. These devices are basically evoked, electro-encephalic, epidermal conduits that help me reach someone's subconscious mind. In essence, within the deep recesses of an intelligent person's brain, I can effectively communicate by thought."

"Say, what?!" Brian gawked at Baouzhe with his mouth agape.

"Your species and the people from my world all have a very similar anatomical arrangement, classification, and organic process," Baouzhe explained. "Impressively, even at the most basic cellular level of stimulation and response, our biologic behavior is remarkably identical." She smiled. "We are not that dissimilar, overall. We require oxygen and water and food to live, just like you do. To no surprise, that is why our worlds are almost a mirror image of each other." She continued to gesture. "In short, because of our profound biological similarities, we were fortunate to discover that my special gift could be used as an advantageous utility here."

"Okay, so..." Brian was utterly speechless, not knowing exactly what to ask next, though he had many questions. "Okay, I know the brain and neurons conduct electrical activity. But..." He was promptly interrupted by Baouzhe.

"Yes, I am familiar with your conventional medical capabilities, somewhat. Your human kind is capable of recording the basic lower level electrical activity of the brain. I know it is an effectual clinical tool. However, that method is not even close to, say, using the antiquated form of Morse code in order to successfully communicate, compared to my ability. My complex and unique ability is capable of isolating and interconnecting our brainwaves to telepathically share an intellectual, simplistic, common reference language. In effect, it is practically like having the total capability to stand in front of someone and comfortably talk to them. Even though they are, in reality, many miles away."

"No shit." Brian gawked.

"It is a very unique and complex process that can only be done when both the receiver and I are in a deep sleep. As you can imagine, it is not very practical to converse in this manner." She took in a quick, short breath before continuing. "Nevertheless, this method of communication has been very remarkable and quite effective up to now. I am very satisfied with the progress we have made together, Brian, and my superiors feel the same. This is truly a historic moment, because it is the very first time this method of communication has been used to contact and converse with your human kind. In fact, this is the only time we have communicated with any human on earth, Brian. You are the first."

"Wow, that's really remarkable, very nice and, I'm really impressed. So," Brian cleared his throat and then asked, "can you communicate with everyone on earth this way, in their dreams?"

"Only you, Brian."

"How is that possible?" He asked, intrigued.

"You have been…" Baouzhe paused for a moment and shifted in her chair. "…you have been fitted with a very tiny device that allows us to communicate in our sleep, Brian. The device works as an evoked, electro-encephalic, epidermal conduit." There was a slight pause. Brian stared, expressionless.

"I hope you do not mind," Baouzhe continued, smiling. "It was a necessary and tolerable risk. You must understand it was very important for us to do so. But do not worry, Brian, the device is so small, like a very tiny mole on your skin… well," she paused for another second, "there are three epidermal implants, actually. One just behind each of your temples and, there is one more on the top on your head." She pointed at a spot on her own head and smiled at him.

"Say what?!" Brian rubbed his temples in agitation, trying to determine if he could feel something unusual on his skin.

"You cannot feel them now, Brian," Baouzhe said, trying to calm him. He was still asleep and experiencing all this in a dream. He stopped rubbing his head when he realized this. She continued, "The bi-phase encephalic-transmitter implants are harmless. They pose no risk to your health. They do not control your behavior or thought processes."

Next, Baouzhe did something very much unexpected. She reached across the small table and placed her soft hands on top of his and then grasped firmly.

"Brian," she said, "I know we did not have your permission to put those on you. I…" She almost stuttered. "I apologize. But I tell you now, you will be just fine." Baouzhe continued to smile, looking into his eyes as she spoke frankly. "Brian, when all the people of my world hear how much you have cooperated and how much you have helped us on this historic mission, I know they will greatly honor your noble effort and involvement. You will one day find out that you are a brave, unselfish hero to them. You will be like an adored celebrity to the people of my world."

"Just for helping you on this mission? Just for helping you find somebody, the subject?"

"Yes, Brian." She squeezed his hands again and smiled appealingly at him.

At that moment Brian realized that no matter if he was asleep and dreaming of the exotic Asian woman, or standing inside the ellipsoid looking into the eyes of the other amberous humanoid woman, the aliens were an enthralling and intoxicatingly beautiful duo. That was fact. The way Brian felt about the extraterrestrial travelers was a clear advantage for the alien world that had sent them to Earth, even though they couldn't have predicted that he would find them so appealing.

"I'll do it," he said.

"You will still help us?" Baouzhe's smile was so big and beautiful that it was infectious. Brian smiled back at her in return.

"Yes, I will help you and your people."

"Wonderful! And we are happy to help you, as well."

"Well, I'm not sure what we really need even though we earthlings do need a lot of help." The young man chuckled. "It's like I said earlier, probably the best thing you can do for now is just stay out of sight."

Baouzhe acknowledged his comment with a respectful nod of her head.

"Let me ask you something. So, every time I dream of you, we are basically communicating with our thoughts, right?"

"That is correct. Whenever we are here together at this location, this restaurant, we are communicating. We talk now, only within your dreams, Brian."

"Ah…" Brian grinned, "I see. So, what about the other times? I mean, I do remember at least one other dream with you and your friend, the other alien woman. I remember you both were in it."

"Any other conversation with me outside of this subconscious visualization and locality is a mere sequence of images in your sleeping mind that appear involuntarily, a mixture of imaginary elements influenced by deep emotions and fantasy."

"Got it," Brian said. "So, what you're basically saying is, if we're not here talking together at this restaurant, then it isn't real. I mean," he waved his hand about, "if we're not here talking together, then, we aren't actually communicating for real."

"That is correct. We talk now." Then, with an engaging hint of a grin she said, "Tell me about your other dream, Brian. What exactly did you subconsciously visualize about?"

"Oh, nothing in particular, I guess."

Baouzhe peered at him and then grinned. "I am curious, Brian. What does the human mind dream of?"

"Well, as a guy, I can tell you, I'm always happy to dream of a beautiful girl like you." He playfully grinned in return.

"That is interesting." She stared at him, studying him across the small cozy table in the exact way the creature did in the waking world. The familiar impression of her demeanor was intensely sobering to him. "And, what did we talk about in the other dream? I am very curious, Brian,"

"Uh…" Brian was fidgeting a bit in his seat. He adjusted his posture, sitting more erect and then spoke frankly, "Well, we weren't really talking." He cleared his throat, "From what I can remember, I kind of walked in the bathroom in my parent's house and found your friend, kind of, well, standing in the shower. She was, you know, kind of… naked."

"That is interesting." She stared at him with a raised eyebrow.

"The reason I'm mentioning this to you is because it all seemed so real. Just like now."

"Tell me, what did you see, Brian?" She smiled, candidly interested in what he had to say.

"Well," Brian paused and continued in the most gentlemanly tone of voice he could, "I saw her… you know, her, stuff." He grimaced. "I saw her private parts." He tried to be matter of fact, but lowered his head to avoid her eyes.

"I see," she replied coolly.

"It seemed so real, Baouzhe." Brian casually shared his experience with his beautiful dream-world alien lady friend, "I was actually kind of embarrassed when I saw her. You know? Everything was so detailed, and so vivid."

"I see," the young Asian lady again coolly replied. "Did she look very different from a human female, in your dream?"

"Yes, well, you know. She doesn't really look that much different, all in all. I mean, her skin color is very different from us, and her body is shaped a little different, but anyone can definitely tell she is a fully developed, healthy, attractive woman. You know what I mean?" Brian fidgeted, uncomfortable with the way this conversation was going.

"I see. You said you saw everything in detail. So, was there anything else you noticed that was very peculiar about her anatomy that is very different from human females, besides the fact that she is not from this world? I am asking, because I am curious about something. Tell me more."

"Uh…"

"The reason I am asking is, well, let me start by saying I am somewhat familiar with the physical anatomy of your species, Brian. I know your kind is born with different shades of skin color and hair color, for instance. And, I can tell you the one thing about her species that is so unique is her hair. Her species has a natural highlighted accent seen as strands, or streaks. She, for example, has a very beautiful and remarkable brownish hair color with naturally accented blonde highlights. There are actually many women of her species on my planet that have similar type of occurring highlighted pattern. And there are a variety of other colors, as well, such as a reddish highlight or a violet highlight. There is even orange. However, her blonde color highlights are quite rare, actually. Her hair pattern, I must say, is considered very attractive on my world."

"You can say that, again."

"So, tell me some more details. Tell me specifically what else you saw that was vivid and distinguishing. I'm very curious."

"Well, there was one thing kind of different that kind of caught my eye, I guess." Brian acknowledged quietly. "The, uh… The pubic hair between her…" Brian pulled at his collar and fidgeted nervously in his chair. "She had an interesting… well, I don't know. She just looked different than earth women, I guess."

Baouzhe took a slow, deep breath and then sighed, looking down at the table.

"Only the females of her species may develop, during puberty, a unique, distinguishing mark on their private parts, as you call it. She happens to have a very unique blonde streak situated almost directly down the center of her pubis. I am assuming that is what you observed and appreciated that was so vivid. Is this correct?"

"Bingo, yep!"

"Brian, I think you may have involuntarily accessed a memory from my own experiences kept somewhere in the recesses of my mind. You probably recalled the way she looks, exactly as you saw her in person. And, I am assuming you also visualized her as she really is, when nude, including some specific detail, just as I have seen. You may have simply mentally interposed what you have seen and what I have casually seen, combining the two experiences into a contrived, voyeuristic fantasy you were able to visualize in your subconscious."

"Say what?" Brian was somewhat embarrassed, but very intrigued.

"Somehow, you are able to know exactly what she looks like based on your brief and limited familiarity, in addition to what I must have seen before."

He looked down rather than at Baouzhe, and nodded.

"This sort of side effect is not dissimilar from some of the experiences I have heard about from a few of the other deep sleep cycle interaction research subjects on my home planet. It probably won't come as a surprise to hear that this type of thing has actually happened before, though to a much lesser degree."

"Okay," Brian said, "so, basically what you're saying is I just saw something you have seen, and remembered. And I just combined it with my dream, making it into a fantasy kind of thing."

"In effect, yes."

"I'm cool with that," Brian said with a hint of a grin.

"Yes Brian, I am sure you are… cool with that. Now, if you do not mind. We start now. You have much to learn."

Chapter Twenty Five

Brian picked up his glass and gulped down what was left of his cold beer. In response, Baouzhe smiled, lifted her glass to her glossy red lips and swallowed the rest of hers, as well.

"Damn," Brian said, "you go girl!"

Baouzhe returned the glass firmly to the cozy table for two with a slight thud and replied, "Time for you to learn, Brian. Are you ready?"

"Wait." He raised his hand.

"Yes, Brian, what is it?"

"You never told me her name." He smiled. "What's your friend's name?"

Baouzhe grinned and then graciously imparted the long awaited information. "Meihtu."

"May-toe." Brian smiled as he unsuccessfully tried to say the name the way Baouzhe had.

"Meihtu." Baouzhe replied brusquely, then she repeated the name slowly so he could hear the pronunciation better, "Me-to."

"Meihtu," he said, grinning. "I like that."

"Give me your hands, Brian," Baouzhe said, interrupting his thoughts about the exotic humanoid woman's pretty name. "Give me your hands and close your eyes." Brian brought his attention back to Baouzhe as she took hold of both his hands in her firm grasp and then said, "Now, close your eyes and clear your thoughts. This is very difficult for me to do. You learn now."

"Wait," Brian insisted, as he opened his eyes in time to see the sultry exotic dreamscape version of Baouzhe grimace back at him with one eye open and the other shut tight. Her face showed just a slight hint of frustration in that instant.

"What is it now, Brian?" She leaned her head to one side.

"So, will I also be able to speak to Meihtu after we're finished? Is it because she is unable to dream and communicate like you that you will teach me a way to talk to her?"

Baouzhe let go of Brian's hands and gestured as she spoke.

"When we saw you in our interstellar vehicle on the evening of our surface landing, Meihtu actually tried to establish communication with you first, by speaking one of your earth languages, Brian."

"Say WHAT!?" His jaw dropped in surprise.

"You see," the beautiful young lady patiently replied, "on our planet we speak about twenty different languages, and we logically assumed, long before the very first probe was dispatched from our planet to this one, that we would detect a very similar language here on Earth. However," she raised a finger as she intelligently asserted, "we found out something quite remarkable, and to this day is peculiarly inexplicable to most prominent linguistics on my world. During the first years of meticulously monitoring your various radio and other simplistic communication bands from deep space, we advantageously discovered a striking similarity."

"What is it?" Brian looked intently at Baouzhe.

"You see," she continued, "not only do you have over a hundred different spoken languages all over this beautiful world of yours, but we also documented many different and fascinating dialects within a single culture's language. And, well, to put it simply, we discovered many of those variances in language occur in the country of China. Much to our surprise, Brian, we heard languages there that are quite comparable in resonance to ours. And, as we documented and studied more of the recorded, bundled human verbalization data coming from the huge and diverse country of China over many years, we discovered something else. Amazingly, we observed that our language was somewhat analogous to Tibetan, Brian." Her eyes were wide and excited.

"No shit?"

"Yes, it is true. I will also tell you this. In order to communicate with your people in the future, we have been studying and learning many different ways to converse. For instance, our Mission Commander, Meihtu, has learned and become proficient in speaking Cantonese. That is the language she tried to communicate with you in. Although we knew you did not live in the quadrant of your world where that language is mostly spoken, we thought we should at least try."

"What?" Brian leaned back and put his hands on top of his head, fascinated.

"She can also speak a little Mandarin, and I think she even tried that with you, too." Baouzhe nodded in recollected consideration and then said, "There are several people studying different earth languages on my world right now, Brian. When the time comes, we want to be able to speak to many people at once. It will be more respectful to do so, we believe."

"Are you serious? How is that even possible? How are you learning our languages without actually being here? That must be very difficult, if not impossible."

"It is having the opportunity to learn that is the greatest challenge," Baouzhe said. "We have a special, dedicated research group on my planet that was exclusively assigned the honorable task of learning several of your world's languages and communication media. And, true, the task is not uncomplicated, by any means." She paused in slight contemplation for a second before continuing.

"I will tell you some details. Many years ago, in order to help facilitate this challenging endeavor, we had a few cloaked intra-atmospheric probes placed circumspectly for observation purposes. Some were well hidden in the highest trees, located only a few miles away from populated areas in select rural areas of China. The elite purpose of these probes was to continuously listen, and gather intelligent information. Their basic objective was acquiring and observing any human conversation. We theorized the information obtained would help us in our efforts to study exactly how humans learn their own language. Indeed, we learned a lot, and very quickly at first. It did not take us long to comprehend some of the basic, vocalized, interchange data we observed and recorded. We learned a lot about human behavior through your spoken and even unspoken communication mannerisms. We observed conversations between many humans, between both the young and the aged. We were so fascinated to observe this, even from afar. Also, we realized a great deal of language is basically learned at home, to no surprise. So, we carefully monitored several homes where some young children live in order to assimilate the learning process of language in the very beginning stages of the lives of you divinely human people. In addition to that, we patiently monitored a few schools where learning first begins, the same schools where some of the very same human children we were already studying attended." Baouzhe continued to gesture.

"Over much time, we were basically educated and we fundamentally learned language along with the children." She smiled delightfully. "It is very fascinating, yes?!" The beautiful young lady's eyes were still wide and excited.

"When you say 'we', you're talking about that special research group of yours, right?" Brian asked.

"Yes, that is exactly correct, Brian! Yes!" Baouzhe politely and gleefully acknowledged.

"So, is Meihtu, or should I say, Mission Commander Meihtu part of that special language research team you mentioned?" Brian asked with a handsome grin.

"In essence, yes."

"I see. So…" he changed his posture and gestured very enthusiastically, broadening his grin and raising a brow, "…where's the person that speaks American, Basic English 101, man? You didn't bring that guy on this trip?" Brian chuckled. "You take years to hide a probe in a tree and learn Chinese like a baby, and then you land in America and can't speak to a brotha'?" Brian laughed. "What's up with that?!"

"We originally had no plans to contact anyone on this mission. In fact, having our whereabouts discovered would normally be cause to abort the mission, Brian. Although we are continually preparing ourselves for that anticipated official moment when we can meet everyone someday, we really were not expecting human contact right now." Baouzhe's courteous explanation was almost apologetic.

"I'm just messing with you," Brian playfully bantered, waving his hand about. "Don't be so serious, space girl. Maybe you should've hung a probe somewhere in south central L.A. so you would know how to talk to people around here. Hell, nobody's going to understand your Chinese here unless you're in Chinatown, girl." He laughed aloud.

"Meihtu tried to talk to me in Chinese? Damn, I mean, it sounded a little familiar, I must admit, but, not THAT familiar!"

"Cantonese and Mandarin," the beautiful young woman iterated kindly. "She tried to communicate with you in those earth languages before I successfully did, in your sleep."

"Yeah, right," Brian said. "Well," he leaned forward, smiling from ear to ear, "shit, y'all should've been watching some reruns of *'Sanford and Son'*, or *'Fresh Prince of Bel-Air'* or, something!" He could not help giggling at his own humor.

"What do you mean, Brian?" Baouzhe turned her head to one side, baffled.

"Nothing, nothing…" He chuckled again and cleared his throat. "Will I be able to communicate with you guys, you know, even after you're gone?"

"We do not have a plan for that."

"Okay. So let me ask this, are you on that special language team, too, since you're about to teach me something?"

"In essence, yes."

"So, what do you speak?" he asked, pointing at her. "Don't tell me." Brian waved his hand animatedly, again. "Nigerian or, Tibetan or, uh, Korean, or something like that, I bet." He started to grin, "If it's Nigerian, then well, shit! Maybe I'll just have to take a trip to Africa next year. You know, take some time to really learn the culture. So I can be ready next time!" He chuckled again. "I'll go and hide up a tree for a year! Just like your floating probe-drone whatever you call them!"

Baouzhe reached across the cozy table for two and grabbed hold of his hands in response.

"Shhh…" She politely hushed him and said, "close your eyes and I will show you now, Brian."

He graciously did as she requested. Eyes closed, elbows resting on the cozy table, the two leaned toward each other. Brian was quiet, trying not to think of anything. Only the pleasant sounds of gentle laughter and casual conversation from people enjoying themselves inside the restaurant area could be heard on the patio now. Brian lowered his head and no sooner had he done that and started to relax than he felt a little dizzy. His head felt heavy and he wanted to rest his forehead on the table. He could feel Baouzhe squeezing his hands, and he could hear her breathing rate slightly increase. He was beginning to feel a little more disoriented now and not certain if he could sit straight for very long. He felt he was losing his balance, and he was thinking about saying something to the pretty young lady opposite him, the delicate dreamscape semblance of the extraterrestrial creature. *Maybe I should tell her how I'm feeling right now.* He considered doing so, but his thoughts simply faded away.

· · · • ● ● ● · · ·

The very next thing he was aware of was waking from a deep sleep. When Brian opened his eyes it only took a second for him to realize it was early morning, and that he was comfortably stretched out on the double bed in the guest bedroom. He instinctively looked at the digital radio clock on top of the nightstand. The time was 6:36 a.m. He sighed, and then recalled the most recent dream he had. He could still see Baouzhe's beautiful face and candid, reflective expressions so vividly in his wakened mind. Brian smiled at the thought. She was very appealing to behold, albeit in a dream. That was why he looked forward to going to bed at night. He really enjoyed meeting the extraterrestrial creature in his dreams. It was because of their pleasant encounters that Brian appreciated the beast much more now than before.

He wanted to document everything they discussed so he could have an accurate record of their most recent encounter. There was much to put in writing. There was so much that he had learned about the aliens from this most recent, intriguing dream. He was looking forward to getting started. Brian sat up straight on the side of the bed and yawned. He was feeling quite hungry. However, he did not want to waste time cooking a large meal for breakfast. He wanted to write in his journal as soon as possible. He gave some thought to whether he should have hot cereal or cold cereal. Regardless of his culinary choice, the first thing he realized he needed to do forthright was relieve his bladder. Brian stood up and proceeded straight to the guest bathroom.

The instant he caught a glimpse of his reflection in the mirror he suddenly remembered there was something he desperately wanted to see. *The implants!* He had forgotten all about the alien, technological skin inserts. He looked in the mirror and raised his hands to his face. Cautiously, Brian softly massaged both temples right next to his closely groomed hairline and thought he felt a tiny bump. Brian leaned towards the large mirror and inspected the right side of his head and, although he wasn't completely certain, he thought he saw what appeared to be a very tiny mole located by his temple. Although he could not see the left opposing implant, he knew they were both there; one on the right and one on the left.

Brian rubbed the top of his head, searching for the third alien implant. Again, he was not completely certain, but he thought he felt something very peculiar there at the top of his head. *It must be the other one. Baouzhe said it was there.* He grinned at the idea that there was a foreign device in his body; a mechanism that opened his mind so the aliens could observe and engage his deep thoughts. *Yes, indeed, you definitely got tricks, space-wolf!*

After having breakfast and going through his usual grooming routine, Brian sat down at the computer desk in the family room and began to document in his journal everything he could remember. When he recalled the segment of their conversation about the skin implants, he raised a hand to his head and gently rubbed the spot of the right implant and once again, grinned and silently shook his head. Then he put pen to paper once more and continued to write. His written recollection of the occurrence was remarkable, to say the least. He even wrote down some of their dialogue, word for word. The task came very easy to him. Brian noticed he was writing at a pace and with an effort that almost seemed programmed. The written words came fluently from his brain, flowing to pen, filling the detailed journal with purposeful alacrity. It was as if his hand knew what to write without any suggestion from his mind. The invigorating circumstance he was experiencing right now, along with his keen recollection, was a potently cerebral, existential awareness. Brian smiled, and laughed aloud as he systematically wrote about their delightful encounter. Before he knew it, he was done. He had effortlessly finished writing about the dreamscape occurrence much faster than the first time he carefully documented the details of his previous dreams.

After the task was successfully completed, Brian silently read what he had just finished. He was very pleased. Then something quite extraordinary suddenly occurred. No sooner had he read the last sentence of his detailed journal than he had an entirely obscure recollection that acutely rushed to his mind, just like a flame spurting, top-fuel dragster thundering down a quarter mile strip.

"Quintessential, q-u-i-n-t-e-s-s-e-n-t-i-a-l… quintessential" he suddenly blurted and spelled aloud. *What the…* He was not certain why he had just spelled that particular word out aloud. *Why in the world am I thinking about that?*

Brian shook his head, somewhat confused. Then, at that very moment, he remembered a particular spelling competition from his sophomore year at Bishop Montgomery Catholic High School and how it had been one of the most intense moments of his young, teenage life. Two contenders remained. He was representing the sophomore class, and Tyler Bellhogan was doing the same for the junior class. Brian was given the word Quintessential to spell in the final round and he failed the attempt. However, Tyler got it right when it was his turn, and the juniors went on to win the school spelling competition that year. From that moment on, Brian was always apprehensive when he had to spell that word, especially aloud for someone that needed to know. Brian remembered that one afternoon a nurse at the hospital was working on a crossword puzzle and had asked aloud how to spell that same word. He was walking by on his way to a patient's room, but stopped in his tracks and concentrated intently. It was almost as if he was back in high school competing in that infamous, intramural spelling challenge. He confidently gave the nurse the correct spelling then in the very same way he had just said it out loud. *Okay, that was weird.*

When Brian finished recounting the chronological events of this historical alien encounter he was experiencing, he hid the journal in his leather backpack. He knew it would be safe there along with the Polaroid camera and the pictures he took in the ravine. He was happy. It felt good to be able to express in writing the experiences he'd been having getting to know the kind aliens. Brian felt more at ease now about having exclusive knowledge of the extraterrestrials' covert mission on earth compared to his initial reaction. He had been overwhelmed, paranoid and apprehensive, and had felt compelled to keep himself overly busy in an effort to distract himself from the continuous thoughts of the alien visitation. He no longer felt anxious or harbored misgivings about the aliens' stealthy arrival. He was very much at ease now. Indeed, now he patiently looked forward to the next opportunity to contact Baouzhe and Meihtu. He had no clue as to when or how that next event would occur, he just knew it would. Those were the basic, simple facts. Therefore, he decided not to think about it too much.

· · • ● ● ● • · ·

Brian kept himself unadventurously occupied the rest of the morning completing most of the routine chores around the house his mother and father had kindly requested of him before they disembarked on their relaxing vacation in Hawaii. After cleaning Mr. Doodles' litter box, one of those delightful chores,

Brian entertained himself for a while by playing with the frivolously vain, youthful tabby. Who needs to watch television when you can watch a happily engrossed, fixedly curious cat chase his favorite toy around, a slightly faded day-glow pink ping-pong ball? Brian had a few good laughs watching the determined, self-involved cat at play. That was pure, free, fun for the impromptu, ambassador of Earth.

Brian rewarded his mother's playful tabby with a few treats before leaving the cat in the garage. Brian knew Mr. Doodles would come walking through the pet door in search of dinner and, of course, more treats later on in the evening.

"See ya later, Doodles," Brian said affably as he stepped through the door to the laundry room and closed it behind him. Suddenly another obscure thought rushed into his mind. He stood perfectly still, holding the doorknob, and suddenly blurted out, "Aaron Burr, Vice President!"

No sooner had he said that aloud than he distinctly recalled the occasion when he was asked who the third Vice President of the United States was in a little pop-quiz session during his 9th grade history class. The teacher was randomly selecting students and asking them relevant questions from their homework reading assignment. Brian recalled how the teacher asked what individual had previously served in office as Vice President who was also involved in a historically customary single-shot duel that resulted in the fatal shooting of Alexander Hamilton, the founder of the central bank, which was the First Bank of the United States. Brian recalled how the teacher had pointed directly at him for an answer. The very moment he was singled out, his adolescent mind drew a complete and utter blank. For the next few seconds, which seemed like an eternity, the entire class had their hands stretched high towards the ceiling in eager anticipation of a chance to answer the question. "Aaron Burr," he finally responded, embarrassed.

Brian started towards the kitchen, chuckling at the memory from high school that was humorous now. As he reached for the doorknob of the door leading to the kitchen, he had another obscure thought suddenly rush to mind and then flow directly out of his mouth.

"Bacteria are unicellular and prokaryotic, and a prokaryotic cell is an organism that doesn't have an enclosed nucleus."

Brian knew this was an interesting moment back when he was taking an exam at Mount San Antonio College in Walnut, California. It was his first year of study in the Respiratory Therapy curriculum. He was taking a general studies requirement in biology that he would eventually use as transfer credit for the University of Southern California. He incorrectly answered a multiple choice question on that exam, and for some reason, now he was verbalizing the correct answer for question number fifteen on the fifty question mid-term exam. *That's odd.*

He looked down in bewilderment at the floor and then slowly turned the brass doorknob on the kitchen door, swinging it open. He looked up and instinctively jerked backwards, away from the creature filling the other side of the doorway.

"Good God!" he shouted. The shock sent Brian's fight or flight response into seriously high gear while simultaneously rooting him to the spot. "How did you get in here?!" A surge of adrenaline rushed through his body and his muscles tensed in a swift physiologic response that evoked another flood of words. "Damn, you scared the hell out of me!" He drew a deep breath and shook his head. "Whew!" He tried to compose himself. "Please don't do that again!" He let out a loud breath and then chuckled at his reaction.

He was accustomed now to seeing the delightful sultry semblance of the creature appearing in his deep sleep, but not having the beast surprise him by suddenly appearing in his kitchen on the other side of a door he was opening. It took a moment before Brian could make the mental shift that this werewolf looking creature was actually Baouzhe. The two very different beings were actually the same person. Brian looked into the eyes of the beast and she looked back. Brian could immediately appreciate the familiar look in her eyes. It was exactly the same as the sexy Asian woman in his dreams. This was Brian's new friend standing before him now, the same person that he had become very fond of during his sleep. She, the creature, stood silently at the doorway. Then she smiled at him.

"How did you know I was here?" Brian asked while looking at the creature's sharp-toothed smile. He was still feeling the after effects of the shock. As soon as the words left his mouth he remembered the nearly invisible floating ball that she used to secretly observe things. *Oh, it has to be around here somewhere. I completely forgot about that stupid thing.* Brian instinctively turned his shoulder and started looking around him in search of the clandestine airborne gadget. *I wonder where dad keeps his tennis racket.*

The waken version of Baouzhe, the actual person of his dreams, promptly caught his attention again with a slight grunt of a sound. Brian returned his attention to his new friend just as she raised her hands about chest high. He stared for a moment, perplexed, and then assumed that Baouzhe realized he knew how she had found him. He assumed that she would quickly recall it by using her wristband device. She did not.

Baouzhe very slowly started to gesture with her hands. Her arms and wrists moved in a graceful manner that seemed rehearsed. At first, Brian was confused by this strange behavior. She repeated the gesture. He tilted his head to one side, frowning slightly. Then, as if a switch turned on inside his head, he instantaneously understood what she was doing and interpreted the motions of her hands.

"Can you understand me?"

Brian didn't know how he understood, in fact, he was mystified on that point, but he instinctively knew she was using sign language and somehow he was able to understand. Brian raised his hand and pointed at her as he spoke aloud.

"You want to know if I can understand you?" He smiled and then said, "Yes, yes I can." Then, at that very moment, he got the inclination to respond in a more appropriate way. His eyes widened as he raised both hands in front of him and, very slowly at first since he didn't know why he could sign with his hands but somehow knowing he could, he gestured back.

"Yes, I understand you." His generous although

slightly nervous smile immediately gave way to appeasing laughter when he realized he had successfully replied back to the creature using the same method of sign language she had used. *So, this is what you must have taught me in my sleep. You definitely got tricks, my friend!*

The wolf-like interstellar alien, Baouzhe, chuckled ever so slightly as her hand gestured, `Excellent!`

"Yes, excellent!" Brian exclaimed with pure glee. He quickly gestured, `We talk now.` Brian nodded confidently at her.

Baouzhe stood silently at the open doorway looking into his eyes. Her expression was no longer daunting. It was a different look. She did not stare warily at him as before. The look in her eyes was not the brazen, disturbing, and dissecting maroon glare Brian was distressingly accustomed to. Not anymore. The extra-terrestrial creature's teeth no longer looked intimidating to him. She seemed completely different now. To him, she was a very intelligent and sincerely genuine person. The expression on her face was a look of honest, welcome familiarity. The creature was truly his friend now, both in his dreams and in the waken world. Brian felt assured of that fact, and he smiled at her.

Baouzhe gave him another sharp-toothed smile and then slowly nodded her head once in affirming response.

Chapter Twenty Six

Brian was actually very happy to see Baouzhe after the initial, terrible shock of unexpectedly finding her standing on the other side of the door, of course.

"It's good to see you here, for real, outside of a dream," he conveyed by hand signals, and then shut the door behind him.

The creature grinned. Her hand gestures said. "It is good to see you, too." Her alien, wolf-like grin became a little more serious as she then asked, "You will help us?"

Brian nodded affirmatively several times.

Baouzhe continued, "Good. Please come with me. We have much to do. My companion and I must leave soon."

The extraterrestrial creature reached out and gently took Brian by the arm. Just as Baouzhe pulled on his arm for him to follow, there was a distinct hissing noise followed by the agitated growl of Mr. Doodles. Brian looked down just in time to see his mother's cat quickly retreat back through the kitchen pet door. Brian looked at the alien female and noticed a definite look of surprise in her eyes. She looked at him. Brian just shrugged his shoulders in response, thinking, *What can you do? Maybe you should go see Doodles in his dreams; he might like you better, too!*

Baouzhe took Brian's hand again and lead him through the kitchen. As soon as he passed the refrigerator he got another surprise; a very pleasant surprise. Meihtu was standing in the family room, beaming in obvious anticipation of once again meeting with the handsome impromptu ambassador of Earth.

They stood looking at each other in childlike delight as if they were old friends who had not seen each other for several years. Brian wanted to race to Meihtu and embrace her tall slender body with a very warmhearted hug. The thought came quickly to mind, and he turned his head to look at Baouzhe for some sort of 'go-ahead'. Baouzhe was already smiling. Then, just before Brian could turn to look at Meihtu again, he got a very welcome response. The exotic humanoid lady embraced him. The greeting hug lasted for only a few seconds, but it was tender enough to deeply warm his soul for a very long time. They stood close. They faced each other and held hands, smiling contagiously at one another in innocent, heartfelt delight. Then Brian raised his hands and gestured effortlessly with his newly learned communication skill.

`"It's very nice to see you, again."`

Meihtu's response was immediate. "It's very nice to see you, too." She hand gestured, and then in a gentle tone of cordial clarity she smiled and said "Bwiy-ann" in her heavy accent.

Brian simply smiled, almost speechless from her kindhearted reply. Peculiarly, her enunciation reminded him of how the creature had first pronounced his name in his lifelike dreams. Brian finally broke the short moment of silence with a warm reply of his own.

"Meihtu."

Brian was so happy to be in the presence of the aliens, again. He knew there was much to discuss. Accordingly, they wasted no time getting better acquainted. Within a few minutes they were all sitting in the family room on the matching velvet fabric of the sofa and loveseat, cheerfully exchanging simple pleasantries by using the silent, extraterrestrial sign language. There was no more of the curious staring at each other in a loss for words since now they had a practical means to effectively express their thoughts and concerns. Now, the immense gap of obscure miscommunication was abridged. Brian was at ease, and casually entertaining his celestial friends who had peacefully come to visit his world from millions of miles away. Brian realized they were very far from home, and that they had a very challenging mission to complete. He reasonably supposed the aliens must feel a little isolated, being so far from home, so he sincerely wanted them to feel welcome on his home world even though he was the only person who knew of their covert presence. He was very polite. He offered them something to eat several times, however, they politely declined. The aliens did thank him for the food they tried the other night, and happily expressed how the samples were very tasty. They mentioned that they had very similar dietary delights on their own world that they would like to someday share with him. Baouzhe even disclosed the incredible fact that the foodstuff they sampled the other evening was actually already on their emergency edible extemporizations list in case they ran out of their own supply of provisions.

Brian also asked if they were comfortable several times, and if there was anything more he could do to make their visit more pleasant. Meihtu and Baouzhe assured him they were quite content. This delighted Brian. Indeed, he could fully appreciate that they were very much at ease now to be in his company. The extraterrestrials were so relaxed and openly communicative now that Brian felt, in a way, as if he was practically part of the alien crew on this clandestine, interstellar mission.

The next concern openly and directly addressed by the kindly aliens was the whereabouts of the remaining subject. Brian agreed it was a pressing matter needing immediate attention. They got right to it. Meihtu had accessed the same colorful image of the swaddled human newborn on her armband device that Brian had previously seen, and showed it to him again. She articulated that the infant pictured on her display device was the remaining subject. Brian nodded as he acknowledged, precisely remembering the very moment he saw the image. He knew that she would look very different now, as an adult. Meihtu conveyed that the reason she showed him that picture was because that is what the subject looked like when the previous mission crew members made their first, covert contact with her. Meihtu also quickly expressed by sign language that she wanted to show him what the female subject looked like more recently.

As soon as Meihtu finished gesturing to communicate all this, she accessed the more recent image of the subject on her armband device. Then, she smiled as she showed Brian the covertly acquired snapshot. He leaned forward to peer at the woman pictured on the sleek, high tech gadget display. Baouzhe gestured that the most recent recorded visual evidence of the subject Brian was looking at had been taken from a very stealth and high orbiting alien satellite a few years ago. No one could tell that just by looking at the displayed image, however. The image was impressively sharp and crystal clear, as if someone standing right beside the woman had snapped the photograph.

Brian reached over and gently grabbed Meihtu's wrist as he studied the image closer. Meihtu, who was sitting close to him on the couch, obligingly leaned against him to make the task much easier. Brian took pleasure in the immediate closeness. He could smell her delightful, fragrant, alien scent. It was almost a total distraction, though a welcome and amorously pleasing one. He had to concentrate on what he was doing.

"I know this woman!" Brian said aloud as he looked up at the aliens.

They stared back at him in obvious anticipation.

"Oh, uh, I mean…" Brian quickly began to sign what he had just discovered. "I know this woman!"

Upon receipt of his hand gestured information the extra-terrestrials promptly began to speak in their own alien tongue to each other. They were very excited. They were practically speaking over one another. One would start to talk and before finishing, the other enthusiastically interrupted. Indeed, they were obviously and without question, quite thrilled. Then, they turned their attention to the handsome young gentleman.

"Where is she?" Baouzhe rapidly gestured at him with the most peculiar smile that resembled a canine wearing a grin.

Once more, Brian looked at the image of the woman and reflected on the times he had seen her. His pleasant thoughts gave way to a sincere, compassionate smile upon his face, in recollection of those cordial moments. She was a very kind person who always smiled at him whenever they occasioned to see each other. Who could know she had been closely observed for most of her life by an unknown people from an unknown society millions of miles away? Brian was totally surprised to see her candid image pictured on the alien device. He never would have guessed that the extraterrestrials were looking for her. Now, because of whom she was, and what she meant to the aliens, Brian was completely involved.

The slim, fair skinned Caucasian woman pictured on the display area of the device was an attractive lady who stood about 5 feet 7 inches tall and weighed about 134 lbs. Her face was in clear view on the display. Brian could see her large, beautiful brown eyes, and her long, curly, natural blonde hair. "Wow, this picture is so clear," he said, his voice a mere whisper, so in awe was he of the impressive capability of the alien technology.

"This is Mrs. Webley," Brian said, pointing at the image of the woman on the display screen area of the armband the Commander was wearing. Then he looked up at his extraterrestrial friends. They stared back at him in obvious anticipation.

Brian quickly signed, `"She's the wife of my neighbor."` He looked directly at Meihtu and enthusiastically supplemented, `"The man who visited this house when you were here last time. That was her husband, Mr. Webley!"`

· · • ● ● ⬤ ● ● • · ·

Her maiden name was Eleanor Francis Maribel. She was born on October 5, 1947 in Sacramento, California, and that is also where she mostly grew up. She attended high school there and graduated in 1965. Soon afterward, she moved to southern California where several of her aunts, uncles, and favorite cousins resided. She worked for a small law firm as a secretary in Riverside, California from July 1965 to August 1966. She really enjoyed living in southern California. She and her cousins were very close. They were a very sociable group of young adults with many close friends who all enjoyed going to fun places together. Some of the things they really enjoyed doing together included county fairs, church socials, school picnics, and late afternoon country hayrides. One of their favorite annual gatherings was the Riverside County Orange Blossom Festival. That was where she met the man she would soon marry. They met while he was on vacation, back home in Riverside, in the spring of 1965. They married on August 13, 1966.

Her husband, Mr. Vernon Mark Webley was a very quiet and simple man. The tall, silver haired, Caucasian gentleman stood 6 feet and one whole inch tall. He was slightly overweight at 215 lbs. although you could not really tell just by looking at him. Vernon was born in Riverside, California on June 11, 1943. He was always a quiet and well-mannered person, even as a little child. He grew to be a very humble and shy young teenage gentleman who graduated from Riverside High School, class of 1961. After finishing high school, the Vernon was eager to see the world and make an honest living for himself. He wanted to do something he could be proud of. It was no surprise to his parents and close friends when he decided that he wanted to serve his country. Accordingly, he wasted no time staking his claim in life, as he decided right after finishing high school to join the ranks of the Armed Forces. Vernon joined the Air National Guard, where he was soon assigned to the 187th Aero-medical Transport Squadron stationed in Cheyenne, Wyoming. He had a very respectable career proudly serving his country from 1961 to 1984. He completed one tour of duty in Thailand from 1964 to 1965, and another tour of duty in Vietnam as Staff Sergeant from 1965 to 1966. After the last tour of duty, he spent the remainder of his military career in Cheyenne, Wyoming.

Vernon and Eleanor were living in Cheyenne, Wyoming as a newlywed couple by late September, 1966. Eleanor found employment very quickly and worked as a Telephone Operator for the county area code from October 1966 to mid-July 1984. She liked her job very much, and she enjoyed living there during that time. The Webleys considered staying in Wyoming after Vernon was honorably discharged from the Air National Guard in the summer of 1984. However, they soon decided to move to southern California so they could be closer to family. The

Webley's packed everything they owned and moved to Lake Arrowhead, California in September of that same year.

Vernon started working as a truck driver for California Navel Oranges Citrus Company. He was able to start work very quickly after he and his wife moved, thanks to several of his family members who were senior employees at the large and successful brand name company. Vernon always enjoyed working there, ever since he was first employed, from September 1984 to present. As for Eleanor, she soon found another job that she enjoyed very much, as well. She started work that October as a 9-1-1 dispatcher for San Bernardino County. She remained in that same rewarding career until her untimely demise in May 21, 2001 from breast cancer.

Eleanor and Vernon had two beautiful daughters who were both born in Cheyenne, Wyoming. Katrina Marylyn Webley was born September 5, 1967, and Frances Lynn Webley was born January 23, 1969. They were very good children who grew up to make their parents very happy and proud. The daughters eventually married and had several adorable children of their own. The daughters were very close to their parents and it wasn't surprising that their grandchildren often visited Vernon and Eleanor. If the daughters were not visiting, then they often called their mother to share entertaining stories of the daily adolescent exploits of their vivacious children. Within seconds of answering her phone, Eleanor could be heard laughing heartily to the point of gleeful tearing about something grand and humorous thing her lovable grandchildren had done that day. Vernon always knew when one of his daughters had called just by the sound of his wife's happy response on the phone. She could not wait to share what she heard with grandpa, too. Those were some of the most tender moments they shared as a happily married couple, so deeply in love after many years together. There was no question Vernon and Eleanor shared a wonderful life together. Without doubt, Eleanor was survived by many beautiful people who loved her ever so dearly because of the wonderful wife, mother, grandmother, and woman that she was.

· · · • ● ⬤ ● • · · ·

"Her name is Eleanor Webley," Brian somberly communicated. "Unfortunately, she died a few months ago. I'm afraid her life force has terminated, as you logically assumed in my dream." He looked directly at Baouzhe as he acknowledged the regrettable fact.

"That is very unfortunate. We are sorry to hear this news," Meihtu responded.

Baouzhe glanced at her Commander before communicating to Brian, "Can we please obtain some type of validation for our records that documents this unfavorable information? Anything we may witness to the fact, while keeping the respectful observations of your divine culture in mind, would be most acceptable."

"Sure," Brian immediately responded, "I think that won't be a problem."

He thought for a second and then replied, "I believe she was cremated. I think her ashes are kept at Mr. Webley's house. Would you like to see the receptacle that holds those remains?"

The aliens looked at each other and then Baouzhe replied, "She was cremated. No wonder we haven't been able to receive any data at all. Yes, we would like to see the receptacle that holds her ashes. Yes, that will be acceptable."

Brian thought for a minute. *I bet with their technology they can somehow get that floating ball in the house and see where Mr. Webley keeps the urn.* He looked up towards the ceiling as he contemplated the means.

"Bwiy-ann." Meihtu caught the young man's prompt attention with her thick-tongued accent. Then she immediately signed, "We know the place where the subject lived." Meihtu glanced at her space traveling companion before she supplemented, "We have been observing that place of residence since we arrived." She paused for a moment before continuing.

"We should tell you of a recent incident during our observation before we continue our mission."

"Incident?" Brian responded aloud with an inquiring, furrowed brow. "What incident?"

Meihtu gently took hold of Brian's right hand in her soft, appeasing grasp. She looked at Baouzhe and nodded once, quickly. Then she returned her alluring gaze back to Brian and looked into his eyes. Brian sensed the uneasiness the two extraterrestrials shared right now and had a feeling they had something important to tell him.

Baouzhe was tasked with dutifully disclosing the events to Brian, so she did. She started slowly gesturing with her hands, clearly and straightforwardly communicating by sign language the peculiar events that took place. She conveyed that an inconsequential complication had transpired recently during their remote observation of the Webley residence. Their clandestine presence had been awkwardly discovered.

Baouzhe informed Brian that when the stealthy, buoyant observation unit had been suddenly detected, the aliens had to immediately take a less than favorable recourse. The creature stated that what actions were taken were done as a necessity, for everyone's common wellbeing, both extraterrestrial and humankind alike. She informed Brian that the two male humans who detected the presence of the hovering probe were subjected to a very low intensity pulsation of electrochemical energy and rendered temporarily unconscious. Baouzhe communicated that while Mr. Aguirre and his son were laid out cold on the very lawn they had come to work on, the method was not only safe, but preferred, since it was specifically designed to innocuously erase their memories of the event.

This was very alarming to Brian. In fact, he was simply at a loss for words and didn't know how to respond so he stared into the distance, focusing on nothing. However, before the mild expression of concern on Brian's face turned to a much more overwhelmed look of panic, Baouzhe quickly acknowledged they never meant any of that to happen and there was no harm done to anyone. She communicated that she understood the event could easily be interpreted as a hostile attack. She wanted Brian to fully understand that hostility was certainly not the intent of their actions that day. The kind creature assured their discovery and their reluctant recourse was purely happenstance. Baouzhe let Brian know that the incident was a completely unexpected departure from their main objective. She admitted the success and safety of the mission was at risk for compromise at that instant. Regardless, they had specific measures to safely and effectively employ for such isolated instances. She insisted the two males were unharmed, and they were being monitored for any side effects from the abrupt encounter. Meihtu gently squeezed Brian's hand. She looked at Baouzhe and nodded once more and returned her attention to Brian.

"You're sure they're okay, the two guys? And, you're sure they don't remember anything that happened afterward?" Brian quickly responded in alien sign. When he returned his hands to his lap, Meihtu again took hold of them in her soft grasp.

"There seems to be no immediate adverse effects from the encounter," Baouzhe calmly insisted.

"Please, believe me. We actually have excellent knowledge concerning human anatomy and physiology. We developed the precise, safe technology and practice long ago, during the planning stages of our first surface contact mission. We essentially learned what was safe to utilize long before the subjects were ever monitored. Please know our methods have been tested on our own people. Only after much time of confident testing and research did we use low intensity electrochemical energy as a method to incapacitate people. The methods are truly harmless. The process is proven technology. In fact, we used similar tactics to carefully sedate our subjects in order to implant the epidermal monitoring devices on them."

Brian wanted to be certain there was no danger posed to him or any other human on planet Earth `"No humans were ever harmed, or killed during all your travels and observations? Is that correct?"`

Meihtu reached for his hands again as Baouzhe began to gesture.

`"No humans have ever been harmed. Not one human, or any other animal being or insect. You have our honest affirmation that this is true, we promise it is fact,"` Baouzhe quickly responded with her convincing canine smile.

Meihtu released the young man's hands and calmly articulated, `"If there has been any harm done to any human as a result of any of our missions, I will be the first from my planet to surrender myself as someone to be held completely responsible."`

She paused a slight moment before adding, `"I apologize that we've been gathering information about your world in secret. Unfortunately, it is necessary to silently hide in the shadows, for now. Making ourselves known to everyone on this world would unquestionably result in a catastrophic mistake at present. Someday, though, I wish for the people of our societies to become friends, and totally trust each other. When that day comes, I know that your people will be eager to learn everything about us. Please know that I will be happy to become a reciprocal subject for your people to study whenever that time comes. I promise."`

"Well," Brian said, "I guess it's cool." Then he gestured, `"Okay, I really appreciate your honesty."`

He looked at Meihtu and kindly said, `"I look forward to the day when our worlds unite in friendship."`

`"So do I."` Meihtu responded with a warm smile. Then the two extraterrestrials respectfully bowed their heads in earnest acknowledgement.

Brian's thoughts returned to the connotations of this

particular undertaking. He wanted to help the aliens validate the whereabouts of Mrs. Webley's mortal remains. "I have an idea," he offered after pondering the circumstances. "Can we use that small observation probe to go inside their house to help with the task? And, if so, would you allow me to use your vision equipment so I can help find where the remains of the subject are located in their house?"

The aliens looked at each other before Baouzhe responded, "We were able to covertly situate the same type of observation probe you saw and mention now inside their home last night. It is positioned in a room that is similar to this one." The creature made reference to the family room they were comfortably sitting in presently.

"As I mentioned," Meihtu acknowledged, "we have been observing that place of residence since we arrived. We have been observing the subject's spouse, as well." She smiled. "When he entered his home last evening, the probe secretly followed him inside."

Very clever, indeed, Brian thought to himself as he nodded in acknowledgement.

The next thing he noticed was Baouzhe taking something out of her utility vest-pack. The pack was situated next to the velvet loveseat Baouzhe was comfortably sitting on. Only now did Brian notice the utility equipment was there. Baouzhe produced the night vision eyewear Brian was familiar with. He observed quietly as Baouzhe handed Meihtu her technologically advanced glasses first, and then she quickly put on her own pair. Baouzhe then gestured to Meihtu. Brian knew she wanted her Mission Commander to pass the other pair of alien glasses to him. Meihtu obliged willingly and very happily. She smiled as she handed her pair of glasses to Brian. As soon as Brian took the technologically advanced eyewear, Meihtu made a simple gesture for him to put them on. Brian did so.

The first thing he noticed was nothing really different,

actually. The alien lenses revealed what he was already looking at before he placed them on his face. Brian saw the two extraterrestrials before him in the family room, in a slightly wider angle view. Then Meihtu pressed her narrow finger about the wrist area of her armband device a few times. Suddenly, the view of the family room and his two alien friends sitting comfortably, faded away. His vision was quickly transported away from the cozy family room to someplace else.

Through the incredibly advanced vision eyewear, the view was, again, simply astounding. Once again, Brian's human eyes were privileged to see what the two extraterrestrials are capable of covertly observing. His heightened optical environment was superb and easily recognizable. He could easily distinguish everything in extraordinary detail. There were the same familiar, small alien symbols flashing about within his field of view. He noticed that immediately. In addition, there was something else acutely familiar about what he saw. It occurred to him that he had seen this place before. Brian quickly recognized that he had a flawless and intensely clear view of the inside of the Webley home.

Chapter Twenty Seven

"Wow!" Brian responded, instinctively turning his head to get a quick look around the inside of the Webley residence.

Amazingly, when Brian looked to his left, the view punctually changed to that direction without the slightest hesitation. As he looked to his right, the view observed from the alien glasses immediately panned right. He looked up and saw the ceiling. *What?* Brian silently admired with an ingenuous grin. *How does this thing work? How do they do this?* Brian looked down and saw the floor.

"These glasses can follow where I look?" he signed as he pointed at the stylish alien vision equipment on his face.

"This is really amazing!" He chuckled, "Oh yes, I really have to get me one of these!"

The two aliens started to talk to each other in a very quiet tone of voice. Then, the next thing Brian unexpectedly noticed was a 'picture box' appear just to the left of his view. He quickly recognized the image of Meihtu within the bordered visual effect.

"Whoa, there you are, I see you." He smiled and waved as soon as he saw Meihtu.

She waved her hand once and smiled in return. Brian quickly deduced the image of her was most likely being captured by the same type of floating observation probe within his parent's house. He presumed that the cleverly cloaked drone was probably floating right over his head, judging from the angle and profile of Meihtu's displayed image. For a slight instant, Brian felt like swatting over his head at it, just to test his theory.

Meihtu wasted no time keeping everyone focused on the mission. She quickly started to sign what she needed him to do next. She asked him to look for the receptacle holding the remains of Mrs. Webley.

Brian responded in their alien sign language while still looking through the technologically advanced lenses into the quiet, unoccupied Webley residence.

"I will look for it now."

Although he could not see his own hands moving about while gazing through the futuristic lenses, Brian was confident the linguistic gestures he made were correct and intelligible. She gestured back her appreciation along with a lovely smile.

The clandestine drone Brian was observing was cleverly situated within the family room of the Webley home. Brian was presently looking to the right of his forward view just above the bordered picture-in-picture effect of Meihtu's displayed image, directly into the Webley's quaint dining room. There was some natural sunlight entering through two windows in the dining room that bathed and illuminated the interior of that portion of the house just perfectly. Next, Brian slowly panned his vision that was secretly coming from the alien technology towards his left. Without any sense of hurry, he carefully gazed from the dining room towards his left, into the family room, where the floating alien drone was cleverly located. Brian noticed he was looking at everything from an elevated point of view. From this visual vantage point, he was able to see both the dining room and family room superbly. Brian had logically assumed that the floating orb he was observing everything from was most likely positioned in the northwest corner of the cozy family room somewhere up close to the ceiling.

As his vision panned to his left, he noticed something very familiar. There, positioned close to the decorative cherry wood lip molding on top of the fireplace mantel was what appeared to be a cremation urn.

"I think I see it!" Brian announced excitedly upon his

immediate, happenstance discovery, "It's right here in front of me!" He happily expressed his amusement aloud. "I'm looking right at it." He started to chuckle. "Wow, how about that? It's right here!'

Meihtu raised her hands quickly as she started to gesture, asking what he saw and what he was saying. Brian immediately focused his attention on the small image of her moving her hands about within the bordered picture-in-picture effect as she silently queried of him.

"Please tell us, did you find her, the subject's remains? It appears you were successful."

She suddenly began talking aloud in her native tongue, almost as if she were making an announcement for someone within earshot. Brian also heard Baouzhe speak up as if to make a comment.

Brian signed back 'blindly' in reply while still gazing at her perfectly displayed image within the alien lenses; "Yes, I see the receptacle that holds her remains."

"That is good. It did not take us long at all to find it." Meihtu replied with an agreeable grin.

The three of them together, working as a team, had successfully found the supposed urn retaining the late, Mrs. Webley's earthly ashes. Now all they needed to do was somehow verify that the vessel did, indeed, contain those cremated remains. Those human cremains would be the only tangible evidence that the beloved wife, mother and grandmother was indeed deceased. Unfortunately, it would also confirm that the subject's assemblage of elemental streaming data was consequently, officially terminated.

With all of that in mind, Meihtu was quick to devise a plan to obtain proof of that fact. It only took about forty minutes for the team to coordinate their efforts and assertively strategize a way to accomplish their objective, so that accordingly, they would effectively attain that verification.

Within minutes after their hand gestured discussion and carefully devised planning, Brian drove down the road to the Webley residence. He didn't give a second thought to the fact that he left the aliens alone in his parent's home. In fact, out of practically anyplace on the planet, he preferred they were there, out of sight. This way, he knew they would not be inadvertently discovered by some unbeknownst stranger. Brian was contented with the fact that his kind and considerate extraterrestrial visitors were sitting comfortably there, intently monitoring his progress.

Brian parked his truck close to the curb in front of the Webley home. He exited the vehicle quickly with his carefully calculated objective in mind and proceeded quickly from the road towards the garage where the sidewalk began and ran up to the front porch. He stopped walking for just a moment when he stepped onto the short driveway. He placed the leather backpack he was carrying down on the cement driveway. Next, Brian carefully retrieved the alien eyewear from the fancy protective case that the kindly extraterrestrial Mission Commander had provided to him. He recalled how Meihtu had instructed him to put the vision enhancer on as soon as he could, in order to communicate with her.

Before placing the fancy reflective copper lenses on his face, Brian had a quick look around him. The immediate surrounding area was pleasantly quiet. He did not notice anyone watching him or standing close by. Indeed, no one was observing him now, save for the secretly located aliens. Brian glanced upward into the sky, just above the mountainous horizon. He turned completely around to get a full, panoramic view. He was looking for something.

Then he grinned as he slowly put the alien eyewear on. Brian was facing south as he did so. The superb view through the alien technology was not much different than the view through any sophisticated pair of expensive designer sunglasses. Except, the alien lenses displayed everything in more like a detailed, wide-screen, live video presentation. The effect was very similar to the visual experience Brian had back in the family room, sitting with the aliens. The rich, slightly tinted, blue sky he beheld was gorgeous and brilliantly clear.

"These are really nice!" he remarked in candid admiration. The unique visual experience was truly, delightfully amazing.

Brian turned so he could look directly towards the Webley home. No sooner had he faced the house than he suddenly caught a glimpse of something very peculiar out of the corner of his left eye while gazing through the lenses. Brian had anticipated that somewhat, and so he slowly turned a little more to get a better look. By doing so his suspicions were confirmed. As soon as he faced more towards the north he found what he was looking for. There, within the privileged exclusive view of the alien vision enhancer, was something quite remarkable, and also, just a bit sobering.

Located not very high above and rather near to him, was a small, soundless, hovering object. It was spherical in shape and it had a strange, stark grayish appearance as viewed through the extraterrestrial copper lenses. Brian stood perfectly still as he stared at the peculiarly ominous, floating thing. There was something about it that made him feel just a tad uncomfortable. He did not know why. Meihtu had told him it was there, but Brian still felt a little threatened at the moment for some reason. Perhaps he felt apprehensive because it was so silent, and only visible through the alien eyeglasses. Maybe it was the mere sight of it hovering motionless in mid-air that disturbed him. Brian was not really sure what bothered him most about it. Its dark and motionless presence just somehow stirred up a deep, disturbingly brusque feeling inside him.

The overt sight of it seemed to be an insinuation, "Here I am, floating in the air. So, now that you see me, what should I do to you?!"

The image of the unknown object through the fancy lenses was accented by some alien jargon that was visible in a bold, orchid color text. Brian had no doubt the information displayed in his enhanced visual field was technical data about the strange thing. He logically surmised the flashing extraterrestrial words and symbols probably displayed detailed information to the adept vision enhancer user about the clandestine hovering object and what it was doing. Brian had not a clue what the hovering probe was truly capable of. However, he had enough of an idea to reasonably believe it was probably some type of tactical military device. He knew it was not to be trifled with. Brian recalled the incident the aliens had informed him about and how this orb had knocked the lawn maintenance workers unconscious and wiped away their memories of seeing it. Nevertheless, he was not too worried. After all, he was part of the team now, and the floating thing would not harm him. They were working together on the same mission. Still, Brian just felt a little apprehensive at the moment. He stared at the dark, grayish object hanging silently in mid-air and did some mental calculations. *I'm gonna need a bigger tennis racquet!*

Brian figured it was not very far away from him. He also figured it was probably actually similar in size to a large beach ball rather than what he had first perceived. It just seemed ominously larger, for some reason. Brian pulled the fancy alien eyeglasses down low enough for his eyes to peer over the reflective lenses. As expected, and to no surprise, there was nothing there to see. At first glance, nothing appeared to be out of the ordinary. It was just another beautiful day outside amongst the valley of the towering evergreens within the gorgeous mountainous resort area. Then Brian centered his scrutinizing gaze upon the approximate spot in the air where the hovering, mysterious grayish object should be. Doing so, he finally caught a glimpse of something very unusual.

Damn! There it is! He silently grinned with a slight hint of self-assured accomplishment. *I see you now!* What his eyes beheld not very far at all up in the air was basically unfathomable. If he was not consciously looking for it, he probably never would have seen it. No wonder he did not notice it before he put the fancy eyeglasses on. *Clever, very clever, but, I see you now.* Brian chuckled, albeit a bit timidly.

The spot in the air where the alien object was silently hovering was slightly dissimilar than the beautiful blue sky around it. With the use of only the naked eye to perceive it, the object did not have any distinct borders to outline its whole. It was void of color and lacked an outside or an inside. The beautiful blue sky was visible behind it, and the light of day shown easily through it. What Brian was looking at was more of a visual distortion rather than a solid object. What he was looking at was something that occupied space, but was visually devoid of perceptual presence. Brian was now looking at a focalized transparent variation that had a definite shape, which seemed to be defined only by its vaguely observable, undulating margins. The naked eye detection and observance of the concealed floating thing was unnervingly captivating.

I don't know how you guys do it, but it's clever, very clever. When Brian repositioned the fancy alien eyeglasses on his face again he saw the hovering object in its entirety, detailed and clear. Brian actually liked the fact that the buoyant observation unit was not able to hide from him now and that he had the capability of seeing it. This pleased him, greatly. *You can't outsmart me now, can you? And, you can't hide now, can you?* He grinned. *Yeah, that's right!*

The very next thing he became aware of was the image of Meihtu waving her narrow hands in an effort to get his attention. Brian immediately focused on her image situated near the lower right hand corner within Brian's field of view. He began to sign in response to her efforts to get his attention. He was facing directly towards the ominous hovering object as he silently communicated. He did so, per her request. Brian was told to always face one of the observation units so the extraterrestrials could see him sign clearly. It was the only way they could effectively converse.

The young man calmly gestured, "I see the observation probe. It is here, just as you told me. I'm going to enter the house now. I will look under the doormat for an extra key first, as we discussed. Some people I know like to leave another key under their doormat in case they accidentally lock themselves out. If it is not there, I will try the master bathroom window, as planned."

He was simply confirming he would carry out the plan they previously agreed to if he could not locate a spare key. Baouzhe had already informed the young man that the bathroom window located at the rear side of the house was observed to be slightly open. It was formerly decided that location was most likely the best opportunity to inconspicuously enter the premises.

`"Good, let's get started before someone soon discovers our intentions, please. Thank you."` Meihtu replied, followed by a quick smile and a nod.

Brian took another look at the daunting hovering thing through the fancy lenses and then focused his attention on the mission at hand. He picked up his backpack, placed the alien eyeglasses back inside the fancy case, and walked quickly towards the front door. Brian proceeded along the narrow cemented pathway directly to the front porch. He knelt down on one knee and, just as he started to reach for the small welcome mat in front of the wooden entryway door, an obscure memory suddenly came to mind.

Brian recalled a very particular conversation that his mother had with Eleanor several years ago. He recalled overhearing them talking while he was visiting his parents one Saturday afternoon. Brian was eating a snack and watching television in the family room at the time. He distinctly remembered the two ladies laughing and casually talking about everything going on in their lives, as friends often do. The women were sitting in the living room at first. Then their conversation brought them to the family room where Linda wanted to show Eleanor some recent photos of Houston, her handsome grandson. He recalled how the two ladies were standing, facing the picture frame floor screen as they laughed and chatted happily. Brian remembered the reason for Eleanor's visit was to inform his mom that she and her husband, would be out of town visiting their grandkids for a couple weeks. Eleanor asked Linda if she could keep an eye on their home, and if there was any reason she needed to go inside, there was always an extra key hidden on the front porch. It amused Brian that somehow, at that specific moment, he had remembered that particular conversation, and because of that unimportant chat almost four years ago between two neighbors he now knew where the key was hidden.

Brian abruptly stopped reaching for the mat and instead, reached for the small potted Rosemary plant located next to him on his right. He grasped hold of the pottery and tilted it to one side. There, under the clay pot, was the extra key to the front door.

"Here it is," he half whispered with a broad smile. He did not have to tell the aliens. Brian knew they had to have figured it out by now, and that he was correct in his assumption about the presence and approximate location of an extra key.

He smiled and stood confidently to his feet and then approached the front door. So far, everything was going exactly as planned. It had not taken long at all to find the key and enter the cozy northwest style, two bedroom, two bathroom home. He did so without hesitating and without even a second thought. Brian opened the door and then quickly glanced around outside to see if anyone was looking before shutting the door behind him. There was no one to be seen.

Brian walked quickly past the short hallway to his left which led to the guest bedroom and bath. He breezed by the small entryway closet on his immediate right. He focused all his attention straight ahead on the fireplace on the east side of the family room wall. He saw the fireplace with its stone mantel and cherry wood lip molding and, sure enough, there was the cremation urn on the mantel. It was positioned exactly where he last saw it as seen from the clandestine perspective of the alien's buoyant observation probe, covertly hidden inside the Webley residence. As soon as Brian stopped in front of the urn, he peered over his left shoulder. He looked directly at the spot where he figured the floating ball should be. He could see something peculiar high up in the northwest corner of the quaint family room.

What Brian discovered was an object like the one he saw at his parent's house. It was the same type of gadget, having the shape and size of a billiard ball, strategically positioned inches away from the ceiling. The hovering orb was difficult to see clearly due to its distortive camouflage. The clever color pattern was practically indistinguishable from the soft fulvous paint on the walls of the comfy family room. The exacting disruptive coloration allowed the floating object to practically vanish from foreground view. The silent floating orb perfectly melded with the surrounding walls and ceiling, just like the floating device Brian was very familiar with at his parent's house. Quite frankly, he knew that if he was not looking for it, he probably never would have noticed it was there.

Brian placed his backpack on the carpeted floor and quickly retrieved the alien vision enhancer. When he put the shiny reflective lenses on, he saw the covert floating orb drone in plain view. Just like the larger version he discovered outside the Webley house, this smaller observation unit was accented by some technical appearing alien jargon. It also had a dark grayish metallic appearance, like the one outside. *I see you, too!* Brian smirked as he pondered; *I wonder how many of these stupid things they've brought with them on this trip to earth.*

The next thing Brian suddenly noticed was the familiar 'picture box' image of Meihtu promptly appear within his field of view. Brian knew she wanted to establish communications with him. He turned to face the floating observation unit so his space traveling companions could clearly see him. At that moment, Meihtu glanced up from looking at her armband device and looked directly at Brian. He realized she was looking directly at the other floating ball in his parent's family room.

"Can you see us? We can see you." Meihtu hand gestured and smiled at him.

"Yes, I see you, too." Brian returned a handsome smile and replied.

After he responded, the small image of the smiling Meihtu faded away, giving him a full visual field of view once more. Next, Brian turned back around so he could examine the cremation urn. The sentimental receptacle was very beautiful and heartwarming to behold. The viridian urn featured a polished monochrome glaze, and it was decorated with a very handsome pink floral metallic appliqué. It was ornamentally, and quite securely, propped atop a perfectly shining brass base. Brian could not help but smile out of respectful sentiment at the sight of the beloved memento.

"Please pardon the intrusion Mrs. Webley. My friends from

outer space would like to pay their last respects, if you don't mind," Brian expressed in a tender tone of voice, "They miss you. We all miss you." Brian smiled. Then he carefully reached for the urn and proceeded to gently remove the lid.

It was very lucky for Brian that the crematorium had prepared the beloved remains of Mrs. Webley according to her husband's request. Normally, the urn would have been sealed shut with a small amount of epoxy adhesive. However, Eleanor's last wish was to be scattered on the shores of beautiful Lake Arrowhead in spring, her favorite season of the year. Respecting her wishes, Vernon planned to hold a simple, private family vigil the following year to honor his late wife's last request. He planned to gather the family together on a day everyone could meet next spring, and they would all take turns scattering her ashes on the lake shore, in the water. As a result of this request for the intended ceremonial occasion, the urn lid was not bonded. Vernon had received his late wife's ashes from the crematorium in a clear, durable, plastic bag adequately sealed with a simple twist tie and enclosed in the beautiful, glossy urn.

Brian carefully placed the urn lid on the mantel, and then gingerly untied the small twist tie. Then he carefully opened up the plastic bag a little, thereby exposing its cherished contents to the air and light of day above the urn. Brian took three steps back. This had been precisely requested of him by the exotic commander. After complying, he turned and faced the small observation drone which was still located up in the far corner of the family room. As soon as he did so, Meihtu reappeared within his alien technologically enhanced view. Brian adjusted the extraterrestrial eyewear on his face slightly, and then he waved at the alien orb drone with a smile.

"Are we ready to proceed?" Meihtu asked.

"Yes, commander," Brian promptly replied.

"We have another scientific observation probe there with you. It was positioned behind you, when you were searching for the key. It quickly followed you inside the house, as soon as you entered." Meihtu signed. `You may have seen it, already."

"I didn't notice. I guess it snuck in behind me." Brian said aloud as he simultaneously signed his reply.

As soon as he was notified of that, Brian focused his attention on the flashing alien jargon as seen through the shiny copper eyeglasses. He noticed there were a few more symbols appearing within the lenses since he entered the house, but he did not really think much of it.

"Come out come out where ever you are," he whispered, looking around the room. When he faced toward the small entry hall by the front door, Brian noticed some of the bolded orchid alien symbols suddenly outline something peculiar up in the air, very close to the ceiling. Sure enough, located just inside the small entryway was another buoyant observation probe, very similar in shape and size to the other floating orb in the same room.

"How many of these things do you guys have?" he jested, shaking his head. He had not actually asked the extraterrestrial commander that by signing. He did not need to. He had already assumed there were probably more of these things floating around than the ones he already knew about.

`Now we will begin." Brian noticed Meihtu gesturing in the small 'picture box' as she signed to him.

Brian lowered the shiny copper lenses slightly to see if he could find the newly discovered floating orb in the entryway with his own eyes. He looked, much to his surprise, just in time to see the clandestine object uncloak. He watched how the visually disruptive, soft fulvous camouflage motif instantly changed to the recognizable dark grayish color scheme he was familiar with as observed through the alien lenses. As he repositioned the fancy eyeglasses on his face, he noticed the descriptive alien symbols and wording flashing next to the object, as before. Brian was intrigued, and watched the alien floating orb smoothly maneuver around him to his left about arms-length away. As it passed by, Brian distinctly heard the familiar muffled humming sound. It was a very similar low pitched harmonic vibration just like the sound he heard the night the strange ellipsoid spacecraft landed. Only the sound coming from the floating orb drone was much fainter.

Impressively, everything was going along exactly as planned. Brian quietly observed how his alien friends commenced the task of scientifically ascertaining the unfortunate condition of their remaining subject. From a few paces away, he watched the small grayish object hover into precise position directly over the open cremation urn, at about the width of a hand above it. Then, without any delay, the floating device began discharging several visible hairline beams of bright, focalized light directly into the exposed sentimental vessel. The alternating amaranthine and crimson colors of the laser like beams flickered in synchronized succession faster than Brian could count. He stood patiently waiting while the alien analysis of the human ashes proceeded. Indeed, this was a very critical stage of their mission. Brian was very well aware of that. He smiled, knowing he was undoubtedly participating in an historic event that would someday be shared with all people on both worlds. Then, before he knew it, the task was complete. The mysterious floating observation probe hovered motionless. The small laser light show had ended, lasting less than five minutes.

Next, the familiar image of Meihtu reappeared within Brian's view once again. She glanced up from her armband device and smiled at him. When Brian turned to face the other observation probe in the far corner of the room, Meihtu began to sign.

"We have completed our examination and have substantiated everything we wanted to know. Please allow the two observation units to depart with you, during your egress. You may now return to your home."

"I'm on my way," Brian coolly replied by human voice and alien hand gesture.

He made sure he resealed the precious contents of the cremation urn and secured the lid, leaving everything as it was as when he first arrived. He looked upon the urn once more before leaving the family room and quietly thanked Mrs. Webley for her service. "You're very special to us all, Mrs. Webley. Thank you for what you have done for the people of this world, even if you never knew." He bowed his head once, respectfully, just as the aliens did.

Brian gathered his belongings and made his way to the front door. When he opened the entryway door, he crouched down to let the clandestine floating observation probes leave the premises as requested of him. He watched attentively through the vision enhancer as both alien probes passed directly over him and went right out the front door, climbing high into the summer sky. Immediately after that, Brian locked the door and returned the spare key to where he got it. He took one final look at the larger observation unit which was still hovering in the exact same spot where he had last seen it. "I still see you," he said boldly, walking to his parked truck.

"Well done young man," Brian said out loud, "That was a piece of cake."

He patted himself on the shoulder, started his vehicle, and then headed home.

Chapter Twenty Eight

The gracious extraterrestrials rose to their feet as soon as Brian opened the front door, and when he walked into the family room, greeted him with sincere, enthusiastic smiles of approval. Both aliens respectfully bowed their heads once at him. Then, Meihtu walked to where he stood and embraced him with a warm, welcoming hug.

"On behalf of all the people from my world, I thank you. You don't know what this means to us. You have helped us, immensely," expressed Meihtu by signing, followed by a respectful nod, and a slow, yet very considerately attempted pronunciation of his given name, "Br-i-yaan." She smiled.

Brian blushed. "My pleasure," he responded humbly. "I want to be part of this team."

"You are, for sure." Mission Specialist Baouzhe quickly assured him.

Brian smiled as Meihtu hugged him again.

Over the next half hour the team held an in-depth debrief of their mission, using sign language to discuss everything that had proceeded exactly as planned. Meihtu was quick to praise both her celestial and earthly subordinates for their committed efforts. Everything was done in the name of science, for both worlds. It was done for the common good of all peoples, worldly and extraterrestrial. Although the aliens sadly lost both earth subjects within the short span of a year, the data obtained over many years was, nonetheless, indispensable. Each of the team members was very proud they were all working together, especially Brian. He felt truly privileged to be a part of this historic undertaking.

The silent, hand gestured conversation continued, then quickly progressed into the next precarious topic of discussion. There was another alien objective brought to Brian's attention by the beautiful extraterrestrial commander, and it was something Brian had to consider very carefully. Her request was something quite unexpected, though not incredibly surprising. Baouzhe passionately concurred, and said that the benefits of the commander's request would modestly exceed the miniscule risk involved. The aliens wanted to observe humankind without the use of any cloaked observation devices. They wanted to study humans behaving naturally as they do in their own physical environment, from a perspective uninhibited by technological interpretation. It was Meihtu, actually, who desired to do such, with her own celestial eyes.

"You want to..." Brian rubbed his chin and lightly nibbled his bottom lip as he contemplated the precarious prospect, "You want to observe my people, in person?" He continued to rub his chin, grimacing in forethought at the slightly imposing request. "You want to see the people of my world without using one of those invisible floating things?"

"Yes. That's correct," Baouzhe politely affirmed. "We have a very carefully thought out plan to help us accomplish this task. We honestly feel it is in our best interest to do this, now that you have become our liaison, our trusted companion." She nodded respectfully.

Brian contorted his face a bit. "Well, I guess that would be alright, as long as there's no chance of you guys being discovered by anyone."

"You will understand better if you let us explain our plan." Baouzhe smiled smartly, exposing her sharp teeth. "I would be very happy to tell you about it, if you permit me."

"Okay, tell me, what's your carefully thought

out plan?" Brian deferentially and open-mindedly replied. "What does it entail?"

The two aliens looked at each other and smiled at his welcome inclination. They were happy to explain. What the intelligent and technologically advanced aliens posited was to observe earth's humankind in broad daylight. The plan was for Meihtu to accompany Brian in his vehicle, and simply ride around the neighborhood for a little while. It was wholeheartedly agreed upon by the aliens that it would be a very nontechnical and uncomplicated task to successfully execute. That was it. That was the carefully thought out plan.

"Are you serious?" Brian half jested aloud, with a generous hint of stupefied caution in his tone of voice. "Are you serious?" He promptly followed by extraterrestrial sign language with the same expression of unbridled apprehension. The smiling alien females just looked at each other quietly after Brian reacted candidly to hearing their supposed carefully thought out plan.

"Is this a joke?" Brian questioned while chuckling anxiously, "What if something happens? What if somebody sees you?"

"We trust nothing will go wrong. All we want to do is, watch." Baouzhe enthusiastically responded with her awkwardly cute little wolf-like smile.

"We are prepared for just about any contingency. You must trust us. We will not let something bad happen to us, or anyone else," Meihtu calmly reinforced by sign.

"My worry," Brian quickly responded, pausing for only a slight moment as he pondered the likely opportunity for everything to go perfectly wrong, "my sincere concern is, you look so different from the people of Earth."

He looked at both his alien friends, up and down, as he frankly expressed himself.

"All anyone has to do is, look into my truck and they will notice." Brian raised his eyebrows, and with eyes wide signed, "People will see something they've never seen before, and they will stare at you. They will point. They will follow us. They will surround us. Then, panic will break out. That's my guess. If you get discovered, it will be uncontrolled hysteria, for sure."

Meihtu and Baouzhe stood quietly still, staring at Brian. He knew they fully understood the consequences of being discovered. Yet, something about their demeanor suggested to him the aliens would not be discouraged.

"I mean," Brian continued, "maybe if it was..." He paused for a moment as he tried to think of the alien translation for Halloween. There was none. Brian then hypothetically supposed, "Even if we were walking around in the middle of a huge costume party, like a neighborhood block party, during one of our very popular seasonal traditions that we all enjoy for fun here, people would be even more curious as to how real you both look. They would want to take pictures, and probably want to talk to you, even more so." He shook his head. "And as soon as people found out there's no wig and makeup, and when they find out who you two really are, well, trust me; there would just be some mass hysteria going on!"

Baouzhe promptly replied to his grave concern.

"Yes!" She nodded at him and smiled assuredly with that same peculiar grin of hers, confidently proclaiming, "Yes, Commander Meihtu has a costume!"

Meihtu also smiled as she clasped her hands together excitedly, seemingly eager for her space traveling companion to inform Brian that very enlightening, weighty news. Brian frowned in confusion as Baouzhe and Meihtu faced each other and held hands. They were unquestionably expressing what seemed to be a moment of celebratory glee for a few seconds, as if they simply could not contain their jubilance any longer. Brian tilted his head to one side. The aliens chatted excitedly in their celestial tongue and, practically hopped in place, bending slightly at the knees in rapid succession. It was a very peculiar thing for Brian to watch. He did not understand their celebratory behavior. Brian was certain he communicated the words in his head correctly. I don't get it. Did they, or did they not understand me? He was lost as to what had just transpired.

The slight moment of celebration quickly ceased, followed by a waning array of giggles from the extraterrestrials.

`"We'll tell you now. We will tell you our plan,"` Baouzhe signed as she smiled again.

"Br-i-yaan," Meihtu expressed audibly in her soothing tone of voice, also with a smile.

Then the two aliens proceeded to inform Brian how they intended to remain covert during this next planned excursion. The celestial voyagers had brought with them on this mission certain equipment that would allow Meihtu to observe humankind in person. The specialized gear was only to be used if the precise occasion arose. Baouzhe would remain behind and monitor the progress of the observation excursion. Brian gave this some thoughtful consideration. The fact that Brian was now particularly well-acquainted with the aliens deemed this an opportune occasion, especially since Brian had wisely not disclosed the presence of the extraterrestrials to anyone. This opened up an opportunity that the aliens felt they could not afford to let pass by. So they again impressed upon Brian their peaceful intent, the overall mission, and promised not to hurt anyone or even remotely endanger anyone's life. Their scientific excursion into the mass public was promised not to be a blundering, irresponsible endeavor. They were reverential. This was an honorable mission of peace, and the aliens made it clear they were accountable for all their actions on this historic delegation to earth. Brian thought for a moment and came to a decision.

`"Okay, let's do it!"` he enthusiastically signed.

Brian admired the aliens and he sincerely wanted to help these intra-galactic, foreign friends; and so he did. After learning their simple plan, Brian was persuaded. It did not take long at all for him to become fully engaged in assisting the aliens.

· · · • • ● • • · ·

The time was now 6:32 p.m. Brian and Meihtu had spent the last ten minutes driving around the beautiful, Lake Arrowhead shopping area, where most of the tourists from the lower valley were gathered. Brian was amazed at how well Meihtu was prepared for this particular covert digression, and impressed that she took the chance and the daring opportunity to secretly mingle among earthly humans. He was delighted that he had agreed to help them accomplish this task. Brian reasoned that he would do the same, given the circumstances, if he was clandestinely visiting another world and civilization. In a way, Brian was actually a little jealous of the alien adventurers. He wished he could have the same opportunity. He truly admired their gallantry.

To no surprise, the proposed, scientific venture proceeded carefully, exactly as planned. Brian was content and at ease as they drove around. He actually enjoyed watching Meihtu observe humankind from his vehicle. Compared to his earlier reservations about this little pleasure trip, he was now convinced this was the right thing to do.

Brian and Meihtu were traveling northbound, approaching the main intersection leading to the popular, scenic lakeside drive, when he had an impulsive notion. Without giving another thought to what he was about to do, he smoothly swerved his truck into a vacant spot close to the curb, near the signal light. He came to a stop close behind an unoccupied, economy sized car situated not very far from the southeast corner of the intersection. It was a sudden, spontaneous deed that was very much unexpected.

Although his intentions were completely good, this was not something that was briefed and consensually agreed to beforehand by the team. Brian seriously had not thought of parking the truck in broad daylight until right now. If the aliens had mentioned the idea of doing something like this, he probably would not have even considered it. However, it seemed like a good idea, and Brian just wanted to offer his beautiful celestial friend a different perspective to observe everything. Although there was no formal discussion about what he was doing, it was not something Brian considered too risky. To him it was just something different to do.

The very next thing Brian did was also not at all expected. He turned off the ignition and the subtle drone of the Toyota Tacoma's engine abruptly ceased. Thus, there was no immediate escape from anyone who might accidentally discover the mysterious extraterrestrial inside the inconspicuous, stationary motor vehicle. Their vulnerability had suddenly been declared with that one quick turn of the key, and the subsequent quiet that followed. The stillness was sobering.

Meihtu turned to look at Brian as soon as she realized what was happening. She swiftly, although gently, reached over from the passenger side of the truck and grasped the young man's right arm while he still had his hand on the ignition key. His response was encouraging. He took hold of her hand in his. Brian reassuringly appeased her unspoken concern with a tender squeeze of his hand. He smiled and simultaneously nodded his head once. Although her face was craftily concealed from public view, the look in her appealing bronze eyes told him she trusted his actions.

Meihtu's wardrobe fully resembled an elegant abaya and niqab ensemble. The pleasantly loose fitting, black and tan garment was most ideal, and it completely and artfully concealed her shapely alien physique. Her delicate alien feet and narrow hands were also appropriately covered in matching shoes and gloves. There was only a very thin opening of her face veil that barely revealed her alien eyes. Underneath the veil, her face was creatively disguised with an ingenious alien cosmetic to make her skin appear more human with a deep olive skin tone. She calmly returned her gaze out the passenger side window of Brian's static vehicle.

As long as she avoided direct eye contact, no one would notice something was different about her, save for her mysteriously alluring bronze eyes. All the same, her outer appearance was not at all uncommon for the thriving and colorful ethnic diversity of

California. Brian was certain her costume was perfect as soon as he saw it. He had considered so, after she tried the garb on for him in a sort of 'dress rehearsal' back at his parent's home.

This was certainly a very different perspective than the one Meihtu had while riding along with Brian. Now, instead of quickly motoring past everything, all the people she contentedly observed were passing by more slowly. She could silently sightsee from this new vantage point, while her subjects walked past the truck at a much more appreciable pace. This was a tempo much more suitable for people watching. Brian could tell she was very pleased with his impromptu decision. He could tell from her composed, enthusiastic posture and mannerism.

Brian noticed her breathing rate increase slightly at the mere sight of everyone walking by very close to the vehicle, practically at arm's reach. Meihtu was blissfully enthralled. He noticed how she turned her head just slightly in close examination of the people walking by. Her curious gaze quickly shifted from person to person, like a famished song sparrow searching for insects and seeds in the early morn. Brian smiled. The sight of her so astutely observing everyone else was amusing to him. This was indeed, a very rare and wonderful opportunity for the aliens, Brian had rightly figured.

Then another impulsive notion come into his mind. He wondered how she would respond. He considered telling Meihtu how to lower the passenger side window. Having the absence of tinted auto glass to look through, essentially a physical barrier between her and the people walking by, would be somewhat liberating, Brian figured. Yet, he had something else even better come to mind. Brian smiled at the exciting thought of it. He cleared his throat as he gathered the daring nerve. He got her attention with a light touch on her hand.

"I want you to really enjoy this experience. Do you trust me?" Brian smiled, as he quietly and eagerly signed.

Meihtu acknowledged with a firm nod of her head.

Brian slowly opened the driver's side door of the truck. As soon as the mechanical action of the opening door softly sounded, Brian suddenly heard the resonance of faint alien chatter coming from Meihtu's communication earpiece that immediately and quite distinguishably intensified. Brian figured the truck was under careful, close observation by at least one of the stealthy floating observation probes. He reasonably assumed that Baouzhe had questioned, and quite possibly even objected, to what was going on. The raised alien tone of voice duly suggested so. There was also something else very peculiar about the sounds Brian faintly heard emanating from Meihtu's earpiece. It sounded like there was more than one voice. It sounded to Brian like there was someone else talking to her, as well as Baouzhe.

Meihtu spoke softly in response to the voices Brian heard. Her reply was short. The chatter suddenly ceased. Then she nodded once at Brian and signed.

`"You may proceed."`

Brian felt a deep confidence in their friendship that he could not explain. He was certain she understood him even without speaking a word of her extraterrestrial language. He was certain she understood his intentions, even without using the slightest expression of alien sign language. He did not have to, because of an honest, unconditional solidarity that firmly existed between them. They shared an unspoken, unique, intimate under-standing. They fully and unquestionably trusted each other.

Brian opened his door with a handsome smile and exited the vehicle. He casually walked around the front of the truck, keeping Meihtu in view. This also allowed him to remain in her watchful view. He walked around to the passenger side of the vehicle, all the while keeping eye contact with her. He leisurely opened her door and extended his hand to her. She trustingly took hold of his hand while staring into his encouraging eyes. There was not even the slightest hesitation from her. She stood up, leaving the sheltered confines of the parked vehicle. He gently pulled her close to his side as he reached around her and shut the passenger door. The look on Brian's face was confident and reassuring. He wanted Meihtu to completely enjoy this moment. Brian knew this was the experience of a lifetime for his beautiful extraterrestrial companion. He could feel his hand being squeezed firmly by hers. She was very excited!

Brian silently looked his alien friend over once to make sure her wardrobe was intact and that nothing looked out of the ordinary. He was confident everyone else around him perceived only that she wore the customary garb commonly worn by conservative women in the Arab Gulf.

There they stood, shoulder to shoulder, comfortably close to each other. The experience was a magnificent and remarkable moment of discovery for both of them. This was truly incredible. Meihtu was standing among the esteemed humans, and Brian was standing next to a colossal, historic secret. The young man remembered what his alien friends had told him, how he was basically involved in a truly extraordinary undertaking. This was an important mission, indeed. The more he thought about the significance of this reverent moment, the more quietly excited he became.

Meihtu stood silently out in the open next to her trusted earthly companion and gazed at the people before her privileged alien eyes. The early, summer lit evening was a gorgeous one, and the mountain air was clear, crisp, and pleasant, very much like it is every day in that pine forested resort area. If there was any day to give an extraterrestrial visitor an exclusive tour of daily life on earth, this was definitely a good one, with an outstanding locale, no doubt. The homely, small town milieu was picturesque. The mere sights and sounds of everyone walking about completely filled their senses. The celestial alien and earthly gentleman said nothing by alien sign language, although they were collectively experiencing everything in wonderful enormity. Perhaps, for the first time, Brian looked upon his own kind in a tender way, simply awe inspired. He started to feel very proud of the fact that the people of earth had greatly impressed the highly advanced aliens. The fact that the aliens would risk being discovered so they could simply observe humans in person is what astonished him most. He could not remember a single moment that made him feel the way he did right now. This moment was as wonderfully historic as any moment recorded in any of the textbooks he'd ever read in school. Brian smiled at the pleasant thought of it.

Many different people strolled past the silent pioneer duo standing next to the parked truck. Some were local residents. Most of them were day-trippers and shoppers. Most did not pay any attention to the fact that Brian's companion was completely covered from head to foot in a traditionally conservative Arab garment. The few that noticed did not realize the garment worn by the alien humanoid was not a genuine ethnic assemblage. Certainly, no one had the slightest clue as to who was underneath the costume. No one knew of the fantastic, secretive undertaking happening right now; a simple observation trip.

One particular young boy did think something was peculiar, though. As he slowly passed the two quiet onlookers, he noticed something odd about the woman. The young boy was old enough to know that there are people that come from many different, wonderful cultures from all around the world. Respectfully, he was mature enough to appreciate the fact that some people just dress a little differently than others and that is normal. However, the boy could not help but notice something very different about the way the costumed commander appeared. It was something separate from the way she was clothed. More specifically, through the small slit in the veil covering the commander's face, he caught a glimpse of something that was conspicuously strange. From where the young boy was, the light of day hit her beautiful alien eyes at just the precise angle, and for just long enough, for him to see the shiny bronzed color. He definitely was not accustomed to seeing anything like that, never before this very instant. The young boy turned his head forward for a moment as he continued walking in stride with his older sister and his mother. There was something definitely different about that woman to him. He could not help himself. The curious boy turned his head to look back at the commander once more. Just as he did, he felt a firm tug on his arm from his mother.

"It's not polite to stare!" She put her face close to his and whispered loudly.

The boy said nothing. They continued on. He did not look back at the alien commander again.

Brian noticed the boy and saw how the youngster tried to take another look. He also noticed how Meihtu quickly averted her observant gaze from making direct eye contact with the boy. She bowed her head slightly and looked down at her feet for a moment. It was an effective, subtle evasive tactic. No need to worry. The observation team had not been compromised. The paired surveillance twosome remained undetected, and their present situation was very collected. Brian quietly watched the boy and his family saunter away, virtually disappearing into the small crowd of other shoppers and sightseers walking about. Meihtu unworriedly returned her gaze to people watching once again.

Brian looked at his alien friend to make sure she was still completely concealed. He noticed her gloved right hand suddenly reach underneath the upper concealing garment. No sooner had he noticed her gloved hand underneath the upper garment than he heard her suddenly gasp. He flinched and raised his head to look at her. He was very curious to know what she was reacting to, and why.

He followed her gaze across the street and immediately saw what was happening.

Chapter Twenty Nine

Brian noticed a little girl across the street had stepped off the sidewalk of the nearby intersection and was heading towards the crosswalk on the other side of the street. She was walking alone. She was alone, because the signal light had turned red for pedestrian traffic. Everyone else had stopped, but the little girl had not. The very moment Brian witnessed that, someone screamed.

"Tiffany!" a terrified woman shrieked.

Brian's eyes widened at the tragedy that could unfold right before his eyes when a brand new Chevrolet Suburban came out of nowhere, packed full of a family out sightseeing on this beautiful day. The Suburban approached the intersection in the same lane the little girl, Tiffany, was in. In fact, the monstrous vehicle was headed directly for the cute little redhead girl who had just stepped off the curb.

In a split second Brian saw the girl, the Suburban, and the rapidly disappearing distance between the two. The little girl froze in her tracks when she saw the car. Her panic and fear were obvious, and Brian immediately felt an awful pang of grief when, in that second, he knew there was not enough time for him to reach her even though he would gladly sacrifice his own life to save hers. His body tensed reflexively and he wanted to scream. But, like everyone else watching, he covered his mouth with his hands to keep from doing so.

The brakes on the large vehicle locked up the tires and a loud screech and the smell of burning rubber filled the air. Someone screamed and it was all Brian could to not do the same.

In that instant, Meihtu nudged him. She pulled her hand out from underneath her garment and Brian saw something extraordinary dangling from her tightly clenched grasp. It was sparkly and wondrously beautiful. In her hand, the extraterrestrial commander held a mysterious alien jewel.

In a fraction of the time it takes to blink an eye, the remarkably beautiful ornament emanated an intense pulse of sheer silvery light. The instantaneous radiance was blinding, and completely visible even in the summertime light of day. Brian blinked and reflexively leaned away from the flash of bright light. He partially shielded his eyes with a raised hand but kept his bemused eyes focused on the wondrous celestial jewel.

At the exact moment that the inexplicable dazzling light flashed, Brian heard and felt a very deep, single pulsation throughout his corporeal mass. The sensation was singularly discomforting, an enigmatic percussion experienced deep inside his skull that seemed to resonant within his very soul. In that fraction of an instant, he felt a little numb and was not sure if he could move.

Then there was a second flash, a strobe of bright silvery light that also resulted in another pulsation he felt deep in his head. The second occurrence was stronger and a bit overwhelming, to the point his knees nearly buckled. He felt very much disoriented. Still, his gaze remained fixed on the glimmering object, the extraordinary alien gemstone.

Brian could see all of its wondrous detail. He noticed how the bewildering jewel twinkled vibrantly as sparks of pure white light blossomed from the center outward. It seemed to reflect daylight within it in the most brilliant way, sparkling like the quick burning wick of a lit firecracker. Brian instinctively knew something was suddenly very different about his immediate surroundings. Something bizarre was happening, something completely abnormal from anything he had physical knowledge of, and he knew it had something to do with the alien jewel. He felt very strange, profoundly obtunded.

While still gazing almost helplessly at the jewel, Brian immediately noticed something else after the second reverberating pulsation. The mysterious gem was sparkling reflected light within it noticeably much slower than when the first flash had occurred. There was something quite remarkable happening right now, without question. Brian didn't know what it was, but he knew something was going on, alright, and that he was exclusively privileged to it all.

Meihtu had the mysterious gem stretched out almost at arm's length in plain view. At that moment, whilst still inexplicably entranced by the mysteriously imposing gem, Brian sensed something. It was a feeling that immediately seemed somewhat familiar to him, for some strange reason, though he did not exactly know why. Though Brian had no whole recollection of the alien gemstone, he logically realized it was something of great consequence. He wondered if he had ever seen such a marvel as this beautiful gem. Brian could not recall if there was ever a specific moment. He did not know when.

Brian became slightly more aware of his immediate surroundings. The first thing he noticed was the normal summertime light of day was now much darker. Also, the myriad of sounds of a bustling street corner filled with the many voices of excited tourists and automobile clatter was somehow completely absent. The normal sounds of daily commotion were simply gone. Instead, Brian could now sense the lively flow of blood rushing through his veins, within the core of his body, and all throughout his extremities. He could slightly feel and hear the pulse of his own heartbeat inside his cranium, in place of all those other usual external noises all around him. Brian's breathing rate increased a little. He was very aware of it. His skin tingled all over, and he was beginning to feel a bit euphoric, as well. It was a very peculiar, surreal experience.

Brian did not notice Meihtu switching the grasp of the gem from her right hand to her left hand. He flinched when Meihtu suddenly yet gently grabbed his arm and broke his engrossed stare, so she could get his prompt attention. He was so extremely entranced. Brian could have stared into the very center of the handsome jewel, forever, or so he thought.

Brian glanced away from the gemstone almost reluctantly.

When his attention shifted to his surroundings, he noticed that the world around him was inexplicably, incredibly different. All the usual lively colors of a typical, late summertime day had somehow become profoundly indistinct. In fact, all the elemental colors of life in general were altered. The entire world viewed through the young man's eyes was bathed in a fantastic shade of anil. It was as if Brian was viewing everything through indigo tinted sunglasses, except he had no such eyewear on. The disorienting visual sensation was just a little bit unnerving and very curiously bizarre to Brian. He had never, ever, experienced anything like this before.

That was not all there was to be anxious about, however. There was much more, something more extreme and visually perplexing than the unnatural coloration of the entire world all-around him. Brian looked around and found himself at a complete loss for words, for what he saw was impossible to fathom. His mind simply could not digest the fact that everything as far as the eye could see around the small space where he and the commander stood, had come to a complete stop!

The world around them hung suspended in a supernatural stillness and, almost as disturbing, was the complete lack of noise. Brian's eyes grew wide and his jaw dropped full open at first sight of the scene around him. He promptly turned his head to the exotic commander for an immediate answer. He wanted her to say something. He wanted her to explain to him anything, some type of an exposition, in an effort to appease his indubitable stupor. *How could this be happening?!* He wanted to say something, but felt too dizzy and dim-witted to formulate words into conversation. Brian was absolutely speechless! For a moment, he felt as if he must be dreaming. He was not.

When Brian gazed at his trusty alien companion next to him, he suddenly noticed that Meihtu appeared the same as the rest of the surrounding view, having a deep shaded tint about her; as if an indigo tinged shadow had been cast over her. Brian, on impulse, looked down at the ground. He promptly observed his own appearance from his feet to his hands. He, too, appeared in the same eerie tinted coloration as his celestial friend. He shut his eyes tight and shook his head in an effort to clear his mind, and his vision. When he opened them again, there was the same look about the world. Everything still appeared static, in a dynamically shaded, bizarre hue. The only thing slightly different was Meihtu and himself. Brian noticed they were both visually darker in shade than the rest of the motionless world around them. It was as if they were standing in a different shade of light, or lack thereof. It was as if the two of them were standing underneath the shadow of something. Brian looked up towards the sky out of complete, naive curiosity. Then it suddenly occurred to him that, indeed, there was a shadow.

There were three distinct emanated shadows, to be precise. However, the source of those mysterious shadows was what immediately grasped his full attention. Brian was looking up into the sky at something exclusively remarkable in comparison to anything he had ever witnessed in his entire life. There were three distinct objects completely visible in the indigo tinged daytime sky above. One object was located almost directly overhead, one was located towards the west horizon on his left, and one was oriented more towards the east horizon, off to his right.

Brian stared at the ashen object above him. It first appeared to his visual senses as a circular object, like a large disk, or a wheel. He concentrated his focus on it and quickly realized that the thing up in the air looked more like a distant planet. It was similar in appearance to the moon, only with a distinct shadowy halo around it. As he observed the planetoid object closely, he noticed a ring of silvery white light that rotated from left to right around it. The thin ring of light turned about the lunar object like a slender ring rotating around a marble toy in the center. Brian had no explanation for what he was witnessing. Though the spectacle was without explanation, it was marvelous to witness. Brian looked at the lunar form to his right, and then he looked at the one to his left. They were both very similar to the bizarre, ashen colored planetoid object above him.

Brian noticed how the dark halos encircling each of the objects were the same hue as the lack of light he and Meihtu were standing in. He glanced at his hands once more, and then down at the ground, noticing this time that he and Meihtu were standing directly in the middle of a darkly shaded, circular area. He intuitively reasoned that each of the dark halos directly facing him from the three lunar forms had something to do with the shade they stood in. The observable effect of all three of the planetoid forms completely blanketed the two covert observers, uniformly casting a full shadow several feet in diameter around them both.

Brian was profoundly perplexed as to how the celestial objects in the sky could somehow cast a dark anil shadow upon him and his extraterrestrial friend, Meihtu. *How could there be a separate shadow cast by all three of those moons on the same exact spot, and so precisely? What in the world would cause* that?

Brian pondered as he gazed up into the atmosphere. Nothing came to mind that he knew existed. The fundamental suggestion that this could even possibly happen was simply mind boggling. Brian looked into the sky, visually searching for anything that would bear evidence as explanation to what he was experiencing right now. *The earth has only one moon, I thought.* Brian thought about how the Earth's natural satellite, the Moon, was sometimes visible to the naked eye during the day. *Which of the other planets in our solar system are this visible at daytime? And, if they aren't from our solar system, then where are those planets or moons from? And, how far away are they?* Brian grimaced while contemplating the approximate location of the astral objects.

Brian focused his attention on the planetoid object above him. As he gazed at the darkened halo around it, he began to realize something else that seemed very peculiar, in addition to everything else going on that was so remarkable. The dark halo phenomenon encircling the lunar form looked more and more to him like a hole. It looked as if there was a hole in the sky, to be more specific. It was as if the planetoid object was visible through a distinct hole that had somehow been perfectly incised into the sky above. Brian thought of the phenomenon as a peephole, allowing his eyes to somehow see through a small opening in the vast atmosphere, deep into outer space. He peered at the astral objects, visually comparing one to the other. All three seemed to each be situated within that same type of phenomenon, an apparent hole in the sky.

He had absolutely no idea what was happening, or how it could be. The strange shade originating from the planetoid objects was narrow in bandwidth, and focused, much like a trio of search lights coming together to bathe would be prison escapees in the dark of night. Except, these were not beams of light, but rather, beams of shadows. Meihtu and Brian were standing under those incredible shadowy beams of dark hue.

"What the …?" Brian finally uttered, jaw wide open in astonished stupor. His head was still curiously turned upwards towards the heavens. Brian stared at the phenomenal object located almost directly above them. He tried to complete his intended sentence, a simple query, but all he could say once more was, "What the…?" He pointed to the indigo tinged sky above about the same moment Meihtu gently grabbed hold of his other arm.

She began to speak. Of course, her alien tongue was completely incomprehensible to him. However, her tone of voice suggested there was something of an urgent matter to attend to. She methodically raised her right arm and pointed with her thumb. She was trying to redirect his captivated gaze across the street. Brian was so engrossed with the alien gemstone, the planetoid objects above them, the shadowy silhouette they stood in, and the color of the entire, catatonic world around him that he'd forgotten about everything else going on. Brian saw Meihtu pointing at something, or rather, someone. He did not know who.

Brian stared at Meihtu with a confounded look, not knowing what to say or do next. He was completely baffled. Meihtu made another gesture for him to look. Brian looked where she was pointing almost out of curiosity. What could be more important than three unexplained planets completely visible in an indigo tinged sky? What could possibly be more important than everything in the entire world coming to a complete halt?

Then, as if he had suddenly been slapped and awoken from

a hypnotic trance, it suddenly occurred to the young man. *The little girl, Tiffany.* Brian focused his attention on the child, the monstrous vehicle, and the impending doom that was about to occur. He had temporarily forgotten about all that.

"Oh shit!"

Chapter Thirty

Meihtu gently grabbed Brian's arm again and gestured for him to follow her. He smiled, and obliged. As he stepped forward, Brian took another look at the mysterious astral objects above. He noticed something distinctively peculiar. All the outlining rings of silvery light around each stellar object rotated in sync with each other. *How incredible!* Brian continued to gaze at the remarkable celestial objects in the sky above them. As he did so, he realized something else coincided with this incomparable visualization. He could hear a subtle, rhythmic pulsation that seemed to precisely coincide with the synchronized revolutions of the silvery rings. *I can't believe it. Just, incredible!* Brian shook his head and silently observed the cosmic effect. He almost tripped as he watched the radiant, thin ring of light rotate around the astral object above him a few times. It was a spectacular phenomenon to behold.

Meihtu took hold of Brian's hand and uttered something to him when he stumbled. He quickly composed himself and walked in stride with her as if nothing happened. He was only slightly embarrassed, figuring she was probably telling him to be careful. He squeezed her hand and she gently squeezed back in response. The covert surveillance duo simultaneously stepped off the curb and in-between the truck and the other parked car and then onto the street.

From there, Meihtu lead the way. She held up the brightly sparkling, mysterious gem directly in front of her, just like a bright lantern guiding their way in the still of a dark night. Brian looked at the beguiling gem for a second, and then he quickly glanced down at the ground. He was quick to notice, and quite fascinated to perceive how the shadowy planetoid silhouettes followed their every footstep. As they walked, the two observers remained exactly positioned within the center of the dark, indigo tinged shadow.

As they slowly walked, Brian took a more observant look at the world immediately about them. Its frozen state was simply astounding. He had so many questions that he wanted to stop and ask Meihtu. He wanted to know how this phenomenon could happen. He wanted to know if Meihtu had positively commanded it, and if she was in complete control of it in some way. He shook his head. The young man could not believe what his eyes were seeing.

"My God, how can this be happening? Everything is just, stopped! How can this be? I don't understand," Brian muttered, as he gaped at the eerily silent and unmoving world around him.

He particularly noticed how everyone around them was posed, just like a candid photograph. Brian turned his head in every direction to be certain he got a good look. He noticed that some of the people were watching, or had seemingly just taken notice of the unfolding tragedy that was about to happen. He could tell by the shocked expressions on their faces.

The terrible split second of horror was captured in time, like a picture snapped at just the precise, awful moment. There was an elderly couple sitting in the outdoor seating area of a popular, trendy coffee house. Their eyes were open wide, completely filled with terror and, ghastly affixed onto the doomed, little redhead Tiffany in the street. Another couple had taken notice, probably after hearing someone scream. Their heads were turned back to look. Brian noticed how the young woman had desperately grabbed hold of her boyfriend's arm. Brian could tell, just by the way her clenched hand had a firm hold of the young man's bare arm, she was frantically trying to get his attention. The young couple had just walked past the little girl near the corner. They were heading south, and were very close to the trendy little coffee house. They both had the same look of pure shock, just like everyone else who witnessed what was dreadfully happening this precise, wretched moment. Brian could clearly tell from the expression on the young woman's face that she was about to scream. The only noise was the rhythmic pulsations of the astral objects above them. They were headed directly for the girl standing in the street amidst an eerie backdrop of rigid onlookers frozen in a precise moment of time.

Brian looked at the large Suburban that was heading directly for Tiffany. He noticed at once, how the large vehicle was starting to bow forward into its front tires. When he glanced down at the wheels, he could see a faint plume of smoke from the rubber being left on the road as the brakes tried to stop the large, sport utility rated tires. Brian glanced into the front windshield. He saw the panic in the wide-eyed expressions of the driver, a middle aged man, and an unpleasantly surprised front passenger, a young woman. The driver was clutching the steering wheel and leaning back aggressively against his seat as though that pressure would help stop the car.

"How can this be?" Brian queried. "This is not possible."

Meihtu suddenly stopped. It was so abrupt, Brian bumped into her. He was still looking at the Suburban. When he returned his attention to little Tiffany, he noticed the shadowy phenomenon that he and Meihtu were standing in was just about to contact the girl's feet. He looked at his friend. Meihtu crouched a little and leaned forward with a tight grip on Brian's hand. He placed his other hand on top of hers. He knew she wanted to proceed very cautiously, although he did not know why. The covert observation duo was very close to the little girl now.

There she stood, right in plain view before them. Brian could clearly see her time-frozen, terrified posture. She was strikingly rigid, with both her hands raised up, about chest high. Her facial expression was one of complete panic. Indeed, Brian was now uncomfortably, intimately close. He was able to clearly observe the uninhibited shock and expression of doom on Tiffany's face in this last, horrific second.

"What are you going to do?" Brian calmly inquired as he stared at his alien friend. "You're, going to help her, aren't you?"

He felt certain of it. He trusted Meihtu and was completely at ease now that something wonderful would be the outcome. He smiled. Commander Meihtu was entirely focused on what she was doing. The task at hand would, in essence, be nothing short of an incredible miracle, as Brian would soon discover. She took another very careful and deliberate step forward towards the petrified and eerily motionless Tiffany. Brian quietly shadowed her movements and positioned himself very close behind his celestial friend, following her footsteps precisely. As soon as he moved in closer to Meihtu, she relaxed the grip of her long narrow hand on his. Brian let go of Meihtu's hand and then grasped tightly onto her concealing garment. He leaned his shoulder forward and to the right slightly, keeping close watch on the presumably doomed little girl. Brian had no idea what was about to occur. However, he assumed by the way his celestial companion cautiously proceeded, that it was something of great significance.

His assumption was correct.

As soon as the indigo shadow converged on little Tiffany's right elbow and right foot, there was an immediate and very tremendous happening. Suddenly, an erratic array of flickering bright lights like miniature bursts of lightening erupted at each exact point where the darkened shadow contacted the little girl. The arcing pulses of lighted strands blossomed as they sparked, stretching out from the contact points like naked branches on a tree. The brilliant eruption of light was quite animated, especially in comparison to the solemn, inert world outside the darkened borders of the shadow, which was everything else surrounding the covert observation team.

There was something rather spectacular that Brian took particular notice of during this brilliant manifestation. The stream of bifurcating light emanated a distinct photo lucent outline as it pranced about the contact points of origin on the motionless, little redhead girl. The pulsing strands of pure light sparked outward in a conspicuous pattern, precisely forming a perceptible dome that completely surrounded Brian and Meihtu that exactly outlined the planetoid shadows on the asphalt. The visualization of this exceptional occurrence was quite extraordinary and a bit humorous. The luminous effect that encapsulated them made Brian think he was standing inside a grand-sized cake dish cover. He chuckled.

"Whoa!" he said, absolutely bemused.

There was something more to appreciate. As the miniature bursts of lightning sparkled around them, Brian heard a crackling sound, as if a tiny firecracker string was going off in a delightful fury. The unremitting noise and the visualization of remarkable light effects excited him. It was all quite the commotion to behold.

Meihtu proceeded at a steady, very careful pace now. Brian dutifully followed. As the darkened margins of the strange shadow passed over the little girl, the flickering, erratic strands of bright light advanced, precisely and uniformly. Brian observed again how the wondrous lighted effect exactly bounded the contour of the darkened shadow on the asphalt. He was curious about how the border of bright light flickered, perpendicular to the surface of the street.

What's happening right now? What can cause this? How can this be? Brian peered at the margins of the mysterious shadow. He was at a loss for all simple conversational words at the moment.

As the planetoid shadow moved across Tiffany, the border of bright light simultaneously and quite amazingly passed through the little girl, inch by inch, at the exact pace that Meihtu progressed forward. As the light advanced, the erratic strands pranced outward in a dazzling and vigorous display.

As the brilliantly sparking perimeter effect of light strands moved from right to left across Tiffany, she became more and more encapsulated within the perceptible 'dome' that completely surrounded Brian and Meihtu. With each step, Meihtu was advancing the circular planetary shadow so that, in essence, Tiffany was nearing the center. Soon, Tiffany would be right where Meihtu and Brian were; under the stark, shadowy beams of the mysterious planetoid objects in the sky.

"Whoa!" Brian's excited voice could just be heard over the clattering noise of the phenomena.

Then, as soon as the bordering flicker of light approached the midsagittal division of the little girl's body, there was a sudden, bright cyan radiance that completely encapsulated Tiffany. The brightly colored glowing effect moved all over her body in visually beautiful, synchronous, iridescent waves. Brian could not help but smile in awe at the fantastical display of emitted light and dynamically shaded colors. The stunning effect seemed very reminiscent of Saint Elmo's fire to him; a phenomenon he had only read about and witnessed on television. All of these sights and sounds became the most unique experience Brian had ever observed. It was both overwhelming and enjoyable.

When the mysterious shadow was completely cast over Tiffany, there was another peculiar episode. The miniature flashes of erratic light filaments and associated noise ceased. The cyan light engulfing Tiffany was no more. It was suddenly eerily silent. Brian stared at the motionless little girl. Now, all three of them were standing under the combined shadow effect of the three celestial objects above them.

Tiffany was still perfectly poised in candid terror. Her pretty little dismayed eyes were locked onto what seemed to be an awful destiny. Brian looked to his right once more to get another view of what she saw. Having moved closer to Tiffany, he had almost the exact grim perspective she had. There was nothing between them and the big Suburban except flat asphalt. From this perspective, he began to feel a bit anxious again. The uncomfortable view and closeness of the approaching Suburban at this angle was unbearable to look at, even though the vehicle was serendipitously suspended in time. Just the thought of what would soon occur began to deeply disturb him.

He looked away and focused his attention on Tiffany. *Please God, let us help her!*

Then Brian noticed something most remarkable happen. Tiffany's eyelids began to flutter. Then her jaw began to quiver and her body suddenly convulsed for a total of one and a half seconds. Her little forehead lowered, and the long, red hair on her head that came down to her shoulders fell forward. As soon as she bowed her head her hair completely covered her face. Her tensed shoulders drooped and her body suddenly relaxed. She looked like she fainted. Brian flinched, thinking he should grab hold of her before she fell, but she did not.

Tiffany slowly raised her head and brought her hands up to her forehead, smoothing the long hair away from her pretty freckled face. As soon as she did so, she got another full view of the approaching Suburban. Although still an ominous sight, the large sport utility vehicle was expediently frozen in time and absolutely harmless now on a corporeal continuum of which Tiffany was at this very instant no longer part of. That did not matter. She still reacted to the very dreadful sight of the Chevrolet Suburban.

She flinched at the sight of her apparent oncoming death. The instant she started to react, Meihtu said something to her. Tiffany immediately turned her head towards Meihtu and Brian in reflexive response. The smartly cloaked alien woman repeated her firm utterance once more. Meihtu was successful in capturing the frightened little girl's complete attention. Though her words were not at all comprehensible, Meihtu's foreign tongue seemed to be an abrupt, welcome distraction.

Tiffany was ready to make a leap towards safer ground, towards the strangely clothed alien woman, but after taking barely one fleeing step, she suddenly froze in her tracks, startled. She gasped.

Tiffany seemed to forget about her oncoming doom for a moment, so focused was she on the people who showed up out of nowhere and were coming towards her. The strange looking one was completely hidden from head to foot, including most of her face. But the really strange thing about this person was the bright light sparkling and shining on her chest.

It was some type of wondrously sparkling jewel and Tiffany wanted to look at it some more. So she did. It looked so very beautiful, like Christmas! Tiffany stared. She stared deep into the center of the bright gleaming gem. She wanted to look at all the sparkly light that twinkled inside. So, she kept looking, entirely focused on the wonderful jewel. Just like that, Tiffany could care less about Brian or the woman with all the clothes. Nothing else mattered to her now. The only thing Tiffany wanted to do right now was stare at the beautiful, dazzling ornament. So, she kept looking.

Brian noticed how the cute little girl became instantly entranced. The sight of her staring at the bizarre jewel brought that same feeling again that seemed somewhat familiar to him for some strange reason, though he did not know why.

"Does she still see us?" he asked, just above a whisper. "It looks like she doesn't even notice we're still, right here, huh?" His query was more of a reservation made out loud than an actual question.

There was, of course, no reply from Meihtu. She was quite occupied at the moment. One glance at his celestial companion and Brian knew. Meihtu was quite engrossed in completing what she had started. She had a method to her determined intention. That much seemed sure.

Meihtu raised her gloved right hand and with her palm facing forward, made a silent, deliberate gesture, as if she were slowly pushing something away from her. In essence, she was. Amazingly, Tiffany, with her eyes still hypnotically affixed upon the wondrous celestial jewel, took a generous step backwards.

Meihtu slowly began to move forward at a steady, very careful pace once again. Brian dutifully followed. As Meihtu took a step forward, Tiffany took a deliberate step backwards. Meihtu started slowly at first, but she soon picked up the pace just a bit. They all walked together, in precise unison. As they walked, all three of them remained exactly positioned within the center segment of the large, dark indigo tinged circular shadow. The enchanting sounds of the rhythmic pulsations of the astral objects above them could still be heard as they stepped across the asphalt together.

As they approached the curb, Meihtu slowed her pace. When Tiffany was close to the edge of the curb, Meihtu made another methodical gesture with her hand, opening it near her chin with the palm facing up. Tiffany, with eyes locked onto the beautiful gem, hesitated for just a second, then she raised her left foot and took a bold step backwards, planting her foot on the pavement of the sidewalk almost exactly where she had stepped off into the busy intersection. Meihtu took a few more steps, and Tiffany resumed her retreat in silent cadence. Brian watched in amazement as his beautiful celestial friend confidently marched the cute little girl rearward, merely by entranced suggestion.

Then, when the borders of the mysterious shadow neared Tiffany's mother, Meihtu abruptly stopped. She proceeded to raise her hand again and made the same gesture as before, pushing away. Tiffany responded and silently stepped backwards by herself. She stepped all the way back, right next to her mother. Tiffany stopped walking when she reached the very inside margins of the mysterious planetoid shadow. She did all of this without taking a single look back, behind her. She did all of this unknowingly and unreservedly while gazing deep into the core of the glowing alien gemstone. She was completely rapt.

Meihtu made another gesture with her free hand. She lowered her hand, palm facing downward. Tiffany's response was immediate and uncomplicated. She stood erect and very still, with her arms and hands stretched out at her sides. It was an impressive sight. Tiffany reacted just like a soldier commanded to attention. It was actually quite entertaining for Brian. He shook his head.

"Damn, this is some trippy shit!" he muttered with a grin.

Meihtu stood for a slight moment just looking at Tiffany, who was facing her directly. Then Meihtu mumbled something in her extraterrestrial language and nodded once, quickly, before reaching behind her back to touch Brian. When Meihtu's gloved hand made contact with his hip, she patted him a couple times. He looked down at her hand still on his hip. He figured she was giving him a signal. Brian took a few steps back.

What followed next was in effect the opposite of all that had just transpired. Meihtu crouched a little and leaned back very carefully, taking deliberate steps backwards, away from Tiffany. As soon as the border of the indigo shadow converged on the little girl's back, the bright flickering lights erupted once more. The stream of light emanated the same, distinct photo lucent outline, the perceptible dome, which completely surrounded Tiffany, Meihtu, and Brian.

Meihtu and Brian stepped back further, and as the planetoid shadow withdrew away from Tiffany, the planar light effect passed through Tiffany's body once again, at the exact pace that Meihtu walked backward. Then, the same bright cyan radiance encapsulated Tiffany like Saint Elmo's fire, just as it did before.

When the mysterious shadow completely withdrew from Tiffany, the miniature flashes of erratic light filaments and associated noises ceased. The encapsulating glow was no more, and it was suddenly eerily silent. She was entirely stationary as everyone else was outside the shadow. Tiffany no longer existed in the present, the now, as Brian and Meihtu did. Rather, Tiffany was occupying space in the soon to be; a place frozen in time.

Brian stared at the motionless child, who was now standing next to her terrified mother. She was no longer suspended in a state of desolate, horrifying shock. Quite the contrary, the look on Tiffany's face was almost amusing to Brian. Her perfectly still, arrested emotion was profoundly different now. She was completely catatonic, like the rest of the world. However, the look in her eyes was not one of horror, common to the rest of the surrounding bystanders who were aghast at what was about to happen to Tiffany. In stark contrast, Tiffany's eyes held a helpless, wanting gaze, searching deep into the light-filled alien gemstone. Brian peered at her innocent eyes in a focused trance, staring deep into something that was no longer in her view. The cute little girl with red hair and freckles was still entranced in an idle instant of time, completely bedazzled.

Alas, in the moment Tiffany was just returned to, there would be no beautiful ornament to gaze upon anymore. Brian wondered what that profound moment of instant realization was like. He wondered what Tiffany would be thinking. He wondered what Tiffany would remember.

As he and Meihtu stepped away, Brian thought about everything that had just taken place. To him, this particular phenomenon seemed much more than just a dazzling display of erratic light and sound. Indeed, the dizzying visual causality seemed to have partitioned time, exclusively dividing what was happening now from what was yet to happen.

Brian remained at a complete loss for normal, intelligent, conversation. He was terribly stupefied, and the look on his face frankly expressed that emotion.

Chapter Thirty One

Meihtu kept a firm hand on her handsome human friend, as the two made their hurried retreat back across the street. Brian took another look at the very extraordinary astral objects above and noticed something distinctively peculiar. The outlining rings of silvery light around each stellar object rotated in sync at a slightly slower pace than before, and the coinciding, subtle rhythmic pulsation seemed to reverberate slower.

That sounds a little different than before. Brian grimaced in reflective thought as he peered into the indigo tinged sky and then stumbled once again as he studied the wondrous cosmic effect.

Meihtu uttered something to him. The alien phrase sounded slightly familiar this time around. Brian quickly composed himself and walked in stride with her as if nothing happened. They both chuckled. He figured Meihtu was probably telling him to be careful as she had the first time. She squeezed his hand and he gently squeezed hers back in response.

The two of them returned to their side of the street where the Tacoma was parked. They walked close to each other as they approached the passenger side of the truck. When they stopped at the door, Meihtu said something and judging from the way she spoke and the light tug on his arm, Brian figured she wanted to hurry. He surmised things were going to return to normal, and perhaps quite quickly. Brian figured she would 'command' it, real soon.

They were still exactly positioned within the center of the

dark, indigo tinged circular shadow, which now included Brian's truck. Brian gazed around the anil hued world that was mysteriously spellbound. It was truly quite the impressive sight and something he could appreciate much more now that he had witnessed what just happened. Brian was completely astounded, even more so, now that he had seen the miraculous alteration of Tiffany's dreadful dilemma. Brian clearly comprehended the awesome capability and purpose of this auspicious extraterrestrial phenomenon.

The cleverly shrouded alien humanoid woman clenched the long silvery necklace and raised the sparkling gem off her chest. At once, and as before, the beautiful jewel emanated an intense pulse of pure silvery light. The effect was also just as extreme. Brian reflexively leaned away from the flash of striking bright light and simultaneously shielded his eyes with his hand. At the exact moment the dazzling flash occurred, Brian heard and felt that familiar, very deep, single pulsation throughout his body resonating inside like a clock tower bell. The sensation was not as discomforting this time. Still, it made him feel a little numb all over and just a bit disoriented.

Then there was the second flash immediately after the first. This strobe of bright light sent another single pulsation deep inside Brian's cranium and then throughout his body. The second flash effect was a little stronger than the first. This time however, Brian was not as overwhelmed with the intense, physical sensation. While still quite resounding, his legs stood firm and he retained his balance.

A sudden, pounding effect filled Brian's ears immediately following the second flash and pulsation. The effect resonated like claps of thunder. He winced at the unfamiliar and unexpected resonance and blinked his eyes against the brilliant light. Suddenly, a rush of air from all directions blew at Meihtu and Brian for just a fraction of a second, then ceased.

In the blink of an eye, a myriad of sounds erupted and, once again, the street corner bustled with the sounds of traffic coming from automobiles on the street and people making their way along the sidewalk. All the usual vivacious sounds and colors of a typical, late summertime day in the picturesque mountain lake area were fully restored. Suddenly, screams filled the air and a split second later, the sound of screeching tires. Brian's eyes immediately shot to where Tiffany had been standing.

Brian's eyes widened once again at the cataclysmic misfortune rapidly unfolding before him and everyone else. He once again heard and saw the large Suburban lock up its tires in a vain attempt to avoid hitting the child. Everything resumed, right on cue, from the precise awful moment before the initial brilliant flashes emanating from the beautiful alien gemstone.

It was as if Father Time was saying, *"Now then, let's see, where were we? Ah, yes!"*

This instantaneous continuation of time and events from the exact moment it was stopped by the light from the jewel was absurdly profound and comprehensive. The immediate restoration of events, along with the piercing sensations of sight and sound sent a chilling premonition, a morbid sensation through his body straight to his bones. Brian looked helplessly at the Suburban even while he knew what the altered outcome should be. Nevertheless, he simply could not help but feel a bit of remorse for what everyone else was bearing witness to. He knew they still perceived that an awful tragedy was about to take place. That is what was supposed to happen. But the mysterious powers of the jewel had changed the child's fate. What was seen, and what was supposed to happen had been altered, Brian hoped.

He gazed anxiously at the Suburban as it swerved to the left slightly, screeching to a desperate halt. Gasps and screams of profuse dread could be heard from all around the street. The large vehicle heaved forward and then rocked back onto its rear suspension, coming to a complete stop. An eerie silence fell amongst the pungent smell of freshly chafed tire rubber and smoke that hung over the crowd of distressed onlookers.

For just a moment Brian wondered, *did she make it!?* Everything happened so terrifically fast. He could not see Tiffany.

"What happened?" he asked, craning his neck while his eyes desperately searched for Tiffany.

He was a little disoriented. As soon as his perception of time was restored, all he had seen time-frozen in place changed in an instant. Consequently, he had some reservation as to the altered fatality of events, but the feeling only lasted a fleeting moment. The child was unharmed.

"Tiffany!" A woman's voice, the child's mother, could be heard over the voices and reactions of horrified, then suddenly confused onlookers. Over the stirring commotion her raised voice was an exclaimer of relief and shock.

"Oh my God!" Tiffany's mother cried out and then broke into loud sobbing as she wrapped her arms around her daughter.

"Is she alright?" Another woman's voice bellowed from close proximity, "The little girl, where is she? I can't see her."

Brian looked towards the origin of the frantic inquiry and immediately realized it was the front passenger of the Suburban. The woman was leaning out the window, cupping her hands around her mouth so her voice carried out into the crowd. The other passengers in the large vehicle were also leaning out their windows in an attempt to see what was happening in front of the car. The older gentleman who was driving the large vehicle said nothing. He just kept shaking his head, visibly distressed.

"We're okay! She's fine!" another voice bellowed back.

It was unclear to Brian who answered. There were so many people surrounding Tiffany and her mother right now. Brian assumed it was a young man standing very close to Tiffany who was looking her over, checking to make certain that the little red head girl was physically uninjured while he spoke reassuringly to her. Brian assumed he was a Good Samaritan, or perhaps he was also a healthcare professional like himself. Brian noticed the confused look on Tiffany's face. Her expression was quite uncharacteristic for someone involved in such a dreadful situation. It was almost as if she didn't have a clue what just happened.

What followed was somewhat anticlimactic, though welcome, given the circumstances. The people in the brand new Suburban waved and then continued on their way. The automobile traffic that had safely come to a sudden stop behind them resumed as usual with a few looks of concern at the little girl. Generally speaking, the scene of sudden, impending despair had changed in an instant. Anyone who noticed the incident had a slightly altered perception of the events. Nobody would remember exactly where Tiffany was standing when the Suburban's large wheels began to brake. The event was perceived as a near disaster that was unpredictably averted. Everyone simply continued about their business almost as if nothing had happened at all. The effects of the mysterious jewel were profound.

Brian, once again, heard the ordinary sounds of people walking and talking as they did on any other typically gorgeous day like today, albeit, minus the dreadful commotion. Brian could only distinguish a few comments within earshot that were about the incident.

"My, my, that was really close!" someone expressed aloud, and then chuckled. "Good God! A miracle!"

"Yeah, she really must have jumped back on that curb, huh?" another person said. "She was in the street one second, and gone the next! Wow! That was a miracle!"

People continued to walk along the sidewalk, passing by the covert duo. Brian heard a few more comments and thankful praises to God above from strangers that there had not been a tragedy today. Their conversations quickly faded as they passed by.

Indeed it was! It was a miracle! If only you knew! Brian smiled in silent thought. He was so excited, but he knew better. He could not tell a sole, or risk compromising his appointed mission as part of the stealth observation team. Not to mention jeopardize the safety of the extraterrestrial landing party, his dear alien friends. Brian continued smiling, though he kept his jubilant feelings unvoiced. He looked up into the early evening summer sky and sent his silent words to the heavens above, *Thanks for sending my special friends here in time to save this girl.*

·　·　·　•　●　⬤　●　•　·　·　·

Brian felt a slight tug on his left arm. The craftily concealed Meihtu stood patiently next to his truck, discretely pointing at the passenger side door. Brian noticed the beautiful celestial gemstone was gone from view, hidden beneath her ethnic style apparel.

`"We should go now."` Meihtu signed to him. Her gloved gesture was followed by a quick, slight nod of her niqab covered head. Brian nodded his head in silent reply.

He reached for the handle and opened the passenger door, making a polite gesture for his exotic alien friend to enter the Tacoma. Meihtu promptly sat down and made herself comfortable. Brian smiled at her as she fastened her safety belt and then took a quick, discerning look around. He was curious. *No one has a clue!* He grinned uncontrollably as he watched people across the street walking about minding their own business.

"Did you see that?!" He wanted to cry to the world what his beautiful alien friend had just done.

He wanted to shout, jump up and down with unadulterated glee. Alas, he could not do so. Brian knew better. He knew there would be very serious consequences to that action; world changing consequences.

As Brian stepped around the front of the truck he anxiously glanced once more at the people on the sidewalk on his side of the street. For some peculiar reason he suddenly felt very odd, as if he was being watched. True, he was fully aware of the cloaked, alien drone that was probably hovering silently close by keeping the observation team in precise view. He knew that. Yet, he sensed something else for some strange reason. It was one of those weird occasions when you just know you are being watched. He felt a bit uneasy. Maybe it was just the fact that everything he had just witnessed, though out in plain view, had incredibly transpired entirely unnoticed by every single bystander. Perhaps.

Brian took a random look at a few of the people in the small crowd of tourists walking past. No one really looked back with interest, except one individual, an elderly man with wiry, white hair. He was standing by himself next to a small antique gift shop near the corner. Brian looked down at the ground as soon as he made direct eye contact with the unassuming old man.

Is he looking at us? What did he see? Does he suspect something? Brian stepped onto the asphalt and walked around the front of the truck and then slowed his pace a bit.

As he turned towards the driver's side of the truck, Brian purposely peered over his shoulder to get one more look. When he did, his curious eyes found the expressionless eyes of the old man staring right at him. Brian immediately turned away, deliberately trying to remain incognito. He did not want to draw any unnecessary attention to what he and his extraterrestrial companion were doing. Brian swiftly got in, buckled up, started the engine, and put the truck in gear. He glanced for traffic, and then without much delay, drove away from the curb. As the Toyota passed the gift shop, Brian's peripheral vision told him the old man was still watching him, staring at them through the pedestrian foot traffic. Brian did not look back.

Brian turned left at the next available street and headed west towards his parent's home. He glanced at his alien friend. Her head was down and slightly forward. Brian could tell without seeing her face that she was tired. Her body language suggested so. Meihtu had not said or gestured a word since they drove off. As they drove away from the beautiful mountain lake area into the picturesque summer sunset, he wondered if anyone was actually able to see them; or, more so, suddenly not see them. He wondered what effect the flash of intense light seemed like to the bystanders.

What was it like for someone standing close to us? What would they have seen if they were looking right at us? What did that old guy see? Brian shrugged his shoulders. *Oh well.*

As long as no one had obviously noticed and approached them after it was all over, well, that was good enough for him.

Chapter Thirty Two

It had been a long, truly eventful day, a day full of new, wondrous surprises and spectacular experiences. The day's events had completely exhausted Brian, so when he got back to his parents' house he lay down and took a nap on the large, comfortable couch in the family room. He woke up some time later and yawned, thinking back through everything that had transpired earlier. He laid his head back and stared at the ceiling thinking about his alien friends.

Meihtu went out the back door and disappeared in a shrouding cloud of mist not long after they arrived at Brian's parents' house. She returned to the clandestinely located ellipsoid spacecraft where Baouzhe was now waiting for her. Specialist Baouzhe was preparing their interstellar vehicle for departure. Brian was home alone now, sitting quietly in the dark of the early evening. He recollected how tired his celestial lady friend appeared after they had returned to the house. Brian surmised the extraterrestrial phenomenon he had witnessed was physically taxing on his exotic alien friend. That was probably the reason they both left the scene of the occurrence so quickly.

Meihtu hadn't communicated a word aside from a smile.

"Well done. I thank you. I will contact you soon." Was the only thing the Meihtu had said by sign.

He thought again how exhausted Meihtu looked. *It must take a lot out of her to do something like that.*

·   ·   ·   •   ●   •   •   ·   ·

Brian was startled when his phone suddenly started ringing. He reached over to the coffee table next to the sofa and grabbed the cellular phone, recognizing the familiar ringtone.

"Hey Brandon, what's up my brother?" Brian happily greeted.

"Brian, oh my God!" The unexpected angst in Brandon's voice trembled on the other end of the line. "Where are you? Oh man, Houston and Donnette…"

"What, what is it? What's going on?" Brian interrupted, feeling anxious all at once just from the sound of his brother's voice.

"They…" There was a short, uncomfortable pause that seemed like an eternity to Brian's waiting ears, "they were in an accident!" Brandon finally divulged, grief-stricken.

"What?!" Brian stood up from the couch immediately as he exclaimed, "Say what?! Please, no. Tell me they're all right!"

Brian's throat suddenly went dry and his hands started to quiver.

Brandon took a deep breath and cleared his throat. Brian could tell his older brother was trying hard to compose himself. He could feel the utter fear and sheer helplessness in Brandon's voice.

"A social worker called me from the hospital." Brandon raised his voice a bit as he iterated, "your hospital."

"What do you mean? Where I work man? Shit!"

"Yeah." Brandon cleared his throat loudly again. "They took them both there. Donnette just arrived by ambulance. But, Houston…" His older brother's voice broke slightly as he forced himself to continue, "they flew my boy in, man. They brought him in by air ambulance!" Brandon coughed as he fought back the tears.

"I guess they want to keep them together or something like that. Is that right, man? Brian, please help me."

"Man, I don't know what to do. They're my whole life!" Brandon sniffled.

"Okay, okay, look." Brian tried to remain calm for both of them. He wanted to ease his brother's anguish and calm

Brandon's distraught nerves. Unfortunately, the younger brother could not even think straight himself this very moment. His own mind was in a complete state of shock.

"Shit." Brian shook his head.

He looked down at the floor and rubbed his forehead, desperately trying to find the words to say to his brother right now. This was all so unexpected, as well as terribly upsetting. Brian wanted to say something appeasing and reassuring. However, he knew better. If EMTs and paramedics by physician's request would forego transporting a child to a nearer emergency facility for immediate care in order to take the child to Pleasant Hills Medical Center, that meant the patient was in extreme distress and perhaps gravely injured. Especially so if a patient was taken by helicopter. Brian knew on special occasions, greatly depending on the acuity of the patient's condition, the Inland Air Medical Transport helicopter was capable of flying those missions. The helicopter was very capable of landing on scene at a traffic accident in an effort to quickly transport the most severe patients to a dedicated trauma center nearby.

"What am I going to do, man?"

Brandon's words sounded completely helpless and reflected such angst. He seemed so distraught, incapable of making a decision as to what action he should be taking in the moment.

"Did you call mom and dad, yet?"

"Yes. They're both crying, man." Brandon coughed.

"Mom is hysterical. They're making immediate plans to return home as soon as possible. Same with Rhonda and Stewart. They're coming, too."

Brian could only imagine how distressed Donnette's parents were.

"Alright, at least they all know and they're on their way. They all need to be here and help us be strong," Brian said.

"Okay, Brandon," Brian tried to inflect a calming tone as he said "so tell me, what happened man?"

Although he needed to know, the younger brother was very afraid to hear what his brother was about to say. Brandon took another deep breath.

"Donnette and Houston were out visiting friends and doing some errands today. Donnette decided to drop by the babysitter's house on the way home to pick up a toy Houston left there yesterday. Donnette left Karla, the babysitter's place and was headed home when the accident happened. Man," the older brother sobbed. "I was told they were hit by a drunk driver! The social worker says they were hit head on not very far from Karla's place!"

"A drunk driver?" Brian shook his head. "Goddamn it!"

"Yes," Brandon confirmed, and then divulged with a hint of disbelief in his tone of voice, "I was told the drunk driver was an older lady who was basically uninjured. Like, not a scratch… man, ain't that something?" the older brother asked.

"But, how can that be? I was told both cars were totaled! And that drunk woman didn't even need an ambulance! How is that? Shit, man! Ain't that a bitch?"

"I don't know." Brian shook his head, feeling deeply dismayed. "I don't know, but it does happen that way sometimes. Damn!"

"Anyway, the drunk driver, I heard she got arrested, right then and there at the scene!" Brandon continued in a calmer tone of voice. "This all happened within the last hour or so. I'm on my way, Brian. Can you meet me at the hospital?" Brandon sounded more anxious now, "I really need you there brother, please."

"I'm on my way," Brian immediately responded. "I'll make some calls and try to find out what's up. I'll try to find out, you know, how they're both doing."

The younger brother supplemented, "Everything is going to be all right. Just concentrate on getting to the hospital safe yourself. Okay man?"

"Yes, okay," was all Brandon said before ending the call.

· · · ● ● ● ● ● · · ·

Brian made a quick call to the hospital to see if he could get some information. He called the Emergency Department and was immediately connected to the social worker, Victoria

Simmons, who was on call that evening. His absolute fears were confirmed. His dear nephew and sister-in-law were there. Both had been admitted to the hospital. Victoria confirmed the fact that Donnette had been transported by ground and Houston had been airlifted to the trauma center; the very place where Brian worked. Hearing this dreadful news again from a professional he worked with made him feel a bit nauseous and even slightly faint. Before he ended the call with the kind social worker, Brian requested that she inform staff of his relation to the patients and that he wanted everyone to know he was grateful for their compassion and care for his very dear family members. The social worker most caringly obliged to do so.

Next, Brian contacted his friends working the evening shift in the Respiratory Therapy Department. He found out his friend Danny was working in the PICU. Brian was pleased that someone he knew who worked exceptionally well and whom he could depend on to help provide the best care possible was there for his injured nephew. Brian actually felt relieved just knowing that his sister-in-law and nephew were transported to one of the best trauma centers in southern California. He felt the emergency department physician on call had made the best decision bringing his family members there.

Next, Brian took the time to try and contact his alien friends before leaving. He hastily signed in different directions towards the walls of the family room, hoping to relay his urgent message to the clandestine floating ball, wherever it was.

"I must go to the same hospital your subject was taken to. The same place I work at. Some of my family members have been severely injured. My sister-in-law and my only nephew."

· · · • ● ● ● • · · ·

Brian felt certain the aliens were able to see his urgently gestured message. He was very confident they would be able to understand what was happening. After he relayed his message, Brian swiftly gathered his wallet, keys and mobile phone and then ran out the front door.

Before long, Brian was speeding down windy Highway 189 on the south lanes leading out of the beautiful mountainous resort area. He had a tight grip on the steering wheel. He was careful not to drive recklessly, as the curves were sharp, many with occasional tall embankments, not to mention several with steep drops into jagged rocky chasms below. Fortunately, there was very light traffic this early in the evening, allowing Brian to keep up the pace. He stared quietly at the road ahead, lighted only by his headlamps. His thoughts reflected over and again on the laughter and smiles of his beloved nephew Houston and the little boy's mother, Donnette.

How badly are they injured? Are they going to make it? Oh, sure, they'll be just fine. I know it. Brian shook his head. His emotions contested his thoughts. *God, please let them live!* He pleaded silently, and then clenched the steering wheel tighter.

There was a car ahead, situated on the shoulder of the south lane. It appeared to be disabled, as the vehicle's hood was raised. As Brian's truck neared the scene, his headlamps lighted the area and he noticed steam rising from the engine under the raised hood. The young man instinctively slowed down. Being stranded in the dark was not a good thing to happen to anyone, anywhere, but especially up in the wilderness mountains. Brian knew that for certain. He glanced at the stranded vehicle as he slowed his truck.

As his truck passed the four-door, early model Cadillac sedan, Brian noticed two young men standing in front of the car looking quite concerned about their vehicle. One of the guys began to flail his arms about, clearly agitated. As Brian stopped along the soft shoulder and put his parking brake on, he heard someone swearing. Brian chuckled and turned off the engine. *I'd be pissed, too.*

Brian had barely exited his vehicle when he said, "You guys look like you could use some help. Are you stranded?"

He walked casually towards the car behind his truck. He smiled at the two young men who turned around to face him.

One young man had on a baseball cap turned backwards. The other, a skinny young man, had his cap on forwards. As Brian stepped nearer, a third man, with a clean-shaven head, got out of the driver's side of the stranded 1987 Cadillac Seville.

"Hey, you guys need some help?" Brian asked again.

"Yeah," the clean-shaven-head man replied calmly as he approached Brian and the other two men near the front of the car. "Yeah man, I can use some help right about now."

The man peered around Brian, looking towards his parked truck. "Is that yours, homes?"

"Yes," Brian said.

The stranger standing close to Brian now silently nodded his head in acknowledgment. He was close enough that Brian could just barely discern a very peculiar tattoo above the man's left eyebrow. Brian was beginning to feel a little uneasy all of a sudden. His helpful mood all at once dissipated when the men started looking around as if they wanted to make sure no one else was present. Brian stared at the tattoo. The illumination from the headlights of the stranded car allowed him to see the tattoo above his eyebrow was a mix of numbers, letters and symbols inscribed in a small, cryptic font. The tattoo also included some small symbols that resembled stars.

Oh, shit! Brian tried hard to show absolutely no expression when he recognized the facial graffiti as a gang insignia. More specifically, the branding appeared to be affiliated with a prison gang. Brian had watched enough reality television and documentary news programs to be in the know. Suddenly he wished he had not stopped. In fact, he wished he was somewhere else at this very moment. Anywhere else.

"Hey, homes," the man said, "that's a nice truck, man."

"You guys need a ride?" Brian begrudgingly asked, trying to find something to say.

All he wanted to do was drive off as fast as he could. He just had a bad feeling. Although the driver's side door of his truck was unlocked, Brian felt his truck may as well be in another state. He knew he could not get to the driver's side door before being tackled.

The clean-shaven-head man reached behind his back and nonchalantly revealed a Taurus 9mm, blue steel semiautomatic pistol that he held up close to his chest, covering it as much as he could with his free hand. Although the pistol was not pointing at Brian, he knew the way the gun was brandished that the strange man was not to be trifled with.

"Give me your keys, homes," the gunman demanded, almost politely. "Don't do nothing stupid. Just give me your keys."

The two young accomplices moved quickly and stood closely behind the stranger with the gun. Again, they glanced around the area quickly to make sure there was no one watching.

"We need to borrow your truck, man. And hey, you know what? You can have this Caddy," one of the men behind the gunman said, and laughed.

"Shit, we don't want it no more!" The skinny one snickered.

The clean-shaven-head gunman had nothing else to say, yet.

"Yeah, you can have this car since we got your truck now." The skinny young man taunted annoyingly.

"We stole that car anyway, shit, we don't need it. We can get any car we want, man," he bragged, "so we'll take yours homeboy!" He leaned forward as he looked around the shoulder of the gunman to scoff at Brian.

"Hey, don't do nothing stupid, man! Just give us your keys, man." He quickly and very animatedly pointed over the gunman's shoulder at Brian.

Brian raised his hands in a gesture of silent surrender and then said smoothly.

"Okay man, be cool. The keys are in the ignition. My wallet is on the seat, too."

"Good! Let's go! Leave him with that piece of shit!" the armed robber said, "I like trucks better anyway."

The other two laughed loudly. The skinny young man had more to say, a blunt warning.

"Don't try to come after us, man. Don't make my friend here have to bust a cap, homeboy!"

More laughter followed his spirited threat. Brian kept his hands up as the perpetrators made their way toward his truck.

They walked together along the driver's side of Brian's Tacoma, still glancing about as if they were going to be caught.

What Brian did not know was these men were all wanted by the City of Long Beach Police. They had very recently committed several very serious crimes, each involving victims being held at gunpoint. In addition to their recent crimes, all three were wanted for parole violations. They had recently stolen the Cadillac to drive up to the mountain resort area. Reason being, they intended on hiding in a small hotel somewhere for a while. They wanted to stay out of sight for at least a few weeks, or until they ran out of the cash they'd stolen. The trio of ignorant delinquents almost made it to the tranquil resort area, and probably would have succeeded had not the early model Cadillac Seville they stole overheated on the drive up the mountain. The fugitive perpetrators were trying to turn around and head back down the mountain when the car quit running. That was precisely when Brian came along.

"Let me drive, man." The young man with the cap turned backwards prodded. "I never get to drive. I don't want the middle, neither. I got long legs."

The three men had all stopped at the driver side door of the Tacoma.

"I'm driving," the gunman replied. He casually held the pistol at his side with the barrel of the semiautomatic weapon pointing down towards the gravel.

"You two assholes get in on the other side." He gestured with a quick nod. The gunman's posture seemed a little more agitated now to Brian. His young accomplices laughed in response and merrily complied, jovially walking towards the front of the vehicle.

The skinny young man looked back at Brian, "I'm watching you, fool! Don't do nothing stupid, man!" More laughter from the delinquents followed the lewd threat.

Brian just wanted them all to leave in his truck at this point. Although he was frightened, he felt somewhat fortunate. At least they hadn't taken anything else, or tried to harm him. Even during this volatile, anxious moment, Brian thought of his injured nephew and his sister-in-law. He desperately wanted to see them.

How can this be happening to me now? All the way up here in the middle of nowhere, too. I got car-jacked! Unbelievable! Damn! So now what? Brian felt totally helpless. He really needed to get to the hospital as fast as he could. If only he had not stopped, this would not be happening to him. If only he had ignored his very kind compulsion to help those in need. *So now what?* He frowned.

Then, without any warning, the early evening quiet suddenly echoed a sharp, cracking noise that came out of nowhere. At that precise instant a glistening, bisque colored sphere of light appeared from above along with a blinding, violet-green flash of light. The dazzling phenomena appeared above Brian's truck in the blink of an eye just as the crackling sound rang out. The immediate sound and sight of the bizarre disruption was frightening and loud. Brian flinched.

Before the three male fugitives could blink, an intense, electrically glowing arc of beautiful light very similar to lightning, bolted violently out from the mysteriously glowing sphere. The bright flash of electrically charged light stretched out in three distinct arcs, instantaneously and simultaneously striking each of the startled fugitives on the very top of their heads. There was a distinctive whack heard as the trio of bolts smartly smacked all three of the delinquent men. Each immediately and forcibly reacted to the overwhelming cuff of electromagnetic energy. Brian observed in awe as the forward progress of all three of the perpetrators was immediately halted in choreographed unison. All three had the same involuntary physical response. Just for a second they kicked their legs and flailed their arms almost as if they were performing in a Hip-Hop dance contest. It was almost humorous. Brian couldn't help but smirk. Then, in an instant, the stricken degenerates toppled over like helpless rag dolls, face first into the gravel.

·   ·   •   ●   ●   ●   ●   •   ·   ·   ·

That was it. Just as fast as it started, it was over. An eerie moment of calm followed. Only the faint sound of the wind could be heard rustling through the trees. There was no sound at all from the incapacitated and ignorant fugitives. They'd been rendered completely unconscious. Brian instinctively looked up over his truck into the air where the strange phenomena had mysteriously and instantly appeared. Alas, there was now nothing at all to be seen in the darkened sky above, except the early nighttime starlight. Brian gazed back down upon the stricken, laid-out perpetrators with his mouth agape.

"Stupid bastards! You got what you deserved!" He shook his head and chuckled aloud.

Brian walked towards his truck. The first victim he approached was the gunman. Brian stood directly over him, staring down at the incapacitated offender face-down in the gravel.

"You don't look so tough now, you stupid bastard!"

Brian noticed the gun lying in the gravel in close proximity to the perpetrator's right hand. Brian considered what he should do. He did not want these derelicts to encounter some other innocent person and take advantage of them. Brian figured if the gun was found by the police, it might be connected to a crime. So, he did not want to take it. However, he did not want to touch it and leave his own fingerprints to connect him to any crimes, either. Then an idea came to mind.

Brian stepped over the unconscious offenders and went to his truck. He retrieved a rag from behind the driver's seat that he used to check the engine fluids every so often. Brian went back to where the gunman was lying and picked up the pistol with the rag. Brian looked around once and then walked to the disabled Cadillac, placing the weapon on the floor of the vehicle just behind and underneath the passenger's seat. He looked above his truck where he thought the floating orb drone would be.

"Thank you!" Brian signed his appreciation.

He quickly ran back to his truck and got in. Brian started the engine, put the Tacoma in gear, and drove away. He left the derelicts face down in the gravel without a second thought as to their disposition. Frankly, he didn't care if they were breathing or not, although he knew they were most likely only incapacitated, and justly so. Most likely that same daunting, clandestine, floating sphere he had observed smartly positioned outside the Webley home had put them down for a while. Brian smirked. *Thank you!* He looked around, but he knew the floating alien thing was not to be seen. He knew the aliens were using the daunting thing to follow him and protect him.

"Thank you, ladies," he said aloud to his alien friends.

As Brian sped up, he took one more look into the rear view mirror. The victims of the alien floating sphere were still on the ground, unconscious. Brian thought about what he should do next. That's when he considered calling the local authorities to inform them what had happened to him. Brian wanted to make sure the fugitives were no threat to anyone else. He glanced at his backpack in the passenger seat. Inside the front zipper pocket was his mobile phone. He decided to make a call to the police as soon as he got closer to the bottom of the mountain drive. Brian knew that cellular coverage was sporadic in the San Bernardino mountain resort area.

Brian had driven not even one minute, constantly rubbing his chin, deep in thought about what he would say to the police. He was a little worried about talking to the police because they would most likely ask him how he overcame three guys. *That would be difficult to explain.*

Then, he saw something very complimentary to his situation. A California Highway Patrol cruiser was approaching in the opposite lane. The timing could not be more perfect. There were no side roads between the stranded vehicle and the patrol cruiser, so Brian knew there was a very good chance the incapacitated derelicts would be quickly discovered by the Highway Patrol. Brian smiled.

"Talk about perfect timing!" he exclaimed cheerfully, "Thank you Lord!" He smiled, again.

"Thank you, Lord!" Brian clapped his hands a few times and then grasped the steering wheel as he approached an upcoming curve. He could not help but laugh, practically to the point of tears. He drove on. It was not long at all until he could see the fast approaching, telltale red and blue lights of more emergency response vehicles speeding up the opposite lanes of the narrow highway. As the flashing lights approached him, Brian observed four other Highway Patrol vehicles sweep speedily past, sirens blaring, on their way up the hilly drive behind him. He knew the perpetrators had been discovered now.

"Go get 'em!" he said pumping his fist in the air. "Yes! Go get those bastards!"

Chapter Thirty Three

Brian finally arrived at the hospital. He talked to some of his friends who were working that night to find out what they knew about Donnette and Houston's condition. Before long, he made his way into the PICU to visit his beloved nephew. Confirming the condition of Donnette as being mostly alert and stable, he planned to see his dear sister in-law next. When Brian entered the private room number two located in the PICU station-one desk area, he at once recognized the young boy lying motionless on the specialized medical bed used in this wing of the hospital. He also noticed his brother was practically collapsed over the waist of his seriously injured son. Brian could hear Brandon sobbing from the doorway.

Brian walked towards Brandon, arms outstretched to embrace his distraught older brother. Brian took a good look at little Houston and quickly assessed the boy's physical condition. His young nephew was lightly sedated and sleeping now. In the quiet, the very familiar sounds of the intensive care life monitoring equipment could be easily distinguished in the dimly lit PICU room. Brian noticed that the boy's vital cardiac and respiratory data displayed on the various intensive care monitors indicated a stable and relatively normal condition at present. He sighed heavily in relief at this reassuring sign. Aside from the neck brace and various lacerations from broken glass all over his upper body, little Houston did not look as bad as things had seemed. Nevertheless, he and his mother had been in a horrible accident requiring vehicle extrication. Houston had actually lost consciousness before the Inland Air Medical Transport helicopter landed on the scene to transport him away.

The mood this evening was solemn indeed, with circumstances no family ever wants to endure. The older Morris brother laid his head down again on his son's lap. Brian sat in a chair pulled up close to the large PICU bed so that he could touch his dear nephew. Almost an hour passed with the two brothers saying little to each other, or to anyone else that stepped in to check on Houston. Several coworkers who were close to Brian that were on shift that evening visited briefly, providing a heartfelt embrace and offering their services in any way they could to support him and his family. The show of support and caring was just what Brian needed to be strong for his young nephew and the rest of his beloved family.

Brian considered everything he had seen concerning his nephew's condition at this point in time and comprehended that the young boy was stable at the moment, however, he also understood that the next twenty-four hours or so would be very crucial. Brian was considerably worried, having worked enough in intensive care with relevant experience to know that acute brain injury can suddenly deteriorate a child or an adult's health condition in the most grave manner, and very suddenly. Houston's respiratory system and central nervous system could become critically exacerbated in response to the acute head injury sustained. Brian knew that Houston's entire well-being was terribly at risk right now. Brian was certain there would be more clinical lab work, x-rays, and computed tomography (CT) scans ordered to closely assess just how young Houston was responding to treatment and recovering from the trauma. Moreover, Brian also comprehended this was a crucial window of recuperation time post trauma, where the outcome was indeterminate. Nevertheless, Brian had to have faith. He had to be strong for everyone.

"Brandon." Brian said against the background noise of monitors and automated intravenous pumps that sounded almost like a melodramatic music score in the otherwise quiet room.

"Houston is going to be alright, bro." Brian gently rubbed his brother's back. "We will all get through this, together."

Brandon sniffled. "Thanks brother." He reached out to his brother and Brian squeezed his hand tight.

Mounted on the opposite wall at the foot of Houston's bed was a television. It was on with the volume turned down to a low, quiet tone. It mostly served as background noise, a quiet distraction. No one was really watching it. Brandon all but ignored it. Brian looked at it occasionally. He happened to glance up at the television just at the moment when there was a soft drink advertisement playing featuring country music star Garth Brooks. Everyone seemed so happy and carefree in the catchy tune of the commercial. The popular country music sensation and pitchman happily sang the company's well-known slogan as Brian just stared. He wished he could be so happy now. Then the night shift unit secretary, Catherine, entered the room. There was a message.

"Brian, dear," she spoke softly, "there's someone downstairs in the main lobby looking for you. The evening lobby receptionist just called and informed me. I told her you were here and you'd get the message."

"Oh." Brian was a little startled at Catherine's unexpected entry, but responded politely. "I'll go down. Thank you."

She nodded. Brian got up and rubbed his nephew's leg and then patted his big brother on the back.

"I'll be right back, bro. I'll go see if it's our family starting to show up. The news is probably out to everyone we know by now."

"Okay." Brandon said without lifting his head or moving the slightest bit.

Brian quietly exited the private, dimly lit intensive care room and made his way down the hall to the elevators. He had only a short wait until one arrived. Brian was mentally distraught and dreaded having to greet somber faces. He was digging deep to find the strongest and most inspiring words he could muster to greet his family and dear friends. He searched for the perfect words to say to them during these dire circumstances without completely collapsing emotionally himself and physically dropping to the floor. Brian loved his nephew so dearly.

Almost reluctantly, he pressed the button inside the elevator. He shut his eyes and clenched his teeth. *Be strong.* He bowed his head as the doors closed and the elevator descended down to the lobby level of the large medical center. *We will all get through this, together.*

The elevator doors opened and Brian proceeded towards the main lobby area. He recognized the very kind lobby level receptionist sitting at her desk, Lucy Zhao. She was politely conversing with someone in her native Mandarin language. When he glimpsed who she was chatting with he stopped short in absolute disbelief.

His jaw instinctively dropped in response to the very slender and tall woman dressed completely from head to foot in an elegant abaya and niqab. Her eyes were hidden behind stylish reflective sunglasses, which he recognized as Meihtu's technological eyewear. Brian's eyes widened at the idea that the person waiting for him in the lobby was his beautiful celestial friend. Brian continued to walk towards the main lobby reception desk, utterly astounded and speechless.

"Lucy, good evening," Brian timorously announced as the kindly receptionist turned toward him.

"Hey there," Lucy smiled, "There's someone here to see you," the receptionist gestured with a nod.

"Yes, thank you." Brian's response was not as timid. More hurried now, he consciously reached for the gloved hand of the clandestinely disguised Meihtu.

"I'll take it from here," he said with a tight smile. "She's a dear friend of mine."

Brian gently pulled Meihtu close to his side and turned to walk away from the main lobby reception area.

"Good night Lucy," was all Brian said without looking back.

The kindly receptionist smiled brightly and waved at them both.

"Okay, see you, good night, Brian." She also said good night in her native Mandarin tongue to the kind celestial alien in disguise.

As Meihtu turned her shoulders slightly to respond, Brian purposely tugged at her hand again, though gently, redirecting her attention towards the elevators they were hastily approaching. She was only barely able to utter a grunt of a reply as he hurriedly pressed the button to summon an elevator. One of the doors to an empty elevator suddenly opened. Brian very swiftly led his friend forward into the vacant elevator. They looked at each other as the elevator doors quietly closed.

`"What are you doing here?!"` Brian's response and hand gestures were immediate, and accompanied by an absolutely flabbergasted look on his face.

Meihtu's response contained no signed words. Instead, she earnestly wrapped her arms around Brian and pulled herself to him, placing her forehead on his chest. She hugged him firmly, dearly, and then looked up into his eyes and smiled. Brian couldn't actually see her looking directly into his eyes because of the sunglasses, but he knew. He said nothing. But he smiled and he hugged her firmly in return. Somehow he knew in that moment that everything really was going to be just fine. His celestial friend always just made him feel a little more at ease and more confident in any situation. Truth be told, Brian was actually very grateful she would risk so much to be by his side.

Brian's thoughts aptly reflected on his travels to the hospital and how he was able to arrive without harm. He thought of the very punctual visual revelation of the cloaked alien floating probe device hovering deliberately in the middle of the air above his truck earlier that evening. The mysterious alien floating drone had resolutely saved him without any annunciation or fair warning, unbeknownst to the unsuspecting, armed and dangerous fugitives who were on the receiving end of its implicit wrath. Brian was actually very happy to see her. He smiled at her again.

`"Thank you for helping me,"` Brian gestured, but also said the words. `"I would not be here if you hadn't helped me."`

He smiled again. Brian's thoughts also reflected on the little girl, Tiffany, standing in the middle of the street. She would certainly not be alive now if not for the presence and intervention of his alien friend.

Meihtu responded quickly. `"We want to help you. But, I would also like to request something of you, please."`

She turned to look just as the elevator doors suddenly opened to the floor of the pediatric ward.

`"We also need your help, if it is agreeable to you, please?"` She continued as they exited the elevator into the serene and vacant pediatric ward.

"Brian!" she clearly vocalized, but still with a heavy alien accent, then gestured with alien sign language. `"I will help your nephew!"` She nodded once.

Brian was very impressed to hear his name come from her delicate, celestial lips. `"Yes, yes, what is it? Of course, whatever you need."`

Brian's sincere reply was very evident in his eyes and his expression. He was very concerned what it was that his alien friends could need. He took hold of her delicate, long gloved hands as they quietly stepped away from the elevator doors. Brian smiled at her.

Meihtu responded, `"It would be wonderful to have your nephew provide new valuable data to us, especially now that we have lost both of our only subjects. This is a very unique opportunity for us. It is very special, because you are considered part of our observation team now."` She nodded her head once.

`"Instead of finding another random subject, we would like to observe your nephew. It would be a much better option because he is very young and he is also your family. Would you do that for us? Can you give us your authorization? Can we study data from your nephew please? I promise no injury` will come to him from our harmless, scientific observation."

"Oh." Brian answered aloud without giving the question a second thought. "Yes! Yes, that would be very cool!" Meihtu stood quietly in poised anticipation of his answer.

Then Brian replied again, this time by alien sign. "Yes, that is acceptable. I know he will be unharmed and it is very safe to do so. On behalf of my family, I approve." He nodded once. Then, he supplemented. "It is an honor for us to help!"

Meihtu responded quickly. "Thank you very much!"

She hugged him again, firmly and dearly. The beautiful alien woman looked directly into the young man's eyes through her reflective, advanced technological eyewear. She nodded her head once.

Meihtu and Brian were approaching the PICU entrance. The adjoining hallway to the entrance, just past the waiting area, was silent and vacant this evening. As the two got close to the PICU, the remotely controlled, automatic security doors suddenly started to open wide to let out a young couple, parents of one of the admitted pediatric patients who were just leaving the PICU.

Brian was about to step aside in order to allow the couple to exit as the doors swung towards him and Meihtu. However, at that very instant, Brian felt a very familiar purposeful, nudge against him. Meihtu was leaning forward, her gloved hand raised, and in her hand was the mysterious and incomparably powerful celestial jewel!

At once, the sparkly ornament emanated the intense pulse of glaring silvery light Brian had observed earlier when the Suburban was bearing down on Tiffany. Brian was not aware that she would use the jewel, so the discharge of pure light was unexpected, and it was practically as startling to him now as it had been the first time. Brian instinctively blinked and flinched at the exact moment of the supplementary resounding pulsation. The slight numbing sensation returned for a second and Brian shut his eyes tight, clenched his teeth and tensed all his muscles in preparation of the second flash from the bewildering gemstone that he knew would be more intense. Doing so, Brian felt less disoriented, and he stood sturdier on his feet this time around.

Brian opened his eyes, fully expecting a change in the aggregate perception of the entire world around him. He instantaneously recognized the immediate quiet, the acute vacancy of normal sounds around him and realized he again had the strange sensation of lively blood flow rushing through his veins. In that same instant, much like what Brian had seen before, everything around him was completely saturated with an anil hue. The sight was just as extraordinary and mesmerizing this time. His skin tingled all over, and he was beginning to feel a bit euphoric. Though somewhat anticipated, the recurring episode was still very peculiar and surreal.

Brian did not look back at Meihtu or the mysterious, celestial jewel. In some way, he felt this experience would not be as disorienting if he did not gaze deeply into the powerful, bewitching gemstone. He kept his gaze forward this time. Brian could clearly see they were once again existent within a monochromatic silhouette world, instantaneously frozen in time. Almost directly before him were the young parents that were exiting the PICU. Both of them were completely static now, their posture entirely frozen within the peculiarity that the celestial gemstone inexplicably inflicted. The couple was slightly embracing each other, each had an arm around the other.

As the clandestine observation team walked past them, Brian noticed the young couple was still looking towards the floor. Brian perceived the parents had a somewhat concerned, yet relieved expression about them. Perhaps their child was doing better, recovering from whatever trauma or illness had occurred. Brian wondered.

They continued past the catatonic young parents as they walked through the PICU main entrance. Brian immediately recognized the darkened indigo tinged shadows that had been cast over the two of them. Brian looked down and observed his own appearance. He quickly recognized and recalled they were both now standing underneath something incredible.

As Meihtu and Brian passed the large security door entrance,

Brian glanced up towards the ceiling. He observed something somewhat recognizable, though to say the least, extremely peculiar. There were the same three distinct emanated shadows. However, this perception of the phenomena was a slightly different experience than the other one. Each of the deeply shaded elongated shadows was now creating a bizarre tunneling effect in the ceiling. The odd visualization was very disorienting to Brian. It was as if there were three large holes channeled completely through the hospital structure directly to the sky above. Beyond the tunneling shadows was something else that Brian also recognized. Seemingly high above, beyond the structural boundaries of the hospital, and distinctly visible, was the source of the tunneling shadows. There were the three planetoid objects high above in what appeared to be the evening sky. The planetoid objects were each exactly oriented in the same position above Brian as he had observed before. One lunar object was located almost directly overhead, one was oriented towards his left, and the other one was oriented towards his right. He could clearly still see how each of the planetoid objects was distinctly bordered with that eerie shadowy halo around it. Also present on each lunar peculiarity was the steady revolving outline of trim, silvery white light. Brian, as before, was speechless.

The clandestine observation team continued to walk forward. They were just now passing the PICU front reception desk immediately to their left. There, Catherine sat motionless with the unit telephone receiver in her hand. Brian almost chuckled at the sight of her in a catatonic state, bathed in monotone anil. She was always so busy, bubbly, and talkative. It was truly a bizarre sight to see her so eerily and tranquilly still. They continued past the PICU reception desk in the station-one area. There were five private intensive care rooms per station area. Immediately to the right of the observation team was private room number one. Brian looked into the first room immediately to their right. That room was empty. He returned his gaze to the hall as they continued walking with the subtle, rhythmic pulsations from the revolving astral objects overhead.

Something ahead caught Brian's attention. There was a RN

poised in front of room number two who definitely appeared to be hurrying into that private intensive care room. Brian noticed how her long, curly ginger hair had been caught mid-bounce up off her shoulders, now motionless in time. Brian was absolutely amazed how her progress had been perfectly captured in static time, mid-stride. Her right foot was lifted up behind her a bit above the floor and her left heel was slightly raised. She was leaning forward pushing something. Brian's anxiety started to build when he noticed what it was. He did not know who the nurse was, but he definitely knew what she was doing, and why. She was pushing the station-one crash cart into private room two where Houston was. That metal drawer utility cart was only used in case of dire circumstances. It contained limited stocks of specific medicines, medical instruments, and various other supplies used specifically for cardiopulmonary resuscitation, more commonly referred to as CPR.

"Oh no!" He exclaimed aloud. Brian's anxiety increased tenfold and was still on the rise.

Chapter Thirty Four

Brian walked faster toward private room two. Meihtu closely followed with one hand on his shoulder. As they entered the room Brian could see the drama unfolding. The apparent sudden and desperate turn of events was now vividly captured in time, all of which transpired while he was away for only a few minutes. He saw his brother Brandon being ushered to the door by the RN taking care of Houston tonight. The nurse, Bob Renhold, was pointing with one hand towards the door and the other hand on the back of Brandon's shoulder. The RN, clad in loose-fitting blue medical scrubs, had an expression of urgency about his entire posture. Nurse Bob was very experienced, having worked over 15 years in the PICU. Brian could appreciate whenever Bob called for someone to help him with a child in critical condition. This would have been one of those moments. If Brian was available and heard Bob calling, he would stop whatever he was doing and promptly go see what patient Bob was assessing and wondering about. If Bob ever thought a child's condition was not looking real good and was possibly getting worse, the child's condition was usually deteriorating.

Brian saw the look on his brother's face. The time-frozen expression of anguish, panic, and disbelief stopped Brian in his tracks. He noticed his brother's tears and he stared helplessly at his older brother. He just wanted to hug Brandon and make things better. Brian felt so completely helpless right now. His own eyes started to tear up.

"Brandon," Brian muttered, his voice cracking, "it's going to be all right, brother!"

Then he felt a nudge from his celestial lady friend. She grabbed his arm and was now firmly nudging him to move toward Houston's bed. Brian immediately diverted his attention to the task at hand. He thought of what Meihtu had said. *She said she wanted to help Houston. Does she know how? Does she know what's wrong? Maybe she can't. What are we going to do?* Brian's muscles tensed. His hands trembled and his stomach physically ached.

There were two other people in the private intensive care room. As the clandestine observation team walked past Brandon and Bob, Brian saw the resident doctor on call, Carl Spies, and respiratory therapist, Danny. He was not surprised to see Carl, who Brian thought was a very competent physician if he set aside the fact that the doctor was dating his ex-fiancée, Gina. Brian was also very happy to see Danny, his trusted colleague, standing next to the doctor.

The night shift Registered Respiratory Therapist was standing at the head of the bed looking at something on the wall. His anil hue frozen posture suggested he had just started to reach for the resuscitator bag and mask that was connected to the oxygen flow meter. Brian looked at Carl. The doctor's gaze was frozen on the cardiac monitor. The sophisticated cardiac and vital statistics monitor was situated on the wall above, towards the left side of Houston's bed. Brian looked at the monitor, too. He at once noticed something very acute, immediately recognizing the problem that caused the precarious situation.

Little Houston's heart rate signal appeared to be decreasing, indicating 40 beats per minute at present. That was a critically slow heart rate for a small child his age. Compounding the situation, Brian also noticed Houston's respiratory rate had decreased. The monitor was indicating 5 breaths per minute. Both of those parameters, displayed in bright red, were critical and had triggered the alarms. Just by looking at the graphical display and having an understanding of how it worked, Brian knew that the cardiac monitor was displaying those vital parameters correctly. Although the monitored data was as static as a photograph snapshot frozen in time, Brian could practically hear the familiar monitor warning alarms sounding off in his head.

Brian looked at his beloved nephew on the intensive care bed. Houston looked so peaceful, and wasn't exhibiting any obvious indications of pain or distress. He lay supine on his back with his little hands at his sides. His eyes were completely closed.

How could this happen to a beautiful child who's fifth birthday is just weeks away? How can this be? Brian lowered his head and rubbed his eyes, trying to hold back more tears.

He wondered if he and his celestial friend were too late to do anything useful. True, the mysterious powers of the cosmic gemstone had again stopped time which offered some relief. Brian logically surmised that he also had the support of the powerful, invisible floating surveillance orb watching carefully over them. Alas, what good would it all do now, in this particular situation? There was no hurtling vehicle to move out of the way of. There was no adversary to stun and render unconscious. Nothing could stop the inevitable from happening in this particular situation from his perspective. Brian understood without a doubt Houston's extreme situation had only been paused for a moment, but the morose outcome of this situation was inevitable.

Meihtu pulled at Brian to move him aside. The firm gesture slightly startled him, but he took a few steps to his right, allowing room for her to step closer to the bed. Brian noticed that he and Meihtu were still standing under the extraordinary shadowy beams. However, there was something distinctly different this time. The borders of the darkened shadows were delimited much closer to their feet now. The mysterious shadowy beams of the planetoid silhouettes were markedly narrower, focused tighter around them.

Meihtu and Brian stood quietly for a moment at young Houston's bedside, almost as perfectly still as the people and objects around them in their static, monotone environment. The enchanting sound of the rhythmic pulsations from the astral objects above was the only ambient noise. Aside from that, it was eerily still. Brian's mysterious celestial lady friend went to work.

The brightly shining celestial jewel was outside her garments now and rested exposed on her chest. She stepped closer to Houston. As soon as she did so, the dark bordering shadow converged on the right side his body. At once, something tremendous happened that was similar to the phenomena Brian experienced before. A bright flickering light erupted where the darkened shadow contacted the injured little boy. Brian's eyes widened at the pulsation of bright filaments, flickering like miniature bursts of lightning. The arcing pulses of lighted strands blossomed as they sparked, emanating a similar photo lucent outline like Brian saw before. But something was a little different this time. The pulsing strands of pure light sparked outward, forming a much narrower, convex conical dome around him and Meihtu. The illuminated visualization was just as impressive as before. Brian looked around him at the flickering lighted effect and felt like he was standing inside an oversized witch's hat. He was able to smile slightly seeing the amusing effect.

Meihtu raised both of her gloved hands about chest high, palms facing outward, and then stood still for a moment. Then Brian noticed something he had not witnessed before. The darkened, closely delineated margins of the shadows steadily stretched ahead of the alien humanoid woman, although the observation team was no longer moving forward. The vigorously flickering, erratic strands of bright light advanced precisely and uniformly over little Houston. All the while, the incredible lighted effect exactly bounded the contour of the shadowy borders around them. The erratic strands of bordered light flickered perpendicular to the surface of the floor and Houston's intensive care bed. As the border of the erratic strands of bright light advanced over Houston's body, the dazzling filament simultaneously blossomed outward more vigorously. As soon as the bordering flicker of light traversed about halfway over Houston's body, the familiar bright cyan radiance encapsulated the boy. Brian remembered the exact sequence of the lighted phenomena effect. As observed beforehand, there was a brightly colored glowing effect that moved all over Houston in a visually synchronous wavelike manner of sheer iridescent light. It was the same Saint Elmo's fire he'd seen before. All in all, this event was very similar to what happened with Tiffany in the street.

Brian watched and stayed close to Meihtu as she situated the borders of the darkened shadows so the converging shadowy beams of the planetoid objects above were cast directly over his nephew. When the shadowy beams were cast completely over the injured boy, there was a significantly different effect compared to what happened to the little girl. The miniature flashes of erratic light and associated noise promptly ceased, but the cyan light engulfing Houston, remained. In fact, the glowing effect suddenly became much brighter, so much brighter that the entire room was completely illuminated. Soon, even the PICU station one area was illuminated and bathed in the intense light.

The light was so brilliant that Brian had to close his eyes and look away. Amazingly, the bright light persisted and Brian wondered how his celestial lady friend was affected. Oddly, there was no sound associated with the intense, glowing effect. The enchanting rhythmic pulsations from the planetoid objects above them, was all that could be heard. Brian stood still, waiting for any hint from Meihtu to do otherwise.

Then, the intensely glowing effect suddenly vanished. Brian opened his eyes and turned his head to look upon his dear nephew to see what had happened. Indeed, Houston was no longer encapsulated by the intense glow. At that moment Meihtu reached behind her back with one hand and tapped her trusted companion on the hip. Brian knew at once what was happening. It was time to make their retreat. Whatever needed to happen, had happened. Brian had no clue what had just transpired. Perhaps the alien humanoid woman failed in her attempt to affect a favorable outcome. Either way, Brian knew it was time to leave.

The clandestine observation duo slowly backed away from Houston's hospital bed, moving carefully in unison, almost as if rehearsed to near perfection. Then an erratic array of flickering bright light erupted, the same as he had witnessed during Tiffany's dramatic rescue. As the mysterious shadow completely withdrew from Houston, the miniature flashes of light and the associated noise suddenly ceased.

· · · • • ● • • · ·

Meihtu quickly situated herself in front of her friend and picked up the pace as they walked forward towards the entrance of the PICU ward. Brian had a gentle hold on Meihtu's hand as they passed the time-frozen individuals around them, including his brother. As the clandestine duo made their way out, Brian looked back once more at his beloved nephew on the intensive care bed. Houston, now bathed in the same anil hue tinged world about them, looked so peaceful. To Brian, the young child still exhibited no obvious indications of pain or distress. He remained supine on the bed with his little hands at his sides. His eyes were still closed.

Brian did not think about much except his beloved nephew's situation. As the two made their quiet exit out of the PICU, he desperately wanted to ask his friend what had just happened. Not a word was spoken, nor any gesture passed between them. Their next objective was to return to the present world that was currently occupying space in concert with the soon to be world.

Soon, they came to the same elevator they'd arrived in. Brian noticed his celestial lady friend slowed her pace and then they both stopped walking. Meihtu clenched her long silvery necklace and raised the sparkling, wondrous gem off her chest. The beautiful alien jewel emanated an intense pulse of pure silvery light, just as before. Brian shielded his eyes and at the exact moment the stunning flash occurred, Brian heard and felt that familiar, very deep, single pulsation throughout his body. As before, he felt a little numb all over and just a bit disoriented. The second flash was a little stronger, but again, he was not as overwhelmed as before. Then the sudden, pounding sound effect filled Brian's ears like piercing claps of thunder. Just as he winced he felt the slight rush of wind from all directions, billowing their clothing for just a second before vanishing.

At once, and without ill consequence, the world was rejoined.

Brian looked around. The shadows and mysterious planetoid objects were no longer there, and Meihtu and Brian were once again returned to an ordinary world no longer arrested in eerie stillness and shades of anil. Brian looked at Meihtu and fervently gestured.

"Everything is normal? Is my nephew going to be okay?"

The exotic celestial Commander nodded once and squeezed his arm gently. The young man noticed she had already concealed the mysterious gemstone within her garment.

"Your nephew will be fine," she gestured, and then hugged him, holding him closely with her head snuggled against his chest. Brian hugged her back firmly.

"Thank you!" he said aloud, his lips starting to quiver a bit from pure the rush of emotion. He hugged her again, firmly. "Thank you!"

"Brian!" The exotic alien woman said out loud in her thick accent.

Then she gestured, "I must go now. I will contact you again, very soon. You should go and be with your family now. Everything will be fine." She nodded her head once.

"Okay." Brian acknowledged as he pressed the elevator down button.

"Are you going to be alright?" he asked, remembering that using the mysterious jewel was taxing on his celestial lady friend.

"Do you need my help? Let me go with you. I should probably at least do that." Brian thought he should walk with her to wherever she needed to go.

"I will be fine. Everything will be fine." She nodded her head once.

"Okay then," he said aloud and then signed, "I understand" with a sincere smile.

Brian did not really know exactly what he should say, but he did know he wanted her to stay with him. He did not want her to go. Yet, he did not want to jeopardize the mission in any way, either. Meihtu hugged him once more just as the doors to the elevator nearest to them opened. Brian quietly watched his exotic lady friend step into the empty elevator. She pushed the appropriate button for the lobby level. As the elevator doors began to close, Meihtu slowly bowed her head once at him. Brian did the same. The elevator doors swiftly closed and she was gone.

Brian wondered where she was going. He surmised she would make a quiet, prompt egress in the other smaller, more clandestine vehicle Baouzhe had mentioned.

"I wonder where it's at. Hopefully not double parked and getting a ticket." He laughed quietly. At least his sense of humor had somewhat returned during this dreadful hour.

Brian's thoughts quickly returned to his dear nephew's situation and well-being. He turned and ran towards the PICU, passing the young couple who were just exiting through the large automatic security doors. They turned their heads when he ran by and watched him rush into the specialized intensive care ward.

As he breezed past the station one main reception desk, Catherine quickly turned her head to get his attention.

"Oh, Brian, I was just about to page you, dear!" she said while placing the phone receiver back into its cradle. She watched Brian stride into Houston's room. Her present expression was one of great concern.

"Oh Lord, please help that child," she whispered.

Brian entered the private suite behind the nurse pushing the station-one crash cart. The young man did not know what to expect. His heart was pounding, his mouth dry, and he was trembling with nerves. His brother noticed him dart in behind the nurse.

"Brian!" Brandon said with both relief and terror tinging that one word. Brian quickly made his way to his brother's side. He hugged him.

"Man, I'm so glad you're here now!" Brandon replied tearfully.

Bob smiled at Brian and then promptly returned his attention to his little patient.

"Well," the wise and experienced nurse raised his voice a bit, "looks like everything is okay now." Bob wore a very bewildered look.

"I don't know. All I can say is, literally one minute ago, not so good."

He shrugged his shoulders and looked directly at Carl.

Brian was truthfully a bit surprised to hear that. But he sighed in relief. Emotionally, those words brought much comfort. Brian had just beheld the mysterious powers of the celestial jewel. He knew something terrific had happened, but his mind held more questions than answers.

Did it really work? What did we do? How did Meihtu do it? He looked upon his beloved nephew. *Is he really going to totally be all right?*

There was a moment of absolute silence. Everyone, including Brian, was looking at the cardiac monitor now. Astonishingly, all of little Houston's vital life signs and indications were completely normal. The monitor alarms had completely ceased. It was as if nothing at all had happened. Brian looked at Carl. The young resident on-call was almost at a loss for words. He sighed and rubbed the back of his neck.

"Well." He took a deep breath and sighed again.

"Well," Carl collected his thoughts and continued in a calm tone of voice, "he definitely looked worse a minute ago. I mean, he looked like he was going into respiratory arrest, but…" Carl grimaced.

"Well, let's get a blood gas, some labs, and I'd like to get a CT scan, like, real soon!" Carl rubbed his chin. "I better get Neurology in here. I'll go tell Catherine to page the doctor on-call." Carl looked at Brandon and Brian.

"I think we're actually going to be okay here. But I want to get some tests done, just to be certain." Carl continued.

The father and uncle of little Houston both nodded in agreement.

"I'll come back and write some orders." Carl said to Bob, who nodded his head.

"Okay that sounds good. I'll draw some blood work." Bob

replied. "Danny, can we get the blood gas, too, sir?" He asked aloud as he walked towards his patient's vital statistics chart on the small nurse's charting table nearby.

"Yes sir, you bet! I'll go get an arterial line kit." Danny said and quickly re-hung the resuscitator bag and mask back on the wall and patted Brian on the back as he made his way around the bed.

"Everything is going to be fine. I just know it will, my friend." Then Danny smiled reassuringly at Brandon. "Your kid is a tough little fighter. I can tell!"

"Oh, now that is true," Brandon quickly replied, and smiled.

"Thanks, Danny," Brian replied, and then returned his gaze to Houston who was still lying so still on the hospital bed. *How did Meihtu do it?*

"Well, good! I guess we won't need this after all!" Rhonda Tenner, the RN said and then smoothly turned the station-one crash cart around for a quick retreat out of Houston's room. "Ta-ta, toodle-oo!" she smiled.

·   ·   ·   •   •   ●   •   •   ·   ·

At that moment the evening PICU Charge Nurse, Linda Hoffett, RN, quickly walked past Carl and Rhonda and entered the private intensive care room.

"Everything all right here? You need some help, Bob?" She noticed Bob writing a few notes on his patient's vital statistics chart.

"You need me to get some vitals for you while you get caught up on some of that, hun?" She pointed towards the narrow work station where Bob was standing.

"Yes, that'd be great!" Bob smiled and nodded.

She looked about and noticed Brian, who she knew worked the day shift.

"Hey, hun." She smiled at the young man. Brian still had an arm snug around his brother's shoulders. Brian smiled at her and nodded. Then she turned all her attention to Brandon.

"Everything's going to be all right, dad." She winked. Brandon rubbed his face and then smiled in return.

Something very peculiar was happening in the PICU and it was starting right there where Carl was. The young doctor did not get very far out of little Houston's room before he was suddenly approached by one of the other nurses working in the station-one area. "Doctor Spies!" Belinda Jackson, R.N. practically stood directly in the doctor's path.

"Um, you're not going to believe this, but our kid in room five just opened her eyes!"

"What?!" The resident on-call could not believe what he had just heard from the tall, young R.N. That patient had been in a coma for over four days now. In fact, that particular patient had a very poor prognosis.

"Patient Marla Torres?" Carl inquired with a confused look on his face.

"You're talking about room five, right?" He knew that could not be possible. That patient had been gravely suffering from a serious spinal meningitis infection requiring life support measures including a sophisticated mechanical ventilator to help keep her alive and breathing.

"Can you come to her room please?" The young nurse politely requested. She turned and swiftly walked away towards her patient's room.

"I'm going to need more sedation for her. "She's, like… trying to claw out of bed and climb the walls!" Belinda pointed at her patient's room. There was another respiratory therapist, Angela Menendez, RRT, in there now trying to keep the child safely and comfortably still.

"Uh," Carl peered into the room from where he stood, "yeah give her what she needs, you've got standing orders for some sedation. I'll be right there in a minute, I promise."

"Okay," Nurse Belinda responded without looking back at the resident on-call. She quickly began to don the necessary barrier gown, gloves, and mask for entering the specialized, critical care isolation room. She swiftly entered the room carrying the medical supplies she had originally gone out to get for her patient.

"Doctor Spies." Another beckoning call came from another R.N. standing at the entrance to room four.

"Can you come see this patient when you have a moment, please?" The nurse, Susan Nguyen, calmly requested of the young doctor on-call.

"It's nothing urgent, she just, well… my patient, Linda Smith…" She looked back into her room, and then the slightly gray haired nurse of Vietnamese descent politely said, "She's normal now, I think." She looked at the doctor and shrugged her shoulders with a peculiar smile.

"I don't know, her blood pressure, and heart rate, and O2 sat, it's all like, suddenly normal now." She shrugged her shoulders, again.

"She is looking much better, now. It's like, all of a sudden. I don't know. Come see."

"Huh?" Carl grimaced and scratched his head several times, utterly baffled by what was occurring with all the pediatric patients in the ward.

The young six year old patient was suffering from a very aggressive sepsis and pneumonia infection. The patient this nurse was referring to had become more and more clinically unstable over the past twelve hours.

"What? Wait…" But the young doctor was soon interrupted.

"Doctor Spies." Another R.N., Carrie Parlor, was holding the sliding glass doorway halfway open to pediatric room three.

She had peered out of her room to get the young doctor's attention.

"I have this cute child, little Jeremy Noble who was transported here the other day."

Carl turned to face the experienced nurse.

"I think he came by air transport. He's the one with all the respiratory problems." The very talkative and socially amiable nurse smiled.

"He's on 50 percent O2, but, well, he looks a lot better now, a whole lot better! Like, unbelievable! I'm serious! Can you come see when you get a chance, Doctor Spies?"

The nurse looked back into the room at her patient.

"He's breathing and looking very stable now. I just took his temperature and it's normal."

Her soft and deliberate tone raised just a bit, her smile ever present.

"His condition just, well, it suddenly changed! He looks much better now!" She shrugged her shoulders.

"Yes, yes, I know who your patient is." Carl turned his attention to nurse Carrie. He grimaced out of confusion and scratched his head several times.

"Sure, uh, I'll be right there."

"Doctor Spies." The PICU receptionist beckoned. "I have calls coming in from the other rooms on the unit."

She raised her eyebrows as she turned to face him and deliver her message.

"And, they all have something in common to say. It's weird. They all say their kids are doing a lot better now." She shrugged her shoulders.

"They want you to come and see." She shrugged her shoulders, again. The intensive care phone lines began to ring again, seemingly on cue and quite fervently. Catherine dutifully returned to her responsibilities. She answered one of the calls.

"Yes, yes, I told him, he'll be there as soon as he can." She nodded, "Yes, yes, patient Jimmy Ackerson? Yes, okay, that's very good news, nice to hear, dear."

The handsome young physician scratched his head again and grimaced.

"Okay," he said aloud. It was his only reply.

Catherine waved her hand in acknowledgement, systematically answering call after call. Carl was astonished and puzzled and had not a clue what was happening, but it was definitely something remarkable.

Brian did not notice his little nephew open his eyes. He was looking at the cardiac monitor and admiring all the normal vital statistics displayed when he heard his beloved nephew's voice.

"Daddy!"

"Yes!" Brandon immediately hugged and kissed his dear child.

"Yes, daddy is here baby boy!" the loving father laughed and sniffled.

"Look," he smiled happily, "look who's here, too." Brandon motioned towards his brother.

"Uncle Brian is here to see you, too." The father wiped his tears and smiled.

"Uncle Brian." Houston smiled and then returned his gaze to his father.

"Daddy, what's happening? Where is mommy?" The young boy's voice rose. He looked around him and then touched the brace clasped around his neck. He looked lost and bewildered.

"What we doing here, daddy? What's happening to me?"

Everyone started to console the little child at once, echoing the very same words.

"You're fine." The father clasped his child's small hands tenderly.

"Everything is going to be okay. You were in a car accident. But, you're fine, now." Brandon sniffled.

"You're just fine. And mommy is okay, too. She's in another room resting. She will see you, soon." Brandon rested his head on his child's chest.

Brian leaned forward and said, "I'll go upstairs and visit mommy now. I'll let her know you woke up and asked about her." He smiled.

"She'd like to hear that." He rubbed little Houston's legs. "Is that okay little buddy?"

"Okay." Houston answered quietly. "Tell her I'm waiting." Then he raised his voice a little, "But, I'm tough! I'm strong!"

"Of course you are baby boy!" Brandon laughed and hugged his son.

"That's my boy!" He laughed joyfully. Houston was doing what he was told. He was reacting the way he was taught, to always show courage. The young boy could not remember what happened to him at the moment. He was very confused.

Nevertheless, he was feeling no pain, and he was beginning to regain his senses.

"Mommy will see you soon." Brandon kissed his boy.

"Just rest now, son. We will take all these wires and things off you soon, okay?"

"Okay, daddy," Houston replied, gently tugging at his neck brace.

"We need to do some tests, then all this stuff will come off, okay?" Bob reassured with a big smile.

"Everything is going to be fine, Houston." He gently patted the child's legs.

Brian hugged his dear nephew.

"I'll be right back." He smiled. "You just get some rest for now, okay little buddy?" He winked at his nephew. "Feel better."

Houston gave him the thumbs-up sign. "Okay, Uncle Brian. I will, I promise."

Everyone in the room chuckled and smiled in response.

· · • ● ● ⬤ ● ● • · ·

Next, Brian visited his sister-in-law, Donnette. She was awake now from the mild sedation she'd been given, and doing well. She was very happy to see him. Brian informed her Houston had just woken up and he was also doing very well. It was definitely good news. She hugged him and cried uncontrollably. He assured her everything was going to be fine. Brian told her what he observed. Not the mission details, of course. Brian did not disclose any of the details of his clandestine mission with the extraterrestrial aliens, or the mystifying effects of the bewildering celestial jewel. Nothing at all about that occurrence was mentioned. However, Brian disclosed enough to let Donnette know that her son was clinically stable. He reassured her everything was going to be just fine.

Maybe it is time now. Maybe these miraculous events I've seen will prove it somehow. Maybe everyone should know what these compassionate aliens can do for us. Brian seriously contemplated telling them now about the aliens.

There was so much he wanted to share right now. His recent personal experience had compelled him to almost completely change his mind about his desire to hide the aliens out of public sight. He wanted everyone to see what he knew. He only desired it for the good of all his fellow mankind.

Chapter Thirty Five

When Brian returned to his parent's home it was nearly 2 a.m. He was exhausted. He could barely remember the drive up the mountain. But even though he was wiped out, he was comforted by the knowledge that his family was doing well. His beloved little nephew and dear sister-in-law were recovering remarkably well now. He sighed in relief at the thought of it. He sat on the edge of the bed in the dark guest bedroom rubbing his head and reflecting on the evening's astounding events. He especially thought about his precarious encounter with the armed fugitives while on his way to the hospital earlier in the evening. That encounter was one of the least desired and definitely least enjoyable to remember from the evening, for sure. There was, at least, something good to know about what followed after that untimely confrontation. Brian recalled hearing a brief news report on the local FM radio station during his return drive regarding the apprehension of those very suspects by the state law enforcement. All things considered, that situation had turned out well. Brian smiled.

As he sat there in the quiet dark and thought about his parents, he knew he would be hearing from them the next day. They were well on their way back from Hawaii, returning to the mainland to see their children. His parents had managed to get the first available return flight home. Brian laid his head down on the pillow and was comforted to know that. He lay still for a moment and then uttered the name of someone he suddenly remembered, "Harry Williams, Jr."

For no apparent reason Brian suddenly recalled a kind,

elderly scale model enthusiast who was a United States Navy World War II veteran. He was a retired Pearl Harbor veteran, a USN ensign, who had admired and bought Brian's assembled scale model replica of the USS Lexington (CV-2) World War II aircraft carrier years ago. Brian had only met him briefly once at a hobby store gathering. He never saw the elderly gentleman again. For no particular reason, Brian had remembered and said aloud the old man's name.

"That was a cool old dude." Brian chuckled and then fell asleep.

·　·　·　•　●　⬤　●　•　·　·

"Brian," a voice called out to him, "we talk now, yes?"

The handsome young man raised his head from the very familiar small dinner table on the cozy outdoor patio area of the romantic dreamscape restaurant. It was no surprise that the exotic Baouzhe was sitting across from him.

"Nice to see you my beautiful friend! I want to also thank you in person, Baouzhe. I am so very grateful for what you guys did saving my nephew's life!"

The beautiful dreamscape semblance of the celestial alien smiled.

"We are grateful to help, Brian." She respectfully nodded once.

Brian beamed sincerely and said, "Our latest mission was successful. Yes?" He raised an eyebrow, inquiringly.

"Yes, Brian. Thanks to you, it is all a great success."

She reached across the small table and took gentle hold of the young man's hands.

"The mission would not be a success without your help." She gently squeezed Brian's hands as she smiled and kept gazing into his eyes.

"You are truly a divine person, just as the prophets have said."

"Say what?!" Brian eyes widened.

"Yes, Brian." Baouzhe looked directly into his eyes with all sincerity.

"It has been said that there would be a human, a very kind man, who would help guide us on this journey. Someone who would help us do great things for his divine peoples. Now, I see that prophesy is true," she said kindly.

"Some of what has happened on this mission, including the very events of this evening, was actually foreseen in limited detail. But, nevertheless, it is now all true." She looked down at the table.

"I originally imagined it would be someone else to guide us with divine clairvoyance and wisdom on this mission, if prophesy was to be true. I envisioned someone different. Perhaps an elderly human being by your standards. I didn't expect that person would be you. In fact, I thought your chance encounter with us had disrupted destiny. I was wrong, Brian. Please forgive my doubt, ignorance, lack of faith, and disrespect."

She nodded once very respectfully and lowered her head.

"It's cool, space-wolf!" Brian sniffed and smiled teasingly in reply. She smiled back.

Then a question came to Brian regarding the mission.

"Is that why…" he paused for just a slight moment, "is that actually why you did not abandon the mission earlier? Is that why you did not erase my mind of our encounter, or something like that?"

He leaned forward and made direct eye contact with the exotic dreamscape semblance of the extraterrestrial being.

"I mean, I know you knew that no one would believe me if I told them about the encounter in the woods. And I remember you telling me about how it's all low risk, and such. But, were you kind of guided by a prophesy? Like, you were relying on it, or something?" Brian had a feeling he already knew what the response would be.

"Well…" her posture tensed a bit. "There was great debating about the matter, to be honest. Different tactics were quickly considered and discussed that night. We considered our emergency egress option and our exit strategy to abort the mission."

"There was a joint consensus to continue the mission as planned. Continue the mission as destiny would have it. Yes, Brian." Baouzhe calmly asserted.

"Really? No kidding?"

"You see, Brian." The alien dreamscape woman smiled just a bit more and her tranquil voice filled his ears. There was absolute assurance in her tone, leaving no reservation or doubt of her intended words.

"There were some military experts on my world that guaranteed the mission would be covert. They said it would be a highly classified operation that nobody on this planet would even slightly notice. We rehearsed and meticulously prepared for every possible contingency, keeping stealth operation a primary objective. But, as you know, that was not to be. The moment we landed, things quickly changed. We were immediately discovered by you, Brian." She made direct eye contact with Brian.

"It has been prophesied there would be one human to guide us and assure our success on this particular mission. That history would be made on this mission." She grabbed hold of Brian's hands firmly.

"Prophesy has been fulfilled, Brian. Thanks in all, to you. Yes, even I see that now."

Brian glanced down at their joined hands on the cozy table.

"I don't know what to say." He chuckled nervously.

"I'm no prophet, for sure. I don't feel chosen or divine or anything, either." He shrugged his shoulders as he made eye contact with her. "I'm just a man."

Baouzhe smiled at him. "You are a very great man, now. A hero, Brian."

"Well, I don't know about all that." Brian shrugged his shoulders again.

"So, what happens next?" Brian respectfully inquired, trying to graciously change the subject.

Baouzhe leaned back in her chair and composed her posture,

crossing her legs as she did so. Then she looked directly into Brian's eyes again with a deliberation that suggested just a hint of temperate affection.

"You are a divine people. And you are truly a kind, considerate gentleman. I have learned so much from you, Brian."

"Very nice of you to say that, Baouzhe. You are a very kind people and I have learned so much from you guys, too."

Brian was feeling quite modest and responded with a smile and a slight nod.

"You must understand I could not really disclose this revelation with you. There was still much to be determined before now," Baouzhe revealed candidly.

"Yes. I understand," Brian respectfully agreed.

"Now, with our mission objectives completed to this point, we will plan for our immediate departure, Brian." Baouzhe paused.

"We will monitor the young child relative of yours for years to come. When the time is right, Brian," the alien dreamscape woman leaned forward, "when it has been discussed and decided upon, we will plan and initiate an official first contact with your species. This matter has been confirmed very recently."

"No way!" Brian's eyes widened. "Really?"

He was actually happy to hear that exclusive information. Brian was beginning to wonder now if the aliens should no longer remain a secret. He had been feeling differently about that. Brian could fully appreciate the wondrous prospect of the celestial jewel effects. He started to feel everyone should know the extraterrestrials as he had gotten to know them.

"So, they really want to send you guys back?"

"Yes, Brian," the beautiful young Asian woman replied candidly.

"When the time is right for that, yes. And I'm certain those plans will include you, too."

"Seriously? How will I know?" Brian leaned towards the small cozy table.

"When will I be contacted, again? Can I really be a part of that event? Can I..."

"I really cannot answer any of those exact details, Brian," Baouzhe interrupted.

"I just know we will return someday," She leaned towards the table, "when the peoples of this world can stop fighting each other and come together for one tremendous worthy cause. That is when I suspect our worlds will meet. There has to be peace on this world for some time, first. No attacking each other. No fighting wars. No destroying humanity. No destruction of this beloved world." She leaned back into her chair.

"That is what I know."

"Yes, I understand." Brian replied. "That's kind of what you said before, and I agree. I suppose that makes sense."

He then thought of the most recent great conflicts in history, the World Wars of the previous century. He considered the past great conflict and the current ongoing, hostile situation between North Korea and South Korea. He thought a little more about the past and remembered some of the Memorial Day documentaries he had seen before on cable television. There had been at least a decade of extreme fighting during the American occupation in Vietnam. Brian also thought of the most recent Gulf War in the Middle East, about ten years past now. That was the last major conflict involving the United States of America, to his recollection.

"I know as humans," Brian thought for a second before continuing, "...we seem to always go to war with each other somewhere on this planet." He looked around as he pondered recent history.

"But I don't think we've had anything really significant in the news involving this country for many years now. Not since that Desert Storm war, I think." He scratched his head.

"I mean, there's always some little guerrilla warfare or skirmish somewhere in the world. But, America has been at peace, mostly, at least since the attack against Saddam Hussein over there in Iraq. But that Saddam dude is like, being cool right now." Brian shrugged his shoulders.

"I think it's all good, now." Brian looked up as he pondered the current world events. He shrugged his shoulders again and looked at her.

"There must be continued peace, Brian. And something must be done of great significance to benefit all mankind during the peaceful period," Baouzhe calmly asserted.

"Then our worlds will meet." She nodded her head, respectfully.

"Wait." Brian's tone of voice suddenly changed, to some extent to an inflection of slight desperation.

"Maybe I've been seeing this all the wrong way. You should probably make contact with us sooner, maybe even now. Look at what you're capable of." Brian began to gesture in animation. "I mean, look at what you guys can do! You saved my nephew! You saved that little girl!"

Baouzhe looked at Brian in confusion. She tilted her head to one side as she considered.

"That is not consistent with your previous desire and your insistent articulation for us to remain entirely secret, Brian." The inflection in her tone of voice substantiated the look on her face.

"Yes, yes," he said, pointing at the exotic alien woman in his dream world.

"But, that is before I knew and witnessed what you are totally capable of! With those miraculous type attributes, our people will be so grateful! You will make such a huge and wonderful impact on our society. That capability you have will demonstrate you are very peaceful beings. You guys are from a world that is so loving and so giving, and I see that now."

Brian's eyes were wide open, beseeching.

"You will change things in a positive way. Yes, I see that now. That special capability you possess should be shared and demonstrated as a means to bring us all together, perhaps."

Brian smiled. He was being sincere. He had changed his mind about keeping the aliens out of sight. He wanted so much now to share his wonderful experience with anyone who would listen to him, and believe.

"Maybe it is time." Brian gazed around his dreamscape surroundings.

"Maybe, the recent events will prove it somehow. Maybe you could show everyone how you do that. Maybe that's also part of the destiny you speak of. After all, we are at peace in the world right now, mostly. So maybe the time is now." Brian was profoundly sincere. He continued to smile.

Baouzhe had no response. She sat almost perfectly still, staring at him. Brian recognized the familiar posture. It was the same gaze the alien wolf-like creature bestowed on him. The same look.

The young man continued.

"Maybe, you could show them, show the entire world. Show them all what you guys can do!"

Brian was excited about his newfound inspiration.

"Show the world your miraculous powers, Baouzhe." He was being genuine in his convincing supposition.

"It will bring us all together. It has to, when everyone sees it. I don't care what people believe in. It's positive, it's good, and it's for the betterment of mankind." Brian calmed his voice.

"This has to be a good time, now. Maybe, this is what God wants."

"Let us not speak for The Creator," Baouzhe serenely insisted.

"Brian," the beautiful exotic semblance of the alien creature calmly replied, "I believe you speak with the sentiment of having witnessed your related child recover from calamitous circumstances." She still had not changed her physical posture with her composed reply.

Brian stared at her. What she said was correct. He knew that. All in all, Brian knew it was still too early to consider an official first contact with the aliens. However, there was so much he wanted to share right now. His personal experience had compelled him to almost completely change his mind about it. Brian did not want to hide the aliens. He wanted everyone to see what he had discovered about them. He only desired it for the good of all people on planet Earth. Alas, he knew better.

"Yeah." He looked down at the small dinner table. "I guess you're probably right about all that." Brian cleared his throat.

"Brian," Baouzhe said, "the things you have witnessed." She

leaned forward slightly, keeping her alluring lean posture with her eyes fixed on his.

"They are no small accomplishment. Those tremendous actions affected by the utilization of the sacred jewel can occur only during certain cosmic gateways. That power and capability is only called upon by a very select, small group of people on my world. Meihtu just happens to be one of them, Brian. I wanted you to know that."

"Woah! Say what?!" Brian leaned forward and his jaw dropped. "You're kidding me now, right? I knew what I saw was like, a miracle or something, man!" He shook his head.

"Damn, it was crazy!"

At that moment music began playing. Inside the restaurant a jazz cover band started their set of musical entertainment for the evening. A woman began to sing a cover of *The Girl From Ipanema* by Stan Getz. The woman's sultry voice was exactingly smooth and engaging. Brian continued to stare at the table. He listened to the pleasant sound of the melody and wondered if he would ever be able to share the extraordinary experiences he'd had getting to know the extraterrestrials with other people he knew. Deep down inside, he knew he must honor the requests of his celestial friends to keep knowledge of the recent events secret. Until such time it was proper to disclose their existence, Brian had to remain absolutely quiet about it all.

"When the time is right, Brian, you will know." The exotic dreamscape semblance of Baouzhe leaned forward and took gentle hold of his hands again. She was more relaxed, and she smiled at him.

"You must keep this mission and everything that happened a complete secret, Brian." Baouzhe leaned forward further and made direct eye contact with him.

"Do you understand and agree, Brian?"

"Yes, just as we had discussed and agreed upon previously." Brian nodded.

He leaned back into his chair. As he released her soft hands, Brian noticed something. Baouzhe was slightly swaying to the rhythm of the jazz music coming from inside the dining area.

Baouzhe was looking down at the cozy dinner table where they quietly sat. She was still smiling.

"You like that song?" Brian pointed his finger up to denote the pleasant sounds they were both enjoying.

"I find it very pleasing," the exotic Asian lady replied.

"You have music like this on your world, Baouzhe?"

"Yes, Brian," she answered, "Very similar and just as pleasing." Brian stood from his small chair and extended his hand.

"Do you dance on your world, too?"

Baouzhe smiled at him. She quietly stood up without saying another word and approached him, closing the neutral distance between them in a short instant. Brian took hold of her hand about chest high and drew her near, while simultaneously placing his other hand just under the back of her small shoulder. The two began to move as one, softly swaying to the beautiful melody that filled their ears.

· · · • ● ⬤ ● • · · ·

Brian wondered if and when he would ever see the two alien space travelers from *dwellers of the lifeful planet* again.

"I hope we can meet again, soon." Brian smiled, looking directly into the tantalizing dark eyes of the lovely woman semblance, Baouzhe.

His thoughts then quickly reflected on Meihtu. Brian wondered if she was thinking about him, too. He wished he could speak to her. But, he understood if he would be unable to see the exotic mission commander now. At least he had developed a good friendship with Baouzhe. Somehow, Brian thought that would be of benefit and help him get closer to Meihtu.

"Baouzhe, will you please say goodbye to Meihtu for me?"

Baouzhe looked up at him and smiled. She brought her rhythmic, slow dance pace to a gentle halt the very instant Brian felt a tap on his right shoulder from behind him. He turned slightly out of curiosity, expecting the familiar restaurant server, probably patiently waiting to take an order of food and beverages. However, to his very pleasant surprise, it was Meihtu.

What an unexpected surprise. Yes, indeed. Meihtu was standing there smiling in great anticipation of seeing the handsome young man, again. She was no longer clad in ingenious disguise. The Mission Commander bore no signs of rank; she was not wearing her standard military style flight suit garb. Rather, she was stunningly dressed in a creamy white chiffon long sleeve maxi dress with an elegant mock turtleneck. The cascading evening dress with the snug fitted waist and darted bodice astoundingly complemented her exceptionally unique celestial physique. She stood there in his dream world in full display of pure elegance.

"Hello, Brian." Meihtu broke the silence with her beautiful smile.

The young man did not answer right away. He was slightly preoccupied admiring her at the moment. His unyielding gaze upon her had apparently taken away his ability to speak. He looked her over again and again. Brian perceptively noticed how the length of her left leg was fortuitously exposed through the side slit of her evening gown. Brian appreciated every detail, including her strappy, pearl white three-inch heels. The open-toed footwear tastefully complimented the silky smooth, deep amberous skin tone of her delicate narrow feet.

"Whoa." Was all he could manage.

Brian looked directly into her eyes now, smiling brightly. They stood looking at each other in a very familiar, sincere delight. Without another word, Brian stepped closer and gently embraced her tall, slender body with a very warmhearted hug. Meihtu kept her eyes and her complete attention affixed on his direct gaze. Brian took hold of her right hand about chest high and kept her snug next to him.

"Hello, beautiful," he responded in a whisper. Then the two began softly swaying to the romantic melody being played in the dining area of the dreamscape restaurant.

Brian turned his head to the right to look at Baouzhe. The

beautiful semblance of the alien creature was smiling happily at the two.

"How did you do it?" Brian asked as he returned his gaze to Meihtu's eyes.

"How are you both here? And, why didn't you come visit me sooner, Meihtu?"

"It is not easy. There is much associated risk," Baouzhe promptly replied.

"We must have someone watch out for us while we visit you this way. This manner of communication requires us to both be asleep at the same time in order to talk, Brian."

"Oh, I see." Brian nodded his head as he thought about it.

"Hey wait, what do you mean by that? You have to have someone…" He was curtly interrupted.

"Brian," Baouzhe spoke up as he and Meihtu continued to slow dance. "We have some assistance here on our mission. We are not alone."

Brian stopped dancing. He turned to face Baouzhe as he spoke, a bit concerned at her revelation.

"What do you mean by that, exactly?"

Meihtu smoothly regained his attention in her familiar calming tone. Her words could now be understood clearly, with only the slightest hint of an Orient tongue.

"Brian, we have a small, very specialized, secretly hidden team located on the far side of your moon. They are only there in case of an emergency. Like, if we need help to be immediately extracted and abort our mission," she said reassuringly. "They mean no harm."

"Uh-huh, okay, I see." Brian was not sure what to think. But, it did make some sense to him.

"That's okay, I guess. At least you finally told me." They continued to dance, slowly.

"It is not an aggression force or an invasion army," Baouzhe affirmed aloud. Meihtu shook her head in simultaneous accord.

"They are a rescue team, basically." Baouzhe nodded her head in affirmation.

"Okay." Brian did not know what else to say.

He almost did not care. For that matter, he would listen to anything being said to him now, so long as he could hold Meihtu close to him.

"Okay, it's cool. It's all good." He shrugged his shoulders.

Then Meihtu said, "Brian, I do not know how to thank you for everything you did for us." She hugged him as she continued.

"This world will continue to change, more so for the better someday, because of people on this world like you, Brian." She looked at him.

"When we return, I hope I can see you again. I want for us to always be friends, Brian." She smiled.

"Is that agreeable, yes?"

"Oh, definitely!" Brian chuckled.

"Yes, you can count on that, Meihtu. I'll always be your friend. Both of you." He looked at Baouzhe and nodded.

As the music changed to an upbeat, smooth jazz improvisation instrumental piece, Baouzhe responded.

"I look forward to our next visit with you, Brian. I am hopeful there will be a formal first contact with your world soon."

"Good." Brian smiled in reply.

"I can't wait for that day to come. And I'll be ready to introduce you guys to the whole world." They all shared a light-hearted chuckle in response.

Brian returned his attention to Meihtu and gazed deeply into her exotic alien eyes. There was no place else he wanted to be right now. He could fully appreciate the way she looked at him. Indeed, Brian knew she wanted to be right there with him, too.

"Thank you so much for everything. I can never ever return the miraculous favors, those feats I've seen, those things you did so willingly for the people of this world. You basically saved my nephew's life." He had never been more sincere.

"Brian," Meihtu responded in her familiar soothing tone.

"We have been successful because of you, my wonderful, kind friend." She smiled. Then she closed the miniscule distance between their stance embrace and kissed him lightly on his parted lips, a gentle sweet acknowledgement.

Brian was not expecting that even though he truly wanted it.

He was caught off guard. He wanted to kiss her again, to return the favor more suitably. *Wait, I can kiss better than that.* Meihtu continued to smile at him.

"Well, uh…" He was at a loss for words at the moment. He did not actually know what to say.

"It is time." Baouzhe spoke up as she placed a gentle hand on Brian's shoulder.

"We leave now, Brian." The young man turned to face Baouzhe. Her expression was just a bit more serious now.

"I am really very happy we met you, Brian," Meihtu said. "And, I know we will meet again. When that time comes, we will be sure to contact you first, okay?"

"Yes, yes," Brian replied animatedly, "I want to be the first to know. And, if you need to visit again in secret, please come find me. You know, like, if you have another mission. I want to help you guys again. Really, I do. Anytime, just come get me." He nodded at them both.

The celestial ladies looked at each other and chuckled lightheartedly, smiling happily and sincerely in reply.

"Okay, Brian," Baouzhe acknowledged, nodding her head once.

Without any doubt, they really appreciated having befriended such a trusted, kind gentleman. Mission Commander Meihtu and Mission Specialist Baouzhe, as well as their other comrades and superiors were all fully aware that under different circumstances their mission outcome could have been absolutely disastrous at this juncture. During their surreptitious visit here, there were certainly several instances where the mission could, and probably should, have been aborted. However, their destiny would be fulfilled as their home world prophets decreed.

"Good." Brian continued to nod enthusiastically. He was sincere about helping them if ever another occasion arose.

"Good bye, Brian." Baouzhe stepped towards the handsome young man and gave him a reassuring hug.

"Until we meet again." She smiled, "Then, we…"

"Yes, I know," Brian looked at her with raised brow as he

lightheartedly interjected, "we talk now. Yes, okay, good." He hugged her tightly.

"Take care of yourself, Baouzhe."

As Baouzhe stepped away, Meihtu took hold of the young man's hands and brought herself up very comfortably close to him. She looked into his eyes and then hugged him tightly.

"Until we meet again, Brian, you are my very special friend." The warmest smile he had ever seen from her graced her lips. The sincere look in her eyes assured him that they would someday meet again.

"Until we meet again." Brian smiled and half-saluted. "Take care, Commander Meihtu."

She let go of her tight embrace about his chest and smoothly stepped away from Brian, still smiling and looking deep into his eyes. Then the celestial ladies turned to each other.

"It is time," Baouzhe spoke clearly. "We leave now."

Meihtu gave an acknowledging nod as if it were a spoken order. The two exotic celestial ladies began their egress, quickly and quietly walking from the small outdoor patio area into the larger main dining area. Brian watched them moving through a small gathering of patrons standing around listening to the music and happily conversing amongst themselves. Just before the two celestial ladies disappeared into the crowd, Meihtu turned to look at him one more time. They made direct eye contact. She smiled at him. Brian smiled back.

Then the ladies disappeared into the crowd.

Chapter Thirty Six

When Brian awoke the sun was already up. He lay there on his back perfectly still on the comfortable bed of his parents' guest room. The last thing he recollected was watching the two dreamscape extraterrestrial ladies walking away through the crowded restaurant dining area. He recalled Meihtu's beautiful smile. Next, he looked at his watch. *Monday, September third, two-thousand and one and counting, until we meet again.* Brian stared at the date information presented on his watch. *Well, that Cold War stuff my dad used to talk about is over, so there is no longer a nuclear apocalypse threat from the Russians. And, these are pretty peaceful times right now.* Brian considered 2001 was almost over and it was reasonably a good year. He thought of what peaceful opportunities would come next year. *I wonder what worthy cause mankind could do together that Baouzhe was talking about. Something to benefit all mankind during times of peace. Was that what she said? Something like that.*

After eating a light breakfast Brian sat down at the computer desk in the family room with his journal. He read what he had already written down and then he continued to document the rest of the events as well as some other details he could remember. Brian raised a hand to his head and gently rubbed all the spots where the skin implants were unobtrusively located. He grinned and nodded. *I hope they keep working.* He devotedly returned his pen to paper and continued to write in his journal. His written recollection was still remarkable, making the task very easy.

Then Brian closed his eyes as he recalled each delightful detail of his dear, alien humanoid lady friend, Meihtu. He fully recollected her uniquely beautiful feminine physique and smiled at the memory of how her flight suit hugged every curve of her alluring and shapely figure. He recalled the way she looked the night before, absolutely breathtaking in her lovely evening dress. Brian chuckled as he struggled to remember the dream of her in the shower. The details of that fantasy were not as clear to him as his other encounters. The thought of the shower encounter still made him smile, though. Meihtu was remarkably exotic and stunningly beautiful. Yes, she was different by earthly standards, yet wondrously striking in comparison to any human woman Brian had ever seen. *I wonder how soon it will be before they come back to earth.* Brian wished he knew the answer. He wanted to know how long he would have to wait. He wondered if Meihtu was thinking of him right now.

He sighed aloud. Then his thoughts returned to his family, especially his nephew Houston. Brian planned to drive back to the hospital later. That way he would be closer to the airport and ready to pick up his parents when they came in. *I'll use my mom's car today.* Brian yawned aloud and stretched his arms.

"Crazy man, it's just crazy."

His thoughts returned to the recent remarkable and miraculous events that had occurred. He thought about what it all amounted to, and the ultimate purpose of the alien's visit. *I truly do believe we can have peace. I believe we can all do good things and be kind to each other in this world. If we all think that way, we can be that way. And, when that time comes, man's history is going to change.* He smiled, thinking about the near future and what it might hold. *I'll be waiting. And, I'll be ready, Meihtu.* Brian bowed his head and prayed for their safe travel home.

· · · • ● ⬤ ● • · · ·

Up on the PICU floor in Houston's room the day shift RN, Darla Lipscombe, had just taken report from the off going nurse Bob. She was writing in Houston's bedside chart in the quiet of the morning shift. She would most likely be transferring the young boy out of the PICU later that day. Houston's condition had improved remarkably. In fact, all the other patients on the ward had also gotten miraculously better last evening. Many of those other young patients would be transferred out of the specialized intensive care ward, too. As nurse Darla wrote her notes, she tried to be as inconspicuous as possible so her patient could have a little more time to rest. Darla would be waking Houston soon in order to do her usual dayshift routines. She sat quietly at the small counter desk, reading and preparing notes for the day. Houston and his father were both sound asleep and did not notice she was there. Something else went unnoticed. Nurse Darla did not notice the shadow on the wall behind her just over her head. A very unusual shadow was being cast from something outside the large window in front of her on the other side of the patient's room. That was the same direction that the light was coming from, the rising morning sun.

What was being cast on the wall behind her, just above her head, was a very peculiar appearing shadow of refracted light. Most of the refracted light appeared at a common focal point at the center of the shadowy anomaly. It was uniformly circular all around, and motionless except for a thin halo of full and then fading grayish light surrounding the midpoint of the anomaly. This faintly pulsating, indistinguishable oddity that was a mixture of light and shadow had a circumference of about 28 inches and it was approximately 9 inches in diameter.

Suddenly Darla stopped writing. She looked around the room and then stood up. She remembered something. She had left her freshly made coffee at the nurses' station outside Houston's room. Careful not to make too much noise, Darla turned around to make her exit to retrieve the coffee. As she walked out of the room, she passed right by the mysterious shadowy occurrence being cast on the wall just to her right. She never noticed it was there. As she exited the room, the faintly pulsating reflected oddity against the wall blurred out of view.

The End

Acknowledgments

To my project consultant, Barbara Lynn. Thank you for giving me the confidence and support during the critical process of developing and publishing my creative composition. You greatly facilitated getting me through this experience and, delightfully so, thanks to your obliging patience and invaluable experience. My world is a better place now because of you!

To my editor, Cindy Draughon, 'the book doctor'. Your keen evaluation, constructive criticism, and professionalism was supreme. You definitely gave me the confidence and the encouragement I needed to take this project to the next level. I learned so much during this process of developing my skill, by working with someone so skilled and experienced as yourself.

To my illustrator artist, Andra Maria Moisescu. Your talented dexterity captured the vision of my characters, superbly. Thank you for your dedication and hard work.

To Henning Morales. To the forever, number-one hustling dirt merchant in work ethic and character. I must give a shout out to you. Your own motivational true story moved me. An absolute testament that anyone can achieve their goals and find success in life if they only dedicate themselves and believe. No superpowers, superhero tights, or cape necessary.

As iron sharpens iron,
so one person sharpens another.

Proverbs 27:17

www.ingramcontent.com/pod-product-compliance
Lightning Source LLC
Chambersburg PA
CBHW070931100726
47908CB00001B/171